Playing For Keeps

Playing For Keeps

Stephanie Salinas

TANGO 2

Tango 2 is an imprint of
Genesis Press, Inc.
315 Third Avenue North
Columbus, Mississippi 39701

Playing For Keeps

ISBN 1-885478-91-7

Manufactured in the United States of America

FIRST EDITION

To my family, with thanks and love
for believing
To Layne, who countless times went
above and beyond mere duty and
friendship
With special thanks to the wonderful
people of Genesis Press for their hard
work and dedication
A special thank you to Doug Frasier
and Rosa Strang for technical advice
and support
And of course, thanks to the ladies of
The Dragonfly Table

Prologue

Waiting around always pissed him off. Being stuck with someone else's timetable meant that any number of things could go wrong. He liked things quick, neat, and clean. Of course, he thought with dark humor, his precision and timing were what made him so valuable in this line of work. With eyes as cold and compassionless as the gray winter day around him, he quickly scanned the people standing by the grave. They had no idea what lay in wait. They were too wrapped up in their sorrow to be mindful of the tempest headed their way.

All but one or two of them, that is. The one or two who had damn good reason for concern. He narrowed his eyes and concentrated on the four most prominent figures beside the man's grave. One of them, the petite blonde woman, lifted her head and swept the area with a furtive glance, as if she could feel the pale, silver eyes studying her. He smiled in wry amusement. Someone had once called his eyes "soulless—the eyes of the damned." They'd probably been right. At any rate, that person was no longer making comparisons. Death could be so inhibiting that way.

The sound of a vehicle pulling into the parking lot near the entrance grabbed his immediate attention. Ahh, at last. The final player was about to assume a position on the field. He watched the familiar figure get out of the car and cross the cemetery lawn to the grave. Picking up his cell phone, he hit memory dial, waited, then entered a series of digits guaranteed to scramble the call and ensure total privacy. The phone rang only once before he heard a terse, "Yes?"

"She's here," was all that the man with the strange eyes said. Then he hung up.

Chapter 1

The tightly gathered band of mourners steeled themselves against the cold winds sweeping across the barren landscape. The normally lush lawns of Bishops Bluff Cemetery still wore their dreary winter coat, damp and muddy in spots from the recently melted snow. Left to its own devices, the rocky soil of southern Oregon lent itself more to the cultivation of sagebrush and juniper than to the carefully nurtured lawn of the hillside cemetery. The gray sky and bleak horizon suited the grim company surrounding the grave. The man being buried was a highly regarded, influential man. Several bank presidents, a senator, a cyber mogul, and numerous other businessmen were among the noteworthy. Alongside of them stood ranch hands, farmers, and laborers. They all shared a common bond on that hillside—the respect they felt for the departed, Thomas Arlington Bishop.

Not one heard the arrival of a rented sedan above the voice of the preacher and the whistle of the wind. Huddled together, with their collars turned up against the breeze, not one heeded the approach of the young woman. She was dressed in black like most of the mourners, but her clothing selection no doubt raised the eyebrows of the most liberal in the group. Her stride was long and purposeful as she crossed the cemetery in her tight black jeans and heeled boots. She tossed her head of tawny hair and pulled a pair of Ray Bans from the pocket of her black leather jacket, apparently finding them necessary, despite the dull overcast sky. Turning up her collar, she took a place at the outer edge of the circle.

The crowd began to stir as her presence was noticed. It started with the turn of a few heads, and continued, ripplelike, toward the tightest cluster of people at the graveside. The crowd parted, allowing the young woman a clear view of the man's family, and them a clear view of her. The murmurs heightened in anticipation of the effect her arrival would have. All eyes turned to the petite blonde woman protectively wrapped in the arm of a tall, fierce-looking man. His shaggy dark hair, ruffled by the wind, danced in front of his eyes, momentarily hiding the young woman from his view. Nevertheless, his eyes locked on her, and there was no mistaking the hatred emanating from them.

The woman at his side tensed visibly and gave a small cry. To her right stood another man, his face impassive, his arm around a teenage girl. The girl's eyes were red and swollen from tears, yet of all the faces gathered graveside, hers was the most compassionate as she looked toward the recent arrival. She started forward, but the petite woman held up a hand signaling her to remain where she was. The teenager gave the hand a mutinous look, but stayed put. The rest of the people whispered and murmured, some even forgetting where they were, to point in avid curiosity. The service ended, but there was a moment of awkward indecision as the crowd waited to see what would happen next. The woman and the two men exchanged looks briefly, then led the teenager directly past the young woman without speaking or acknowledging her in any way. Some shook their heads in sympathy; others clucked disapprovingly at the black-clad figure. But different opinions aside, one fact was irrefutable. Hallie Bishop had come home.

Once Marlene and Genna were inside, with the car door secured against the chilly wind and prying eyes, Tyler Nighthawk paused to look back at the grave of his friend and mentor. The crowd gradually dispersed, leaving one lone figure. Shoulders square, body erect, the young

woman stared at the coffin in front of her. The proverbial
bad penny, he thought. It was just like her to put on a
show by arriving at her father's funeral dressed in clothes
more suitable for street walking. Did she come when he
was ill or when he lay dying? Hell no. The selfish little
tramp didn't give a shit. As usual, she was too wrapped up
in herself to give a thought to the man who, for reasons Ty
couldn't figure, never stopped loving her. "I know what
you're up to, Hallie." he snarled through clenched teeth.
"Tom wouldn't believe it, but I know it's you and I'll prove
it. You won't get away with it. This time he's not here to
plead your case, and if you give me any trouble, I'll bring
you to your knees. Whatever it takes," he vowed. He
opened the door and took his seat behind the wheel, then
addressed the three people reflected in the rearview mirror. "I suppose it was too much to hope that she'd stay
away."

The man nodded and the woman said, "I know, I know.
But when she didn't respond to the telegrams, I thought for
sure... " Her voice trailed off.

"Don't worry, Marlene," Ty said. "It'll be all right. I
know how to deal with Hallie." He started the car and
pulled away, but not before turning his cold, narrowed
gaze on the woman at the grave a final time.

Long after most of the people went home, Hallie remained
beside her father's coffin. It had been left above ground
after the service ended, waiting for the friends and family
to depart and leave so the grave diggers could conclude
their work. Most people would find the actual interment
of the body too unnerving to watch. Hallie wasn't most
people. To her, it was a much more upsetting idea to leave
her father above ground, all alone with strangers, as the
wind whipped around his coffin. So she stayed. There

were few to witness the steady stream of silent tears that coursed down her face; few to see the frozen mask finally shatter and leave her shoulders heaving with the racking sobs of grief. Two men, one in the uniform of a deputy sheriff, came forward to wrap protective arms around the woman who had once been their closest friend.

Two miles outside the town of Bishops Bluff, an unmarked dirt road veered from the highway through the tall sugar pines and sage bushes. It was the turn to the Bishop spread, and it ran for miles before the actual ranch house and outbuildings came into view. The land had been in the Bishop family since the claim was first staked in the early days of the Oregon Trail. All in all, there were fifteen square miles of brush, forests, streams and pasturelands. In the middle of it all sat the ranch. The original homestead was demolished at the turn of the century by Tom Bishop's grandfather. He'd made a healthy fortune in the lumber business and wanted a home suitable for the founding of a dynasty. He'd built a very large, four-story Victorian home, complete with turrets and a glassed-in widow's walk. The structure would have looked at home on a San Franciscan hillside, but out in the middle of nowhere, it looked like what it was meant to be—ostentatious. Tonight, light shone through the various windows in a random pattern as the occupants of the house sequestered themselves to privately deal with their grief. One man kept vigil downstairs, silently preparing for a storm that would soon rage more fiercely than anything a northwest winter could hurl at them.

Tyler Nighthawk watched the rain blow against the library window. Of all the rooms in the house, this was his favorite. He could still feel Tom here. They'd spent years together in this room, first as cautious strangers, taking

each other's measure, then as teacher and student explor-
ing the wonders of the universe, and finally as surrogate
father and son. He'd spent some of the happiest hours of
his life here—and some of the darkest.

"Tom," he said softly to the dark sky, "what would have
become of that cocky little punk if you'd never given him
a chance?"   He sighed and turned back to the fire, his
hands shoved in his pockets, remembering himself at a
sullen sixteen. Life was never fair, but it seemed he'd been
dealt more than his share of bad cards. When he was a
small boy, his father, a mean, hard-drinking son-of-a-bitch
on a good day, had finally pushed his luck and gotten ten
to twenty for felonious assault. Within six months he was
dead, a victim of a prison fight. Ty's mother had never
been what you'd call a survivor. Perennial victim, yes—
survivor, no. She'd met Ty's father in her early teens and
defied her family to run off with the handsome, smooth
talker. Their first night together, he'd bloodied her lip to
show her who was boss. Things went downhill from there.
Later booze made it easier to forget the battering brute she
lived with and the cries of a hungry, frightened child. After
Ty's father died, so did the dubious income he'd provided.
His parents had never legally married, so there were no
widow's benefits, and the benefits for Ty hardly did much
except cut the welfare amount. As his mother continued
her slide into the deeper stages of alcoholism, their shack
became a clearing house for a long procession of
boyfriends, some married, some not, some more abusive
than others. The rent was paid, sometimes there was food,
and his clothes usually came from the church barrels.
There was no time or money for toys, books, Christmas, or
birthdays. The only time one of his mother's notorious
dates gave him something, it was in preface to asking Ty to
pull down his pants. His mother had come back to the

room in time and chased Ty out the door. He shuddered at the memories. The school yard had been hell—pure hell. By the time he was eight, he was pretty much on his own. His mother would sometimes be gone for days at a time. In a way, that was preferable to her drunken wails and the steady stream of friends in and out of the house. As he got older, of course, the taunts grew in frequency and malevolence. By the time he was fourteen, he'd been expelled from school for fighting, truancy, and a general bad attitude. He was belligerent, uneducated, and a whole lot of trouble by the time he made Tom Bishop's acquaintance.

Ty wasn't sure what had finally been the last straw. Nothing had happened that day any different from any other day. He'd been standing on the ravine bridge just outside of town when it occurred to him that it really didn't matter if his life ended now, or later. There were no changes on the horizon, no miracles to expect. Suddenly, he was more terrified than he ever remembered being in his dismal life, and, as with most people who find themselves in that position, he had realized he had the luxury of nothing left to lose. He made plans. All he needed was some money to finance his escape. He'd try a big city. Los Angeles would be perfect. The weather was great, they had fantastic beaches and lots of opportunities for a young man fast on his feet. The scheme took shape in his mind over the course of the rest of the day. All he needed was one big, fast score. Though he was good at hustling pool and shooting craps, he knew from experience that the local games wouldn't provide the amount necessary to keep him in style until he got on his feet. The kind of score he needed for that could only be found at one place in town, the Bishop spread.

By the time he got to the ranch that night, he'd been

soaked to the skin and was shivering so badly he could
hardly make his hands work. Everything was sealed up
tight due to the severity of the weather. The ranch house
and all the outlying buildings sat in darkness; the corrals
vacant. Anybody with any sense at all had long tucked
themselves safely away, leaving the night and the storm to
a desperate and frightened boy. He'd been shaking so
intensely that he had had a difficult time holding the flashlight steady, one he'd stolen earlier that day from Falk's
Feed and Seed. He'd held his breath as he checked all the
windows on the ground floor. Finally, when it appeared
he'd have to run the risk of breaking a pane of glass, he had
come upon the window where he presently stood looking
into the night.

He paused in his reflections to take a sip of bourbon
from the lead crystal glass in his hand. He glanced around
the warm, book-lined room again. This was were he'd met
Tom Bishop, and it seemed only fitting that it was the place
to say goodbye. The fire had been little more than glow-
ing embers that night, providing inadequate light for a
close study of the room beyond the window. Ty had been
barely able to make out two large leather chairs flanking
the mantle and a desk. Necessity made him bold that
night, as the thunder crashed so fiercely. His boldness had
made him careless, and in the quirky fortunes of life, his
carelessness was the best thing that could ever have happened to him. After navigating the window ledge, he'd
crept softly into the room, scanning the interior with the
flashlight. From behind him, a man cleared his throat. Ty
whirled to face the leather chair where the sound had
come from. With a shaking hand, he'd brought the flashlight up to shine on the face of the man seated in the
leather chair. Thomas Arlington Bishop.

"Well now, young man," Tom Bishop's slow, calm

voice began, "would you be kind enough to lower your light, please." Ty had automatically complied. Most people had found themselves meeting Tom's requests; even business rivals, who later often asked themselves why. There'd just been a way about the man. "If you'll kindly be seated," Tom had indicated the chair across from him, "I think introductions are in order. Then we will have a little talk, you and I." Tom had been aware of the water pooling around the feet of the boy in his study, but he hadn't seemed perturbed in the least by it, and gestured again to the chair. Thus began Ty's life in this house. He'd never gone back to his mother's place again. Indeed, he'd had very little contact with her from then on, until the time of her death. But in many respects, he'd had more than enough. Disgust curled Ty's lip as he remembered his mother's disastrous appearance at his engagement party. Tom had always tried to place himself squarely between Ty and his past, and for the most part, he'd succeeded. His jaw now hardened at the memories of shocked faces and quickly muffled laughter. Though not a single person in Bishops Bluff had ever dared say a thing against him within Tom's earshot, Ty had always known what remained unsaid.

Bishop money had supported Ty's mother until Ty himself had the means to assume the obligation. In retrospect, it hadn't made the slightest difference in how she'd lived the rest of her life. He glared angrily through the darkness, as inevitably, thoughts of his mother led him to thoughts of Hallie Bishop.

Damn that woman anyway. Hadn't she wreaked enough havoc in all their lives? Two weeks ago as Tom began his decline, Ty had prepared himself for her return. When she didn't respond to the letters or telegrams, he'd figured that Hallie, being Hallie, didn't give a shit. The mere fact that her father lay dying and wanted desperately to see her meant nothing to her. Hallie always operated with her own agenda, and damn the consequences to anyone else. He knew that from personal experience. Ty glanced toward the clock on the mantle. Seven forty-five. That meant she would probably be showing up here anytime. Thankfully, she'd waited until everyone had gone home and Marlene and Genna had retired for the night. Poor little Gen. She had actually stopped in about half an hour ago to see if he'd heard from Hallie. The kid had no clue that she was eagerly waiting for the fox to come to the hen house. She was crying out for a sister who was a pure figment of her imagination, carefully fostered by Tom, God rest his soul, in an effort to hold on to his own delusions. Headlights flashed at the front of the house. She was here.

Moments later, Mrs. Hudson, the housekeeper, knocked softly on the library door and opened it to usher Hallie into the room. At Ty's nod of thanks, she cast a wary glance at the woman standing in the middle of the room and hurried out. No sooner had the door closed on them, than the young woman stalked across the room to stand nose to nose with Ty. "All right, you son-of-a-bitch," she said coldly. "Why the hell didn't you call me before it was too late?"

Chapter 2

"All righteous indignation, aren't you?" Ty's eyes narrowed to chips of green ice. "Not too heavy-handed, just the right touch of anger without being too showy. That's a nice choice of outfit too," he sneered, as he took in her appearance from head to toe. "Somber color to show the proper respect, yet suitable for trolling bars after the funeral." He tossed back the contents of his glass and set it sharply on the nearby liquor tray.

Hallie's gaze met his without so much as a flinch. "I asked you a question, Nighthawk, and unless you want me to scream the whole house down, I suggest you answer it. You know I'm perfectly capable of it, and right about now, nothing would give me greater pleasure."

"And nothing would give me greater pleasure than to wring your scrawny little neck if you try. Marlene and Gen are finally asleep, and you're not going to disturb them." Ty placed a none-too-gentle hand on her upper arm and guided her to a chair. She shook him off.

"You're wasting some valuable time here, *cabron*. I don't intimidate worth a damn these days."

He glared at her, carefully taking stock of his adversary. Some battles were best saved for the cold light of day, he reflected. He would pick the time and place. "Very well," he said coldly. "It seems that we both have some explaining to do." He sat down in one of the chairs, quietly waiting for her to follow suit. He was pleased to see she was disconcerted, however mildly. After a few awkward moments, she seated herself across from him. "Now then," he began, "let's cut through this charade and come to the point. What do you want?"

Hallie stared at him, dumbstruck by his colossal arro-

gance. How could he ask that question? What the hell did
he think she wanted? She mentally chastised herself for the
stupid question. Leopards didn't change their spots; at
least not according to this family's rules. She let a tired
sigh escape, and not for the first time, questioned whether
she had the strength and resolve necessary to get through
this. Hallie leaned back into the chair. Maybe it would
have been better to wait until morning after all. Nighthawk
hadn't even tried to disguise his feelings about her. His
hate and disgust were evident. Say what you would about
the man, at least he wasn't a hypocrite.

"Look," she began, "I want to know why no one bothered to call me. I was his daughter too. You didn't have
the right..." She stopped abruptly, not trusting herself to
keep the pain and anger from her voice. It was never a
good idea to let Nighthawk see a weakness. He would be
on you in an instant.

His eyes glittered dangerously across from hers. "Cut
the crap, Hallie. You can't pretend your way out of this.
Four telephone calls and two wires don't all just happen to
get waylaid. I'm not a complete fool, and it would go better for you to remember that from now on." Ty took his
time giving her a leisurely appraisal before he spoke again.
"Now then, I think all we need to do is come to terms.
How much do you want?"

It took a moment for his words to sink in, through the
turmoil and unreal quality of the day. The dirty bastard
wanted to buy her off! There was no, "Terribly sorry, it was
an oversight that never should have happened," no words
that even attempted to explain his unexplainable position.
He not only dismissed her accusations as if they were of no
more consequence than an annoying insect, but he had the
unmitigated gall to propose a payoff. Hallie's anger
straightened her sagging shoulders and pushed to the back

burner all the sorrow and grief that had threatened to overcome her.

"You vile, disgusting pig," she ground out between her teeth. "What on God's earth makes you think you can talk to me like that?" She shook her head in disbelief and muttered an oath in Spanish. "I've seen some cold, sorry sons-of-bitches in my life, but you..."

"I'll just bet you have, sweetheart." Ty bit the words out, making the last one sound like anything but an endearment. "I warned you not to play me for a fool. I don't have any of Tom's sentimentality where you're concerned, so you might as well save your breath. I'm not about to justify my behavior to you." Ty's mouth curled in a contemptuous sneer. "I hope the party that delayed you was a good one, because the price of admission was pretty damn steep."

"I wasn't at a party, Nighthawk. I was out of town. I didn't expect that much change in Dad's condition in less than two weeks. Last I heard, the prognosis called for another year, perhaps more," Hallie stated evenly. "Anyway, Mrs. Verdoza knew where I was. Unfortunately, her husband was rushed to the hospital with a heart attack. She wasn't at my house to get the message or the wire." Hallie focused on his eyes, determined to hold his gaze no matter how difficult he made things for her. "As for four messages and two wires, well, let me point out that my answering machine is working fine. There were exactly six messages, two from Mrs. V, three from my agent, and yours—the most charming and descriptive of all, I might add. The one wire came about five minutes after I'd gotten home. Seeing that Mrs. V and my agent's messages didn't mention anything about Dad, I doubt you guys tried very badly to find me."

"Always the injured party, aren't you? Wasn't everything terribly convenient?" he murmured.

Hallie sighed in exasperation. "Well gee, Nighthawk, I'm not sure, but I don't think Mr. and Mrs. Verdoza planned this. I could be wrong, but I don't think the heart attack was staged simply to throw you off track."

"That's hardly the point, is it? Let's try to keep to the subject at hand. How much will it take to get rid of you?" He got up and poured himself another glass of bourbon, holding the decanter out to her in inquiry. She shook her head in answer, and he returned to his seat. "I've got quite a tidy sum set aside. I'm sure it will do for a down payment. I'm also prepared to arrange a reasonable quarterly allowance. I'm sure Marlene would agree to it for certain 'concessions' on your part."

Hallie felt as if someone had jammed her in the stomach with a pitchfork. This was a thousand times worse than she'd imagined, and she'd imagined some pretty horrendous stuff. Hold on, she told herself. Come on, *chica*. Don't let him get you going. If you blow your cool, you'll lose a lot more than just your temper. Hallie struggled to keep her emotions in check. You can pull this off, she scolded herself. The sorry bastard can't say anything half as bad as what you've already said to yourself. She gathered her resources from all the times she'd walked onto the stage; her attitude, her style, the whole rock 'n' roll persona she'd affected, which had made her notorious worldwide. She relaxed, took a breath, and stepped into the spotlight. Draping herself artlessly in the chair, she adopted her best husky bad girl voice and said, "What makes you think I have a price?"

"All whores have a price," said the cold voice across from her.

She responded in the only way the legendary "Gal Hal" Bishop would. She threw back her head and laughed. It wasn't sharp or high-pitched with tension, but rather the rich sultry sound of a confident, seductive woman. Ty felt his temper begin to boil as her laugh rolled up rich and full of mockery. He also hated the fact that her laughter could be so pleasing to the ear.

"Well, Nighthawk, you should know," she said, trying to catch her breath, "Tell me, have you raised your rates to keep up with inflation?"

Ty's knuckles whitened around the glass he held. He spoke between clenched teeth. "I'd be real careful right about now, Hallie, if I were you. You see, I'm operating on an average of about three hours of sleep a night for the past two weeks. Patience isn't my strong suit in the best of circumstances. The last thing I want to be doing tonight is trying to clear the trash away from the house. I'm prepared to give you three hundred and fifty thousand right now, and a quarterly draw of fifteen thousand just to get you to keep your distance." He returned to his seat, then continued speaking. "With that and any royalties you get, you should be able to live in comfort. I'll have my attorney draw up the necessary paperwork tomorrow. As soon as you sign the documents, you can have your money. Then I want you gone. Is that clear? No contact with Genna or Marlene. Even one phone call and the deal is off. You don't see a penny." He leaned forward in the chair. "Hallie, do it my way or I'll make your life a living hell."

She forced herself to meet his glare and respond with a mysterious little half smile. Her insides had turned to jelly, and she didn't think she'd be able to stand, much less walk out of there if the need arose. "You're so sure of yourself, aren't you?" She looked him over in annoyance. "I don't want your money, Tyler, and if you picked up a copy of the *National Inquirer* occasionally, you'd know I do just fine making my life a living hell all on my own, thank you very much. Remember, old son, I told you I don't intimidate worth a damn."

He returned a smile that had all the warmth of arctic tundra. "Don't bother waiting for the will, Duchess," he drawled, using the name he'd taunted her with as a child. A month before he died, Tom sent for his lawyer to make what he termed some significant changes to his will. The guy spent the afternoon hunched over a laptop in Tom's room. I can't say for sure what the changes are, but they came hot on the heels of a phone call from you. I don't think, if memory serves, that Tom was in a very pleasant mood after that particular conversation."

Hallie blanched visibly. Did their row shorten his days? She'd called him three days later and tried to patch things up. He'd seemed to regret their harsh, angry exchange of words as much as she did. She thought they'd made real progress in trying to settle their differences once and for all. Hadn't he mentioned that to anyone? Hadn't he mentioned they'd both agreed she should come home around Easter for an extended stay? He'd even offered to have her converted bunkhouse, the one he'd set aside for her use years earlier, redone and outfitted with anything she needed so she could work while she was home—a milestone in their terminally uneasy relationship. Home. It was an odd word for a place she'd all but turned her back on years ago. The range of her emotions flashed briefly across her face before she was able to successfully mask them.

The chink in her armor pleased Ty. It proved to him that he'd hit the nail on the head where she was concerned. He'd shaken her confidence, and now she would be more easily managed. "Delay the decision, Hallie," he said coolly, "and the offer goes to a hundred fifty thousand and five thousand quarterly. After the will is read, it goes to zip."

"Keep your damn money, I don't want it, and, for the record, I don't need it." Hallie's voice grew louder with each word. "You can take your preconceived notions and shove them, Nighthawk! I had a message waiting for me at the hotel from Dad's attorney." She drew a shuddering breath in an effort to calm herself. "Apparently my presence is requested at the reading of the will tomorrow. So get used to it. I'm staying. The only reason I came here tonight was to get some answers. I didn't want tomorrow to be any more difficult than necessary." She narrowed her eyes, then jabbed her finger in his direction. "But if you want to throw down the gauntlet, bucko, you can just bet I'll pick it up."

Ty rose to stand over her. "Listen you little—" His reply was cut off by the sound of the library door opening. A tall, lean man slipped quietly into the room, closing the door behind him. He shook his head at the couple by the fire.

"I could hear you all the way upstairs in my room. This has got to be one for the record books, even for you two." He took in Hallie's appearance in a wistful gray gaze. "Hello, Hallie," he said. "Long time no see." There was a gentle rebuke in his soft words.

"Hello, Walt," she replied coolly. "It's nice to see you too."

He stepped across the room to her and extended his hand. His sandy-colored hair held well-established streaks of silver and gave him an air of distinction, Hallie noted, though he hardly looked his forty-five years. She took his hand, surprised by its warm reassurance. Perhaps she still had one friend left. "You look good," he said, "under the circumstances."

"Thanks. How is Genna holding up?"

Walt shifted uncomfortably under her question. "About

as well as can be expected. Even though she knew, like the rest of us, that it was only a matter of time, she wasn't prepared for it. It was a little sooner than any of us expected. The doctors said at least another year to eighteen months."

"I know. When I talked to him last, he sounded good; tired, but good."

Ty snorted derisively. "And you knew so much about his illness, didn't you?"

"Please, Ty," Walt began wearily. "This isn't doing any of us any good. I came down here to quiet things down, not bring you reinforcements. We're all pretty tired and sad. I think we all could use some rest. Hallie, don't take this the wrong way please, but I think it would be better if you left now. I don't want my sister or niece any more upset tonight. This day has been hell for them." He reached down to take her hand again. "I'm sure it's been hell for you too," he amended belatedly.

She allowed herself to be assisted to her feet, her eyes never leaving Ty's face. *Later*, she promised him silently. Aloud, she said, "I think you're right, Walt. I'm exhausted. Nothing that's been said here tonight can't wait for another time. I've heard it all before, and I'm sure I'll hear it all again several times before I'm through."

Ty spoke acidly as she stepped away from the men. "Through? Sweetheart, I'll make sure you're through before you even get started." Walt forestalled any parting shot Hallie would have made by placing his arm around her shoulders.

"Come on, Hallie," he said, giving Ty a very pointed look, "I'll see you to the door." They left the room without further comment, and he stopped them in the formal entry, turning her to look at him. His handsome face studied her intently.

"Thanks for the escort. Were you afraid I'd steal the silver?" she asked.

"I don't think I deserved that," he said reproachfully. "I'm sorry, Hallie, if you feel angry and misused, I truly am. But facts are facts. Marlene and Genna are very important to me, and whether you choose to believe it or not, you are too—in your own way." His hands gently massaged her upper arms. "Are you going to be okay tonight?"

"Hell, Walt," said Hallie, drawing a ragged breath, "you know me. I'm always okay." Her voice lacked the bravado she strived for. He was right. She had no right to take her pain out on him. "Look, thanks for the concern, but I'm just going to crawl into bed and try to forget for a few hours."

"Are you sure? There's an all-night coffee shop on the highway. We can go there if you need to talk. I really don't like the idea of you being alone tonight, but the situation here makes it impossible for you to stay." Hallie detected a genuine note of regret in his voice that soothed some of the ache in her heart.

"Don't worry about me," she said, doing a credible job of keeping her voice light. "If I can't sleep I'll watch TV. If I'm lucky, they'll be running a Hitchcock marathon or something."

Walt gave her an affectionate smile. "Still a Hitchcock fan, I see."

"Of course. I'll be fine, really." Impulsively, she reached up and hugged him. His arms enclosed her, and she rested her head on his shoulder. She wanted to stay there, feeling safe and secure in the arms of someone who cared how she felt and what she was going through. His hands gently rubbed her back as he murmured assurances. For whatever reason, maybe the nuance in a word, or the fingertips that slowed in their movements just a fraction too long, Hallie began to feel a little uncomfortable. If anyone saw them like this, they'd probably get the wrong idea, and the scene that would follow would make the one in the library almost pleasant by comparison. She removed her arms from his neck and pulled back. He held her a moment longer, then let her go.

He caught her chin with his hand. "Call me if you need me. My private line is in the book. I take it you're staying at the hotel?" She nodded. "Fine, I can be there in twenty minutes, half an hour tops. I mean it, Hallie. Call me if you need anything." He kissed her cheek and said good-night.

Walt watched the sway of her hips as she walked down the porch steps, then with a sigh, turned off the light, locked the door, and rejoined Ty in the library. Ty's mood looked even uglier than it had a few moments ago, and he barely waited for the door to close before he was on Walt. "What the hell was that shit?" he snarled. "I thought we agreed—"

Walt cut him off. "Never heard of good cop, bad cop? Really, Tyler, you should watch more detective movies," he drawled as he crossed to the decanters of liquor and measured a generous portion from one of them into a glass. "If one of us manages to convince her we're on her side, it'll be easier to catch her with her guard down and get to the bottom of the troubles we've been having. Unfortunately, after tonight's little episode, you've pretty well finished off that role for you."

"I see your point," Ty said grudgingly. After a moment he asked, "How far do you think you'll have to take this 'good cop' thing?"

"Not too far, I expect," Walt mused. "I wouldn't really mind taking it all the way, so to speak. She's quite lovely, the spitting image of her mother. Don't tell me you're totally immune to that body of hers?"

"Pretty poison, Walt. Watch your back. She takes after her mother in more than just looks," Ty said contemptuously. "She's every bit the lying slut her mother was—if not more so."

"True," Walt admitted, then sipped from his glass in a thoughtful manner. "But I'm surprised by your vehemence, Tyler. Elena's reign of terror here ended long before your time."

Ty's lip curled in disgust. "That doesn't mean I never saw her in action when I was a kid."

"Really?" Walt asked with renewed interest. "Just what did you see?"

"Enough to know that Elena Bishop wasn't particular about who she slept with, or how many. The way I understand it, her daughter's just got a broader playing field— that's all."

"At any rate," Walt said with a hint of irritation, "of all of us, she probably finds me the least offensive. We were on friendly enough terms last time I saw her. It shouldn't be much of a stretch to convince her she can trust me."

"The attorney wants her at the reading tomorrow."

"What!" Walt turned back from the table where he was standing. "I thought you said Tom changed his will!"

"I never guaranteed anything, Walt," Ty said, a distinct chill in his voice. "I made what I considered to be an informed guess, but only Tom and his attorney know for sure."

"This is great! Talk about a wolf in the fold," Walt fumed. "And just what do you propose we do to control this situation?"

Tyler Nighthawk smiled unpleasantly. "Whatever it takes, old man. Whatever it takes."

The night clerk at the front desk looked up and smiled at Hallie as she stopped to check for messages. She returned the desk clerk's smile and nodded as she accepted several slips of pink paper from his hand, grateful that he made it unnecessary for her to speak. Hallie didn't believe she could get through one more condolence and not totally fall apart. Right now she wouldn't trust her voice to deliver more than harsh, agonized rasps. She went to the modern elevators on the left, struggling to ignore the ornate iron cage that graced the rambling Victorian hotel. When she'd been a little girl, she'd loved riding it to the second floor ballroom, her small hand tucked in her father's large, comforting one. That was in the old days when she'd been just a little thing of five or six and the apple of her Dad's eye. After her mother had run off into the night to join her lover, only to end up with her car wrapped around a tree. Before Marlene had come into the picture. Before Tyler. Before Hallie's imperfections and shortcomings had become too numerous to ignore, causing an irreparable breach between father and daughter. Before anyone in town just had to look at Hallie's face to know she was Elena Bishop's daughter. Tonight, riding the old elevator would be her undoing.

She reached her hotel room, and after a series of fumbling attempts to use her key, gained the sanctuary of her suite. Feeling utterly beaten and desperate to close the chapter on this horrible day, Hallie slumped to the couch. Tomorrow would be round two, and it promised to be even bloodier than the fiasco tonight. Sick with grief and remorse, the only thing Hallie wanted to do right now was turn tail and run. It was one of her best talents.

She'd already made up her mind to leave the next morning after the will reading. It was a bad idea to hang around much longer than that. With a few hours of sleep and a chance to regroup, she could face her family, such as it was, and try to make some kind of tenuous peace before leaving town. She crossed the room to the kitchenette and retrieved a can of diet cola from the refrigerator.

As far as Hallie was concerned, there were plenty of questions about her father's death and far fewer answers. During the past six months she'd had more conversations with her father than in the previous six years. Not all of the phone calls had been pleasant, but for the first time in more than a decade her father had made a sincere effort to bridge the bitterness and distrust that separated him and his elder daughter. He'd succeeded in extracting a promise from Hallie to come home and make peace before it was too late.

Shortly before his death her father had told her that certain financial inconsistencies had been found in many company holdings. Further investigations had determined that large amounts of cash were being mysteriously siphoned off by a person or persons unknown. How it was being done and where the money was going were a complete mystery. He needed her support, he'd said. Tom Bishop had been a proud man, and swallowing his pride and anger to express his need must have cost him dearly.

When he had been initially diagnosed and treated for terminal cancer four years ago, Tom had made a decision to forego much of the lengthy and debilitating cancer surgeries and drug therapies. He'd pointed out to everyone that the end would be the same anyway. He'd strongly felt that the quality of life was more important than the quantity. With her fellow band members in agreement, Hallie had left a half-done music video and postponed a much ballyhooed concert tour to rush to her father's bedside. Unfortunately, as he had at countless other times, he'd responded to Hallie's efforts on his behalf with hostility and anger, finally demanding that she leave his home until she could accomplish something with her life other than shaming her entire family with her lifestyle. Thankfully, no one had been privy to the viciousness of that particular speech, and Tom's pride had never let him confess it to a soul. When Hallie, crushed by her father's belittling attitude, left the ranch, Marlene, Walt and Ty simply believed she'd finally gotten bored with the role of dutiful daughter and gone off in search of new thrills. Her father, as usual, never referred to the incident again. He had, however, let her know at every available opportunity what a source of disappointment and shame she'd become to him. The public face he'd presented, though, was quite another matter.

The recent years of Hallie's career had been the most successful and scandalous of any. The results of which were the sensational breakup of the band, Loreli, and a permanent rift between herself and her best friend of many years, lead singer Cassie Donovan. Throughout that entire period, Tom had excelled in publicly playing the stoic father, drawing admiration from all who knew him for his loving and forgiving nature where his daughter was concerned.

She took a long drink from her soda. No matter how old she got, she still felt like the lonely, frightened little girl, who'd so desperately fought to recapture her father's heart and had only succeeded in driving it further out of reach. He'd never forgiven her for looking like her mother, the beautiful and sensual Elena Valascez, and had always believed Hallie to be equally lacking in morals. The fruit never falls far from the tree. God, how she'd hated that expression. She'd heard it often enough from both her father and Nighthawk.

Hallie's lips quivered. She'd come so close to reclaiming her father's love. So close to receiving his acceptance if not his approval. Not close enough. Shit! Hallie shook her head, refusing to descend any further into the self-pity that threatened to close in on her. All afternoon she'd fought off the guilt and gloom and she would continue to do so. For one of the few times in her life, her father needed her, and she couldn't afford the luxury of bemoaning her situation. He'd wanted her help and this time she wouldn't disappoint him. She'd find the strength to stay for the fight. God help anyone who got in her way.

Chapter 3

Hallie lay on her stomach swatting ineffectually at the bedside phone, as it delivered the shrill rings of her morning wake-up call. She glanced bleary-eyed at her travel clock, barely able to make out the six a.m. on the digital dial. Pushing herself up on her knees, she muttered and picked up the receiver. Hallie thanked the operator, hung up the phone, and sat back on her heels waiting for the fog in her brain to lift. Slowly, the memories of the last few days came into focus. Death upon death. First her manager, Sye, then her father. Unconsciously, Hallie wrapped her arms around her pillow, hugging it close to her. She wished more than anything that she could crawl back under the covers and pull them over her head, but she'd made her decision last night. Come hell or high water, no one was going to run her off. No one, especially not a heartless prick with a very personal ax to grind. "Look out, Tyler," she said softly, as she got out of bed, "the bitch is back, and she's got very sharp teeth."

She treated herself to a full thirty minutes in the water and steam of the shower as she came up with a game plan for the day. The scent of the apple shower gel and shampoo she favored drifted throughout the bathroom, calming and soothing her. She could have easily stayed under the warm spray for another half hour, but she had important matters to attend to, so, reluctantly, she turned off the water and reached for her robe.

Hallie flipped through her clothes twice before settling on faded jeans and a simple charcoal-gray, scoop-necked cotton sweater. A brown leather bomber jacket would complete the outfit. It was hardly the sort of ensemble a normal person would wear to the reading of a will, but

Hallie didn't want to be a hypocrite, and she could well imagine what Nighthawk would say if she showed up brandishing full mourning gear now. Hallie inspected the jeans carefully for intentional razor rips and holes. Once she'd reassured herself they weren't going to shock the family with anything but tightness, she threw them on the bed with the rest of her clothes. She turned to look in the vanity mirror and frowned, picturing the ruthless curl of Ty's lips as he looked her over and found her lacking, no matter what she wore. Hallie felt a burning sensation over her skin as she imagined those deep, brilliant-green eyes of his sweeping over her. He always had had a way of making her terribly aware of his presence. Against her will, she was drawn to another place and time.

After her mother's death, her father had refused to allow even the smallest traditions of Mexican culture to be observed on the ranch. It had been one of his methods in his ceaseless campaign to eradicate the memory of his beautiful first wife. Other than letters and one visit to her Tia Augusta in that fateful fifteenth summer, her friend Pepe Ramirez and his family had become Hallie's sole link to her Latino-American heritage. Through the years, on feast days and other holidays, Hallie had been able to pretend, for brief snatches of time, that she was part of the warm and boisterous Ramirez family. On *Dia de los Muertos*—The Day of the Dead—it had been Pepe's mother who had first instructed Hallie on how to wash and tend her mother's headstone. She helped the little girl assemble the altar, complete with a sugar skull and the various things her mother had enjoyed in life. Hallie smiled gently now, remembering the laughter and affection that she'd received from her friend's mother.

By the summer Hallie graduated from high school, the situation at home had become intolerable. In his obsession with Hallie's morals, Tom Bishop, with Tyler Nighthawk's assistance, had made his daughter a virtual prisoner. She'd been forbidden from playing her guitar in public, as well as seeing her best friends, including Pepe and his family. To be shut away from the only sustaining joys she had in her life had been more than Hallie could bear. For her it became an issue of survival. So she'd run.

She'd been gone about a month, and nobody had managed to track her down—or so she'd thought. She was backstage in a run-down theater, in a less-than-savory area of Chicago. Seventeen, angry, and rebellious. Two weeks later she would meet the three people who would forever change her life, but right then, she'd been alone, hungry, and desperate for life to give her some kind of break. Only the desperation for a chance made her put up with the sleazy pawing of the concert promoter. She'd managed to keep him at bay through most of the week, but prior to the show, he'd caught her in the dimly lit, grimy corridor that led from the dressing room to the stage. Hallie could still smell the mingling odors of pot, the unwashed bodies, and the decay that permeated the building. He'd pressed her against the wall, letting his hands explore her as he described in detail the things he would do with her after the show.

For all her bluff, the white spiky hair, black leather, and studs, the Hallie of that time was still a virgin. She remained frozen, too scared to do anything. Suddenly, the weight of his greasy body was lifted away from her. She'd seen him fly through the air and land none too gently several feet down the hall. Tyler Nighthawk loomed over him in a murderous rage. He lifted the whimpering man to his feet by the front of his shirt and proceeded to knock him cold. Then he'd come looking for Hallie. She remembered his hands grabbing her arms in a vice-like grip. The words of relief and gratitude died on her lips. He shoved her angrily against the wall again, but this time Hallie didn't feel sick and frozen with fear. A curious warming sensation started in the area south of her navel and laced its way lower. She was sure Ty had felt something too, because he'd automatically pressed himself closer, his breath getting shallower. Her face tilted upwards to him, and her lips parted slightly of their own volition. His mouth came within an inch of hers. Ty had suddenly drawn a sharp breath and seized her wrists in a punishing grip.

His eyes had traveled over her, taking in her outlandish appearance. "So this is how you achieve a career in music, huh? You'll spread your legs for just about anybody, won't you? Like mother, like daughter, huh, Hallie?" he jeered. "God, Tom's right. He said it was your choice, and I guess if you want to spend your life in the gutter, it's none of my damn business." He pushed himself away from her, then turned his back and left.

"Nighthawk," she sighed to her reflection, " you always were an asshole." They'd known each other since she was seven years old, and in that whole time they'd rarely exchanged a pleasant word. He'd made no secret that he thought she was not worth the trouble it would take to blow her to hell. It was a view he'd helped convince her father of, and she'd never forgiven him for that. Even during the insane time at fifteen when she actually thought she was in love with him, she still resented him.

Teenage crushes rarely made sense. Hers had been no exception. She'd just woken up one day and it was like seeing Ty for the first time. Somewhere along the way the sullen, gangly teenage boy had been replaced by a rugged, virile, young man. He was tailor-made for a lonely, naive girl, eagerly waiting for her first tall, dark, and handsome

anti-hero. Was it her fault she never did anything in half
measures? Yes, Ty had plenty of reason to hate her. Still,
she hoped one day to find the means to make him understand why she'd done what she'd done. He wouldn't forgive her—who could—but perhaps he'd hate her just a little less.

Hallie began to apply her make-up base with more
vigor than usual. She continued her cosmetic regime, eyeing the final results with satisfaction, then began digging in
her jewelry chest for accessories. She placed several
expensive rings on the table and chose four of them. The
effect was more sedate than her usual seven. A knock at
the door signaled the arrival of room service and her breakfast. After showing the rather awestruck bellhop where to
set things, she left him to his task, grabbed her clothes from
the bed and raced to the bathroom to change.

～❈ ❈～

Marlene Bishop motioned Tyler to join her as she sat in
one of the library's wingback chairs, calmly conversing
with her brother, Walt. She was a vision, Ty observed,
even in the uncompromising morning light. Her silver-
blonde loveliness seemed only enhanced by the stress of
her recent bereavement. Lack of sleep had cast small shadows beneath her eyes and given her a fragile, ethereal quality. She'd come to Tom Bishop an innocent young woman
of twenty, a welcome respite from his tempestuous years
with his first wife, Elena. Twenty years had had little effect
on her beauty.

"Do you think she'll show this morning?" Walt asked Ty
as he approached them. There was no doubt who he
referred to.

Ty shrugged. "Hard to say. I called the hotel about five
minutes ago, and they said she'd already checked out."
He'd been half-expecting a call from Hallie accepting his

offer of money, but so far, nothing. Now she'd run herself out of time. He muttered under his breath. No doubt she was planning a grand entrance.

"Perhaps she decided to return to LA right away," Marlene suggested hopefully.

"I wouldn't count on it," Ty replied. "She seems to be under the misconception that she's welcome here, that Tom left her a sizable portion of his estate." He added sarcastically, "Perhaps that explains why she's been helping herself to the Bishop Company money. Waiting for her father's death was merely a technicality."

Marlene shook her head. "Granted, I believe my step-daughter's capable of just about anything, but there's no proof she's the one responsible for the missing funds."

Walt snorted. "Who else has reason and motivation? She hates us all and Tom most likely cut her off without a penny." Marlene nodded, clearly troubled by the notion that Tom's older daughter would operate solely out of malice.

Their conversation was interrupted by the sound of sobs and a low-pitched female voice offering words of comfort. Ty grimaced as the identity of the speaker came to him. He glanced toward the library door to see Genna entering in the sheltering arm of her sister. Tom's attorney followed them closely.

"Good morning all," Hallie said. "The black sheep's here, so we might as well get started." She looked around at the room's occupants, her gaze coming to rest on her father's second wife. God, the woman never aged! Hallie half suspected that somewhere on the property, there was a portrait of Marlene gracefully aging away a la Dorian Gray. She took in the sleek, navy-blue Armani suit and matching heels. Marlene Bishop would be at home in any drawing room in the world. Hallie had always envied her the poise and elegance that came to her as naturally as breathing. Maybe it was easier to look that good, she mused, when you had only two brain cells to rub together. "Hello, Marlene," she said. "You're looking prosperous. Nice suit." The other woman merely nodded in acknowledgment, the slightest whitening of her already pale skin being the only indication of Hallie's direct hit with her scornful remark. Walt moved closer to his sister, silently offering protection from Hallie's verbal thrusts. Ty took a step toward Hallie, as if to separate her from Genna, but the young girl's woebegone expression and tight hold on her sister stopped him in his tracks. Only Genna seemed oblivious to the undercurrent of tension running through the room. Hallie tipped her head in acknowledgment of the men, and steered her sister to the couch abutting the north wall of the room. She gently placed her sister on the sofa and removed her leather jacket before seating herself.

Hallie placed an arm around her sister once more and said, "You holding up all right, kiddo?"

Genna gave her a watery smile and replied, "I'll be fine, Hallie. I just wish this was all over. I just wish things could go back to the way they were."

Hallie nodded in understanding. She wished she could go back too. What Genna didn't realize, though, was how much of the past Hallie would change if she could. She felt Ty Nighthawk's infamous eyes watching her from across the room. He was warning her silently. Returning his stare, she challenged him. Anytime you think you're man enough. About then, the attorney cleared his throat, giving the signal he was ready to proceed.

Hallie waited on the edge of her seat as the bequests to the ranch hands and house staff were read. Next came the charitable donations. Her anxiety built. The outcome would have little impact on her financially, but that's not what she was waiting to hear about. There was no question in her mind that everything would go to Gen and Marlene. Whatever she felt about Marlene, the woman was her father's wife and she was entitled. What Hallie really hoped for was some message to her from her father— something that would indicate his love, his forgiveness. Instead, what she heard made her fists clench and the hair on the back of her neck rise. She jumped up from her place beside Genna, ready to come out swinging.

Chapter 4

No one spoke for a moment. Then all hell broke loose. Hallie was on her feet in an instant, oblivious to the questioning hand Genna laid on her arm. This was preposterous! She couldn't have heard that little twerp of a lawyer correctly. "Everything but five and a half million is to be divided into three equal portions, and those portions in their entirety go to Marlene Bishop, Hallie Bishop, and Tyler Nighthawk." Her father had disinherited one daughter for that deceitful bastard Nighthawk! She wouldn't stand by and let this happen.

"No way in hell!" she hollered, then whirled in fury to Tyler. "You miserable, self-righteous son-of-a-bitch."

Ty jumped to his feet as well, ready for war. He was as shocked at receiving one-third of the considerable remaining estate as she was. In all the years of Tom's bottomless generosity, nothing had ever made him anticipate anything like this. He marked the fire flashing in Hallie's eyes. She was livid. Why had Tom left Hallie so much and Genna nothing. Guilt washed over him. What had Tom been thinking? He couldn't accept the bequest, of course. The cold fury in Hallie's face let him know there was no way she'd let him accept it either. Genna had laid a restraining hand on her sister's elbow, but Hallie either didn't notice or she didn't care. A dawning realization swept over him. She wasn't enraged for Gen's sake. She was furious that her sister's rightful portion would be forever out of her pernicious grasp.

The attorney could see a situation that was rapidly spiraling out of control. He needed a cool head and a firm hand to bring things back to order. "That's quite enough, Miss Bishop!" he boomed over the uproar. "Kindly remember where you are, if you please."

"For God's sake, Hallie," cried Marlene. "Do you have to turn the reading of your father's will into a three ring circus too? I don't think I can take your theatrics another minute." She began to weep quietly into a delicate handkerchief. Walt placed comforting hands on his younger sister's shoulders and threw Hallie a murderous look.

"Sit down, Hallie," Ty said ominously, taking a step toward her. She lifted her chin mutinously, daring him to make her. Genna pulled desperately at her sister's arm.

Hallie's highly emotional state almost made her miss the attorney's next words. "$5,000,000 will be held in a trust fund for Genna Bishop until she reaches the age of 25. The trust fund is to be administered by Tyler Nighthawk, who in the event of the death of Marlene Bishop will become the sole guardian of Genna Bishop until she reaches the age of majority."

Hallie couldn't believe this. Not only had the unscrupulous vulture displaced Genna, but now he had control of her purse strings as well. She emotionally flinched from the realization that her father and stepmother would rather see her half-sister sheltered with anyone but her. But she had enough anguish to deal with at the moment; she'd deal with her pain later.

"Miss Bishop," the attorney continued, addressing Hallie disdainfully, "your father had some things in particular he wanted you to have." He cleared his throat, and Hallie held her breath. This could be what she had been waiting for. "Prior to his death, your father had me make the arrangements for a construction crew and a decorator to redo the guest bunkhouse. The arrangements have been completed, and work will start tomorrow. He left the bunkhouse to you with the hope that you'll stay and make it your permanent home this time." Hallie's face became a

frozen mask. She swallowed with difficulty and stiffly suffered the enthusiastic embrace of her sister. She heard Ty's
snort of disgust and Marlene's startled exclamation. "There
are also some boxes of things that belonged to your mother. Your father thought you should have those. And one
last thing. He left you the concert grand piano. That was
your mother's as well." He spoke of the items casually, as
if they were mere trifles instead of rare and precious links
to her mother. Since her mother's desertion and subsequent death, Hallie had been denied access to anything,
save the piano, that would remind her or anyone else of
Elena Bishop's very existence.

The attorney went on to discuss some of the provisos
set forth in the will. Of the three shares of the estate, no
single piece could be imparted to another of the share-
holders, nor could any shares be given to anyone or con-
veyed in any manner by the inheritors prior to their death.
In short, they each owned one-third of all Bishop holdings
until their death. He also relayed a short, pointed message
to Tyler. Tom Bishop, the attorney informed him, wanted
Tyler to accept his inheritance without reservations. He'd
thought of Tyler as the son of his heart, if not of blood.
Hallie received no message. She sat there trying to remember to breathe as waves of agony threatened to tear apart
her very soul.

Genna touched her sleeve and spoke softly. "Hallie,
I'm awfully glad you're back. I've really missed you. We'll
finally have the chance to be, well you know, like real sisters."

Hallie struggled to pull herself out of her despair. She
turned to smile at her sister, touched by the genuine love
in the younger girl's face. It was much more than Hallie
had hoped to see, given the influence of Marlene and Ty.
She looked at Gen's gentle, trusting face and thanked God

that at least she now had a chance to stay and become a small part of Genna's life. She could put up with whatever they dished out. Genna was worth it.

"Thanks, sweetie." She hugged the girl tight, holding the fierce pain in her chest at bay. "I can't tell you how great it's going to be to finally have the opportunity to get to know you too."

"It gets sort of lonely here sometimes, you know? Dad was ill for so long, and Mom and I don't always get along the best." Genna grinned shyly. "It'll be great to have someone to talk to."

"Yeah!" Hallie grinned. "Someone to gossip with, tell secrets to, someone around here who actually likes my music." Genna laughed.

Mrs. Hudson entered the library, disapproval clearly stamped all over her. She addressed Ty in a loud clear voice, including Hallie with a jerk of her thumb. "This one has a phone call. Some man," she said, disgust in her voice. "Calls himself 'Randy'." Ty made a contemptuous sound and nodded, as if granting the housekeeper permission to give Hallie her call. "This way," the woman said to her coldly.

Hallie rose from her seat and paused in front of Ty before following the housekeeper's stiff form out of the room. "Thanks for being so magnanimous, Tyler," she said. "I'll try to hold the heavy breathing to a minimum."

"What are we going to do, Ty?" Marlene asked brokenly, as she watched Hallie's retreating figure. "How could Tom force Hallie down our throats this way?"

Ty placed a protective arm around the woman's sagging shoulders. "Don't worry Marlene. I told you I know how to deal with her. She won't be here long," he vowed grimly.

Hallie fumed as she followed the unbending housekeeper to the telephone. It was worse than she'd thought: Nighthawk controlled everything. She had no doubt that, without his approval, she wouldn't have been allowed access to a phone. The beneficent, all-powerful OZ, from whom all bounty and privilege flowed! She'd just have to see about that. "Make it brief," she was instructed none too kindly as the woman departed.

Hallie picked up the phone and said with feigned lightness, "Hey, Rand-man. *Que pasa?*"

"Hello, gorgeous," said the deep, sensual voice on the other end of the line. It belonged to a man that millions of women all over the world fantasized about, threw underwear and room keys at: her former fellow band member and best damn bass man in the business, Randy Raveneau.

Hallie relaxed at the sound of his voice. Since the band breakup they'd only spoken a few times and had always strained to keep the conversation pleasant and civilized. After Sye Greenway's funeral last week though, they'd screamed, ranted and raved and called each other horrible names until they were exhausted. The death of their manager had forced them to deal with resentments and anguish too long denied. After the storm passed, they'd held on to each other tightly as only dear friends can, shed their tears and forgiven each other. "How are you doing?" she asked softly.

"Question is, babydoll, how are you?" The concern in his voice was a balm for her bruised and battered emotions.

"Ha! Enough said," she answered bitterly.

"All is not forgiven, I take it?"

"Are you kidding? All they did was run out and get a bigger score card." She sensed his worry and tried gallantly to lighten the mood. "It seems I've inherited one-third of everything and my mom's piano. Oh, and the bunkhouse I told you about."

"All of which, with the exception of your mother's piano, you need like another foot," he said with irritation. "I'm sorry, Hal. It's been hell for you over the last two weeks, and the last thing you need is me taking pot shots at your family. I just wish you'd do the smart thing for yourself and sign away everything, come back to LA and get on with your life. You've got lots of people down here who love you, Hal." Randy's sympathetic voice washed over her, reminding Hallie that she wasn't totally alone in the world. He understood her, understood her pain and her sense of isolation in the midst of what passed for her family. Part of her knew he was right. Aside from Genna, there was no family for her here. But Genna was more than enough, she told herself. The girl loved her older sister and after all the years of separation, that's all that mattered to Hallie.

"Thanks for keeping an eye on Mr. and Mrs. V. for me," she said, trying to change the subject. "Tell them I love them and I'll be back soon."

"No problemo. Mr. and Mrs. V. are almost as special to me as they are to you. The hardest part of the band breakup was not getting any of Mrs. V's cooking," he joked. She laughed in response, knowing full well her housekeeper had paid more than one surreptitious visit to Randy's house with hampers of food.

"Seriously, Hal, the Verdoza kids are here and I can be up there in a couple of hours if you want me to. Just say the word. I can help you get things settled, meet your folks, you know, keep anyone from hassling you. What do you say?" She knew all she had to do was crook her finger and he would be there—her own personal white knight. It sounded like heaven to her but Randy had his own life and she refused to impose any further on him.

"I appreciate the support, Randy, but I'll be okay, really. I have a few things to go over, but I'll be back in a day or two. We'll get together then."

"Sounds good, babydoll. In the meantime don't let the assholes get you down, okay?"

She shook her head and laughed warmly, "God, I've missed you. You're amazing, you know that?" she said softly.

"That's what all the ladies tell me, honey." There was a moment's hesitation before he spoke again. Hallie braced herself for what she sensed was coming. "I already called Cassie," he said. "She should be checking in with you any time." Hallie sighed. She'd been right. He was trying to play Mr. Fix-It again, God love him. "She's really worried about you." Randy continued.

"Yeah, well it's not like it's her month to watch me or anything." Hallie's heart lurched, but she was unwilling to show how much his simple words had meant to her. She'd truly burned that particular bridge. Her deep friendship with Cassie Donovan was ancient history now. She missed her more than she could say, quite literally. Since their falling out over Cassie's reconciliation with her first husband, Nicholas Montoya, and her subsequent remarriage to him, they hadn't said more than a couple of strained sentences to each other for more than a year and a half. Gossip columnists had a field day accusing Hallie of everything from jealousy of Montoya to sleeping with him. She hated Montoya intensely, and the media, in its continual quest for larger market share, had badly distorted the truth. She'd sooner sleep with a pig.

"Look, if she catches me in, I'll talk to her okay? I know she was upset about not making it to Boston for Sye. Right now I can relate, believe me." She paused for a moment and said, "I want to thank you for offering me shelter from the storm in Boston and flying down to Mexico with me. It was what I needed—we needed."

"You're welcome, Hal," he replied gently. "I've missed you too. So has Cassie. Call me as soon as you're back. I love you, Hal."

"I love you too, Rand-man." She hung up the phone and turned around to come face to face with Tyler Nighthawk looking like a thunder cloud. "What!?" she demanded loudly in her best brat voice.

"This week's lover?" he asked snidely.

"What's the matter, wasn't the wiretap on the phone clear enough, oh lord of the manor?" she said caustically.

"I take it you declined his kind offer to come up here?" he asked in a voice edged in steel. She nodded curtly. "Wise decision." He leaned against the wall. "In light of your father's will, I can't stop you from being here, but I sure as hell don't intend to make it easy for you, Hallie." He straightened himself and casually walked into the sun-room at the end of the corridor, knowing his challenge would make her follow him. He wasn't disappointed. The irate woman entered and prepared for combat. He raised one eyebrow and smiled pleasantly. "If you're going to stay at the ranch, we're going to have to establish the ground rules. Number one: no men. I won't have you parading your lovers around here, letting Genna see God knows what." As he spoke, his voice lowered, emphasizing the unfriendly tone. "Number two: Stay away from Marlene. I can't stop Genna from seeing her 'glamorous' sister," he said, making the adjective sound distasteful, "but I won't allow you to torture Marlene. She's suffered enough. And rule number three," he said, coming to tower over her, "is this: If you so much as bend rules one and two, you'll have me to deal with. I'll take you apart, Hallie."

She lowered her head and brought her eyes up to look at him. She was doing a slow burn. It was a stance and look that made many roadies the world over quake with fear. "Well now, " she said softly, "that was a real pretty speech...real pretty. Let me see if I've got this straight. You say 'jump' and I say 'how high,' right?" Ty nodded, as he narrowed his eyes warily. He'd expected her to take a swing at him and was prepared for swift and immediate retribution. With any luck, she'd be booked on assault charges and cooling her heels in jail within the hour. Hallie tapped her finger thoughtfully on her cheek. "Also, if I'm good and don't cause any trouble, I can stay and nobody gets hurt?"

"That's about it." Ty answered. Was he imagining it, or was she looking at his throat with a feral gleam in her eye? She'd matured, somewhat, and honed her battle skills to a fine edge in the process. The idea was extremely unnerving. His disquiet agitated him even more, and he regarded her fiercely.

"Bullshit," she snapped, jabbing him in the chest. She put her hands on her hips and spread her feet apart as she glared up at him. "Now we'll go over my rules, sunshine. Rule number one: I don't have any rules unless I make them. If I want to sleep with the entire first string of the Green Bay Packers on the roof of my bunkhouse, it's none of your damn business. Got it! As for Marlene, if she stays out of my way, and leaves me alone, I'll do likewise; it's up to her. And as for you—since the minute I arrived yesterday, you've been all over me with your nasty little suspicions and your attitude. I'm sick of it. You push me, Nighthawk, and I'll push you back. Real hard. Any questions?"

"Just one," he drawled. "Tell me, Hallie, how does it feel to know that while you were in Mexico screwing your lover, your father was dying?"

Hallie's face whitened and she shut her eyes for a moment as Ty's words hit their mark. She opened them quickly again to look up at him, her eyes blazing with hate. "Go to hell!" she said. Then she turned and left the room to walk briskly down the hall.

Ty watched her go, feeling dislike, disgust, even admiration—all at the same time. She'd stood toe to toe with him, like a cub hissing and spitting at a full-grown lion. Whatever else he thought of her, he had to admit she had guts. He continued to watch her walk down the hall and felt heat rise in his loins. She also had one incredible ass.

Chapter 5

The next three weeks flew by in a haze of activity. Hallie returned to Los Angeles to make arrangements for leasing her house and to ensure that Mr. and Mrs. Verdoza were suitably taken care of. With their retirement fund, and the pension plan Hallie had provided for them, they would be able to live comfortably for the rest of their lives. Hallie's final present to them had been a condo in Sedona, Arizona, close to friends and family. It was a tearful good-bye when she saw them off in the company of their oldest son. Magdelaina Verdoza and her husband Bernardo had been surrogate parents to Hallie since the day the agency had sent them in answer to Hallie's request for a house-keeper and handyman. Mrs. V had fussed when she didn't eat, clucked over her when she was sick, and worried every time Hallie was on the road for the last eight years. It was hard to let them go, but Bernardo's health required rest, relaxation and the care and support of his real family.

Clancy Redfern, Hallie's personal assistant, made the arrangements for the correct instruments to be sent to Oregon and the rest to be stored. Hallie had an extensive collection of guitars, some original one-of-a-kind show stoppers, some signed by the true legends of the business, and her own personal weapons of choice. She would be taking only four guitars with her at this time: her old Martin acoustic, the new Rickenbacker 650 series, her beloved Stratocaster picked up at Christie's auction house and auto-graphed by Jimi Hendrix himself, and her Gibson Les Paul. She was taking her favorite things to build herself a fortress of comfort and safety against the animosity she would be facing. Clancy helped her pack up what clothes, memen-tos and selected house furnishings that would fit in her new digs, and the rest of it was either sold, donated or stored.

When the movers had taken the last of the items away, Hallie began to give instructions to the endless stream of lawyers, accountants and stock analysts she kept on retainer. She was advised to hire an outside auditing firm to go over the financial records of her father's companies, assured she had every right legally now that she owned one third of each of them. The firm suggested had enough clout so that the mere mention of their name would effectively silence Tyler and Marlene, should they protest. Slowly but surely, the pieces came together, and she was finally ready to return to the ranch.

The renovation of the bunkhouse had been completed, and with the arrival of her amps and recording equipment, all was in readiness. She'd let Randy Raveneau know the latest developments, and had carefully avoided Cassie Donovan's repeated attempts to contact her. The last thing she could deal with was the guilt she'd feel at even the sound of her voice. No, Cassie was well intentioned, but what had passed between them over Nick couldn't be ignored or swept away with a sympathy call.

As for Cassie's own guilt over being unable to be with their manager Sye when he died, Hallie passed along what comfort she could via Randy. Cassie had been in the last month of her pregnancy. Given her age, the proximity to her due date, and the fact that she was carrying twins, her doctor and Nick had insisted she remain at home. As far as the rest of the former band members were concerned, Cassie had no reason for guilt. Unlike herself. Randy and Chuck E. had come just before the end and at least had gotten to say goodbye. Hallie had been with Sye for over a week beforehand.

The man who'd lain dying of AIDS had, without a doubt in Hallie's mind, saved her life. He'd taken a chance

on a scruffy, half-starved street kid who could play the guitar like hell. He'd picked her up out of the gutter, and
between himself and his life partner Toddy, had made her
what she was today. In the times of her worst need, both
those men had been there to take care of her and support
her. Though the anguish she felt over not seeing her father
before his death hadn't diminished over the weeks, part of
her thanked God she hadn't been forced to choose
between the two. Because she honestly didn't know
which she would have chosen.

Clancy, bless her heart, ran interference diplomatically
with the press and her acquaintances during preparations
for the move. She passed on the information to Hallie of
the successful birth of Justin and Juliet Montoya—mother
and babies doing fine. Clancy made sure Hallie's brief
note and the custom-made miniature leather wrist bands,
one in pink and one in blue, were delivered. Hallie was
going to miss Clancy's day-to-day presence overseeing the
intricacies of her life, but Clancy was a city girl at heart and
knew that fax modems and e-mail would make it possible
for her to still work for Hallie without leaving her beloved
LA.

The day before Hallie started her drive back to Oregon,
her feisty factotum arrived unannounced on her door step,
fit to be tied. "We're firing your accountants," she declared
without preamble as soon as Hallie opened the door.
"They're blind as well as inept."

"Oh yeah, Redfern? What's the matter?" Hallie asked
facetiously. "Somebody pee in your oatmeal this morning,
or do you have a legitimate gripe?"

"This is serious, Hal," Clancy returned grimly. She
waved copies of bank statements underneath her employ-
er's chin, then stomped into the now vacant living room.
She looked around at the bare hardwood floor and empty

bookshelves, then back to Hallie. It looked as though she were about to cry and Hallie hoped that wasn't the case because she'd felt close to tears herself all morning. "I don't think you should go back up there," Clancy said, her eyes sad and worried. "I know how much you love your sister, Hal, but as your personal assistant, and dear friend, I think you're making a terrible mistake. Someone is playing a real horrendous game with you." She extended her hand holding the papers toward Hallie. "Your most recent bank statements for your personal and corporate accounts—ten of them in all. Pay close attention to the deposits. That damned accounting firm of yours should have picked up on this right away. Within the last thirty day period, thirty deposits have been made to these accounts."

Hallie shrugged as she accepted the papers from Clancy. "So? I'm surprised there weren't more. You know how many royalties, endorsement and dividend checks we get every month. What's the big deal?"

Clancy made a disgusted sound at Hallie's blasé attitude. "I'm not talking about the usual deposits. They're all there. It's the others that have me worried."

"What others? What the hell are you talking—" Hallie stopped abruptly as she saw what Clancy referred to. Quickly, she skimmed through the other statements and an expression of growing alarm spread across her features. "There must be at least twenty-five deposits here made to each account, all for the same amount."

"I told you, thirty, exactly. All for $9,900. One for each day of the statement period. It adds up to a total of $297,000. Not too shabby, but darned suspicious. Banks are required by law to report any deposit of $10,000 or more to the IRS. Whoever your Santa Claus is, they didn't want to tip off the feds—either that, or they wanted it to look like they didn't. Deposits like these look very suspect to bank auditors, the IRS," she paused then added significantly, "and the district attorney's office."

"Shit!"

"Exactly. Care to guess where these little beauties came from?"

"I'm afraid to," Hallie answered morosely.

"You should be. The Grand Caymans. A numbered account in your name."

If there had been a chair left in the room, Hallie would have collapsed into it. She quickly assessed the possible meanings for the deposits. Hallie had never been slipshod in managing money. To forget an additional $300,000 in income, she'd have to be a blithering idiot. As for Santa Claus, well, Hallie knew she'd never been a good enough girl to get that kind of money in her stocking—or a bad enough one either. The answer was obvious. Someone was setting her up to take the fall for the disappearing company funds. Someone who hated her enough to destroy her life. A deep sense of dread gripped her. Perhaps it was the same someone who felt she'd destroyed his. She moved swiftly to the phone that now lay neglected on the floor. "I'm calling my lawyer," she said over her shoulder.

Unfortunately, her attorney had left town for a long weekend on the ski slopes. Hallie left a desperate plea on her voice mail, knowing it could still be quite some time before Kelsey got her message. "I'm screwed, Clance," she said dejectedly.

"Call Randy," the other woman suggested. "When it comes to finance and investments, the guy has second sight. He'll know how to find out who really put the funds in the Caymans account."

Hallie nodded, not missing the fact that at no time had there been any doubt in Clancy's mind she was innocent of any wrongdoing. She began to dial Randy's number, wondering again if returning to the ranch was the wise thing to do, even though her promise to her father demanded it. With the exception of Genna, no one would be glad to see her. In light of the information about her accounts, it appeared someone was willing to do practically anything to remove Hallie from the picture—as perhaps they had with her father.

❧ ☙

Tyler put the last of his paperwork in the out basket for the secretaries to handle and turned to pack up his briefcase and laptop computer. Thank God for fax programs and modems, he thought. He packed the discs with all the files and records he'd need. Anything else would be downloaded as necessary. Ty planned on working from the ranch now as much as possible. All the better to keep an eye on Hallie.

Marlene had called him at his house in the northwest hills last night to tell him that the contractors and electricians had finished, the movers had brought Hallie's things, and she was scheduled to arrive this morning. There had been no emergency calls from the ranch, so things must have stayed fairly calm. The ranch hands and Mrs. Hudson had been alerted to keep an eye on Genna and run interference with Hallie as much as possible. He wasn't quite sure what to expect. Loud music, booze, and paparazzi hanging from the trees seemed a safe bet. In any event, he'd be glad to get home to observe the mayhem personally.

On the ride to the airport, Ty filled Walt in on the most current information he'd gathered about the company's financial status. There wasn't much new to tell. They both knew that the money trail had come to a dead end. It would probably take several weeks and every marker the

Bishop Company had to obtain the information they needed to bring the embezzler to justice. Ty's money was still
on Hallie. His lip curled in disgust. He'd get the evidence
they needed to get rid of her. And he didn't care what he
had to do to get it.

By the time they reached the ranch it was shortly after
six o'clock, and Ty wanted nothing as badly as a double
shot of bourbon, a shower, and his favorite pair of jeans.
Unfortunately, his fantasy was short-lived. As they drove
past the newly rejuvenated bunkhouse, he saw Genna do
a sprightly jump in front of the picture window in the living room. Hallie obviously hadn't thought to hang curtains
this afternoon. To Walt's obvious amusement, he was still
swearing and sputtering when he parked the car. He gathered his belongings and stomped up the verandah steps,
closely followed by Walt. Mrs. Hudson greeted them at
the door, looking nervous and at wit's end.

"Thank heavens you're back, Mr. Ty, Mr. Walt. That
one," she said, pointing toward the bunk house, "arrived
this morning, lock, stock, and barrel, wanting this,
demanding that. She waltzes herself up to the front door
and demands to see Miss Genna, bold as brass."

"Calm yourself, Mrs. Hudson," Walt began. "I'm sure
we'll get matters straightened out. Things were bound to
be a little bumpy today."

"Bumpy!" the grim-faced housekeeper sputtered.
"She's the most pushy, opinionated piece of baggage!"

"All right, Mrs. Hudson," Ty said. "We get the idea.
What else happened?"

"Well, I tried to do what you said, Mr. Ty. You know,
about keeping Miss Genna occupied and all. She comes
bounding down the stairs and throws herself at that sister
of hers, and they both start squealing and carrying on.
Next thing I know that one says Genna should come help

her move in. I says, 'Miss Genna, I'm going to the market later, and I wanted know if there was anything you wanted. Maybe you could help plan the meals for the weekend?' Then that woman says, 'Great! I need some things too.' 'Well,' I says, 'I work for Mrs. Bishop and not you.' And then you know what?" The woman's mouth worked with indignation. "She smiles all big and cheery and says, 'Well if you work for Mrs. Bishop, then I guess you'd better get to it.' Then she trots off with Miss Genna as bold as anything, waggling her behind in those tight pants of hers." Mrs. Hudson started to wring her hands. "Miss Genna's been gone all day, and it's dinner time. Her mother's real upset."

Ty let out an exasperated sigh. "Did anyone happen to think to go to the bunkhouse and tell Genna it's time to come home?" At the housekeeper's stricken look, Ty swore, left his things in the front hall, and headed toward Hallie's place. He called back over his shoulder, "It's not exactly the other side of the moon, Mrs. Hudson, and even if Hallie bit you, I'm sure she's had her shots!" He stomped toward the bunkhouse, loosening his tie and rolling up his sleeves as he went.

He stopped himself just before he opened the door without knocking. After all, it was Hallie's home, and it was important to respect her rights as long as it was convenient to. He rapped sharply and almost immediately she opened the door.

"Hello there," she said amiably, giving him that sexy, go-to-hell half-smile of hers. "I've been wondering when you'd turn up. I was beginning to think maybe I'd scared you off." She stepped out of the way and gestured him in.

"That'll be the day, Hallie," he said, shutting the door behind him. "I've come to get Genna. You've had enough quality time with her."

"As you can see, she's right there in the living room."
Hallie gave her sister a conspiratory wink.

"Genna," Ty said evenly, trying to hold on to his badly
frayed temper, "it's time for dinner. Get up to the house."

"Ty, we were going to go out for pizza!" the teenager
complained.

"Now Genna," he said sharply.

The girl flounced off the sofa and hugged her sister
goodnight, promising to return early in the morning. After
she'd closed the door behind her, Ty glanced around the
living room at the tasteful and expensive furnishings. He
noted the lamps, accent pieces, and art objects placed
throughout the room in a well designed, yet seemingly art-
less arrangement. The concert grand piano from the main
house was already in place. A lot of the art pieces gracing
the walls were old, original concert posters, some by
famous artists, including one by Peter Max. He noted the
poster from the Philmore West concert hall in the sixties,
advertising Big Brother and the Holding Company and
their lead singer Janis Joplin. He wouldn't have minded
having that himself. There was also one for Woodstock,
with its little yellow bird perched on the guitar neck, and
one for Altamonte. Two shelves of the newly installed
bookcases were devoted to her music awards, and Ty was
annoyed with himself for wanting to take a closer look at
them. "Nice furniture," he said. His attention was drawn
to a large, wall-sized photograph centered over the sofa.
The color photo was of a group of middle-aged to somewhat older men, and one woman. Hallie.

"Thanks. You always talk to Genna that way? Go
Genna, sit Genna, stay Genna, come Genna. You're not
her father, you know."

"Right now I'm the closest thing she's got to one. I suggest you mind your own business, Hallie." He gave her a

level look and turned to go.

"I bet you do. You've got quite a little lord of the manor deal going on here, don't you? Nothing gets done without your okay, and no one lives their life without your all-powerful benevolence." She tossed her hair and glared defiantly at him. "Afraid I'm going to cramp your style?"

"Nothing about you frightens me, Hallie. Sickens me, yes, but frightens, no," Ty responded, curling his lip.

Hallie shifted her weight onto one leg and folded her arms across her chest. The feral look was back in her eyes. "Hey, come on, *chico*. Don't hold back. Let me know how you feel." He had the disconcerting impression she was gauging the distance between herself and his throat. Something must have made her change her mind suddenly because as quickly as the gleam had come into her eyes, it was gone again. She shook her head as if to clear her thoughts. "Look, Ty, for once in our lives, let's try not to get off on the wrong foot, okay?" she said.

"It's about twenty years too late for that, Hallie," he replied coldly.

"You're not going to make this easy, are you?"

"I gave you fair warning that it's going to be hell. You're not wanted here." He gestured to the picture over the sofa. "Might as well go back to where you're appreciated, where you're the center of attention. You're good at that."

Hallie strolled over to the picture and said, "Nighthawk, if ignorance is bliss, then you must be the happiest son-of-a-bitch this side of paradise." She crooked her finger at him. "Come here a minute." When he hesitated, she gave him the crooked smile and an arched eyebrow. "I don't bite little boys the first time they step into my parlor."

He went to her, standing close enough that she could

feel his breath on her face, and said, "I haven't been a little boy in a long time, Hallie. I suggest you remember that
and don't challenge me." The hard glint in his eyes made
her nervous, but she decided to ignore what she'd seen
lurking there, and turned her back to kneel on the sofa and
point accurately at each person in the picture.

"From the left, Jeff Beck, B.B. King, me, Mark Knopfler,
Eric Clapton, Bo Diddley, Eric Johnson, Carlos Santana,
and Brian Setzer. Benefit and tribute concert in Europe two
years ago." She turned to give Ty an amused glance.
"Surely some of those names ring a bell with even a complete rectangle like yourself. Try being the center of attention in company like that. It don't work so well."

"Am I supposed to be impressed?" he asked, the sharp
edge of cynicism back in his voice.

She laughed shortly. "Honey, I have quite a few things
about me that seem to impress men. This photo isn't one
of them." She got up from the sofa and headed to the bedroom. "I'm going out, so I have to shower and change.
Don't slam the door on your way out." She never looked
back.

It was all Ty could do to keep from storming into her
room, shaking her and demanding that she start impressing
him, then and there. His blood was beginning to boil;
unfortunately, most of it was headed straight to his groin.
It was stupid of him to think Walt could ever handle a
woman like her. She'd chew him up and spit him out, and
Walt would never know what hit him. Ty slammed the
front door loudly and stormed toward the main house, with
visions of Hallie doing a water ballet in the shower.

Hallie cringed behind the closed door of her bedroom.
She let out a sigh of relief as the front door slammed, rattling the window glass throughout the house. What the
hell was she thinking, provoking him that way? He could

have come bursting through the door at any time, intent on God knows what. She felt a little flutter in her stomach. Part of her almost wished that he had. Get a grip, Hal, she thought to herself. Hallie had felt an odd little tremor go through her the moment she'd opened the door to find him standing there—looking sexy as hell in a dress shirt with the sleeves rolled up, a blue and red silk tie, loose around the collar, and navy blue suit pants. He was a handsome man and those boardroom-type fantasies really got to her. What was she thinking! This guy hated her guts and didn't much care for the rest of her either. Most of the time, he looked and spoke to her as if she were something distasteful at the bottom of a glass. But every now and then, deep in those jungle eyes of his, she saw a primal animal passion that made her knees shake. Did he hate her clear through? Probably. Did he find her attractive? Definitely. One thing was for sure: He was a cold-hearted predator as far as she was concerned. If he ever decided to act on any attraction he did have, there would be very little she could do about it—and she had to ask herself if she would even want to if she could. "Good going," she said to the walls. "You're fantasizing about a guy who could very well be the one planning on giving you a new address at the federal penitentiary." She grabbed her bathrobe and headed toward the shower.

Some distance away, a telephone rang and an uneasy man scrambled to answer it before it rang again. "Well, it sure as hell took you long enough to me call back! We've got trouble."

"It figures," said the slightly bored voice on the other end of the line. "What's the matter now?"

"She knows. She called me yesterday in a panic. Wanted me to tell her what to do—how to get out of this mess." He began drumming his fingers on the top of his desk. "I told you we wouldn't have enough time," he accused.

There was a resigned sigh followed by a terse oath over the phone. "What did you tell her?"

"Nothing."

There was a very minute pause that spoke as loudly as gunfire, and the blonde man was glad he couldn't see the eyes of the man on the other end. "What did you tell her?" There was a distinct warning in the softly spoken question.

"I told you, nothing. I just said I'd make some inquiries and told her not to worry—I'd help her out. Luckily for us Kelsey Hogan is out of town till Tuesday at the earliest. That may give us some more time."

"It doesn't matter," the man on the phone said curtly. "There's nothing either one of them can do at this point. Everything is proceeding as planned. Bishop won't give us any trouble."

"Are you nuts? Hal can give people nothing but trouble if she has a mind to. You know that better than anyone."

He heard an unpleasant chuckle come over the phone and flinched. "She's not going to be a problem to me. No matter what she does. I can guarantee it."

Chapter 6

By ten o'clock that evening, the air in Pepe's was heavy, tinged blue with cigarette smoke, the smell of nickel-and-dime cologne, and the friction of male and female bodies as they moved against each other on the crowded dance floor. The juke box belted out a popular country western hit as Ty Nighthawk entered the bar. He didn't come here often, only when he was in a reckless, unpleasant sort of mood. He was dressed in his favorite type of off-duty outfit: faded blue jeans and an uptown and expensive version of a pale-blue chambray work shirt. An ornate, but not vulgar, turquoise and silver belt buckle rode at hip level, and he wore black boots underneath the legs of his boot-cut jeans. His jet-black hair was swept back from his face, but for all his good intentions, the shaggy bangs continued to fall over his forehead.

He studied the crowd roaming the bar for a moment, then ambled toward a vacant space at the side. The roadhouse had always drawn a rougher clientele, and he could remember well the days before Ramirez bought it, when chicken wire covered the front of the stage to fend off flying beer bottles. He also remembered carrying a snarling, kicking sixteen-year-old back to the ranch after she'd snuck here to play guitar. For his trouble, he'd received a black eye and several bruises. He ordered a beer and mentally cursed himself for letting Hallie intrude on his "R&R." Dinner had been a complete ordeal, from poor Mrs. Hudson's uncharacteristic scorching of the meal to Marlene's relentless grilling of Genna—the end result of which was the girl's running from the dinner table in a torrent of tears. After the meal was no picnic either. Marlene retired to her room with a headache, leaving Walt and him

fighting in the library. Ty issued a warning about any
intention of romancing Hallie. Walt laughed, ridiculing
the younger man's opinion. He saw himself as Hallie's
ticket to the inner sanctum of the family and assured Ty
that he would have her eating out of his hand in a matter
of weeks, tame as a kitten. Walt also offered to share
Hallie's obvious attributes. The derision in his voice
annoyed Ty. Whatever he thought about Hallie, she was a
worthy opponent, one who had managed to earn a certain
amount of grudging respect and admiration. She was a
fighter, not unlike himself.

The last thing he'd wanted to do was spend the evening
trapped in a tense and sullen house. That decision led him
to Pepe's door. Granted, it was an odd choice of estab-
lishment. Pepe Ramirez was still a good friend of Hallie's
and though he never had refused Ty service, Pepe made no
bones about his feelings toward Hallie's family. Tom had
never approved of Hallie's closeness to the Ramirez family, and Hallie's insistence on accompanying Pepe to fiestas
and concerts had forced innumerable confrontations
between father and daughter. Actually, Tom's almost irra-
tional need to keep Hallie from her Hispanic roots had
been one of the few things that Ty had ever disagreed with
his mentor about. Ty certainly realized the importance of
tracing cultural roots in his own life. Tom had always supported Ty's quests for communion with his Native
American ancestry, even allowing him time off every year
for the state pow-wow in Salem and a retreat to the Warm
Springs Reservation. Ty now wondered about Tom's inexplicable double standard. He presumed it was his disapproval of Pepe, who was several years older than Hallie, as
a suitable companion for an impressionable young girl.
After all, Tom had firmly believed it was Pepe or one of the
Stanton brothers who had first seduced Hallie. Personally,

Ty thought it was the other way around.

He felt a hostile glare seeking him out and turned his head to find Russ Carver and two of his friends looking him over. Great. The place was loaded with people full of love for him! Alcohol and grudges—not a good mix. Carver had never been crazy about him, but after he'd found out about Ty's spring break fling with the girl Russ was dating, he'd loathed him. Ty lifted his mug in salute, then felt a slight tap on his shoulder. He turned to find Sara Brown smiling up at him.

"Are you mad, bad, and dangerous to know tonight, or just plain foolhardy?" she asked. He gave the woman a slow, lazy smile.

"Depends who's doin' the asking." His eyes swept appreciatively over her trim little figure as he said, "Hello, Sara. Can I get you a drink?" She blushed at the interest in his eyes. They'd been casually dating for a little over a year, ever since she'd moved back to Bishops Bluff from Cincinnati.

"I'll have a beer with you, if you're looking for company," she answered, letting the tone of her voice suggest that a beer wasn't the only thing she'd be willing to have with him.

"I am now." The evening was definitely looking up. They'd spend a couple of hours over beer and conversation, and then he'd take her home to her place and her very large, very familiar bed.

He ushered Sara to a small discreet table in the shadows near the stage. Suddenly, Russ Carver's bulky frame materialized in front of them, his hand resting possessively on the back of a vacant chair. "Sorry, Nighthawk," he drawled, "but it appears this table is taken. Guess you'll just have to wait at the bar."

❧ ❧

"Well that's too bad, Carver," Ty said tightly, his cold eyes never leaving the sneering face before him. "The lady and I would like to have a couple of beers and a dance or two. Now we can go outside to discuss this little matter if you want, but," he looked Carver up and down as if he found him to be small and rather insignificant, "I'd take it kindly if you'd just go about your business, and leave us to ours." Carver hesitated for a moment, then at the almost imperceptible tightening of Ty's jaw, slipped his hand from the back of the chair.

"Dirty breed," he hissed. "You got no business with a decent woman." Sara gasped and laid a restraining hand on Ty's arm.

"Move off now, Carver, or Pepe's going to need a major over-haul in here," he said.

With a belligerent shove to the chair, Carver moved away, sliding through the crowd to join his cronies at the bar. Sara stroked Ty's arm. "Let's sit this one out, okay?" He nodded stiffly, then moved to hold the chair for her.

"Anything to oblige a lady. It's been one hell of a day." He signaled the waitress and within moments the table was cleared, wiped, and restocked with icy mugs and a large pitcher of draft. No sooner had the waitress departed, waggling her shapely little behind, than Ty returned to the conversation he'd halted in her presence.

"You know, I still can't quite believe it. Tom had always talked about leaving me a piece of the ranch, but I didn't expect a third of everything he had. I never asked for it. I know he figured Genna would one day come into Marlene's share, but why would he choose some kid he took in over her? Why three equal shares? People are bound to talk, Sara. I'll tell you, Hallie was fit to be tied." He swallowed a mouthful of beer, letting it roll down the back of his throat with satisfaction.

"Tom thought of you as a son, Ty," Sara stated in a soothing tone. "You know that. It's not surprising that he'd give you an equal share with Marlene and Hallie. As you said, Genna's portion will come to her through her mother in time. I'm sure Marlene respects her husband's wishes, and Hallie, well...it's not as if she needs the money, is it?"

"Who can tell with that washed-up has-been." He drained his glass and set it on the table with a loud thunk. "Why else would she move her junk back into her old bunkhouse and decide to stay for the duration. She's lost her band, and probably the record companies aren't beating a path to her door anymore. She has time on her hands, and Hallie with time on her hands is a dangerous commodity. The last thing any of us need is her getting creative with all our lives."

"Ouch!" Sara grimaced. "You sure don't pull your punches where she's concerned, do you? Did you ever think maybe Hallie regrets how things turned out between her and her family? I know you have your problems with her, but I remember her a little differently. Wild, yes, but not mean or devious. The way you talk about her...well, it's as if you can't see any good in her. Almost like you're afraid to." Sara let her voice trail off as she noted the expression on his face.

Ty's jaw tightened with the memories of a father waiting for a word—any word—that his daughter was alive. He saw the note Hallie had sent to his mother scrawled in her impatient, immature hand—the note responsible for shattering his dreams of the future. He saw the bitter, hostile eyes of an angry teenager backstage at a Chicago concert hall. In Ty's mind, Tom had gone to his grave trying to make everyone in town believe in a Hallie that didn't exist. "You don't know what she can be capable of, Sara," he said out loud. "She'll do anything she can to settle a score—real or imagined. No one knows that better than me. What she's just beginning to realize, though, is that she's bitten off way more than she can chew." He changed the subject to something more pleasant, and again chastised himself for dwelling on the things he'd wanted to escape.

The band was heading back to the stage after a break, and the lead singer, a big burly fellow whose voice was a cross between Charlie Daniels and Randy Travis, strolled to the mike to address the crowd. "Ladies and Gents!" he shouted. "It's not every day that I get to introduce a real celebrity!" A collective murmur of anticipation broke over the crowd. "A local gal who's done pretty darn well for herself!"

"Shit!" hissed Ty. Sara patted his arm, an amused smile on her face.

"I'm also real proud to call this little lady a friend of mine." The crowd started to whoop and cheer as their suspicions were confirmed by the figure entering the stage. "Everybody, give a big hometown welcome to Hallie Bishop!" Amid more cheers and foot stomping, Gal Hal took her place with the band.

"Christ, I can't get away from her," Nighthawk growled.

Sara's smile erupted into a laugh. "Honestly, Ty! I swear you think that woman is here on purpose the way you're carrying on! What the hell. Let's dance." With that, she stood and took his hand to draw him toward the dance floor.

Hallie plucked a couple of chords and ran an experimental riff to tune her instrument. She was as excited as any member of the audience. Shielding her eyes against the overhead stage lights, she leaned out toward the cheering crowd and favored them with her famous half smile.

"Hey everybody! Thanks for letting me sit in. I can use the practice." They went wild. She continued to tease as she stroked and tuned her instrument. "Pepe's gettin' pretty uptown now. I don't see any bottles flying around. We used to have to bob and weave pretty good up here." She laughed and pointed to a heavyset bear of a man at the bar. "I see you, Bobby Gillis! Don't you laugh! Rex up here's still got a scar on his leg from you!" Big Bobby hooted good-naturedly and was rewarded by slaps on the back and the offer of drinking to the good ol' days. Suddenly the lights dimmed and Gal Hal Bishop led the band in a slow, sultry rendition of Alana Miles' "Black Velvet."

Her hands moved up and down the neck of the guitar, teasing and coaxing, as her pelvis arched against the body of the instrument. The temperature had risen ten to twenty degrees since the beginning of the song. Gradually, she became aware of one couple, particularly, who danced close to the front of the stage. The woman was tall and sleek with a short, glossy brown bob. The man in whose arms she moved fixed Hallie with an intense, burning gaze. Oh God! she thought, almost blowing a chord. Nighthawk. When he saw the flash of recognition cross Hallie's face, he tightened his embrace instantly around Sara and gave Hallie a mocking smile. His eyes never leaving Hallie's, he altered his dance to a slower, more sensual movement. His hands slid down Sara's figure, skimming the outline of her hips and coming to rest on the curve of her buttocks. He pulled her to him as his hips moved against hers. Sara tightened her arms around his neck, forcing his mouth down to hers.

Hallie's voice throbbed through the club. She wasn't sure where the sexual heat of her singing stopped and the scorching passion of Ty's and Sara's dance began. She suspected Nighthawk was having similar difficulty defining the boundaries himself. It felt as if she were in his arms instead of Sara, moving with him in slow, pulsing foreplay. She tried to break her eyes away from Ty, time and again, only to find herself helplessly drawn back to those eyes, those hands, those hips. As the song ended, she turned abruptly from the mike to take a gulp from a glass handed to her by the waiting band technician. Wonderful, she thought glumly, not only was her evening of relaxation ruined, but she was acting like a goofy high school kid. She took another drink. They made an attractive couple. An attractive sexual couple. She shook her head in an effort to compose her thoughts, mouthed the name of the next song to Rex, and whirled back to the audience with the opening strains of the Stray Cats' "Rock This Town."

Later, back at the table, Ty watched a rivulet of sweat run down Hallie's neck. It traced a pathway to the cleft between her breasts, where they strained against the fabric of her spandex top. Her head was thrown back as the music erupted from the very center of her being. He was mesmerized. The guitar spoke in her hands, crying from the heart. She was a witch with the instrument, a bruja, conjuring places and emotions from some far off, misty shore. Song after song took flight from the stage, arching high over the audience to enthrall and energize them. Hallie was the tour guide and no one was allowed off the bus until she decided. He watched her face, alive with passion from her mastery of the music. If she was this good in a local dive, what was she like in concert with a great back-up band and a state-of-the-art sound system? He hated admitting it to himself, but he'd like to know. He also hated admitting to some of the other things he wondered. What she was like in bed? Did she have the same fire and energy? What did her face look like when she came? It wasn't the first time his thoughts had taken a turn like that where Hallie was concerned, and he was damned if he could understand why his loathing of her only added fuel to an already blazing inferno. He turned to find Sara regarding him thoughtfully. She shook her head and turned her attention back to her mug of beer.

The crowd refused to let her go. After all, it wasn't every night a rock 'n' roll icon played for free at Pepe's Roadhouse. Another set came and went before they let Hallie take her bow and leave. Rex and the boys had an hour to play, and the still bewitched crowd greeted their numbers with more enthusiasm than they usually did.

About twelve-thirty, the place thinned out to drunks and the few unlucky individuals who for one reason or another hadn't managed to make an affection connection. The drunks still hoped to score a couple more rounds, and the singles just hoped to score. Ty looked at the mugs and pitchers littering the table. Sara had gone home an hour ago with the girlfriend she'd come with. She'd angrily muttered something about second-string fiddles and left him to drown his bruised ego in another pitcher and curse the real villain of his ruined evening—Hallie. Everything had been going along just fine til she showed up. He glowered into his beer. After the first dance, he was ready to take Sara home and try some more intimate horizontal moves. Sara was a long, cool drink of water to a man dying of thirst from the dancing and the music. When their last dance was finished, he'd torn his eyes from the stage only to find Sara looking up at him with an expression that was both bewildered and resentful. He brushed her mouth with a consoling kiss and suggested they go somewhere a little more private. She demurred, and in her hesitancy, he read the war she was having with herself, though he could hardly credit the cause.

Later, as they sat at the table nursing their beers and

straining to make even the slightest conversation, the
beginning of Blue Oyster Cult's "Burning For You" hyp-
notically drew his attention back to the stage and to the
woman in the spotlight. The spell was cast, and he was
caught again. He was vaguely aware of Sara leaving his
side to go and talk to someone, a woman he'd thought.
Suddenly she was in front of him again, jabbing her finger
into his chest, informing him of her departure, her opinion
of him and his future chances of her companionship, public or private. He spent the rest of the evening with another large pitcher, watching Hallie.

It had been almost ten years since he'd heard her play
live. When he heard her music, his natural dislike of her
had made him give all the credit for the music to the
recording studio technicians, as if her talent was all elec-
tronically enhanced and therefore as fake as she was. But
sitting here, listening to her live, he knew there was no
denying it. She was magnificent. She could play anyone's
music and still make it uniquely her own. When she
closed out with the Scorpions' "Rock You Like A
Hurricane," and kicked her leg high to the side, a trade-
mark of hers, Ty was sure he, and every other man in the
place, would charge the stage. He knew he wanted what
every guy in the place wanted. The difference was that he
knew what they didn't. The little slut was poison clear
through. His hatred of her was no doubt part of the attraction. She felt it too. He'd seen it in her face as she'd
watched him dance with Sara, and he let the knowledge
roll around his brain for a while. Hallie wasn't a distant
image on a TV screen. She was real, all hot-blooded
female. What were some of the lyrics to that last song?
Something about a hungry bitch... He made a decision. If
the opportunity presented itself to sample what she adver-
tised so freely, he'd make sure he was there to accept it.

Perhaps he'd end up in a better position than anyone to control her.

Hell, he couldn't stand her, but why shouldn't he enjoy what she offered every other guy in the world? Maybe it was the beer talking, but after what she'd cost him in his personal life, she certainly owed him a service call. He didn't care what the sly innuendoes in the gossip columns said about her sexual orientation. After seeing her on that stage, watching her body move, her hips grind, he knew. He thought about her in his bed again. She would claw and scratch and completely lose control, at least for him. He'd make sure of it. There was a sexual tension between them. He'd denied it, fought it for years, but Sara knew. Hell, even Tom had suspected. Lay her. Get it over with. Yeah, why not? Once he'd had her and gotten her out of his system, he could concentrate solely on extricating her from all their lives. It was the ultimate revenge and he would be doing them all a favor. The main problem would be convincing Hallie to overcome her pride and hatred enough to admit that she was as hungry as he.

He wanted her hot, wet and eager, making his revenge that much sweeter. But how do you set up a skillful seduction when the object of your lust can't stand the sight of you? Ty mulled the whole thing over with more beer. Let her think she'd reeled him in too, that's what he'd do. Just when she thought he was well and truly caught, she'd find herself caught in a net of his design. The idea got more and more appealing with each drink. When the little cutie waiting on him announced closing, he decided to head for home, hoping to make it by Deke Stanton's stakeout. Ever since the kid, another friend of Hallie's, had joined the local sheriff's office, Ty had gotten more warnings and tickets than he had in all the previous years combined.

The parking lot was nearly deserted as Ty headed for his

Corvette. A crunch from the gravel behind him made him turn sharply in the direction of the noise. Russ Carver and two of his buddies closed ranks around him. "Well, breed," Russ sneered, "long time no see."

"Well, Carver," responded Ty, nodding his head toward Russ's companions, "looks like you've been working up your courage."

"Shit! I don't need no help cleanin' the pavement with you! What happened, big man? Did ya lose your whore to a bigger bankroll?" Russ, busy laughing at his own humor, had no time to see Ty's fist rushing to his jaw. The blow rocked the big man well back on his feet, and it was only a drunkard's luck that saved him from flying ass backwards. "Ooohh man," he slurred, "we're gonna do a war dance on your head now, Injun!"

"Aw, come on, Russ," said one of his companions. "You're so pissed you can't hardly stand up! Let the guy alone 'n let's go track down some pussy."

The third fellow guffawed in agreement. "Yeah, come on, Russ. I don't want to waste no time poking him in the face when I could be poking Arlette!"

Russ staggered toward Ty. "Hell no! This uppity breed's gotta learn some manners. Thinks now he got money, he's Mr. Big Shot. Well, I'm gonna teach him a lesson, yes sir! Your face ain't gonna be so pretty when we're done."

"Aw Russ," whined the shorter of the two men, "it's late and I'm primed to explode! Val's at home, and if I'm any later it'll be next year before I get any nookie!"

"You mess me up with Arlette, and I'll do some serious damage to your head, Russ," the other man chimed in.

"Okay, okay!" Russ waved impatiently at the group. "Let's just kick him around a little and then we'll go. I'll start."

"Sorry, mister," Arlette's boyfriend apologized as he seized Ty's arm, "but we'll make it quick."

"I appreciate your consideration, fellas," Ty jerked his arm free, "but I have other ideas." He whirled about and fell into fighting stance.

"Hey, mister!" the whiner started up again. "This is gonna take all night if you don't cooperate!"

"I told you he was an ornery son-of-a-bitch," Russ said self-righteously.

They all lunged at once, somehow unable to land more than a couple of glancing blows. Ty ducked and weaved among the tangle of limbs surrounding him. He delivered a well-placed kick to the short one's backside, sending him crashing face first onto the pavement. This annoyed the men enough to make them combine their efforts with more success.

Arlette's boyfriend tackled Ty at the waist while Russ planted a fist in his jaw. Once the short one was up and around, he helped his friend secure Ty's arms behind his back. Russ took aim and landed two quick shots to Ty's face.

"You're gonna pay now, you miserable bastard," Russ crowed. He drew back to punch Ty hard in the stomach. He doubled over from the blow, and they let him slide to the ground. Before any more kicks and punches could begin, a woman spoke from the edge of the gathering.

"Getting a little late for Romper Room, isn't it, boys?" The three culprits turned in the direction of the husky voice. "And somehow I don't think three against one is playing by school rules." Hallie stepped toward Russ Carver. "How's it going, Russ? You finished beating the crap out of him yet?"

"Well hello there, Hallie,'" said Russ pleasantly, as if she'd come across him at the Pak 'n' Karry. "Thought you'd gone a long time ago."

"I've been up visiting Pepe and Josefa in the office. Gosh, time flies. Ramon starts at UCLA this September," Hallie said conversationally.

"Yup, I guess that'd be about right." Russ started to fidget a little. He was always a little tongue-tied around a pretty woman, and about now he felt like he'd just been caught with his hand in the cookie jar. He regarded the man slumped on the asphalt.

"Cody! How the heck are you!" Hallie stepped around Russ and seized the hand of the man on Ty's right. How many little ones have you and Val got now?"

"Uh, three now, Hal...uh Miss Bishop," the man mumbled to the pavement, thankful it was too dark to see his red face.

"Miss Bishop?" Hallie turned a warm smile on Russ. "Do I look like somebody's great aunt? I think we've all known each other long enough for first names."

Russ's companions nodded quickly, relieved that one of the largest land owners, belonging to one of the richest, most powerful families in the state, seemed to be taking the present situation in such an amiable fashion. "Sure thing...Hallie."

"You know, I sure do hate to interrupt you from such a worthwhile cause here," Hallie began, as Ty struggled to his feet, "but I'm pretty tired and he looks like he's going to need a ride home." Ty glared at Hallie. "I hope you don't mind if I take him with me."

"Listen, you scheming little shrew...." Tyler hissed. A painful jab to the ribs from Cody silenced him.

"You rotten bastard, you got no call to talk to a lady like that," Cody snarled. Ty made a derisive snort and all three men gave him a warning glance.

"Hallie," said Russ, genuine concern in his voice, "you

sure you want to trouble with this piece of garbage? We could knock him out for you if you like. Probably give you a whole lot less trouble that way."

Hallie was definitely enjoying this as she appeared to seriously reflect on Russ' suggestion. "Oh, I'll be fine. At least this way he'll get home before dawn, for a change. Let's go, Tyler. You can have one of the ranch hands drive you out tomorrow to pick up your car." She smiled pointedly at the men around her. "Of course I know I can trust all of you to keep your hands off the car, can't I? I'd really get annoyed at the...inconvenience." Russ and his friends hastily assured her that nothing would happen to Ty's Vette. Hallie smiled in satisfaction.

The men were a little reluctant to let her take Ty, more from a sense of chivalry than from a desire to inflict more damage. They even seemed remorseful that their evening's entertainment was inconveniencing her. It was only after repeatedly assuring them it was no trouble at all and that she would be quite safe that they allowed her to take his arm to guide him to her Jeep.

Ty was a stubborn, proud man, but not a stupid one, so he waited until they were almost to the car before jerking his arm away. "Touchy, touchy," laughed Hallie, unlocking the car door for him.

"Shut up, get in, and drive," spat Ty.

"Okay, okay. Just tell me how the hell you managed to get three guys so worked up that they wanted to bash your head in." She started the engine and headed toward the drive as she talked. "I mean, I understand it. I want to just about any day of the week. What incident led up to it, though? Hey!" Hallie braked hard at the entrance and turned to look at Ty. "Where the hell is Sara?"

Ty groaned and put his head back. "At home in bed—alone. Can't you drive without jerking people all over the place? Oh, forget it—look who I'm asking."

Hallie narrowed her eyes. "Pissed her off too, huh? I'm not surprised, given your scintillating personality."

"Listen, for your information, I didn't piss her off. You did."

"Me. I didn't even talk to you guys."

He laughed shortly. "Not with words, no." She looked puzzled. "It was that sexual floor show of yours." He braced himself as the car swerved onto the highway. "Watch it, unless you want your interior covered with beer."

"Nighthawk, you puke in my car and you are majorly dead! Majorly! And as for my floor show," she said, tightening her hands on the steering wheel, "I wasn't doing anything compared to your little exhibition on the dance floor, and you know it. What happened? Being made a public sex object didn't appeal to her? Ha! I knew Sara had too much class for the likes of you." She could feel the malevolence of his gaze from across the vehicle. Hallie shifted a little uncomfortably, knowing she should have chosen her words with more care. "Look, all I'm saying is that you can't go blaming big bad Hal for screwing up your love life."

"You mean this time?" he hissed.

She swore angrily and swerved the car much more than necessary. "I don't believe you, Nighthawk," she shouted at him. "You are such a complete jerk that it defies description," she said, pounding a fist on the wheel. "Eleven years later, and look who's still whining. It's over! Hello, moron, get back on the bus! The rest of us have all gone on with our lives."

"Shut up, Hallie!"

"No!" she barked back at him. "Where do you get off carrying a torch for some cheesy little college bimbo and whining how I ruined your life for all these years." Hell, she thought, so much for her noble intentions of one day explaining gently why she'd wrecked his engagement. She was so mad at him right now, she didn't care if he ever knew. Her anger and lack of consideration over her choice of words would again be her undoing. "I'm sick of wearing sack cloth and ashes because you have some real off-base notions about self worth. Why don't you go ahead and marry some gold-digging tart and end up in a shack like the one you grew up in. It's what you deserve, right?"

"Pull over!" he roared. "Pull over now!" Hallie's taunts made anger, red and hot, explode in Ty's eyes.

"Are you gonna hurl?" she asked, her anger momentarily traded for concern for the car's interior.

"Get this damn thing pulled over now!" He knew he was going to throttle her this time.

"Geez! Okay! Just wait a minute." She pulled the Cherokee onto a side road and stopped far enough from the highway to give Ty some privacy and avoid any confrontation with the police or Russ and his friends.

Instead of Ty jumping from the vehicle as soon as she parked, he leaned across to the driver's side, seizing her upper arms in a vice-like grip. "That's it! I tried to warn you in the beginning not to push me. Like always, you never listen, just had to do it, didn't you? A guy like me doesn't deserve a woman with any class or breeding, huh? The idea of a savage putting his hands on her is enough to make her run screaming for the door."

Oh shit, Hallie thought. He'd totally misunderstood her sarcasm. She had a tiger by the tail and didn't know how to let go without getting eaten alive.

"No 'decent woman' would put up with it, would she?" Moving like lightning, he unsnapped her harness and pulled her roughly across his lap. "Well, baby," he said softly, "we don't have to worry about that with you, do we? The one thing you're not is decent, right?" In the darkness, his eyes bored into hers . She could feel the hatred radiating from them—hatred and something far more dangerous. Panic gripped her, and she felt desperate to escape his touch.

"Get your goddamn hands off me, you bastard!" Hallie snarled, realizing too late that that was the wrong name to call him in his present mood. She struggled to get free.

"Are you sure, Hallie?" His mouth was just inches above hers as she lay in his arms. "What if we just see how eager you are for me to let you go five minutes from now?" He lowered his mouth to hers. The shock of their lips touching temporarily froze her. He shifted his grip, freeing his hand to stroke the hair back from her face. His tongue traced the path between her lips, coaxing them apart. At her resistance, he increased the pressure of his mouth on hers, then lightly nipped her lower lip. As Hallie gasped in surprise, he took advantage of the opening and glided his tongue skillfully into the warm, moist depths of her mouth.

Apples, he thought, fresh, crisp and sweet. She tasted and smelled like apples. Suddenly he felt the call of orchards in the early autumn, and brisk sunny days with enough wind to hold a kite aloft for hours. He remembered that first enticing sip of cool cider, the one that made you want to take another, and then another, rolling them slowly over your tongue to savor every nuance. She was soft and sweet, much different than he had expected, and he found himself deepening the kiss, wanting to taste more of her—having to taste more. He heard her moan softly against his mouth as she met his tongue eagerly with her own. His arms no longer restrained her, but held her, drawing her against him.

Hallie swam in a well of sweet sensation. Ty had

claimed her, releasing with his touch a flood of response. His lips were firm, insistent, leaving her no retreat. Make him stop, she thought, make him stop or it will be too late. It was too late. She wanted more. She wanted his hands moving over her, touching her breasts, grazing across her stomach. She needed to feel his body hard and demanding against her own. She wanted him to find the special center between her legs, the one that would melt all her inhibitions, all her doubts. She arched herself toward him, a slow steady burn building in the area south of her navel. Ty groaned as he slid one hand to cup her breast, feeling her nipple, pebble hard against his palm. His hand reached automatically for the buttons of her shirt.

"Has it been five minutes yet?" The contemptuous edge in Ty's whisper effectively doused the fire in Hallie's belly. The harsh reality of the situation washed over her. Here she lay sprawled inelegantly across the front seat of the Jeep, reclining in the arms of a man whose hatred for her was only surpassed by hers of him. She felt ill. In another minute, she would have been willing to do God knows what with him. She wanted to crawl away and hide. He'd never let her live this down. Ty already thought of her as little better than a whore. Now he'd be convinced she really would spread her legs for any man with a hard-on.

She slapped his hand away and struggled upright in his lap, becoming all the more aware of his hardness beneath her. "I don't think you've got anything to complain about, Nighthawk. Judging from your present condition, that is." She moved to scoot across the seat away from him, and he let her go—a mocking smile curving those too well remembered lips.

"What's the matter, Hallie? Did I stop a little too short of the goal?" he asked coolly. "If you need a little help, I guess I could oblige." His eyes traveled over her, slow and insulting. She swung her arm to wipe the smirk from his face. "Wouldn't try it, little girl," he said, catching it effortlessly, "unless you want to eat standing up for a couple of days."

Hallie's face became blank as she wrenched her arm from his grasp. "Sorry, Nighthawk," she said, in a voice carefully devoid of expression. "I just thought maybe you were a little restless and a sympathy screw was in order." She started the engine and quickly U-turned back to the highway without further comment. On the other side of the car, Ty's thoughts returned to his decision at the bar. She was more trouble than she was worth. She had a smart mouth that had gotten to him on more than one occasion, not to mention her complete lack of scruples and the gigantic chip on her shoulder.

Her kiss had shaken him to his core. He'd expected it to be experienced, even a little jaded, but it wasn't. Experienced yes, sexual yes, but it was that underlying sweetness and vulnerability that had really gotten to him. If he didn't know her, he might believe that fallen angel act. As it was, he'd forgotten his intent to pay her back for her words. He'd kissed her and his hands had moved over her body learning its contours and committing them to memory. Desire for her grew until it became a living, breathing entity all its own, threatening to devour them both. He might have been able to take her then and there, yet something had held him in check at the last instant. Perhaps it was his desire for revenge, but he didn't think so. Revenge would have been well served if he'd had her in the front seat of her car like a common hooker. The satisfaction would have been short, though. When he took her, he wanted to savor it. He wanted the moment to linger so that when it was over, it would really be over, the true satisfaction of a job well and thoroughly done. He looked at the cold, unbending figure behind the wheel and smiled to himself in the darkness. He almost felt a little ashamed of himself when he thought how easy it was going to be to bring her down. Tonight hadn't turned out to be a waste after all. He knew now that she did want him, in the most basic, elemental way a woman could want a man. And it would serve his purposes well.

Chapter 7

About three weeks after the night in the Jeep, the beast from hell arrived. Ty's first indication that something wasn't right was a suspicious lack of activity in the main house when he returned home from a meeting in Portland. Instead of the sound of voices from the dining room or living room, there was only an ominous silence. He called out, and was surprised when Mrs. Hudson didn't come running to greet him and fill him in with the newest of Hallie's sacrileges. Mrs. Hudson's complaints had slowed considerably in the last several days. Most likely it was due to the fact that Hallie had chosen to keep a low profile. Ty had decided to let her lick her wounds for a while before he began the next phase of his campaign to get her into bed.

Today's meeting had been yet another futile attempt to unsnarl the mess hiding the identity of the embezzler. The last thing he needed this evening was another mystery. He called out a hello once more, and heard a soft call from the living room in response. He entered the room to find Marlene serenely turning the pages of a fashion magazine, enjoying the home's peace and solitude that was so hard to come by lately. She smiled in greeting and offered him a seat. He set down his briefcase and sank gratefully onto the sofa opposite his hostess.

They had become great friends soon after Ty's introduction to the family. He'd been wary of them all at first—from Tom and his young bride Marlene to the sulky seven-year-old Hallie. He'd been bitter, resentful, and completely unsure of what Bishop and his wife expected from him. As for Hallie, she was angry and mean, resenting the way her father was forcing a strange teenage boy into her life only a few months after his marriage to a lovely, young woman. On more than one occasion growing up, Hallie had accused him of stealing her father's affection and setting her up for his censure—as if she'd needed any setting up. Thinking back on it though, it must have been hard for a kid to deal with so many changes to her life in such a relatively short time.

He grinned a little tiredly at the woman across from him. "Things seem nice and calm tonight. Where is everyone?"

Marlene stopped mid-page, turned and smiled. "I was just thinking about the quiet before you got home. Walt has a Lions' Club meeting, and Genna went to the movies with a friend. I'm afraid it's a fend-for-yourself night tonight. Mrs. Hudson isn't here either. I can fix you a sandwich, if you like," she said, setting the magazine aside.

"Oh, don't bother, Marlene," he said. "I can take care of it myself later. I'm just going to relax for a little bit." He sighed contentedly and settled further back into the sofa. "It's nice to see things so peaceful here for a change. Sounds like the other precinct is pretty calm as well."

"Well," Marlene began slowly, "I hardly think calm is the most appropriate word to use. In fact," she hesitated, "I'm sure it's totally the wrong word."

"Oh God, what's she done now?" Ty looked at the ceiling, hoping to receive patience from on high, and waited for the bomb to drop.

"Oh, well...Mrs. Hudson and Genna have been running around all day like chickens with their heads cut off. Hallie, too, for that matter. You see, Hallie's friend arrived this morning, and with all the commotion and upset—well, you'd have had to be here to believe it all. I think Mrs. Hudson had to go down there again to set things right one more time. I'm sure she's exhausted."

Tyler shot straight up on the sofa. "Hallie's friend is male, no doubt?" His voice was edged in anger.

"Yes, but I believe he's been..." Marlene began, but Ty was already up and headed for the door, cursing all the way.

"The little tramp was just waiting for me to turn my back for a second so she could move him in! I'll be back, and unless you hear gun shots, don't interrupt," he thundered.

Marlene couldn't understand the change in Ty's mood. Why was he so upset, for Heaven's sake? If Hallie wanted her cat with her, that was her business. It really had nothing to do with Tyler. He would have more important things to be upset about when he found out what had happened. She shook her head and picked up her magazine again.

Tyler Nighthawk's fury gained momentum with every step he took toward the bunkhouse door. Halfway there, he met Mrs. Hudson walking briskly toward him. She signaled him as she passed, but he was in no mood to start a conversation. He didn't want the edge taken from his anger. He'd warned Hallie more than enough. Rule one: no men. The worst thing was that he was more upset about the hitch another man would put in his own plans than from a sense of moral outrage. He'd finally come to terms with wanting her, and before he'd allowed himself to act, there was another guy in the way. He opened her door and quickly stepped inside, carefully leaving the door ajar to prevent warning her with even the slightest noise. A glance around the front room and kitchen yielded no trace of her. She kept her home neat, he'd say that for her. Almost too neat. A survey of the area showed no items out of place, such as luggage, a man's jacket, or a man's pants. Suddenly, his attention was caught by the sound of a soft husky voice beyond Hallie's closed bedroom door. He froze. They were in there together, because he could hear her speaking in soft, lowered tones. He couldn't quite make the words out, so he cautiously moved across the room.

"*Te extrane mucho, mi corazon,*" Hallie's voice crooned from the bedroom. "You missed me too, didn't you?"

Ty clenched his jaw and listened outside the door. He couldn't distinguish a single noise coming from the man, but Hallie was obviously a talker in bed. Her next words made him catch his breath. "You love it when I do this to you, don't you?" The cold fury washed through him again. He remembered Chicago and the grimy little bastard with his hands all over her. Here we go again, he thought. Once a whore, always a whore. It made him ill to think what she might be doing to her lover in there, and not just a little curious. "Oh yeah, that feels great, doesn't it?" He felt himself tighten as the sound of her voice brought unwanted pictures of her naked, astride some faceless, nameless man. He was about to jerk open the door and interrupt their little interlude when Hallie sounded a cry of alarm. "Oh no! No! Don't do that! Not there, please! Damn it, no! Great! Just how am I ever going to get that out?"

Wasting not a second more on useless speculation, Ty charged through the door roaring Hallie's name and ready to nail the perverted little bastard with her. He heard Hallie squeak, and saw her jump beside the bed. "All right, you pathetic son-of-a-bitch," he snarled, "get your ass off that—what the hell is that thing?" An ungodly howl came from the middle of Hallie's bed. Tyler Nighthawk, now grabbing the footboard to stop his momentum, found himself staring at the largest, meanest-looking, ugliest damn cat he'd ever seen in his life. The thing had to be twenty-five pounds if it was an ounce. It looked at him balefully from a single gold eye. The cat was an orange and ginger color, missing one ear and the very tip of the other. Unfortunately, he didn't notice the enormous claws until the animal had charged to the end of the bed and raked them over Ty's right hand. He swore and pulled his hand back.

Hallie swooped down on the furry little monster and picked him up, holding him closely to her. "It's all right, sweetheart. Mama will make the bad man go away." Both she and the animal in her arms glared at Ty. He looked at the quilt on the bed and saw the remains of the cat's last meal mixed with the biggest hair ball imaginable. Hallie continued to croon to her cat.

"Oh sweetie, you feel so much better, don't you, with that big old nasty thing out of you. I just wish you'd have waited 'til I got the towel. That's one mean mother of a stain."

To Ty she said, "You scared the hell out of us. What do you mean creeping into my house like that? I ought to call the police." Her voice was ripe with indignation.

Ty could have kicked himself for his stupidity. He'd made a complete horse's ass of himself and was also in danger of bleeding all over the expensive, oriental rug at the foot of Hallie's bed. She handed him a tissue, then placed the cat on the pillows. "Come on," she said, motioning Ty to follow, "I've got first aid stuff in the bathroom."

"I'll take care of it myself at the house," he said tightly.

"Yeah, right!" she said. "And in the meantime, while you're reading me the riot act over something you think I've done now, you'll bleed all over the place. I don't think so. Haul it, *chico*!"

He swore under his breath and followed her out of the room. She led him to the dining bar that separated the kitchen from the large living room, then headed off to get the bandages and antiseptic. He heard her rattling around looking for things. She called out to him, "Do you mind answering me now?"

"I was talking to Marlene and she said you had a friend arrive this morning who was staying with you." He was glad she couldn't see the sheepish expression on his face.

"Let me guess: You didn't wait for an explanation. You figured it was a guy and came down to catch me doing the old horizontal mambo, right?"

"Something like that," he admitted.

Hallie rejoined him, supplies in hand. "Bullshit, it was exactly like that and you know it." She dropped the items on the counter harder than necessary, and turned to look at him. "So you snuck in here to get a good look." The light began to dawn by the look on her face. "You heard me talking to HB and thought he was the guy!" Her jaw dropped and she glared in disbelief. "You're the pervert here, buddy! Ugh! You thought, wait a minute, I don't want to know what you thought!" She crossed her hands back and forth in front of her as if to ward off unwanted images.

Ty actually found himself smiling at her discomfort. "That's right," he said, beginning to enjoy himself for the first time since he'd walked through her door. "That's exactly what I thought. So tell me," he continued, leaning toward her, "do you talk like that in bed?"

"You're disgusting." Hallie snapped, as her cheeks began to turn pink.

"I don't believe it. I'm actually making Bad Gal Hal Bishop blush," he chuckled. This was definitely getting interesting. "So, do you?"

Hallie savagely tore open a package of gauze pads and dabbed some iodine solution on one. She seized his hand. "Now hold still," she said, giving him a sweet smile. "This is going to hurt—a lot." He barely had time to draw a breath before she rubbed the pad across the back of his hand. "There now," she said, still smiling up at him, "that wasn't so bad, was it now?"

He swore at her and tried to pull his hand free. She was stronger than she looked, and he had little choice but to allow her to finish tending the wounds. Her head was bent over his hand, and he could smell that luscious apple fragrance again. He liked the way the light played on her hair, picking up the reds, golds, and tawny blonde shades that were so uniquely hers. He toyed with the idea of dropping a gentle kiss on the top of her head, but decided against it. "There, all done," she said, and looked up to see him regarding her strangely. Their faces were only a few inches apart. "What are you looking at?" she asked stiffly.

He grinned and moved away. "I'm still waiting for an answer."

"Hell will freeze over first," she responded testily. "Go wait at the main house." She nodded toward the door. "I'll make your good-byes to HB for you."

Ty leaned back against the tile counter top, ignoring the suggestion that he leave. "Where did you get that thing?" he asked nodding toward the bedroom. "Were they having a clearance sale at a research lab or something? Last time I saw claws like that was in a drive-in splatter flick."

Hallie laughed and visibly relaxed. The subject of sex was probably going to be a sore spot between them for a while, but now the conversation had turned to a safer subject. She appeared to be in no particular rush to shove him out the door now. She went around the counter and retrieved paper towels, cleaner and a small plastic trash bag from under the sink. "I've got to clean that mess up or there'll be no hope of the stain coming out," she said, heading for the bedroom. Ty, not waiting for an invitation, followed her. It seemed to be okay with Hallie, as she began to answer his question about the cat. "I found him. It was on a tour we did. He was in the loading area of the concert hall in Baltimore. Like you see, he was in pretty bad shape." They entered the room and HB arched his back and hissed. Maybe he imagined it, but he thought the cat smiled with satisfaction when he fixed his eye on the bandage Ty now sported. "Boy, he sure doesn't like you," Hallie said, as if she suspected the same thing as Ty. She quickly set to work cleaning the bed and removing the soiled quilt. Ty took advantage of her absence from the room to study its furnishings. Rooms always said a lot about their occupants. As in the rest of the house, every-thing was well ordered. She evidently liked neatness and organization, which surprised him, seeing that she'd been the quintessential messy teen. The bed frame was an antique sleigh style, built out of rosewood, he guessed. She liked fine things and took care of them. Interesting. The bed was flanked by a night stand on either side, each holding one of a pair of matching electric hurricane lamps. An ornate silver picture frame sat beside one of them. Ty couldn't resist temptation and decided to examine the pic-ture. The tyrant on the pillows hissed and gave a warning growl. Ty watched him warily as he edged toward his goal. There were seven people in the photo, but he only recognized four of them: Hallie, Cassie Donovan, Randy Raveneau, and the late-great jazz artist, Eddie Melick. Ty had everything the man had ever recorded. He shouldn't have been surprised to see Melick in a picture with Hallie. After all, he'd been married to Cassie Donovan at the time of his death. He stood in the photo with one arm around his wife and the other around Hallie. Raveneau stood on the other side of her. Ty felt a knot tighten in his gut as he thought of all the ugly, sexual rumors surrounding Hallie and her fellow band members.

Hallie stopped in the doorway, watching Ty with the picture. She knew what gave his face such an intent, grim look. Her annoyance grew as she thought of him standing in her home judging her, and with his attitude, tainting a picture she held very dear. "I keep my jewelry chests in the armoire," she said evenly. If she'd startled him, he did-n't show it. He turned to her slowly, his eyes still on the picture. She tried to keep her face impassive.

He gently placed the photo back on the nightstand. "All the old gang, huh," he said, making no apology for invading her privacy. There was a note of contempt in his tone and she suddenly felt very exposed and vulnerable. Why had this man always had the power to hurt as no other man ever could?

She wet her lips before she spoke. "That's right. If you've got any questions though, you'll have to check out back issues of *People*. I've got 'no comment.'"

He smiled and let his eyes roam over her as he crossed to the doorway. She had to stop herself from looking down to see if she was all buttoned and zipped. "Can't help being a little curious I suppose." She knew what he was curious about all right—the same thing most of America had been at one time or another.

His gaze remained heated though he spoke cynically. "I guess if you're going to play the game, though, you have to expect the name."

Anger from the injustice of his remark welled up inside her. She hadn't done anything to deserve a comment like that. Hallie drew a breath to calm herself. "Worked up quite a little fantasy from the other side of the door, did we? That's all it will ever be too—a fantasy."

"Yeah, sure. If that's what you want to tell yourself, go ahead." He was staring at her lips as he placed his arm on the doorjamb above her head. He leaned down until his mouth hovered just a whisper above hers. "But you don't really believe it anymore than I do." In just a split second his mouth could cover hers. He seemed to be waiting for some type of signal to proceed. He never got one. Instead, Hallie bolted under his arm and headed for the kitchen. Ty strolled slowly after her, smiling to himself.

"So what was Mrs. Hudson doing here today?" he asked, as he stood looking over her instruments.

Hallie smiled nervously from the kitchen. "Would you like a glass of wine?" she asked suddenly.

"Why do I get the feeling I'm going to need one?" he said with a tone of suspicion. Hallie took a bottle of wine from the refrigerator and began quickly assembling glasses, napkins, a corkscrew, and a plate of cheese and crackers on a tray.

Ty ran a finger over the bridge of the white guitar in front of him. Hallie was still occupied in the kitchen and the instrument in front of him was far too tempting to resist. He read the brand name and took a guess at the guitar's age. He gave a low whistle and picked it up.

Hallie set down the tray on the wrought-iron coffee table and turned to find Tyler holding her beloved Stratocaster. The man was impossible. No one she knew, except another musician or a roadie, would even try to take a liberty like that. Even the rest of the band kept a respectful distance from her guitars, unless invited. Now a man she considered to be an arch enemy held one of her most prized possessions. She was annoyed, but strangely not nearly as annoyed as she would have expected herself to be. No matter what she thought of Nighthawk, she knew he'd appreciate what he held. Hallie walked up behind him. "What do you think?" she asked him.

He turned and gave her a sheepish grin. "Sorry, I should have asked first. Is this what I think it is?"

Hallie smiled back and said, "You're right, you should ask first. No," she said as he offered her the guitar back, "go ahead. See, I trust you. And you're right," she added, "it is what you think. Jimi Hendrix had it with him at Woodstock. Can't say for sure if he played it, but it was there."

Tyler Nighthawk turned the white Stratocaster over and looked at the scrawled signature preserved under countless layers of painstakingly applied resin. Now this impressed him. He'd been a Hendrix fan forever. It surprised him that Hallie hadn't become totally unglued at his presumption, but she seemed to enjoy showing it to him. He wondered if he would have been as understanding if their positions were reversed.

"Here," she said, turning the guitar over and placing the strap over his neck, "now you get the full effect." She smiled and stroked the guitar neck as she spoke in soft reverent tones. "Most people that are left-handed just restring the guitar backwards with the low E string here. Like me. Not Jimi though. He just learned to play upside down."

He searched her face, caught up in the enchantment in spite of himself. "That's right, you're left-handed."

"Yup," she shrugged in a self-deprecating gesture. "Not only do I happen to be one of the few women in the field, but wouldn't you know I'd have to be left-handed to boot. I never take the easy way."

"So I've noticed," he said, continuing to study the Stratocaster. "I've always heard that some of the chords he did can't be done by anyone else."

"Kind of, he had incredibly long fingers. Combine that

with him playing upside down, and you can see the trouble a standard right-handed player would have."

Ty handed the guitar back to her and watched intently as she replaced it on the stand. Hallie motioned him toward the sofa and he settled himself comfortably, taking a moment to loosen his tie and unbutton his collar. He looked thoroughly at home, and so damn sexy Hallie had to remind herself to breathe. She opened the wine and filled their glasses.

"You didn't need to go to all this trouble. I promise not to murder you for whatever it is that happened. I'm too tired." He rubbed his fingers across his forehead. "I think the adrenal rush from earlier is over."

Hallie fought the impulse to offer a neck and shoulder massage. At this point it would be playing Russian roulette. Instead she said, "Sounds like a rough day at the salt mines."

He took the glass from her hand, "Yes, you could say that."

"Can I ask what happen?" Hallie prodded gently.

"Why are you interested?" Then he laughed, answering his own question. "Sure, you like the idea of me having a bad day, don't you?"

"Not necessarily," she said frowning. "I own part of the business now, and maybe I just want to know what's going on."

"Maybe you do, maybe you don't," he said thoughtfully. She got the impression he was gauging her words on the internal lie detector he employed whenever talking to her. "All right, I'll bite. Some person or persons unknown are removing large amounts of cash from the company holdings. Walt and I have been spending the last month and a half trying to patch all the holes that made the embezzlement possible in the first place. Now we're trying to track down the culprit."

"Any suspects?"

Ty was immediately alert, watching her intently. "One or two. Don't suppose you have any names you'd like to add?" he said, more sharply than he intended.

Hallie took another sip of her wine, afraid she'd really put her foot in it this time. "No. As you know, I've never had anything to do with the business. That was strictly yours and Dad's province." He listened for a telltale note of bitterness in her voice, but heard none.

"At any rate, that's what's going on." Ty took a sip of wine, then leaned forward to sample some cheese from the plate in front of him. "You're planning on attending the meeting a week from Monday, aren't you?"

"Uh-huh." At Ty's cynical expression, she continued, "Fear not, Tyler, I've been known to maintain the status quo for extended periods of time. I promise to leave the Ray Bans in my purse." She crossed her heart with her finger and grinned.

"See that you do, and no acting out like you did at the reading," Ty said levelly. "The last thing we need is more high drama."

"And of course I'm the only one who acted inappropriately that day, right?" She stopped herself before she said any more. "Look, forget it. I'm not going to start the merry-go-round one more time. Do you realize this has got to be the longest period of time we've ever talked when somebody didn't have to jump between us? Forget it, I'll be there scrubbed, pressed, and in control. Unless," she added with a wink, "you do something that really pisses me off."

Ty found himself returning her grin and saluting her with his glass of wine. He drank the last of it and poured them both another glass. This was an alarmingly pleasant place to be, he reflected—not what he expected a home of Hallie's to be like.

Hallie, as if she knew exactly what he was thinking, said dryly, "I always put the altar and the black candles away when people come by."

"I figured that," he said, teasing her back. "I was wondering how you managed to get all those sacrificial blood stains out of the carpet." She laughed, and he found himself drinking in the sound as if it were the wine in his glass. As he watched her, she drew her legs up into the overstuffed chair where she sat and rested her chin on one knee. He was offered a view of one very attractive jean-clad cheek. Yes, he was decidedly too at ease here, and he abruptly set about to change the situation before he found himself kicking off his shoes. It wasn't that difficult to see how she made so many men into her lap dogs. She could be an extremely captivating woman. Putting a heavy note of disapproval in his voice, he said, "So, what's this mess you have to tell me about. What have you done now, Hallie?" He could see confusion, and even hurt, reflected briefly in her face. Instead of it appeasing Ty's need for distance and control, all he felt like was a bully. He reminded himself sternly that a bully was precisely what he needed to be where Hallie was concerned, and that some wine, pleasant conversation, and atmosphere didn't change anything.

"It's about HB, my cat," Hallie replied.

"Oooh, that's a cat. I wondered."

"Very funny. How about I go get him and drop him in your lap? You two could do more bonding." Hallie picked up a cracker and nibbled on a corner, the mischievous sparkle quickly back in her eyes.

"Thanks, I'll pass. Interesting choice of name you gave him." Ty's eyes gleamed at her across the table. "I guess his personality reminded you of someone you care about intimately."

Hallie gave him a hard stare. "For your information, I didn't name him. Two of my friends did. HB doesn't have anything to do with me, though I'm sure you'll disagree. It stands for 'Hell Beast'."

He snorted, "That's appropriate. Next question. How did you get Edna Hudson eating out of your hand? A couple of days ago, she was ready to hire a hit man and now she's been here most of the day. She isn't paid to look after you, Hallie. Hire your own help."

She uncurled herself in the chair and leaned forward. "I didn't ask her to come, Genna did. For your information, I'm not trying to use Mrs. H. to look after me, not that that's your concern since you don't pay her either. Marlene knew all about it. Hell, she was even here herself. Now do you want to use this time trying to bolster your stupid male ego, or do you want know what's going on?"

His fingers tightened on the stem of the wine glass, and for a minute she was afraid it would snap between them. "Cut to the chase, Hallie, I'm tired. What's any of this got to do with me?" His mouth became a firm line.

She was getting angry at him again, and that gave her the courage to be blunt and to the point. "It's got to do with your car, you know, your—"

"My Corvette!" He was on his feet in an instant, slopping wine down his front. His '69 Corvette was his pride and joy. It had been part of his life since he'd bought it from a wrecking yard at eighteen and begun the long arduous process of restoration, one piece at a time. Working on the car had been a labor of love for Ty, a chance to build something of his own from the ground up and not count on the Bishop money to provide for him yet again. Tom had understood Ty's need to do it on his own without financial assistance, and he took a fierce pride in his foster son for his determination. Instead of handing over money, the two of them had spent hours pouring over auto magazines. As Ty's fortunes increased over the years so did the number of Corvette restorations. It now sported a black leather interior, CD player with surround sound speakers, and a brand new, custom paint job. Though money hadn't been an issue for years, Ty had only been able to bring himself to have the vehicle repainted two months ago. Up until then, it still sported the two-hundred-dollar job he'd saved for when he started college. The car represented his commitment to improving himself, overcoming the odds. He coddled it like a child, parking it in the garage under a cover and only driving it when warm weather permitted. "What the hell did you do to my car?" he shouted. Hallie was on her feet in an instant too. She sidestepped the coffee table and stood in the traffic pattern, looking as if she was ready to run. If anybody knew what that car meant to him, she did. "Don't even think about leaving this room, Hallie, or I'll be on you in a second!" He couldn't remember the last time he'd felt this violated.

"I didn't do anything, blockhead. I told you, it was HB." She watched him tensely, wondering if she dared call his bluff and make a break for it. Hallie decided to stand her ground because, in spite of Ty's fury, he wasn't about to go for her throat. But if she ran, it would be like giving a wolf the scent of fresh blood and expecting him to ignore the sheep.

"I'm waiting, Hallie." He bit the words out and moved to stand in front of her.

"He came in on a freight plane this morning with my telecaster, because I figured HB's coming anyway, so what the heck, why not kill two birds with one stone. I'd forgotten it anyway, and I need it for the recording studio gig in Seattle this fall. I never go into the studio without it."

"Whatever the hell a telecaster is! Stick to the point." He shook his head in wonder. Hallie was the only person he knew who, when faced with imminent death, would still indulge her penchant for extraneous detail.

"That is the point, because HB was supposed to be brought to the freight terminal late last night. Well, things got screwed up like they will when you're not there to check the details yourself." She extended her arms out to the side and brought them with a sharp slap to her thighs, to punctuate her exasperation. "And instead of—"

"Is there any point to this idiotic story?" howled the furious man in front of her. "I swear to God, Hallie, you've got thirty seconds to get to the damn point or I'm going to throttle you, and not a jury on the planet will convict me."

She calmly retreated a step and said slowly, "The veins on your neck are standing out. Do you have high blood pressure?" At the growling sound he made, she continued, "All right, all right. HB scratched the paint on the hood and the roof of your car." She winced, waiting for the explosion to come.

"My new paint job," he said. "My new custom paint job. You're telling me that, that fur-covered Freddie Krueger of yours wrecked my new paint job." He couldn't believe how calm he sounded. "Come on." He seized Hallie's upper arm roughly. "You're going to show me, now!" He pulled her with him toward the door. "What business did you have around my car anyway," he shouted at her, "and what the hell did you think you were doing bringing that psycho cat of yours anywhere near it?"

She tried to wrench her arm free, but only succeeded in making him tighten his grip even more. It was painful, and she knew she'd have a bruise in the morning. "It's not there!" she cried out, the pain evident in her voice. "They towed it to the paint shop already!"

Ty dropped her arm like a hot rock. He'd hurt her, damn it! She always managed to anger him more than any other living human being, and how did he respond? Like the brutish pig that sired him! He disgusted himself. Hallie took advantage of her release to put a couple of steps between them. "I'm sorry, Hallie. I lost my temper and I didn't notice I was hurting you," he said in a strained voice. He blew air out through his teeth. "That's no excuse, but please accept my apology." If she grabbed a vase, or a rock, or anything, and tried to brain him, it was no less than he deserved. His gut clenched in the sick disgust he felt for himself, and he thought about fruit never falling far from the tree. He'd taunted Hallie with the expression more than once in regard to her mother. The same was true about him. He looked at the woman he'd just man-handled. Strange as it seemed, she didn't appear fright-ened or even angry. Her expression was one of concern. He could hardly credit it, but the concern seemed to be directed at him.

She rubbed her arm and looked him straight in the eye as she spoke. "I told them you'd call with instructions tomorrow, and to be sure to send the bill to me. For the record, HB squeezed in under the old carriage door. He was frightened and wanted to hide under the cover. I guess the slick surface freaked him and he dug in for trac-tion. I wouldn't have let him get to it intentionally. I do understand what it means to you, just like you understand about the Stratocaster. By the way, any time you want to hold it, that's okay with me."

He stared at her in disbelief. With more eloquence than any hasty words of forgiveness she could have said, she'd given him her vote of confidence by offering access to one of her most prized possessions. It was more con-

sideration than he deserved or expected at her hands.
Hallie continued to meet his gaze as he said softly, "You're
a strange woman, Hallie Bishop. Any sensible woman
would have called the police, and they would have been
right to."

"I doubt it. The way I look at it, you've been hauling or
shoving me since we were kids. Old habits die hard. Not
a very big deal, really." She added with quiet strength,
"You're not your father, Ty. It's not in you." Hallie
glanced down at the floor for a moment, then returned her
direct gaze, full-force, to his. "The problem you've got
now, though, I wouldn't wish on a dog," she said.

"What's that?" His gaze scorched her with equal intensity. Damn it. He'd let her get to him. He'd let her see not
only the anguish, but the source as well. If she hadn't
known his weak spot before, she sure did now. Distance—
he needed distance between them.

"We're not kids any more, and that adds a whole new
element." Her lips curved into the funny half smile that
always did a number on the pit of his stomach. "You still
hate my guts, and it disgusts you that you don't know what
you want to do more—kill me or take me to bed."

He felt his phallus throb between his legs as he said,
"Oh, I know what I want to do, Hallie, make no mistake
about that." His hot, hard eyes slid over her body. "Every
time I see that sexy little ass and those incredible breasts of
yours, I want to fuck you where you stand."

Her lips and throat went dry as she begged a higher
power that he not touch her now. She was already damp
at the thought of him taking her. "Too bad you blew your
big chance the other night," she said hoarsely.

"No, I didn't. You would have stopped me eventually
yourself. You're not hungry enough, yet." He knew he'd
have to leave soon or he would do something he'd regret.

He didn't really want to go, but she wasn't ready to sur-render, and that was an important part of his plan to con-trol her.

Fire flashed in her lion's eyes as she said, "I'm not like-ly to ever get that hungry."

He gave her a slow lazy smile and drawled, "Sure you will, Duchess. It's only a matter of time. Especially seeing how anyone that wants to come sniffing around you has got to get through me first. Stanton included. Face it, I'm going to be the only game in town for you."

"Get out," she hissed. "And don't call me that ridicu-lous name again! I don't know why I even try to treat you like a human being."

He chuckled softly. "Happy to oblige. I'll talk to you tomorrow about the car." He was still chuckling when he closed the door.

Hallie stood shaking for some time after he left. Then she quietly went to the bedroom and spread out the clean comforter. She picked up HB, who meowed and purred his pleasure at seeing her. Holding him close to her chest, she lay down on the bed and curled herself around him.

Chapter 8

Nighthawk strolled slowly back to the main house. This evening's engagement had taught him several interesting things about his opponent in the bunkhouse. Hallie was a complete contradiction in terms, an enigma. Had anyone told him several months ago that he would find her company charming, pleasant, and more than a little difficult to leave, he would have laughed in their face. After this evening, however, he realized that that was exactly the case. He'd long since thought himself immune to any seductive web she might try to snare him in.

Even the name of her band had been appropriate to the sort of woman she really was. Like the beautiful but deadly Loreli of myth, she drew people to her to be smashed on the rocks and devoured at leisure. Now his own desire for her made her even more dangerous than he'd first anticipated. For all his certainty with regard to Hallie's malicious nature, though, a few things still nagged at him. She'd been so damned understanding tonight—hell, even compassionate to him when she'd had a perfect opportunity to have Deke Stanton run him in for assault. He himself had planned to do just that to her the day of the will reading.

Marlene opened the door before he reached it. Mrs. Hudson stood further back in the hallway a little anxiously. "Hallie told you," Marlene said. It was an observation, not a question. At Ty's terse nod, she gestured toward the living room. They went in, and Mrs. Hudson hurried off to bring him some sandwiches and lemonade. "I'm sorry, Ty, but she didn't mean for it to happen, truly."

"I know she didn't." He flopped into the chair he'd formerly occupied. "She told me."

Marlene raised her eyebrows quizzically and sat back down on the sofa. "And you believed her?"

"Yes. I know, I know. I'm the last guy in the world who would cut her any slack, but I know it was an accident. I still want to kill her," he admitted, "but it was an accident."

Marlene smiled. "Strange, isn't it? Who'd have thought that barely a month after her arrival, I would be waiting to rush to her defense, only to find it isn't necessary. One thing about my stepdaughter, Ty: She provokes the most startling reactions without even trying."

That was an understatement if ever he'd heard one. Ty thought about his last words with her. He'd never talked to a woman like that in his life, outside of a bed that was; yet, she could arouse an animal in him that wanted nothing more than to run her to the ground and mate with her in savage passion. He sat up quickly in his seat. He'd better change the track his mind had chosen to wander before his body gave Marlene something even more astounding to contemplate.

"You should have seen her today. She was absolutely frantic. It seems one of Hallie's people was in charge of air freighting a certain guitar that she wanted—and the cat. Somehow, things got delayed and the cat and guitar got shuffled to the side in Portland for two or three days." She paused in her narrative as Mrs. Hudson set down a tray of sandwiches, lemonade, and glasses. She thanked the older woman as she handed the food to Ty. He dug in, winking his appreciation at the housekeeper.

"The animal was in pretty bad shape by the time he got here," Marlene continued. "He was half-dead. He'd only had enough food and water for one day, at the very most."

"Good Lord," Ty interjected, accepting a glass of lemonade from Marlene. "Didn't anyone think to check on him along the way ?"

"No," continued Marlene, punctuated by a snort of disgust from Mrs. Hudson. "Can you believe it? The driver told Hallie that everyone was scared to open the cage."

He glanced down at his bandaged hand. "Impossible," he murmured.

"Anyway," Marlene said in a dismissive tone, "the moment Hallie opened the cage, he took off for the stables. We had a terrible time getting him out of there. The horses were terrified. Poor Zenda started rearing and twisted his front leg. HB was so frightened that he clawed him, and we had to have the vet come out and stitch Zenda up."

"Damn it! Is there any permanent damage?" Zenda was the new black, tobiano paint stallion that the ranch had purchased in an effort to improve bloodline in the stock. A limp wouldn't affect his stud use, but any serious injury might necessitate the horse being destroyed. It would cause a severe delay in their breeding plans, not to mention the loss of a beautiful and spirited animal.

"No, Luther assures me he'll recover just fine. Just as we got to HB though, Luther's collie came in to investigate, and the cat bolted."

"That's where my car came in, right?" Ty said between bites. Both women nodded. He swallowed some lemonade before continuing. "I think I know the rest. He scrambled under the car cover in the garage and got the paint in his panic. Hallie said she'd already had them come and get the 'Vette."

"She was very upset about your car, Ty, and not just because she thought you were going to kill her either," Marlene said earnestly. "I think she was genuinely concerned about how you would feel more than anything."

"Funny as it sounds, I got that feeling myself. I'm just not sure I should accept it at face value."

Marlene shrugged. "I know what you mean. After seeing her shaking and almost in tears over HB today, I don't know what to think either."

"'Scuse me, Mrs. Bishop," the housekeeper said, "but it's like I say, there's got to be some good in a person that sets that much store by a cat. A cat is a darn good judge of character in my opinion. Miss Hallie loves that animal, and there's no doubt in my mind he loves her."

Miss Hallie? When had she stopped being "that one" and become "Miss Hallie"? Of course, Ty realized, Edna Hudson was a woman whose feet remained firmly on the ground in all things except one: She became a cooing, babbling fool over any cat she met. Much like Hallie evidently.

"That could well be, Mrs. Hudson. I know you have her eternal gratitude for calming him down and getting him to the bunkhouse." Marlene smiled and turned to Ty. "He was a pretty sorry looking mess, but, luckily, Mrs. Hudson got him to eat and drink this afternoon, and he got some rest. We suspected a hairball problem late this afternoon, but thanks again to Mrs. Hudson..." She trailed off at the end of her sentence as Ty looked at the remainder of his sandwich. The word hairball brought back the memory of the mess in the middle of Hallie's bed. The ham and swiss on dark rye had definitely lost its appeal. The housekeeper beamed and left them to their conversation. "You know, Genna told me the story of how Hallie found that cat and, Tyler, I've never been so sickened by anything in my life," Marlene shuddered.

"She told me she found him in Baltimore, all banged up."

"Tyler, think about Baltimore for a minute," Marlene paused. "Now, add Hallie."

"I don't get what you mean, Marlene." Ty watched the woman across from him, a puzzled expression on his face.

"She said she was at a concert hall, and he was out back. Wait a minute." He snapped his fingers as the light clicked on. "Five, six years ago." He set the plate down on the coffee table and leaned toward Marlene. "The fan she assaulted. Someone sent Tom a clipping, right?"

"Exactly. She was arrested and charged with assault by some fan who was waiting by a stage door to see her."

"One of her more notorious stunts," Ty said darkly. "I always wondered who the bastard was that sent the clipping, not to mention all the other ones as well."

"But you see, the point I'm making is," Marlene began with fresh intensity, "all any of us heard was half the story. The charges were dropped, and the press hinted at a pay-off by Hallie and Loreli's manager. That's not what happened."

"What did happen?" Ty narrowed his eyes. It had been an unpleasant episode for all of them, Tom's shame, the sly remarks in town made behind his back. He felt his anger surge again as if it were yesterday.

"When Hallie walked out the stage door, she caught that disgusting little pervert pouring lighter fluid on this poor little cat he'd tortured, getting ready to set it on fire."

"My God." Ty felt his meal rise to his throat.

"That's pretty much what the police thought at the station." Marlene shook her head. "Can you imagine? I would have done the same thing. Do you know what's the worst thing about this, Ty?" She looked up at him with large sad eyes. "Tom never knew why she did it. He never asked her. None of us did. We just assumed the worst."

"Look, Marlene," Ty replied carefully, "I see what you mean, but don't get too carried away. Sure I understand her reaction. I think any one of us would have done the same thing in similar circumstances, but let's not forget that one noble act does not a saint make. We both know what she's capable of if things don't go her way."

"Believe me, I know. Today is one of the few times I've seen Hallie have anything close to normal human reactions, at least ones I could relate to." She sat back with a sigh. "I don't know, Ty. I have to admit I found myself enjoying her company today. Maybe that scares me more than anything she's actually done since she came home. Despite everything, she can certainly be amusing and such a breath of fresh air."

"A breath of fresh air that's tried to rob her own family blind, Marlene." Walt stood in the doorway, fighting to control his temper. "I don't believe this!" He came toward them, his stride forceful from the outrage he felt, the outrage that was clearly visible on his face. "Hallie is dangerous, for crying out loud. Did you know Genna's back from the movies? Three guesses where she headed first." He tossed the folder he was carrying onto the coffee table impatiently. "She's trying to drive a wedge between us and Genna, just like a coyote will work to cut off the weakest sheep in the flock. God knows what she'll influence the girl to do!"

Ty leaned back into the sofa and stretched his arms across the back. Walt shifted impatiently on his feet. "I think you're being an alarmist, Walt. I'm here to keep an eye on things—particularly Hallie. True, she's a danger in a lot of ways. For all we know, she is the one behind the thefts—might even have accomplices throughout the company, but frankly, I think it's a damn good thing she's here so we can keep an eye on her." Ty shrugged. "Maybe that's what Tom had in mind this whole time." Ty rose from his seat and walked slowly toward the hall. "You remember what he used to advocate so strongly, don't you?"

"You mean 'keep your friends close, and your enemies

closer'?" Walt answered slowly.

"Exactly," Ty replied, smiling broadly. Then he ambled down the hall.

❦ ❦

The next morning passed quietly enough. Mrs. Hudson came to see her patient and brought Hallie some fresh-baked croissants in the process. Hallie dug into the peace offering immediately, thanking the taciturn woman. Evidently Mrs. Hudson, or Mrs. H. as Hallie had immediately dubbed her, was beginning to suspect some good qualities lurking somewhere inside the young woman—or at least she was willing to open her mind to the possibility. It was too early to tell for sure, but Hallie cherished the fond hope that the woman would give her the chance Tyler and Marlene refused. Perhaps she would finally gain entrance to the charmed circle she'd stood outside of her whole life. Hallie offered to show the housekeeper some of HB's baby pictures one evening, and Mrs. Hudson seemed genuinely pleased at the prospect.

Walt had stopped by soon after Mrs. H left. He didn't stay long. He was warm and comforting, saying he was concerned that she might be feeling a little depressed about the chilly attitude from the main house. Hallie felt things had thawed considerably, but kept her opinion to herself. When Ty drove by as Walt was leaving, he suddenly turned and placed a tender, lingering kiss on her cheek. She'd thought at the time he was merely demonstrating his support of her to Tyler. But as she reflected on the incident now, and remembered the glint in his eye as he watched Tyler's car pass, she couldn't overcome the feeling he was somehow staking a claim.

Hallie spent the rest of the morning and early afternoon at her guitar. She was rapidly approaching the crunch date to head for the recording studio. Her solo CD was sched-

uled for release in mid-December, and she was still working on several of the original songs. There was a lot to be
done before she could even contemplate hitting the recording studio, and she was having trouble with some of the
arrangements. She was used to a lot more input when she
was composing for Loreli or even the jazz arrangements
she did with Eddie Melik, Cassie Donovan's late husband.
She worked hard at her music, and even harder at keeping
the blues away. This time there was no Cassie, Randy or
Sye to bounce a riff off or pull her back from an overindul-
gence of the whammy bar. God, but she missed them.

Unfortunately, Tyler Nighthawk occupied more space
in her thoughts than was necessary—or healthy. She'd
been sure her feelings about him were all in the past, until
the other night. One kiss and every girlish fantasy she'd
harbored about him came rushing back, threatening to
bury her in the spell of carnal promise. Damn him! He
knew she wanted him. He'd always been like a blood-
hound once he caught the scent of anything. How many
times when she was a teen did he catch wind of her nocturnal sojourns to Pepe's and how many times had he
foiled them? Once, she'd even unwittingly lowered her
guitar into his waiting hands just before she slithered herself out the window and down the trellis. Ty caught her
instantly and deposited her, kicking and screaming, in her
father's study.

He wanted her too. *El cabron* was just waiting for
unconditional surrender. He wanted her abject humiliation, and he had insidious patience. He always had. After
all, he'd waited thirteen years to pay her back for breaking
up him and Monica. He'd been telling Hallie since the day
of the funeral in not so subtle ways that payback time had
come—now that he no longer had to concern himself with
sparing Tom's feelings. Her best policy was going to be to

keep out of his way. That didn't seem too likely an option since they'd already had three major confrontations in the month she'd been here, and each one had ended on a heavy sexual note. Hell, they'd ended on a sexual symphony!

Hallie sat at the piano playing "Fur Elise." It had been a particular favorite of her mother, who, according to her Tia Augusta, had wanted to be a concert pianist before marrying Hallie's father. Hallie mentally winced as she remembered her disastrous attempt to please her father by playing it on his birthday. He'd almost broken both her hands when he slammed down the cover on the keys. She suddenly switched to playing "Pathetique," the memory bringing pain to her eyes. Two days later at Marlene's urging, he'd brought her her first guitar—no apology, no remorse, just an unspoken truce and tacit agreement never to mention the incident again. She still played the piano beautifully, but the guitar would always be her first love. Ironically, the incident with her father had been a blessing in disguise. The music fed her soul and pulled her thoughts safely away from her turbulent childhood. Adrift in a sea of contentment, images came and went. She let them roll by as her breathing slowed and her mind cleared. Suddenly, a pair of brilliant green eyes formed in the shadows of her consciousness and the speed and force of her playing increased.

A sharp rap at the door immediately recalled Hallie to her surroundings. She half-expected to find Tyler Nighthawk standing on her threshold and quickly masked the flash of disappointment she felt. Genna whirled by her and merrily danced across the room.

"Cole asked me to the dance," she bubbled. "Oh, Hallie, everything I own is so lame! Maybe you've got something I could borrow?" she asked hopefully. Hallie rolled her eyes. She could imagine what the warden, a.k.a. Nighthawk, let alone Marlene, would have to say about Genna borrowing anything from her older sister's closet.

"Hon, with one or two notable exceptions, you can borrow anything you like from me," Hallie said. "But I think it would be the quickest way to get yourself locked in your room 'til you're 18."

Genna sighed dramatically. "Yeah, I guess so. But would you come shopping in Eugene with me this Saturday? We'll ask Mom to come too, okay?" Hallie could think of lots better ways to spend a Saturday than in her stepmother's company—like having bamboo driven under her toe nails, for instance. But Genna looked so excited and she wanted her sister's company so much. There'd been too many missed opportunities between them over the years and Hallie couldn't let this become one more.

"Sure, Gen," she responded, grinning broadly. "It sounds like fun. You go ask Marlene and let me know the verdict."

"Oh, I know she'll agree, Hallie."

"Agree to what?" asked a cool voice from the front door. Ty leaned against the doorjamb, observing the scene in front of him. He waited a moment for an explanation, and when none was forthcoming, he eased himself into the room. "Agree to what?" he repeated, enunciating each word.

To Hallie's surprise, Genna seized control of the situation. She bestowed a cheery smile of greeting and linked her arm through Ty's. "Hallie and I are planning a shopping trip to Eugene this Saturday." Hallie bridled at his immediate frown. "Mom's coming too, of course," Genna hurriedly added.

"I don't think so, Gen. She has a committee lunch this

Saturday," he said. "You'll have to make it another time."

The girl's face fell and Hallie felt like kicking Ty's butt up around his shoulders.

"I'll take you myself," she interjected. "We'll make a real day of it." The light was back in Genna's face but Nighthawk darkened it in the next second.

"You're not taking Gen anywhere," he stated grimly. "I wouldn't trust you to take her to the supermarket, let alone out of town."

"Luckily, it's not up to you," Hallie snapped. "It's up to Marlene."

Ty snorted. "As if Marlene would allow it either."

Hallie smiled sweetly. "Guess we'll see, won't we. Genna," she said turning to the girl, "run up to the house and ask your Mom. Ty and I have some things we need to discuss." Genna nodded, watching them warily as she headed for the door. Ty and her older sister looked like combatants slowly circling each other, taking one anther's measure.

"Look, Tyler," Hallie began as soon as the girl was out of earshot, "Genna needs this trip. She can use all the attention she can get right now."

"As long as it's the right kind of attention," he said evenly, "from the right source."

"Meaning what? Keep her away from the 'Whore of Babylon' at all costs?" Hallie threw up her hands in exasperation. "You slay me, you know that? You're so busy sitting around worrying about what I'm going to do to her that you can't see the real dangers to her right now."

"Oh, I see the real danger, Hallie," he said pointedly, as he looked at her with eyes of steel. "I'm the one that had to haul my mother out of the ballroom so stinkin' drunk she puked all over me, herself, and whoever else was around." Ty came closer, his face growing colder and angrier with each step. "I'm the one who watched the only woman I ever loved or ever will recoil in disgust and horror from me and the obscenity that gave birth to me. All because Hallie Leigh Bishop wanted a birthday party and her father said no." He stood over Hallie, wanting to smash her to bits.

Hallie bit her lip and held back the impulse to sharply remind him that a young woman's *Quince Ñera* was hardly a simple birthday party. It was a fifteen-year-old Mexican girl's formal introduction into society. It began with a Holy Mass in the young woman's honor, and concluded with a debut ball complete with a court of honor and everything. Hallie'd been bitterly devastated by her father's absolute refusal to sponsor such an event for her. Her bitterness had doubled when Ty, returning home from college, announced his engagement and Tom Bishop had spared no expense for the formal engagement party he'd given his ward later that summer. When Hallie had thrown the event into utter chaos, everyone was convinced she'd done it for spite. Only two people had known her real reason at the time, and one of them had taken it with him to his grave.

Hallie crossed to the front door and pointed to the outside. "Like so many of our conversations, this isn't getting us anywhere. Your opinions of me are carved in stone—no mitigating circumstance, no excuse, just bad-to-the-bone Hallie. Hope they never select you for jury duty, Tyler, because the concept of innocent until proven guilty is something you obviously don't subscribe to."

"Are you trying to tell me one more time how misunderstood and abused you are?" he said sarcastically as he crossed to stand by her. "It doesn't wash, Hallie. Never has, never will."

"Nighthawk," she began wearily, "I've never denied

sending your mother the note and invitation to your engagement party or making sure she got there right on cue. I took complete responsibility for it, and as ugly as it got, I still took the heat because I did do it. I had a very good reason for doing what I did and it had nothing whatsoever to do with Dad refusing me my *Quince Ñera*." She searched his face, hoping to find some inkling of understanding or belief. There was none.

"You had your reasons, huh?" he asked softly. She nodded. "You always do. Just like you had reasons for breaking your father's heart, and reasons for sleeping with every man you came across—even your best friend's husband."

She recoiled as if he'd struck her, and he saw pain fill her eyes. He felt like a total bastard, but tried to remind himself that it was no less than she deserved. Hallie could look so small and helpless sometimes. Part of him wanted to take her in his arms and whisper an apology. He forced himself to ignore the hurt in her incredible lioness eyes.

"I think you know the way out by now," she managed in a shaky voice. "Do us both a favor: Don't bother to come back. If you need me for something, use the telephone."

"Oh, I need you all right, Duchess," he drawled, smirking as he felt her anger flame higher. "I just didn't know you were into phone sex." Like lightning, her fist headed for his jaw. He stopped it just before it connected. "Told you not to try that." He traced the pattern of the ring that graced her forefinger. "You get three warnings, and that was number two." He dropped her fist quickly and was gone. Hallie stood trembling silently. She wrapped her arms around herself, wishing someone was there to hold her.

Chapter 9

On Saturday, the pre-dawn sky over southern Oregon promised a brilliant, sun-filled day. Hallie finished her make-up quickly, pulled on tan kettle-weave pants over a rust-colored body suit. She grabbed her waist-length brown leather jacket and rushed to the living room, expecting her sister's arrival at any moment. They needed to get on the road as quickly as possible if they were to have a full day's shopping. Surprisingly enough, Marlene had agreed to the sisters' shopping trip even though she couldn't join them. Unfortunately, there'd been one stipulation. Ty would drive them. Hallie hadn't been happy about it, but the alternative had been to disappoint Gen and she couldn't do that. Ty had assured them that he had business of his own to attend to and would only be driving them and dropping them off at the mall. She was thankful for that much. Since their argument the other day, she'd avoided him like the plague. Hallie heard their knock and answered the door.

Involuntarily, her eyes ran over Ty's tall frame. God, he looked good in the morning. Frankly, she'd yet to discover a time that he didn't look good. He wore tight, fitted jeans, an unbleached cotton, band-collared shirt and his jean jacket. Her appraisal hadn't gone unnoticed and he grinned impudently at her. Hallie murmured a quick good morning and hurried off to her bedroom to get her purse. Ty waited in the living room with Genna. He noticed Hallie's keys lying on the coffee table and casually pocketed them. There was bound to be a hell to pay, but he needed to establish control from the beginning.

Hallie breezed back into the room. "What did I do with my keys?" she asked no one in particular. Her eyes swept

the room and finally came to rest on the source of the jin-
gling sound coming from Ty's hand. "Oh, thanks," she
said, holding out her hand for her keys.

Ty smiled cheerfully and pocketed them again. "Forget
it, Duchess, I'm driving. I've ridden with you, remember?"

"The hell you are, you presumptuous, arrogant—"

Ty cut her off. "I drive, or we don't go. It's that simple." His eyes challenged her to make a scene and spoil
the day for Genna. He had her, and he knew it. What was
more, she knew it. Hallie wasn't happy, but she'd fall into
line. He studied the expressions as they played across her
face: fury, impotence, frustration, and finally resignation.
Genna cleared her throat and both of them turned to look
at her.

The teenager appeared ill at ease, as if she expected to
receive her head in her hands for daring to intervene, but
she proceeded anyway. "Guys, I've really been looking
forward to this trip. If you can't declare a truce, could you
at least call a temporary cease- fire?"

Hallie was ashamed. Here she was ready to rip his
throat out, and the one person she wanted no harm to
come to was being hurt. "Sorry Gen. Don't worry, I'll
retract my claws for the day." She stared meaningfully up
at Ty. "We both will."

Without further comment, Hallie turned off the lights
and headed them toward the Cherokee. Ty opened the
rear passenger door, and laid a gentle hand on Hallie's
arm, keeping her beside him. After Genna got in, he
closed the door and opened the front one for Hallie. He
caressed her arm briefly to ensure she understood where
he wanted her sitting. She complied, telling herself she
merely wished to keep the peace for Genna's sake. He
was playing with her and she knew it, but, like the moth to
a flame, she felt powerless to call a complete halt to the

game. For better than twelve years, she'd voiced her hatred of Nighthawk like a mantra to protect herself from the fascination he wove around her. The litany didn't seem strong enough today to invoke the necessary buffer she sought between them. She snapped her seat belt in place and folded her arms across her chest, staring straight ahead, her face expressionless. Hallie could feel his mocking smile on her, and she would be damned if she would give him pleasure of so much as a frown in response.

Ty whistled as he slowly walked around the vehicle to settle himself behind the steering wheel. "All set, ladies?" He gave each of them a warm, charming smile. Gen bubbled affirmatively, and Hallie harumphed in spite of herself.

The miles sped away, and they were only half an hour into the drive when Genna fell asleep, leaving Ty and Hallie to keep each other company. Ty pulled into a convenience store on the highway and bought two large steaming cups of coffee for him and Hallie and a bottle of orange juice for Genna to have later. The promise of caffeine served to mollify Hallie, and she was actually polite when he handed her the cup.

"Does this mean I'm forgiven?" he asked, taking a sip from his own cup.

"Yeah, I guess so. The true way to my heart is coffee, especially after last night." Hallie stretched her neck and twisted her head from side to side.

"What happened last night? Did Pet-of-Frankenstein strike again?"

"Of course not, he loves me. He really is a very affectionate cat, you know. He just doesn't like you."

"I'm crushed," Ty said flatly.

"You should be. Mrs. H says cats are very astute judges of human nature. Guess he's got your number, huh?" She smiled sweetly and took a sip of coffee.

"So what was the deal with last night?" Ty said, ignoring her barb.

"Nothing special, just a very long work night. I'm having some trouble getting in the groove for this solo CD. It's not the easiest thing under the best of conditions, but there's no one to bounce things off or hold me back." She added in a confiding tone, "I'm getting more than a little self-indulgent with the licks and bridges, not to mention the whammy bar."

"Self-indulgence is your middle name, after all," he retorted quickly, then instantly regretted his words as Hallie turned back to look out the passenger window again. Great, he thought to himself, every time she started to open up to him, he had this automatic defense mechanism that made him force her to shut down.

He didn't want to know about her, he told himself. He didn't want to feel comfortable spending time with her, even looking forward to it. He wanted sex from her, then he wanted her out of the way. Anything else was purely out of the question. What he didn't understand, though, was why he felt compelled to be so rude and, in most cases lately, downright crude. Ty had dealt with plenty of ruthless, unscrupulous businessmen in his time, but he'd always kept a veneer of civility. He'd never talked to anyone the way he talked to her. He sighed. "I'm sorry, I promised to play nice today, and at the first opportunity I take a cheap shot. Can we try it again?"

"Yes, please," Hallie said quietly. She turned her luminous golden eyes on him, soft with hurt and unspoken pain. In that moment, Tyler Nighthawk would have moved a mountain or slain a dragon for her—anything to take that look from her eyes. He fought the impulse to pull the vehicle to the side of the road and hold her, kissing his apology properly. Instead, he concentrated on the road ahead, fully realizing how she held men spellbound.

He set his cup beside hers in the drink holder, then cleared his throat and tried to make conversation. "How about some tunes? I'll check the dial." He tuned in the first rock station he came to, using it as a peace offering. Hallie bent down quickly between her legs and retrieved a CD case from the floor of the Cherokee.

"I've got some CDs here. What do you feel like listening to?" She began flipping through the contents of the case. "You like jazz, blues, rock, alternative? You name it, I've got everything but Yanni and Zamphier."

"Thank God!" Ty grinned. "You got any Bob Marley?"

She shook a CD at him saying, "Jammin' Mon." As Hallie reached over to pop it in the player, the station's DJ announced the next selection.

"We'll rock the house this morning with a little of the best in classic rock, Loreli's "Stumptown Boogey." Hallie went to hit the play button, only to have Ty's fingers block the way. He shook his head and she sat back in her seat. "Stumptown" was a point of pride with her. She'd written the piece herself and it had made her as famous as "Stairway to Heaven" had made Jimmy Page. It was truly a classic, and lots of garage-band hopefuls cut their musical teeth trying to master its intricacies. As superior as it was, Hallie wasn't sure she was up to listening to the cut in a small space with Tyler Nighthawk, especially seeing as how their cease-fire was off to such a rocky start.

"I want to listen. It's a classic you know." He winked at her, and Hallie felt her heart turn over in her chest the way it had when she was fifteen. As the opening bar started, Ty continued, "Marlene said you played something called "Clear-Cut Rag" for her the other day. Despite her mangling the name, she was very impressed." Hallie laughed and he was struck again by its engaging quality.

"I played without the amp, and it was a pretty sanitized and abridged version at that. I didn't see the point of freaking her out up front." Her hands and fingers moved in front of her, in automatic air guitar. Ty knew she wasn't even aware of what she did.

He chuckled. "You know, I wouldn't mind hearing you do it live, unabridged, loud, and dirty."

"Really?"

"Yeah, really. Actually, I was sort of disappointed you didn't do it at Pepe's the other night." His eyes told her he wasn't making fun of her.

"Not the right sort of crowd. The Scorpions piece went over like a lead balloon. But I played that one for me. And as much as I love the boys in the band, they're not good enough to back me up on it."

Ty threw her an amused look at the sheer egotism in her statement.

"Yeah, I know, I know, but it's the truth. I have certain inflexible standards about my work. The right stuff for the right crowd, and if I can't do justice to the piece, I don't do it, period. I'll play it full forty for you sometime, if you like," she added tentatively.

"I would like." The guitar solo wailed from the speakers. Hal Bishop raw and at some of her best. He glanced over at her again. "You're pretty damn good."

"I'm pretty damn great."

"Yeah, you are, and modest too." They both laughed.

The song came to an end and the DJ's voice cut in. "That was Sassy Cassie Donovan doing the vocal out in front of Loreli. Gal Hal Bishop with awesome lead guitar. Oooh baby, the things she can do to those strings. And, let's not forget the Rand-Man himself on bass. Like just about everybody else out there, I miss 'em like hell. Hey, you guys, literally, get your act together! Check your egos at the door, and lay down some new tracks. Who knows, maybe one day..." His voice trailed off and the Guns and Roses' version of "Live and Let Die" cranked out through the speakers.

Hallie stared out the window in silent misery. Ty leaned over and hit the play button, springing Bob Marley's reggae to life. He knew she was trying to hold in the pain caused by the words of some over-zealous DJ. It was private, deep. And the last thing she wanted to do was share it—and the last person she would want to share it with anyway would be him. According to the gossip columns, Loreli's final tour had been plagued with mishaps, short tempers, and artistic differences. The straw that broke the camel's back came, they said, when Cassie Donovan publicly struck Hallie across the face for sleeping with her husband. The tabloids had had a field day, and Hallie had reportedly abandoned the tour, calling in an army of lawyers to make the breakup final. Though legally she'd been compelled to return and finish out the tour, she'd kept strictly to herself, even refusing to be in the same room with the Donovan woman.

He felt a twinge of guilt as he remembered his dig about her sleeping with her best friend's husband. Granted, she'd brought the whole mess on herself, but he couldn't help feeling a little sorry for her. She didn't look like the cold, calculating siren he'd always believed her to be. She looked like a lonely, sad woman who needed a friend. Ty returned his eyes to the road. Perhaps he could offer her some kind of comfort. It would only further his plans to gain her trust and make her turn to him instead of Walt as a confidant. He frowned. The thought of Walt coming on to Hallie annoyed him more than he could say. He'd wanted to slam on the brakes, jump out of the car and knock

Walt senseless the other day when he'd seen him kiss her on the cheek. It wasn't like it should be any skin off his butt, yet still it bothered him. In the back of his brain, a warning bell clanged, and Ty schooled himself to harden his emotions. He needed to remain cool and uninvolved for a proper seduction. Ty forced his scruples to the back of his mind. After all, he reminded himself, in this case the ends justified the means.

"You okay?" he asked, trying to place the right amounts of concern and distance in his voice. It was remarkably easy.

She laughed shortly, and it was a harsh, bitter sound. "Don't you keep up with the tabloids? I'm always okay. Ask anybody."

"Hallie," he began.

"Save it," she said, as she waved her hand at him while still turned away. She feigned boredom, yet her voice sounded more brittle than anything else.

✦ ✦

Genna and Hallie were practically staggering under the weight of their packages as they entered the exclusive clothing boutique. It had been a glorious day. They'd laughed, talked, shopped and spent. Ty had long since disappeared, having dropped them off hours ago at the mall. He would be meeting them in 30 minutes or so, much to the relief of their aching feet. Two salesclerks immediately came forward to help them with their bags. If they found Hallie's use of sunglasses inside unusual, they kept it to themselves. The clerks smelled money and were more than willing to help the women part with some. Genna had long since exhausted her spending allowance, so despite the girl's protests, Hallie was providing the bankroll. She told the younger girl to go a little crazy and she'd stand the bill. While Genna disappeared into a changing room with an armload of items, Hallie began to idly examine a rack of form-fitting Spandex dresses. She pulled out a thigh-high chocolate creation, off-the-shoulder, and low cut, that would be superb with a certain pair of heels she'd seen earlier. She wasn't an extravagant person by nature; however, she enjoyed nice clothes. Both Cassie and she liked to drop a better-than-average bundle in Paris or Milan a couple of times a year. Most people would have laughed at cleavage-queen Gal Hal in haute couture, but most of her personal wardrobe was night-and-day different from her professional one. She still had a fondness for leather jackets, though.

This dress was fun, and even though she needed it like she needed a hole in the head, she tried it on. It fit like a glove, or more correctly, a second skin. She wore it out of the fitting room to stand in front of the three angled mirrors set up to give the customer either a rude awakening or the confidence to buy. Hallie turned, twisted, and pulled at the dress. It came to just three or four inches below her bottom, and was the sort of dress that pulled you in like a girdle, enhancing all that nature had given you. The sleek lines required the wearer to forego most, if not all, of the usual undergarments. Hallie bent over sharply and looked at her rear in the mirrors. She wanted to make sure there was adequate coverage; the last thing she wanted to do was inadvertently flash a photographer. "Gen," she called, "come see this dress. I absolutely love it, but I don't know. I don't really need it." She heard a movement from behind her, past the view of the mirrors. She swung her hips back and forth a little, checking the dress in the mirrors. "What do you think?"

"I think you should buy the damn dress," came a husky male voice. She whirled instantly and saw Tyler standing to one side behind her, his eyes alight with desire.

"Thanks," she said carefully, "but I think I'll pass."

"You don't buy it, sweetheart, I will."

"It's really not your color," she said evenly. Damn the man. It wouldn't matter if she was wearing full rain gear and golashes, he'd still manage to make her feel naked.

"You know what I mean." His eyes continued their scorching trail over her. He smiled lazily. "Hey, if you can't afford to, I'll be glad to spring for it. I'd consider it my charitable duty to preserving the state's scenery." Just as he'd intended, the remark irritated her independent streak, and he could tell she wouldn't be able to get to the register with it fast enough. He smiled to himself, wondering how and when he would be able to convince her to wear it for him so he could have the indescribable pleasure of removing it.

Genna appeared at his elbow. "Wow! Can you give me your body, please?" she said to her sister.

"My thoughts exactly, Gen," Ty said casually, wrapping an arm around the girl's shoulders. "We'll meet you at the register."

Hallie changed quickly, suddenly anxious to get out of the store. When she handed the salesclerk her credit card, the woman looked at the name and back at the woman standing in front of her. She did a double take and smiled broadly. "This is so great," she said, bubbling over with enthusiasm. "My boyfriend Steve, well, he's got everything you've ever done, Miss Bishop. He loves you! I love you!" she gushed.

"Thank you," Hallie said quietly, "that's so nice of you to say." She smiled at both clerks.

"Steve—you know, my boyfriend—he plays guitar, too." She stopped suddenly and looked up from the tag she was reading with a stricken look on her face. "Oh, I didn't mean he's as good as you or anything. I guess no one is."

"Oh, a few are," Hallie said easily, "and quite a few are better." Obviously, the poor woman expected her to do a personality flip a la Courtney Love, and punch her lights out for being compared to a rank amateur. Damn tabloids. "I'm flattered you and Steve think so highly of me, though." She signed the credit slip the woman handed her. She appeared to want something more, so Hallie decided to help her out and offer. "Do you think Steve would be interested in an autograph?"

"Oh God, yes!" the woman blurted out. "I just didn't want to be too pushy. I'm sure you get hounded all the time."

"No problem, Wendy," Hallie said, checking the woman's name tag. "I'm always glad to oblige a fan, all evidence to the contrary."

Ty stood back watching her be gentle and gracious with both women, generously taking time to put them at ease, as if they were talking to an ordinary customer. He saw her sign one autograph, then another. Luckily there was no one else in the store, or they probably would have been there for some time.

"Hal," Wendy said shyly, "I've just got to ask you one question." Hallie's smile became a little strained as though she knew what was coming. "What's it like to kiss Randy Raveneau?" Hallie froze for a fraction of a second but the clerk, intent on Hallie's possible answer, failed to notice.

"I never kiss and tell," Hallie demurred. At the women's disappointed looks, she added, "Tell me, what do you think kissing Randy Raveneau would be like?"

"Heaven!" they chorused.

Hallie smiled noncommittally, then waved goodbye and left with Genna and Ty.

Ty noticed that some of sparkle had gone from her eyes,

though. If he didn't know better, he would have sworn she was on the verge of tears.

Gen's face glowed with excitement. "Is that what it's like all the time?"

"No," Hallie said, turning in at the shoe store, "it can get a hell of a lot worse." Gen looked confused.

"But you were so nice to those people, didn't you enjoy it?"

"Hon, it's easy to be nice when people are nice to you. It's the not-nice people that make it rough. I see a lot of rude, overbearing people all the time." She stopped by the shoes she'd seen and signaled a clerk.

"Well, I can't believe absolute strangers asked you about kissing Randy Raveneau." The girl frowned indignantly.

"To tell you the truth, I figured I got off easy," Hallie said ruefully. "I've had perfect strangers come up to me in produce aisles or on the street and ask me what he's like in bed. As if I'd know." She looked earnestly at her sister. "No matter what you've heard or read, Gen, Randy and I have never had a sexual relationship. Hallie turned away and held up the shoe to an approaching saleswoman and told her the size.

Ty wasn't sure if he believed Hallie's relationship with Randy had been strictly platonic, but he did know from his own experiences that people could be needlessly cruel. He'd just never thought of it as something Hallie would have to deal with as an everyday matter. He noticed, though, that she quickly tried on the shoes and that this time, she paid for them with cash.

Tyler pulled the car up in front of the main house and started helping Genna unload her packages. He'd dropped Hallie off at her place and told her he'd drive her vehicle back as soon as he unloaded the haul. Gen kissed his cheek to thank him for the lovely day and dashed inside. Ty checked the back of the vehicle once more for any miscellaneous bags before he slammed the hatch. The only two bags left were the infamous dress and the matching heels. He wondered if Hallie would accept a dinner invitation, something intimate, maybe in a suite at the hotel where he could sweet-talk her into removing it. He smiled to himself. One way or the other he was going to win the game with Hallie. She'd end up under his control, and when he could prove she was behind the thefts, she'd be out of their lives for good. There'd be no more waiting for the other shoe to drop, no more wondering when she'd pull the rug out from under Gen, no more verbal fisticuffs or double entendres, no more intensely burning looks from golden eyes, no long lustful gazes at her tight little— He stopped himself, wondering whose side he was really on.

Hallie came out on her porch when he backed her vehicle into the parking strip at the side of the house. She walked down the steps toward him before he had time to shut the driver's door. Ty had a feeling she wasn't about to ask him in for a nightcap. She'd left her jacket in the house and the cool May evening was hardly conducive to a long chat outside. Ty knew Hallie had taken off the jacket and met him outside on purpose. What better way to ensure he didn't overstay his welcome than by pleading cold and fatigue. Well, he'd just have to see about that. They stood at the driver's side, Ty leaning against the vehicle, and regarded each other in the outer edges of the porch light.

"Thanks for driving today, Ty. It meant a lot to Genna," Hallie said.

"What about you, Hallie? Did it mean a lot to you too?" he asked softly.

She shifted uncomfortably for a moment, then said,

"Well, of course. That's why I said thank you." She didn't like the sensual tone in his voice or glint in his green eyes, just barely discernible in the faint light. They made her pulse jump erractically. Hallie cleared her throat. "Keys, please," she said, extending the palm of her hand.

He continued to regard her with a leer. "What's it worth to me?"

"Hand 'em over. It's freezing out here! I've had a long day and I'm ready for bed," she said sharply, heedless of the double entendre.

Tyler wasn't. "You're right," he said, straightening himself up and away from the side of the Jeep. "It is cold out here, and," he murmured softly, "I'm ready for bed myself." His eyes fastened on her chest, admiring her nipples, hardened by the chilly air as they poked against the thin fabric of her body suit.

"Knock it off, Tyler," she said, snapping her fingers at him. "Give me the keys, now please."

He held the objects of desire just a little out of her reach and jangled them at her. "Come and get 'em."

"Are you mental?" she asked. "We had a reasonably good day. Not much bloodshed. Why are you trying to spoil it now?" She looked at him as though she thought he'd had one too many beers again.

He laughed gently, "I'm not trying to spoil anything, sweetheart. I forgot for a minute how scared you are of me, that's all."

She edged closer to him, with her hands on her hips, and thrust her chin up toward him defiantly. "That'll be the day when I'm scared of a pompous, over-bearing jerk like you!"

He grinned. Just as he thought, she'd taken the bait like old times. When she was a little girl, the easiest way to get Hallie to do anything was to call her a scaredy cat. He mentally flinched, thinking of the times he'd employed the tactic to her detriment and his amusement—much like now. He pushed the thought away quickly. If he achieved his goal tonight, he'd make damn sure she had no room for complaint. He felt himself tighten at the prospect of Hallie reaching climax in his arms. "I'll make you a trade," he said softly. "One kiss, you to me, mouth to mouth, and I'll hand 'em right over."

Her eyes glowed in the shadowy light. "Eat shit, you bastard," she snarled. "Just couldn't get through the day without trying to pull one last power play on me, could you? Leave them on the front seat when you get tired." She turned back toward the bunkhouse, but had only gone a few paces when his voice stopped her.

"Knew I scared the shit out of you," he murmured. "You always were such a coward around me, Duchess."

Hallie froze in her tracks. She hated it when he called her that. She turned abruptly back toward him. He could tell she was weighing the pros and cons rapidly, as she always had under one of his challenges. He also knew she'd curse herself for falling for his taunts, but fall she would. Her tawny eyes took on a feral gleam, and he wasn't sure if she was looking at his mouth or his throat. "Okay, cowboy," she said huskily, "pucker up."

She sauntered slowly back to where he once again leaned casually against the Jeep. Her hips swayed as she eyed him steadily with the practiced eye of a huntress. Her full lips parted and she slowly ran her tongue over her top lip. She hadn't even touched him with anything yet, and Ty felt his mouth go dry and his sex begin to harden against the fabric of his jeans. Hallie slowly placed one hand and then the other on either side of his jacket. Her eyes locked on his, and she held them, daring him. Damn, she was a sexy little thing. She seductively ran her tongue

back over the way it had traveled and smiled as she heard
his sharp intake of breath. It was all Ty could do not to
seize her immediately and roll her beneath him against the
side of the car. She pulled him forward by the front of his
jacket until her mouth was no more than a whisper below
his. She paused there, and for a terrible moment Ty was
afraid she would let go and head for the bunkhouse again.
He wouldn't let that happen. Her legs and thighs rested
against him and he knew she could feel his erection growing by the second. Her breasts brushed lightly against his
chest. He was at the point of taking her mouth himself, for
fear she'd change her mind and bolt. Suddenly she made
her move, and she made it with lightening speed. Her
hand dropped from his jacket and reached up behind his
neck to pull his mouth to hers. Her lips moved over Ty's
in a gentle seductive dance, first teasing, then demanding.
Hallie traced the line of his closed lips with her tongue,
seeking admittance. He groaned and opened his mouth to
her, bringing his hands to encircle her incredibly small
waist. Her tongue slipped into his mouth, seeking his. She
enticed it back into her mouth with an exciting dance,
increasing the pressure and urgency of the kiss. She
brought the inside of her right leg up to rub down the outside of Ty's hip. He wrapped one arm tightly around her
waist and bent her back in an effort to bring the juncture of
her thighs hard against him. His other hand covered one
of her breasts, exalting in the feel of her hard nipple in the
center of his palm. God she'd gotten him so hot with one
kiss. His shaft throbbed painfully against the confines of
his jeans. He felt her start to pull away to end the amazing
intimacy. He wouldn't let her. He growled low in his
throat and rolled her underneath him. She pulled her head
away from his.

"My keys, now," she gasped. Her breasts rose and fell

against his hand, both nipples standing proud and erect—and not just from the cold.

"Sure thing, sweetheart," he managed, "a deal's a deal." He placed the key ring on the roof of the car and bent to claim her mouth again. He dropped his hand from her breast to rub her between her thighs. She moaned against his lips. He widened her legs and lifted her, keeping her braced against the side of the vehicle as her feet hung slightly above the ground. Ruthlessly, he ground himself against her. There was no retreat for her now. She whimpered as his mouth continued to take hers, and his pelvis rotated against her. Her fingers tangled in his hair and she parted her legs automatically to bring him closer against her. Her hips began to move with him in the age-old tribal dance. He placed his hands underneath her bottom for support, and wished to God he'd been smart enough to get her jeans off before they'd gotten this far. Ty was close to going over the edge and he knew she was too. He nipped at her throat and neck with his lips. Hallie gasped and dug her nails into his back. He needed to be inside her soon. There was nothing to do but halt the proceedings and hope to God he could get her inside and onto the nearest horizontal surface before her brain engaged and she sent him packing. He broke off the kiss and his motions abruptly, painfully. She slid her feet to the ground.

Hallie's eyes, hazed over in passion, looked at him. She was totally confused. She'd meant to show him that he was the last thing on earth she had to fear. She had wanted to show him she was in control—that she could kiss him passionately, hungrily, and still be unaffected. She'd known from her first approach to kiss him that he wanted her badly. She'd planned to use it against him but had found herself neatly caught in her own trap. One more time he'd humiliated her by calling a halt to everything, leaving her hungry, aching, and very frustrated. She dreaded to hear what he'd say to her.

Ty's breath came in painful rasps. "Just say the word, honey, and we'll go inside, get comfortable, and I'll take care of us both." She said nothing and pulled her eyes away from his as she tried to calm her own ragged breathing. So, he wanted to finish what they had started—correction, what she had started. The only thing that could possibly be accomplished, outside of orgasm, was revenge. Make her want him, take her so he could treat her like the whore he thought she was. No, damn it! She wanted him, but not like that. When she slept with a man, she had to care deeply for him, and he had to at least respect her.

Too late, Ty saw his mistake. He'd given her time to think and question the wisdom of sex with him. Damn it! If he'd just carried her to the bedroom as he fondled her, she probably wouldn't be withdrawing from him now. The only thing that had kept him from trying that very thing in the first place was the trick of navigating the steps to the porch. It was a pretty lousy seduction technique to drop your lover on her ass and break your own neck in the bargain.

"Come on, Hallie," he whispered in her ear, "don't chill on me now." He gave a slow grind against her. "We were both about to come, right here. You know how much we want each other. You know how great it's going to be." He leaned against her and cupped her breast again, but she refused to respond.   "Stop fighting it, baby," he murmured. You're only hurting yourself."

"Sorry, cowboy," she whispered in that husky, made-for-sex-voice of hers. "I don't go to bed with a man unless he likes me. Guess that pretty much eliminates you as a candidate, doesn't it?"

He dropped his hands from her as if she burned him. He had no reason to be offended by what she said. It was the truth, wasn't it? Why did he feel like she'd kicked him in the gut then? So she called it like she saw it, and she just happened to see right through him. So what? He didn't like her, or trust her, or even want her around, did he? He just wanted sex with her, hot, down-and-dirty sex. Right now, he'd do just about anything to get it, except force her or lie to her. He cleared his throat and said carefully, "You're right, I don't particularly like you, but that doesn't change the fact that I'm very much in lust with you. I'm not going to lie and give you pretty speeches to get you in the sack." He narrowed his eyes and studied her face sharply. "First, you're too intelligent to fall for them, and second, I don't need to. You want me in your bed as much as I want to be there. The only problem you've got, lady, is that you want every man in the world to be putty in your hands. That's not me, sweetheart, and it isn't going to be either." He stood away from her, and she slid sideways to avoid brushing against him. "There's no way we'll ever be anything to each other than what we are right now. Sex will just add an exciting new battleground, that's all." He gave her a lazy smile and drawled, "I'd even let you win sometimes."

She turned away from him so that he couldn't see her face. "I'm tired of the need for battlegrounds, Tyler." She walked slowly toward the bunkhouse.

Anger twisted in him like a knife. He wanted to hurt her, needed to hurt her as she had hurt him with her withdrawal and gentle reproaches. He didn't want to notice the sag in her shoulders or the sad note in her voice. Ty didn't want them to matter to him. What he wanted was distance. He embraced his fury, welcomed it as if it were the lover he'd thought lost. He took the cheapest shot he could think of. "Hallie," his voiced crackled through the night air. Her head came up, but she didn't turn to look at him. "Do you think the *Inquirer* would pay me big bucks to tell them what it's like to have you moaning and wiggling under me?"

Hallie remained frozen for a moment. "Yes, Tyler, they would," she said quietly, and finished her solitary walk inside.

Chapter 10

The phone rang about ten o'clock that evening. Hallie hated telephone calls this late at night. Invariably they brought bad news that couldn't wait, and she felt a pre-cognitive knot tighten in her throat as she picked up the phone.

Randy Raveneau's voice responded to her tentative hello. "Hey there, Gal. Where've you been all day?"

"Never mind where I've been," she snapped. "What have you found out?"

Randy laughed. "You know, Hal, you really should go get yourself laid. You're getting just a mite bitchy."

"Please, Randy," she muttered, "that's the last thing I want to hear right now, if you don't mind. Just tell me some good news, okay." She flopped across her bed and rubbed her hand wearily across her forehead. "Did you get hold of Kelsey?"

"Don't I wish! But I only got to talk to her," he said, sighing dramatically. Randy had a weakness for cool, leggy blondes and had been drooling lustily over her attor-ney since he'd first seen her in mediation during the band's breakup. Up until two years ago, Hogan had been one of the fastest rising legal stars in the LA County District Attorney's office. Disillusionment, personal tragedies, and whispered rumors of payoffs had driven her to the private sector and contract law. Hallie was referred to her during the Loreli breakup, when it became apparent she would need her own legal tour-de-force. Kelsey and her law clerks took on a job that would have quelled many a great mind in the legal world—and acquitted it nobly. Since then, no job was too large or small, no situation too dirty. She took care of contracts, corporate filings, and the various and sundry legal difficulties that Gal Hal Bishop occasionally found herself embroiled in. Now she was marshaling the first line of defense against the embezzlement accusations that were bound to come Hallie's way sooner or later.

Kelsey was meeting her in Portland on Monday. They hoped to come up with the correct strategy to locate the original source of the funds used to open the numbered account in Hallie's name. They'd already determined the funds had been transferred from another numbered account, but the confidentiality of depositors was so closely guarded, they hadn't been able to come up with a name. She hoped Randy had been more successful.

"Did you two come up with anything? Were you able to find out who the generous bastard was that created that account in the Caymans?"

"No such luck, baby doll. The best I could do was talk Hogan into delaying this hare-brained idea you two cooked up about flying down to the Caymans and investigating this yourselves. I can see it now—Lucy and Ethel do the islands." He chuckled for a moment, then said softly, "I know you're scared, Hal, but believe me, this is all going to work out. You know I'll do anything I can to keep you out of harm's way." He paused, and Hallie got the feeling he was trying to figure out the best way to phrase his next words. "I've run into a pretty good-sized brick wall on this one, Hal. I don't have the clout necessary to push for names and locations." Hallie swore. "On a more upbeat note, I do have an idea who can get the job done for you." She held her breath, fearing he would say the one name she didn't want to hear at all. "Call Ryker."

Hallie bolted upright on the bed and started yelling into the phone. "No way, Randy! I can't believe you're serious! Like he'd help me. He'd probably turn me in and give them enough trumped up evidence to get me life. The demented son-of-a-bitch would love it too. He hates me worse than I hate him, and believe me, that takes some doing!"

"Are you through," Randy asked quietly from the other end of the line, "or do you want to waste more time ranting and raving? Time is a luxury you can't afford right now, Gal."

"It's pointless, Randy," she said bleakly. "If Ryker is my only shot out of this mess, then my ass is toast and you know it."

"What I know is that you've got to call him. Look, you, me and Kelsey could all spend the next several weeks trying to batter our way to the information we need and still not get anywhere. In the meantime this Nighthawk guy could have you charged, arrested, and halfway to conviction before we learn a damn thing." Randy was right and she knew it. She also knew that no matter how much she protested, she'd end up doing just what Randy had told her to do.

"Okay," she said, reaching into the nightstand drawer for a pen and paper. "What's his number?" Randy gave it to her and stayed on the phone long enough to extract her promise that she'd call Ryker immediately. Then satisfied, he said good night.

Hallie sat on the edge of her bed and studied the sheet of paper in her hand for some time. Suddenly she longed for comforting arms around her. Someone to whisper to her and say everything was going to be fine. Someone like—well, Tyler. She'd spent a lifetime trying to keep all but a select few at arm's length. Now, when she wanted to reach out so desperately to someone, no one was there.

Tyler—God how she wished she could call him. Right now, she wanted nothing as much as his arms holding her, supporting her, making love to her. She shook her head to clear away the seductive images. For a variety of reasons, not the least of which being her suspicion about his desire for revenge, the idea of calling him was impossible.

With resignation, she steeled herself against the fury and humiliation that were to come, then dialed the number on the paper. It rang three times, and Hallie breathed a sigh of relief when his message machine took the call. Ryker was apparently still out for the evening—probably torturing small children and animals, if she knew him. She left a message.

"Ryker, this is Hal Bishop. Look, I've got a couple of questions to ask you." She paused to halt the tremulous note in her voice. "I need some advice and Randy thought...well, he figured...would you call me as soon as you can, please? The number is, area code—"

She was interrupted by a terse, hard voice on the line. "I'm here."

Hallie swallowed compulsively as the sound of his voice whisked her back in time to other unpleasant and dangerous circumstances. Jake Ryker had often been her only source of protection then, and a few times, himself the source of the danger. Unconsciously, she clenched and unclenched her left hand, shuddering as she remembered his fury at her for playing what, at the time, she'd believed to be no more than a harmless prank. The memory of his cold words of retaliation sliced through her soul. "All it takes is a couple of flicks of the knife, Angel Face," he'd whispered, his sinister words freezing the very air in her lungs. "A couple of flicks and it's the end of your career. Hell, you won't even be able to hold a cup, much less play a guitar." He'd never acted on his threat, but one look into his remorseless silver eyes had assured Hallie that he was entirely capable of doing so. She'd made sure never to give him cause for such fury again.

She cleared her throat. "Randy suggested I call you, Ryker. I'll cut to the chase. I need to know how to get confidential information out of a bank in the Grand Caymans." Silence greeted her on the other end of the line. "Did you hear me?"

"Yeah, I hear you. So what's it worth to you?" Ryker sounded cold and detached, not an unusual state for him.

Tension coiled through Hallie's shoulders as she gauged how much information to give him. Ryker would welcome the news of her most recent troubles, and allowing him any knowledge of her weaknesses would be an extremely foolish thing to do. "I'm not asking you to do the job, Ryker," she said carefully. "I just want to know how it's done. I can take care of things myself."

The man on the other end of the line gave a derisive snort. "Sure you can, Bishop. And while you're at it, why don't you steal some top level secrets from a third world dictator—or maybe disarm a nuclear device and save Manhattan? Leave intrigue to the experts, Angel Face. Go restring a guitar or something."

She fought the quick retort that sprang to her lips and replied with an indifference she didn't feel, "Kelsey Hogan and I are flying down to the Caymans next week anyway. I just thought you might be able to save me a little time, that's all." Hallie's inborn stubbornness kicked in and she resolved to find her own way out of this mess. Without his help.

"The hell you are, Bishop!" Ryker snarled into the phone. The vehemence of his response startled her. "You've gotten yourself into some kind of jam again, haven't you? That's what this is all about." Even at this distance Hallie could feel those merciless silver eyes of his narrowing purposefully, watching and waiting. She shiv-

ered. His eyes were eerie, not just because of their unnatural luminescent color, but because they were totally
devoid of any emotion—cold and dead as the Arctic itself.
If taunting Nighthawk was like waving a flag at a bull,
taunting this man was like crawling into the den of a hungry wolf and offering him your exposed throat.

"You got thirty seconds to give me the straight scoop, or
I hang up and leave you out there blowin' in the wind."
His voice had become soft and deadly, with an edge like
cold steel.

Hallie took a deep breath in an effort to calm herself.
He meant what he said. He always did. Randy held the
creep in very high regard and through the years they had
developed a type of friendship. As much of a friendship as
a human being could have with a creature like Jake Ryker.
He was a top-level, ultra-covert government operative.
And as such, Ryker performed jobs for his country, and
occasionally other people with the right price—jobs that
were outside the normal diplomatic and ethical channels.
He was a misogynistic bastard, whose dislike of women in
general was only surpassed by his dislike of Hallie specifi-
cally.

"I knew this was pointless," she muttered. "Why in hell
I let Raveneau talk me into calling you in the first place is
beyond me. You're about as sympathetic as—"

"Ten seconds."

"Okay, okay. Yes, I'm in trouble," she said hastily, hating herself and him for her lack of options. "I know the
why but I don't know the who. It's serious."

"So, say it," he snapped.

She knew what he was demanding and her pride
screamed in rebellion. He wanted her to admit she needed his help. He wanted to make her grovel for a while.
Hallie closed her eyes, hating the necessity of having to

swallow her pride and give him what he wanted. Just as her mouth opened to form the words, she heard a woman's voice issue a whiney protest at Ryker's preoccupation with the telephone call. The woman's words were followed by what could only be the squeak of a mattress and bed frame. The son-of-a-bitch had been giving Hallie the third degree while he was in bed with some bimbo.

The woman beside him whimpered something else in an irritating nasal tone. Ryker barked the word 'quiet' at her. Hallie, flinching at the cold brutality infused in that single word, felt a rush of embarrassment for the woman who'd foolishly offered up her body for Ryker's amusement.

"You are totally unbelievable, you know that?" Hallie snapped, glaring at the air in front of her. Ryker said nothing, but for him that wasn't unusual. He never responded to the obvious. "The only good thing about the band breakup was never having to see your sorry hide again. I need to have my head examined for—"

"Then you must be pretty desperate if you need to ask for my help, Hal." His words sounded like velvet-wrapped pinchers, their grip on her becoming more uncomfortable as he smoothly increased the pressure. "So quit babbling, Angel Face, and tell me what I want to hear."

Hallie swore. No matter what she said, he intended to refuse her request. She'd be damned if she'd humble herself for nothing. Well, if he was going to refuse her anyway, what did she have to lose at this point? "Listen, you moth-eaten son-of-a-bitch, if you want the job—it's yours. Money's no object. But you hear this. If you think I'm collapsing at your fungus-covered feet pleading for your help, you can go screw yourself!"

"Hal," he barked into the phone, but it was too late. She'd already hung up. "Why you fucking little bitch," he said without surprise, as if she'd done exactly what he expected her to do. He set down the receiver. Hal Bishop might be the most manipulative, chain-jerking little piece of ass he'd ever seen, but she certainly had balls. She might be going down in flames, but she was going down on her own terms. Randy would be calling him any minute. He'd bet money on it.

"Get your clothes on," he said to the blonde lying inches from where he sat. "It's time for you to go." He didn't look at her.

"But Jake," the woman started to whine once more, "I thought we were going to spend the whole night—"

"You thought wrong," Ryker snapped. "I got what I wanted, and I gave you a pretty good time in the bargain. Go on, get out." He reached for his wallet, still in the back pocket of his pants lying neglected on the floor. He fished out four twenties from inside and tossed them on the bed. "Call a cab. Use the downstairs phone." He heard the woman get up and begin to dress.

"I've got my own money," she said stiffly, tears in her voice, "I don't need yours."

Ryker shrugged without turning around, "Yeah, whatever." He left the money on the bed and said nothing when she reached for it after all.

She paused at the door of the bedroom and said, "Look, you've got my number, so call me sometime, okay?"

"No," he said coldly, "I don't do return engagements." The woman's breath caught in a sob as she fled downstairs. After a few minutes, he heard the front door slam as she headed outside to wait for the cab's arrival.

Ryker pulled the Yellow Pages from the bedside table. He looked up the airline number and called to make reservations. According to Randy, Bishop and Hogan would be in Portland on Monday. It would be a simple matter to get her alone and follow through with his own plans. No sooner had he gotten off the phone with the reservation clerk than it rang again. "Yeah," Jake said after Randy identified himself, "I figured it was you. I'm surprised you managed to wait this long. She called."

"And?"

"And...I'm meeting her in Portland," Jake replied coolly.

"So, now you believe me?" Randy sounded almost smug.

"I didn't say that. Nothing's changed my opinion since the last time we talked, Raveneau. I intend to draw my own conclusions once I get her alone." He stared straight ahead with cold eyes. "By the way, she has no idea I'm coming—so keep your mouth shut. That's an order."

"Wait a minute," Randy began nervously.

Jake cut him off. "I thought I'd made myself clear. I won't tolerate any problems—from her or you.

Randy cleared his throat. "Look, Jake, just tell me what you're planning to do to her."

The other man gave his characteristic humorless laugh. "I told you at the beginning of this, if you don't have the guts for the answers, don't ask the questions. Suffice it to say that by the time I'm finished with Miss Hal Bishop, there won't be any doubt about where either one of us stands. Now goodnight, Randy." He paused, then added with another mirthless chuckle, "Sleep tight."

⁂

Randy stood at the window looking out at the twinkling lights up and down the valley floor. They usually soothed him and gave him a sense of peace. There was no peace for him tonight. "Oh God!" he muttered to the darkness, "what have I done?"

Chapter 11

Ty looked out the taxi window at the downtown Portland skyline. The clear morning light washed the tall glass and concrete structures in a rosy glow. One of the nice parts of having someone else driving him was that it afforded him the opportunity to enjoy the sights of one of the loveliest cities on the west coast. The traffic was beginning to slow to a crawl as the hour stretched toward eight. Ty had flown in this morning on a red-eye commuter flight, and Marlene and Walt had arrived last night. As for Hallie, she'd been gone since sometime early Sunday morning. Her vehicle was parked in the small fenced lot at the airport in Medford where Ty had left his own.

Walt maintained that she'd left to avoid traveling with the rest of them, but Ty knew it had more to do with the incident between them Saturday night. She merely wanted to make sure she wasn't forced to spend any more time in his company than necessity demanded. He couldn't blame her. He'd been cruel to her—due as much to his own frustrations as his need to keep her from getting any further under his skin. The more time he spent in Hallie's company, the harder it became to remain unaffected by her. He kept seeing the hurt and loneliness in her face. Damn it, she was tying him in knots—making it impossible for him to reconcile the laughing, mischievous temptress with the Hallie that he'd always believed in.

He glanced at his watch. It was still more than forty minutes before the meeting. He wondered where she was staying, and if she'd make the meeting on time—or at all. He made a mental note to find out what her plans were. If he found out where she was staying, perhaps he could make up for some of his meanness. A nice, quiet dinner for two, a bottle of wine and that hot chocolate dress she'd bought. Ty smiled a little wistfully. One thing was for sure: The next time he got Hallie as worked up as she'd been Saturday night, it would be on a bed, where there'd be no time for second thoughts.

The cab pulled into the parking basement of Bishop Tower and stopped at the double glass doors leading to the elevators. Ty exchanged pleasantries with the security guard on duty and asked him to keep an eye out for members of the press. His own personal staff had spent the better part of the last two weeks fielding questions regarding which of the heirs would assume control of the Bishop Company reins. Reporters from the Oregonian newspaper and the local television stations, plus an impressive number of national cable stations, had been invited to a press conference following the meeting. The CEO would be announced at that time.

Ty headed for the Tower's express elevators to take him to the top floor, where Walt was planning a discreet meeting for the three of them to make sure they'd covered all contingencies before the meeting. If Hallie was indeed planning something, today would be the perfect launching pad. Tyler fit his key in the elevator lock. The door opened, and within seconds he was headed toward the top floor, which housed the conference rooms. Walt and Marlene were waiting in one of the smaller rooms for him. Marlene presided over an elegant silver coffee service, and Walt paced nervously in front of the window.

"There you are, finally!" Walt exclaimed. "I've been waiting for an hour."

"Relax, Walt," Ty said, setting his briefcase down and taking a cup of coffee from Marlene. "We have plenty of time to say whatever needs saying before the meeting. We're all aware of what to watch out for."

"Oh really?" The older man's face wore an unpleasant expression. "It might interest you to know that Hallie arrived half an hour ago, and with a woman who looks suspiciously like an attorney." Ty frowned and looked at Marlene for confirmation. She nodded. "Prepare for a royal battle, Tyler. Not only for the C.E.O. position, but for your efforts to prevent the sale of the troubled subsidiaries. She'll tear this company down around our ears."

"Walt, for heaven's sake!" Marlene cried. "Hallie hasn't done anything to suggest that's her intent. If this woman is her attorney, then it's only common sense for her to bring her to the meeting. After all, ours will be there." Ty agreed, but he was still nervous. His personal wishes aside, he still didn't believe there was the slightest chance Hallie was innocent of the embezzlement, as Marlene obviously did. Her attitude toward her stepdaughter had softened considerably since Hallie's return to the ranch, and though for some inexplicable reason the notion pleased Ty, he felt it was dangerous.

Marlene spoke with impatience. "Tyler, I don't plan to go into the meeting blind to any manipulations Hallie might pull, but likewise, I don't intend to go in loaded for bear." She smiled ruefully. "I can't believe I'm actually willing to give her the benefit of the doubt. The last time I did, she put India ink in my hand cream." Marlene grimaced, remembering the incident when Hallie was eight and how Marlene had been forced to wear long gloves to the country club event that evening. Tom had been enraged and taken a belt to Hallie in spite of Marlene's protests. She couldn't abide physical punishment of children. Unfortunately, more often than not, Tom had refused to listen to her where Hallie was concerned. It had been almost as though he were trying to purge some spark or spirit from the child. A name sprang unbidden to her mind. Elena. Marlene shook for head to clear the phantom away. "At any rate, I want to be fair, and the Hallie I've gotten to know in the last few weeks deserves that fairness." Ty's mouth set in a grim line and she knew he was remembering that summer, 15 years ago. She sent him a sympathetic look. "She was only fifteen, Tyler," she reminded him softly. "In most ways still a child."

"Don't, Marlene," he said stiffly. "What she did to Monica and me went far beyond a childish prank. It was mindlessly vicious. I'm not likely to forget it or ever turn my back on her again."

"Morning all." They turned their heads in unison toward the soft voice.

Tyler took in Hallie's appearance. She was dressed in a black-tailored pants suit. Definitely not something off the rack. A simple pearl necklace and matching earrings were all the jewelry she wore. As she entered the room and crossed to the table where Marlene sat, he noticed her hair was fastened in an elegant French twist. The rings on her fingers were gone, and she looked every inch the successful, savvy business woman—and breathtakingly beautiful.

"Hallie," Walt said, coming toward her, "Why didn't you tell me you were coming to Portland early? I'd have been happy to escort you."

"Keep an eye on me, more than likely," she replied archly and winked at Marlene.

The other woman smiled in response and poured another cup of coffee. Hallie smiled back and took the proffered cup.

She turned to Tyler, taking in his sullen expression. "What's the matter, Nighthawk?" she asked. "Visions of hostile takeovers dancing in your head?" She took a sip of coffee, waiting for his counterattack. He merely looked at her. Long and hot. His eyes danced over her body, coming to rest just long enough on the parts he'd caressed and stroked to such sensitivity the other night. Hallie could feel her nipples pulling up and tightening and thanked God she was wearing a jacket.

"Among other things," he said. His inflection and gaze left no doubt to anyone in the room what the nature of his thoughts was. Hallie blushed in spite of her best efforts to appear unaffected.

She turned with relief at the sound of footsteps in the hall, put down her coffee cup, and leaned out to signal someone about to pass by. A tall, slender blonde toting a hefty briefcase and dressed in a charcoal gray suit stood in the doorway. Walt was right. Everything about her cried "attorney." She looked cool, controlled, and suitably dressed for a courtroom kill. Hallie ushered her into the conference room. "Marlene, Tyler, Walt," she said indicating each in turn, "this is my lawyer and friend, Kelsey Hogan. Kelse, this is everyone." The woman nodded a solemn acknowledgment. To the rest of the room's occupants, she announced, "Kelse and I have some things to discuss now, so I'll see you all later." She gave them a jaunty salute, and left the room, delighting in the uneasy looks the men exchanged.

The two women walked down the hall to stand at the large plate window in the sitting area. Hallie looked out on the downtown section, trying to get her thoughts to focus. She'd gotten little sleep over the past two nights. When concern over her father's company hadn't kept her awake, erotic thoughts of Tyler had. Hallie had met with Kelsey over dinner last night to discuss the situation surrounding the embezzlement. Her attorney had informed her as they'd lingered over after dinner coffee that the first stumbling inquiries into Hallie's financial situation had begun. Kelsey felt certain, however, that it would still be several weeks before the investigators would discover the funds in the Caymans and link them to her client. Time was on their side right now. Her advice was for Hallie to relax and let the auditing firm lead them to the real culprit. She approved of Hallie's arrangements to transfer the majority of money from the numbered account and the three million from her accounts in LA, into a client's trust fund in Genna's name to be administrated by her father's attorney. The Cayman account would be left open to prevent the real thief from getting suspicious.

They both agreed Tyler was the most obvious choice to become the new CEO, as he'd been making most of the decisions for the year prior to her father's death. He was the hand-chosen successor, the heir apparent to head the company. Hallie had always been doubtful about any involvement on Tyler's part in an attempt to weaken and collapse Bishop holdings and would gladly cast her vote for him.

"Hal," Kelsey Hogan said from behind her. "Have you spoken to Ryker again?"

"No," Hallie replied emphatically, jerking herself back to the present. "It's useless. The only thing 'Jake the Snake' wanted was to listen to me beg, Kelse. He wouldn't have helped anyway. I could hear it in his voice." She shrugged with affected nonchalance. "It's for the best, really. We'd have killed each other within the first five minutes anyway. Guess it's just you and me, kid."

"It makes me very nervous that he's even aware you're in trouble. You know how sharks gather at the first smell of blood. Hal, I suggest you invest in an M-16 and a suit of armor," her friend said dryly, "because Ryker's nobody to fool with."

Hallie conceded her friend's point and by mutual agreement they changed the conversation to more pleasant topics. Suddenly Kelsey glanced back up the hall. "Uh oh! Raptor alert." Hallie followed the lawyer's gaze to find Tyler striding toward them. "I've got to make a quick call. Good luck!"

"Did I scare Ms. Hogan away?" Ty asked as he approached Hallie.

She shook her head. "No. Kelse had some things to take care of."

"We need to talk, Hallie," he said bluntly.

"I agree. There's something I want to get straight right away," she said firmly. "Kelsey isn't here to pull any fast moves or shady deals. She's simply here as my attorney to look after my interests—no more, no less. I know there's a snowball's chance in hell of you believing that, but it's the truth."

"Forgive me if I keep a 'wait and see' attitude," he said quietly. "Once burned, twice shy."

She sighed in frustration. "Fine, Nighthawk, you made your feelings clear enough the other night. All of them. If you'll excuse me—" She moved to go past him.

He caught her arm. "We need to talk about the other night as well, Hallie, but now isn't the time or the place. I want to know where you stand on the CEO issue. If you're going to oppose me, I want to know right now. You owe me that much."

Hallie turned to him, exhaustion permeating each word. "Would you believe me if I said that I have no intention of opposing you?" She studied his expression. "I didn't think so. I guess you're stuck with 'wait and see'." She left him standing there and walked into the board room.

꧁ ꧂

Two hours later, Ty was eating crow and Marlene wore a somewhat smug expression. Not only had Hallie voted in his favor, but she'd managed to neatly circumvent one of Ty's biggest concerns: the liquidation of distressed Bishop Company holdings.

He'd been astounded when Kelsey Hogan had asked for the floor and even more astounded at Hallie's contrite look under her attorney's watchful eye.

"My client wishes to inform you that she has secured the services of Atwater, Inc., Auditing Systems to conduct a complete financial audit of the Bishop Company and all its underlying holdings," she'd said. "The audit will be fully funded by Ms. Bishop, and as an heir of the Bishop Company, she respectfully requests that any discussion of unloading unprofitable or distressed assets be tabled pending the findings of a full financial systems audit."

Ty found himself smiling in admiration at the neat little package Hallie and Ms. Hogan had passed off. Hallie was obviously an accomplished businesswoman. It was ironic that this facet of her personality was one her father had been ignorant of—he would have been proud. Walt, on the other hand, had been visibly upset.

"Hallie, this is wholly unnecessary! It's insulting to all of us and especially to the memory of your father. We have our own internal auditors, an excellent department developed under the watchful eye of Tom himself."

Walt had given Hallie a disappointed, weary look that spoke of her father's memory and implied Tom's undeserved faith in her. He'd hit her below the belt, and though Ty had done so himself on more than one occasion, he'd felt protective urges on Hallie's behalf. Hallie's mouth had drawn into a grim line, but she'd said nothing.

After the meeting was adjourned, the other board members offered Ty their congratulations on his appointment. Likewise, Walt patted him on the shoulder, though his words of approval rang a little hollow to Ty's ears. He thanked Walt briskly and excused himself, wanting to catch Hallie before she left. He found her in the sitting area, deep in conversation with Kelsey Hogan once more.

Kelsey excused herself shortly after his arrival. There was a moment of awkward silence after she left.

"Looks like I owe you another apology," he said, happy to eat a little crow. "I was wrong. I'm sorry."

"You don't owe me anything, Tyler," Hallie stated succinctly. "What I did, I did for Dad." She had trouble talking around the sudden lump in her throat. "This company, you and Genna were the most important things in his life. I couldn't let him down—not again. Not when he'd asked..." She couldn't go on and spun away from him suddenly.

"Hallie," Ty began gently, "that's not true. Tom loved you very much." He'd known Hallie had always resented his presence in her father's life but not to the extent that she truly believed Tom had had no place in his heart for his own daughter. He was about to reach out and gather her close when she held up a hand to ward him off. Hallie kept her back to him and gave a husky and mocking laugh. He felt a chill run up the back of his spine. She tossed her head back and said coolly, "Save it, Nighthawk. I'm not interested in your opinions." He was suddenly reminded of the night of Tom's funeral, Hallie laughing cynically and with false brightness. Now without anger and grief to cloud his judgment he knew he was watching a stellar performance—a performance from a woman whose heart was breaking.

Any further conversation on the subject was curtailed by the rapid approach of Kelsey Hogan. "Hal, Mr. Nighthawk, we've got a problem. I'm afraid you're going to have to cancel the press conference. Downstairs is crawling with paparazzi and reporters from every sleazy tabloid show in America!" To Hallie she said, "We've got

to get you out of here. They want you to give them a statement for tonight's broadcasts." She pointed her finger
directly at Hallie's face. "I want you to keep your mouth
shut, you hear me? Clancy's not here, so I get to be the
bull dog. Are we clear on that?"

To Ty's amazement, Hallie merely nodded. He'd
expected, at the very least, a string of four-letter words turning the air over downtown Portland completely blue. She
still looked upset. He thought about wrapping his arm
around her shoulders and taking her down to his office for
awhile. She could hide out, and they could talk. He knew,
though, that talking with Hallie was the last thing he'd have
on his mind if he was alone with her. Instead he said, "I
think we should do the conference as planned. We'll
announce that Hallie will be making a statement there, and
while they're beating their butts to get a seat, we'll take her
down the express elevators."

"I doubt they'll take the bait," Kelsey remarked, "but it's
the only shot we've got."

"I could go and make a statement at the press conference and get it over with." Hallie said, having recovered
her emotional balance. She was beginning to enjoy the
idea of the two stiffest necks she knew trying to hatch a plot
to thwart the reporters. "I think a few pointed obcenities
might be surprisingly well received."

"God no!" they both shouted in unison, drawing looks
from those remaining in the hall. Hallie felt like smiling for
the first time in days, and she was loathe to let them off the
hook.

Kelsey sighed in exasperation. "Knock it off, Hal, this
is serious. I'm going to get Walt to call all the building
security people you have. I was less than impressed by
those two dweebs in the parking garage, so I hope you can
do better. If not, we're in trouble." She hurried off in

search of Walt. Hallie chuckled softly.

Kelsey returned moments later with fire in her eyes, her worst fears confirmed. Altogether, there were four security guards, with an average age of well past fifty. "Just how did you people think you were going to circumvent the media circus that was bound to happen?"

"I'd like to point out that company matters are hardly the cause of a press feeding frenzy under normal circumstances," Ty said impatiently. "Hallie's appearance here today is the sole cause. Instead of trying to take us to task for lack of preparation, may I suggest we run the gauntlet and get her out of the building."

Kelsey looked at her client's drawn face. Obviously, none of these people had ever tried to maneuver Hallie through walls of flash bulbs, video cams, microphones and clutching hands. She remembered all too well the regular messes she'd had at the courthouse and outside of her office during the band breakup. Nothing brought the vultures out in force like the breath of scandal, and Kelsey Hogan had learned that the hard way. For the first time since Hal had told her she'd talked to Ryker, she almost wished he'd come. He'd played bodyguard for Hal on more than one occasion. Oh well, nothing could be helped. The best thing they could do was to get her out immediately.

"All right, Tyler, the express elevator to the garage: Let's get a couple of cabs there. There's no way most of those jackals are going to believe she'll be at the press conference. They know Clancy never lets her address them herself."

When the elevator doors opened, Ty took Hallie's arm by the elbow. Kelsey took up position on the other side of her, and Walt took the flank with Marlene. The guards had been mobilized by the double-glass doors, and even Ty

took an inadvertent step back as he saw the throng amassing outside. He thought he was prepared for cameras and
reporters, but he'd had no idea there would be so many.
Let alone the legion of fans. He felt Hallie reach for his
arm with her other hand. Her face had lost some color, but
she held her head high. He patted her hand for reassurance, and fervently hoped they would make it intact to the
waiting cabs.

Suddenly, out of nowhere, a tall, ruggedly built man
appeared at Hallie's left. He came in beside her from the
rear, effectively cutting off Kelsey. At the attorney's startled
gasp, both Ty and Hallie brought their heads around. He
had shaggy black hair, with wisps of premature silver just
starting at his temples, a strong, handsome face, shuttered
to the outside world by the dark reflective sunglasses he
wore. He quickly seized Hallie's upper arm in a hard grip
before she had completely turned to look in his direction.
Ty heard her gasp and whisper a name. "Ryker."

The man gave her a cold smile from his sensual mouth.
If the smile was any indication, he had a great capacity for
cruelty. "In the flesh, Hal," he said, his voice as chilly as a
damp and foggy night. "Let's go." Hallie tried to pull her
arm from his grip, but he only tightened his hold merci-
lessly. She winced and immediately stopped her struggles.

"What the hell do you think you're doing!" Ty flared
angrily. "Let her go!"

Hallie held her breath as Ryker said calmly, "She's coming with me."

"Like hell she is," Ty snarled. The man was scaring the
hell out of Hallie, and he was damned if he would stand
idly by and let some thug just take her. Walt moved forward to add his protest, and the security guards consulted
one another nervously.

The man glanced around, but didn't seem to be partic-

ularly upset with his odds. He bent his head beside
Hallie's ear and whispered harshly, "Ball's in your court,
Angel Face. You want pretty boy here to get hurt?" Hallie
shook her head quickly.

Ty felt Hallie's hand touch his chest. "Please, Tyler, it's
all right. I know him." The man who clasped her arm so
relentlessly noted the placement of her hand and set his
mouth in an even grimmer line.

"Yeah, we're old acquaintances, aren't we, Hal?" His
voice was less than pleasant. Hallie nodded, never taking
her eyes off Tyler. "Now haul your ass, sunshine, 'cause
we're leaving."

"Please, Tyler," her eyes pleaded for him to stand aside.
Tyler released her arm and glared at the man who held her.
Kelsey Hogan, standing behind them, shook her head,
warning him to stay quiet.

"Don't worry," Ryker said in a nasty tone, "I'll take real
good care of her, won't I, Hal? You know the drill, let's
go."

He propelled her toward the doors and Kelsey Hogan's
voice called after him. "Wait a minute, Ryker, I'm going
with you."

Ryker didn't even look at her as he said, "No dice,
counselor, this is a private meeting. Stay put." There was
no mistaking the warning in his voice.

"Ryker," she called sharply, and this time he stopped
but didn't turn around. "Not a thing, do you hear me? Not
a thing, or there won't be a rock in the world large enough
for you to hide under." His response was a derisive snort
to tell her they both knew there was nothing she or anyone
else could do about whatever he had in mind. Hallie kept
her head high as he took her from the building.

Ty watched helplessly as Ryker steered her effortlessly
through the reporters. He definitely had experience. He

kept Hallie tucked close to his front and pushed her through, toward a cab. Kelsey put a restraining hand on Ty when he was about to dash out after them. "You'd only make matters worse," she said. They reached the cab, and Ty and Kelsey watched as Ryker roughly handed her in, climbed in after her, and slammed the door. Ty had a hollow feeling in the middle of his chest. He turned on Kelsey, "What the hell is going on? Who is that guy?"

"His name is Jake Ryker. Let's go get some coffee. I'm sure you've got a lot more questions than that. I'll answer what I can."

The two of them left Walt upbraiding the guards, threatening them with everything from termination to prosecution for aiding and abetting a kidnapper. The reporters let them escape fairly easily. A few terse "no comments" and they were seated in the cab. "So talk. What's going on, and who's this guy other than a friend of Hallie's?" Ty began.

"I didn't say he was a friend of Hal's," Kelsey replied tensely, and for the second time that day Ty found himself irritated by the way people kept calling her Hal. Her name was Hallie, damn it. "He despises her," Kelsey continued, ignoring his frown, "and has from the first time they met. Believe you me, it's mutual."

"Then what's he doing here if he can't stand her?" He wasn't sure he wanted to hear the answer to the question, but it had to be asked.

The attorney hesitated. She had to be extremely cautious from this point on. Tyler Nighthawk was a very intelligent, highly suspicious man. If he caught a single whiff of what was really going on, he'd have both Hal and her arrested before the day was out. She had to give him enough information to pacify him, yet divert the conversation from the more dangerous questions. She worked to keep her voice calm and her manner sincere. If Tyler decided she was lying, he was the sort of man who would have little mercy. "How much do you know about what happened in Hamburg?" she asked.

"That the audience got worked up by the show and charged the stage. Four teenage girls were killed." Ty's face hardened as he replied. "Tom was absolutely devastated."

"Yeah? Well, let me tell you," Kelsey retorted harshly, "the band wasn't in real great shape either."

"It's also my understanding that the band dropped a bundle to pay off the families, then continued business as usual," Ty commented acerbically.

She frowned in impatience. "Sure, business as usual. I'm not going to go there with you, Tyler. Hal is a very private person. She'd be furious with me for telling you anything—but I think you have a right to know for your own peace of mind if nothing else." She cleared her throat and said to him levelly. "After the riot, the German government considered prosecuting the promoters and band members with their version of negligent homicide. There was even talk of mandatory prison time." She could tell from Ty's expression he'd had no idea. "Sye Greenway, Loreli's manager, had connections to the U.S. State Department through his partner, Toddy Benedict. As I understand it, Toddy called a friend of his, asking for U.S. government intercession if it came down to legal action. Our home boys decided to send over what they call a 'housekeeper'—Ryker. His job was to hold off the press, keep the tension from escalating and if the need arose, sneak the band members and their people out of the country."

"Housekeeper." He'd heard the term before—usually in conjunction with mob movies or spy thrillers.

Housekeepers were sent in to clean up missions or hits that had gone very, very wrong. Their methods were ruthless, unorthodox and extremely thorough—removing the obstacles, human or otherwise, with dispassionate precision. A hitman. Dear God, he was a hitman and Ty'd just let the bastard take Hallie away without more than a token protest! Why hadn't he stopped him? He remembered the look of panic in her face. What had that son-of-a-bitch said to her? She'd practically begged him not to interfere.

As if she knew exactly what he was thinking, Kelsey said, "It wouldn't have mattered, you know. He wouldn't have let any of you stop him. Ryker's very single-minded that way."

He noted the bitter expression on her face and realized she had personal reasons for disliking the man. "So what did he do to you, Kelsey?"

She took a deep breath, trying to decide how much to tell him. She decided to play it close to the vest. "Very observant of you, Tyler. I'm impressed. But let's just say he did enough and leave it at that."

Ty frowned, obviously unhappy at her sudden reticence. "What's he doing here and why are you so concerned for her safety?" He jumped on her slight hesitation. "Don't bother trying to tell me you're not. Just tell me straight." If Hallie had been personally involved with this guy, it wasn't a hard stretch to imagine her angering him enough to make him want to harm her. He passed his observation on to Kelsey and waited anxiously for her answers. The hollow spot in his chest filled with a knot of concern and jealousy as he envisioned Hallie in the arms of the man he'd seen today.

Kelsey snorted. "Lovers? Hardly. As I told you, Ryker and Hal don't like each other. It started the first moment they met in Hamburg. He made some derogatory comments and started ordering her around and she—"

"Punched him," Ty finished, a brief smile working at the corner of his mouth, easing some of the tension he felt. "She always did have a mean right cross," he added ruefully. The attorney nodded.

"At any rate, she—or more correctly the band—was his assignment, so killing her wasn't an option. They had a lot more run-ins, as I understand it. When Hal doesn't like somebody, she can get pretty offensive."

"Believe me," Ty muttered darkly, "I know."

"He ended up threatening her and scaring her pretty badly to keep her in line." At Ty's look of alarm she said, "She never explained what he threatened her with but it was enough to make her nervous around the guy from then on. Through the years, until the band's breakup, Toddy and Sye would occasionally hire Ryker to run interference with the press vultures, check out the crank letters and make sure there was absolutely no chance of a repeat of Hamburg. He even got to be on pretty friendly terms with the other Loreli members and their entourage. But he and Hal never made any bones about their dislike of each other."

Ty nodded and fixed Kelsey with a hard stare. "That explains who he is to her but you still haven't told me what he wants with her." He saw a stricken look come over the normally cool and collected lawyer. He turned his head to look out the window, and growled, "Damn it, Kelsey, where has he taken her? What's he got in mind?"

"I wish to God I knew, Tyler," she whispered anxiously.

Chapter 12

Hallie shifted uneasily in the backseat of the cab. Her best bet was to keep as much distance between herself and Ryker as possible. Her arm still ached from his hand and she fought the impulse to massage the sore muscle. "Am I making you nervous, Bishop?" The man seated next to her gave her a disdainful sneer.

"You know you are, Ryker. Why the hell else would you be doing it?"

"You look like hell," he said casually, as if he was making an everyday observation.

The arrogant bastard, she thought. How did he think she would look? He was probably happier than a pig in slop about it too. She decided to throw him an emotional bone that might just keep him off her throat later. "You'll be pleased to know I feel about a thousand times worse than I look." He gave her a humorless smile.

"So what are you doing here? Are you taking the job?" She waited for a reply and moments later she was still waiting. "Well?" she prompted.

"It remains to be seen," Ryker answered levelly. "We've got some talking to do." His sunglasses hid his eyes as he looked at her, but she could well imagine them, flat, dead, passionless.

Hallie leaned forward to speak with the driver. "There's a café on Salmon street. Take us there, please." The driver automatically glanced in the rearview mirror at the man seated beside her. Ryker indicated, with a slight shake of his head, that her request was to be ignored. Hallie caught the movement and immediately pressed for an explanation. "I thought we were going to talk. I think the café is as good a place as any." She tried to keep her voice steady, but with only a modicum of success.

Ryker nodded to the driver, who plainly had doubts
about what he was supposed to be doing. Ryker said to
Hallie, "Oh I'm sure you do, darlin'. I'm sure you do. Too
bad for you I've got a more private location in mind." Her
eyes widened at the decidedly sinister note in his voice. "I
don't want to run the risk of us being interrupted, Hal."

"Where the hell are you taking me, Ryker," she
demanded.

"Where else? Your hotel room."

She turned to look out the cab window, not giving him
the satisfaction of a response. They completed the ride to
the Benson in silence. When the cab pulled up in front of
the grand old downtown hotel, Ryker quickly assumed
control of the situation. He was out his side and around to
hers in what felt like the blink of an eye. He gripped her
arm once more in what would look, to the average passer-
by, like an effort to assist her from the vehicle. In truth, he
was securing her to him, not giving her the chance to dart
away or attract attention. They entered the hotel arm in
arm. He held up his hand to warn off people who planned
to enter the elevator after them. He looked the part of a
secret service agent—still wearing his sunglasses and standing with his legs slightly apart. He let go of her arm, and
his hands now rested, interlocked, in front of him. Hallie
glanced at him carefully, trying to gauge his mood. It did-
n't help. It never did with Ryker. He could open a door
for you one minute, then slam it in your face the next—and
try as you might, you couldn't figure out what had set him
off. She took in his appearance, the distressed leather
bomber jacket, worn and scuffed, not by a manufacturer's
process, but by use. Indiana Jones would have been envious. His jet hair, beginning to prematurely gray, was over-
long and shaggy, brushing the very tops of his broad shoul-

ders. It was brushed back at the sides and forehead from his ruggedly handsome face. Ryker was a tall and powerfully built man, but his frosty, controlled demeanor made him even more imposing. He wore his sunglasses more often than not in public. Nature had given him those exotic silver eyes, more wolven than human. Most people became jittery under Ryker's unshuttered gaze, though Hallie believed it was due more to the lack of any real feeling and warmth in them than to the unusual color. Years earlier, in a moment of drunken camaraderie, Hallie and Cassie had agreed that physically, his eyes were very attractive—it was the dead quality they found disturbing. She shivered, and Ryker gave her a mocking smile.

At her door, Hallie tried to quell her shaking hands so she could manage the electronic lock. Ryker took the card from her and swiftly unlocked the door. He stopped her abruptly to enter the room slightly ahead of her. He gave the front room of the suite a cursory glance, then nodded her in, with a taut jerk of his head. Hallie sighed. He'd automatically gone into guard-dog mode. The sound of the door closing, followed by the ominous click of the deadbolt sliding into place, stopped her cold. She didn't want to turn around and look at him, but she realized she had little choice in the matter. Ryker was not an easy man to ignore.

She turned, and he crossed the room to stand mere inches from her. He removed his sunglasses and tucked them in his shirt pocket. "What have you got to drink around here?" he said, his voice low and smooth.

Hallie pointed to the bar in the corner, and replied in a suffocated whisper, "It's a little early, don't you think? I mean, it's not even noon."

His eyes slid over her body in a lazy and insulting manner. "It's later than you think, Hal." The easy drawl in his voice held a note of challenge. She refused to buckle in front of him this early in the game, and for a long moment she just looked up at him. Ryker gave her the ghost of a smile, and crossed to the bar. He retrieved a bottle of Makers Mark bourbon and two glasses, then sat down in the living room and proceeded to splash the liquor generously into them.

"I don't want a drink this early," Hallie snapped, unable to stand the tension another second.

"You're going to need one before we're done here, Angel Face." He took a quick gulp and held out the other glass to her. She shook her head, and he shrugged as he set the glass on the coffee table. "Don't even think about it, Bishop," he said as he noticed her looking hard at the door to the hall. "You wouldn't make it."

"Quit bullying me, Ryker! I'm about at the end of my rope. Just say what you've got to say!" Hallie threw herself down in a chair opposite the sofa where he sat and pulled the comb from her hair. She tossed it on the end table and ran her hands through her hair in a brief, massaging motion.

Ryker took another sip of bourbon, his mercurial silver eyes sharpening on her movements. "I haven't even really started bullying you yet, Hal. As for what I have to say, that more or less depends on you." She waited for him to continue, but he didn't. He simply sat there studying her.

She fumed over his silence. What made her angrier was the fact that he knew he was annoying her and the bastard was enjoying it. "Damn it, Ryker! Could you possibly give me a straight answer—just this once."

"I think I'm the one who deserves some straight answers. Don't you? After all, Bishop," he said coldly, taking pleasure in his words, "you're the one who came crawling to me for help."

Hallie fought hard to control her temper. Ryker was doing his damnedest to antagonize and intimidate her today. She had to stay calm. It would do no good to get into a knock-down, drag-out fight with him. She'd be the loser. Anyway, during the last several hours she'd come to understand just how much she did need his help. She wanted to make sure, though, that she had to sacrifice as little of her personal dignity as possible. Since he was alone with her he evidently felt no need to temper his words. God only knew what else he figured he could get away with.

Looking him clearly in the eye, she said, "I'll get your ticket to the Caymans this afternoon. We leave in the morning. I'll write you a check for expenses and half your fee as well." She rose from the chair and crossed to a small, elegant writing desk. Opening her purse, she withdrew her checkbook and sat down. Ryker remained silent as she filled out the check and returned to stand in front of him. "Let me know if it's not enough," she said, extending the item to him. He made no move to take it so she tossed it on the coffee table and returned to her seat. Ryker sat sipping his drink and watched her, his eyes icy and unrelenting.

"What makes you think I'm going to the Caymans?" he asked softly, mockingly.

Hallie sighed in exasperation. "If you're not, then what the hell are you doing here?" So much for diplomacy, she thought.

He set his glass down sharply on the coffee table and leaned forward. There was a distinct air of menace about him. "Right now I'm doing a little fact-finding work. You're going answer all my questions and if I like your answers, then we'll talk terms. But listen, you little bitch, if you try waving your damn money in my face again, I'm going take this check and shove it up your ass. Understand?"

Hallie's face paled and she nodded grimly. Then Ryker began his harsh interrogation. During the next half hour he fired question after question at her. She found herself reluctantly telling him everything about her father's calls to her, the mysterious deposits and the meeting this morning. Occasionally his eyes would harden as if he was unsure of her honesty. Of course, Hallie reasoned, Ryker had seen her at her worst and conveniently ignored her at her best. Thank God he knew nothing about Tyler's engagement party or he would never have believed her then. At last, when she was sure she'd scream if he asked her one more thing, he nodded in satisfaction and sat quietly watching her once more.

"Well?" she asked, trying in vain to keep the querulous note from her voice. "Are you going to take the job or not?"

His eyes glinted at her. "We need to discuss terms before I agree to anything, Hal." It always made her nervous when he called her by name. He did it so infrequently. She was usually "Bishop," "Angel Face," or "You goddamned spoiled brat."

"Name your price, Ryker. I'll pay it. We both know I'm not in any position to bargain." The smile he gave her when she said that made her blood run cold. "I wrote the check for ten thousand. I'll double it."

His face fired quickly with rage, and then settled into an unpleasant sneer. "That's your answer to everything isn't it? Just wave enough cash and that'll fix everything, huh, Angel Face?" he asked softly. "Ironic, isn't it, that an overabundance of cash got you into this fix. Pisses the hell out of you, too, that you need my help and I don't need your money."

In the back of her head, a warning bell sounded too late. The next words were already out of her mouth. "It makes me sick to my stomach that I have to ask you for a goddamned thing, Ryker. And you love it. Now, how much?"

He shrugged matter of factly. "Maybe we could work out a trade, few hours of your time." She frowned at him in confusion. "Oh," he said in a studied tone as if it were truly an afterthought, "and the unconditional use of your body. I know lots of rich guys that would pay me big money for the chance to nail you. We could hold an auction. Of course the winner might want to add you to his harem permanently, not that that would cost me any sleep."

She stared at him for a minute, as the import of his words sank in. He couldn't be serious. But this was Ryker and she knew there was little if anything he wasn't capable of. As the astonishment ebbed, fury and hatred took over.

"You're pathetic. Do you hate all women this much, or just me?" she sneered.

"Careful, Hal," he said evenly. "You don't want to hurt my feelings. It would be in your best interests to be extra nice to me. I could make things a lot easier on you." His gaze traveled over her, and a flash of crimson stained her cheeks. Ryker found himself wondering if she blushed all over. Some women did. "Do you want your drink now?"

"Why in the hell do you hate me so much? Other than calling you on absolutely abhorrent behavior, and getting a little bitchy, what did I ever do to you?"

His voice cut the air like a knife. "Pissed me off, Bishop, and that was enough." He snatched his glass from the coffee table and drained it. "You acted like a goddamned prima donna. You were always right, you knew best and what you wanted, you got. To hell with the cost or who got hurt." Hallie flinched at his biting tone. This man would never forgive her for the unwitting harm she'd done in Hamburg, or make allowances for the follies of youth. She watched in dismay as he poured himself another glass of whiskey, this one larger than the last.

"Selfish, that's what you are," he snarled, his lips curling in disgust. "What did you care what you did to Raveneau and Donovan? What right did they have to lives of their own anyway—to make decisions not sanctioned by the great Hal Bishop herself? And let's not forget what a treat you made the last year of Sye Greenway's life." He swallowed hard, then rose to his feet. Ryker walked a few paces from her and turned to fix her with his contempt-filled eyes. "Don't worry, Angel Face, I'll help you. It'll just cost you money—lots of it. I just wanted to make sure you really were innocent of swiping your dear ol' daddy's money, that's all. If you'd lied to me, I'd have turned you in myself." He flicked his eyes over her in dismissal, taking stock of the damage done. Hal's golden eyes held a haunted, faraway look, and the shadows beneath them were darker. He saw the cumulative effect of all the death and catastrophe in her life marked clearly in her face. She was devastated, emotionally bent, but still by no means broken. Ryker felt grudging admiration for the woman. It was the only positive emotion he had ever felt for her other than lust.

Through the years, Sye had hired him to accompany her to various appearances and through sections of the band's tours. Hal hadn't been particularly happy to have his company, any more than he'd been happy to have hers. When he'd arrived towards the end of the first such tour, he'd been astounded at the sight of her. If she looked like hell now, she'd looked dead then—with little sleep, long grueling hours of setups and sound checks and the concerts themselves. Not much surprised Ryker anymore, but the way Bishop had kept going strong in the face of mind-numbing exhaustion had. Raveneau and Donovan weren't exactly lightweights either, but Bishop could run them into the ground and still keep going. How many times had he seen her wandering backstage like the walking dead, knowing to a certainty she'd never be able to pull off any kind of decent performance, only to stare in wonder as she became vibrantly alive under the roar of the audience and the flashes from the light display. She'd come through this, too.

He said with quiet authority, "You're going to make a couple of phone calls: one to the good counselor and another to your new boyfriend." She opened her mouth to correct him, and he silenced her with a wave of his hand. "Save your breath. I don't give a shit." His pale eyes were like bits of stone, closing off all emotion, except those of which he chose to speak. "Let them know you're okay," he continued. "We're talking, and they should stay away 'til they hear from you again. Got it? Nothing more."

She nodded mutely. She was feeling stronger, as though she had a fighting chance of getting through this thing after all. Ryker, though still Ryker, was no more menacing than usual and now for good or bad, he was on her side. She dialed Kelsey's cell phone, and her attorney answered it on the first ring. The blatant relief in her voice when Hallie identified herself was almost laughable from the cool and collected Ms. Hogan. "Where are you? Are you all right?"

"I'm okay," Hallie answered steadily. "I'm at the hotel with Ryker and everything's going to be fine. He's going to the Caymans with us. We're having lunch and working out some of the details."

"Oh joy!" said Kelsey sarcastically. "I'll be there in ten

minutes."

"No, Kelse," Hallie replied gently but firmly. "This is a private meeting. I'll stop by your room around six, and we'll go grab some dinner." She effectively cut off any protest her friend would have made by asking the next question rapidly. "Have you seen Nighthawk?"

"He was having coffee with me here until about five minutes ago, but he had a lunch meeting with a group of Japanese businessmen. If he hadn't, I'm sure he'd be pounding on your door about now. He's pretty concerned, Hal. He left his pager number and told me to call the second I heard from you."

"Call him then, tell him I'm okay. Tell him Randy sent Ryker here to keep the press from hounding me. Be sure you stress that he's not to try to see me here. Tell him to call me later if he has to talk to me."

"Believe me, Hal, he'll have to."

"Just how much talking have you two done, Kelse?" asked Hallie starting to get a little nervous with the idea of her lawyer and Nighthawk getting buddy buddy.

"Oh, this and that. You know better than to ask if I've been indiscreet, Hal," Kelsey retorted sharply.

"Actually, that didn't cross my mind," Hallie said to immediately reassure her. "I just don't want him to know a hell of a lot about anything. He's hardly my greatest fan, and I've told you that he's not above exploiting any information he gets to further his own end. His end, in this case, is to get me off the ranch permanently."

"Now that would surprise me. The way he was acting...well...never mind, I'm not going to argue about it now. I'll let you get back to the beast. He's probably getting restless. Remind him I meant business. He didn't hurt you or anything, did he?" Kelsey asked in lowered tones.

"No, Kelsey, I'm fine really," she said, and Ryker gave

her a mocking smile. "Don't worry so much." She tried to make her voice light, but she must have sounded worse than she thought because Kelsey told her she expected to hear the truth that evening, and abruptly hung up.

"The good counselor was doing her customary cross-examination?" Ryker asked as he crossed the room to join her at the phone.

"Yeah, but she was the one having coffee with the enemy, so if anyone should be cross-examining someone, it's me," Hallie said, sounding testy.

Ryker found himself reluctantly contemplating the man he'd seen with Hal today. She'd referred to him as the enemy and said he wanted her out of the picture. From what Jake had observed at the funeral, he tended to agree. It remained to be seen what lengths the fellow was willing to go to. Jake remained puzzled however, about the dramatic change in this guy Nighthawk's demeanor toward Hal that he'd observed at Bishop Towers. He decided not to take it at face value for a variety of reasons.

At any rate, Bishop certainly hadn't wasted any time finding herself a man since her return to Oregon—which surprised him. In all the years he'd known her, she'd never even had a steady boyfriend, much less a lover. Again, he thought somewhat bitterly, not his business. If he'd really wanted it to be his business, he'd take her in that bedroom and put it to her like he'd wanted to for the past six years. He walked over to her and handed her a glass of bourbon. She frowned at it and shook her head. He gave her a quelling look, and she took the drink, glaring at him the whole time. Yes, she was definitely feeling better. He stood over her until she'd had enough of the contents of the glass to satisfy him, then he picked up the phone to dial room service.

Twenty minutes later Hallie eyed Jake Ryker suspi-

ciously as he held her chair out for her at the table room
service had provided. Once more, he was trying to rattle
her, and was succeeding admirably. He unfolded her nap-
kin and, with exaggerated servility, laid it across her lap.
He removed the covers from the plates of food, took his
seat, and reached for the bottle of champagne resting in the
ice bucket.

"My, my," Hallie said. "Lobster and champagne. You
shouldn't have."

"I didn't. You did—I charged it to you."

To her surprise, she laughed. "You know, Ryker, I'm
going to miss you like a case of plantar warts." She picked
up her fork and began to play with her food. "Kelse and I
will pick you up on the way to the airport tomorrow.
Where are you staying?"

He gave her a twisted smile. "The suite next door to
yours. Where else?"

Her fork stopped halfway to her mouth, and she looked
at him steadily. "Just like old times. My own personal tiger
at the gate. Why? And don't tell me it's for convenience,
because you're the least convenient person I know."

He regarded her just as steadily and said, "Thinking I
might try to seduce you? Sorry to disappoint you, darlin',
but I'm playing this deal real cautiously. Now that I'm
forced to admit Randy was right all along, I think you could
well be in danger—especially with the way you've been
stirring things up." He took a bite and chewed thoughtfully. "That's another good reason for you to keep a low profile and stay the hell away from the islands. You're going
back to the ranch tomorrow and staying put. No arguments, Bishop," he said sternly as she opened her mouth to
protest. "This is my show now—just like the old days. No
more calls to banks or anyone. Hogan or I will let you
know what's going on." His eyes narrowed to mean points

of light. "If I find out you've been doing any more investigating on your own, I'm going to be very unhappy with you, Angel Face. And if I get unhappy with you, it'll make today seem like a birthday party. Got it?"

She nodded and swallowed nervously, remembering well what it cost to defy Ryker. In hindsight, he'd only demanded the same obedience from her that she herself demanded from the young bands she mentored. But obedience was never something Hallie gave easily. Small wonder they'd been at drawn daggers from the first day they'd met. She drew a deep breath and broached the subject she dreaded most. "Ryker, what did you mean when you said 'Randy was right all along'?" The smile he gave her now was wicked, but by no means without charm. She could almost see why otherwise shrewd and intelligent women were captivated by him—almost.

"Randy called me while you two were patching things up in Mexico. When you told him your father wanted you to come home and make nice with the family, he got suspicious. When you mentioned the missing family money, he got real worried. He asked me to check things out." He shrugged matter-of-factly before continuing. "I discovered the account in the Caymans, and the deposits to your accounts in LA right away. Randy was convinced you were being set up. I, on the other hand, figured you were out to extract a little familial vengeance. After all," he said, watching for her reaction, "they did seem less than welcoming at your father's graveside."

Her face went white. "You were there? You were spying on me?" she whispered.

"Of course. I promised Randy I'd get your ass out of the fire if you were really innocent. So I kept an eye on you while I figured out who the major players were." He took a sip of champagne. She remembered breaking down at her father's grave, an intensely private moment. He had to have seen it. She waited for him to make some sort of reference to it, but he didn't.

"Sometimes I hate you so much, Ryker, it scares me," Hallie said softly.

"Aw jeez, Bishop," he chuckled, totally unaffected by her words, "does this mean you don't want to bear my children?"

"I could kill Randy for bringing you in on this without telling me. He had no right." At Ryker's cold look, she said, "I know—I'm lucky to have him looking out for me." He nodded. "I also know, Ryker, that if it wasn't due to your friendship with Randy, you wouldn't have given me the time of day." The man across from her continued to regard her but neither nodded nor shook his head. She sighed. "You'll probably throw this back in my face but thank you for taking the job."

Ryker grunted, "Shutup and eat your lunch. Then we'll make some calls."

The rest of the afternoon passed quickly. Ryker placed calls to people with names like "Jammer," "Stoneman," and "Blade." Evidently he had a broad network of associates from which to draw, and judging from the one side of the conversation she could hear, none had any qualms about operating outside the law.

After the last call, he turned to see her watching him from the sofa. She looked tense again, wary, and he silently scolded himself for not making the calls from his own room. The frankness of the conversations had disturbed her, especially since a couple of his team members had asked what the anticipated body count would be. He contemplated calling Randy from his room, but frowned when he realized he was considering it only to spare Hal's feelings. "Screw it," he mumbled as he placed the call.

Randy answered immediately as if he'd been waiting by the phone. "Settle down, Raveneau, she's fine," Ryker said, sounding a little bored. Obviously Randy had been concerned himself about what Ryker would do to her. "She's right here. Yeah, well it's her room." Hallie winced at the suggestive quality in Ryker's voice. He turned and swept his gaze up and down her. "Okay, okay! Here she is." He motioned Hallie across to him with a crook of his finger. Handing her the receiver, he quickly pulled her to stand between his legs, keeping his eyes steady on her the whole time. His gaze glittered with sexual frankness and that, more than anything that had happened today, threw her for a loop. In all the years she'd known him, Ryker'd shoved, bullied, threatened, even slapped, but he'd never looked at her like that—at least not that she'd noticed.

"Hey, Gal," Randy began gently. "Are you still speaking to me?"

"Yeah, Randy," she replied curtly. "But if I were you, I'd hire a food taster for the next couple of months." She heard him let out a sigh of relief and before long he was regaling her with his own amusing version of the events that had brought Ryker back into her life. Soon she found herself laughing with Randy, and Ryker faded into the background. The only tense moment came at the end of the conversation when Randy asked if Ryker had "hurt her or anything." As if he knew exactly what her friend had asked, Ryker reminded her of his presence by cupping her left buttock briefly, then sliding his hand down her leg. Hallie caught her breath for a second, then answered Randy lightly as she glared at Ryker. "Oh you know Ryker, he's a total pig. What can I say?" Randy seemed relieved that she had nothing to say other than her usual smart remarks. Shortly afterwards she handed the receiver back to Ryker. Nevertheless, he kept her secured between his legs.

"I got you, Randy, don't worry," Ryker was saying tersely. "I'll take care of her. No, she won't. Ah hell! I won't, okay? I've got more important things to worry about right now than that! Bye."

He glared at Hallie, and said, "How do you do it, Bishop? I sure as hell must be missing something. You give that man months of hell on earth because you decide Montoya and Cassie don't belong together, and he still worries like shit about you."

She moved away from him and asked, "Are we done here then?" The tension of the last few days had receded a bit thanks to the alcohol and the fact that Ryker had a definitive course of action planned. But right now she felt drained and exhausted and wanted nothing more than a couple of hours of sleep-induced oblivion.

"Yup, I've got a couple more phone calls to make, but I think you'll sleep better tonight if you don't hear them. Actually, Bishop," he said, noting the fatigue rapidly engulfing her, "sleep doesn't sound like a bad option for you right now. You're about to fall over."

"So I've noticed," she said, giving him a half smile. Ryker found himself not as immune to her as he thought he was. "You can see yourself out." She turned to leave the room.

"I'll make the rest of the arrangements from here. It'll take me a while," he said with velvet-edged force. "You go bag some Zs, and I'll make sure you're not disturbed."

She knew better than to argue, and to be honest, it would be nice to have someone—even Ryker—standing watch. "Thanks," she murmured.

"I'm not doing it for you, Bishop," he responded grimly. "Remember?"

She leaned on the bedroom door for support and met

his turbulent stare. "Yeah, well, thanks anyway." She turned to open the door, but the sound of his voice brought her back around.

"Bishop," he said, more sharply than he intended. "Listen," he began. Hell, he wasn't good at this comforting business, and didn't want to be anyway, he told himself. "I'll get you out of this. Don't, you know, worry or anything."

"I hope so, Ryker," she said softly, her eyes pleading. "Just promise me if I have to take a fall, you won't let Kelsey or Clancy get sucked down too, okay?"

For the first time since she'd known him, Ryker looked as if he were in totally uncharted waters. "I won't let any of you go down, Hal," he said, as if embarrassed by his softened attitude toward her. "No matter what it takes."

Hallie smiled at him gently, "I'll see you in the morning. Thanks again."

He nodded, and was astounded at the feeling of frank relief which hit him as she quietly closed the bedroom door between them. He moved toward the glass of whiskey that he'd abandoned on an end table. Beside it lay the comb Hal had used to hold up her hair. His fingers reached out to touch it with a will of their own. He made a sound of disgust and grabbed his glass instead. Then, muttering to himself, returned to his chair by the phone. Damn you, Raveneau, he thought for the millionth time since the call from Hal a couple of days ago.

Ty looked at his watch, and glanced around his office. It was four-fifteen. Kelsey had called about four hours ago to tell him Hallie was all right. He probably shouldn't have taken the call during the middle of a meeting, but he hadn't been worth a damn anyway until he'd been assured by Kelsey that Hallie was fine. She'd delivered Hallie's message about not trying to contact her until the evening and then only under the most dire circumstances. He felt a flash of anger. How dare Hallie shut him out. Didn't she know how worried he'd been about her all day? Damn it! She'd better have a darned good explanation for keeping him in the dark like this because— He stopped himself. She wasn't holding out on him—not really, and he certainly wasn't due any explanations. The more he thought about it, the more he realized that he didn't know Hallie that well after all. He had no part in her professional life and oddly, the notion saddened him.

He picked up his telephone and called the Benson Hotel. At least Hallie had allowed him that much information. The hotel operator picked up the phone and within moments, Tyler was put through to Hallie's room. He was startled by the sharp male voice that answered.

"Ryker here," the voice barked.

Ty was momentarily taken aback. He knew from Kelsey that this Ryker guy and Hallie had had lunch, but he'd hardly expected him to answer the phone in her room this late in the day. He felt the sting of jealousy, sharp and true, pierce him.

"This is Tyler Nighthawk. Let me talk to Hallie," he said shortly. "Now."

"Sorry," the man drawled, and paused as if to savor the impact of his next words. "Hal's still in bed. Do you want to leave a message?"

"Tell her I called," Ty snarled and slammed the receiver down.

🙶 🙷

Across town, Ryker chuckled. He opened the bedroom door and observed the woman in question still deep in slumber. He noted an innocent, vulnerable quality about her, and briefly contemplated stretching out beside her and taking her in his arms. She'd wake like a tiger, he thought, all claws, teeth, and outrage. He felt himself harden as he pondered how long it would take to have her purring like a kitten. In the next instant, he snorted in self derision and quietly closed the door. After grabbing his jacket from the back of the sofa, he let himself out.

Chapter 13

Hallie grabbed the delicate peach satin robe lying at the foot of her bed and quickly pulled it on over her bra and panties. She flew toward the door of her suite in response to the heavy pounding on the other side. There were only two possibilities as to the source—Ryker or Nighthawk. The idea of either man being in her room was unwelcome, for completely different reasons. She checked the door's peephole and steeled herself for the worst. It was Ryker and he looked anything but happy. He'd probably been trying to call her and couldn't get through. Actually, she was surprised he'd waited this long to storm the door.

Hallie'd meant to let him know she'd returned from dinner with Kelsey as soon as she'd gotten to her room, but the phone had been ringing off the hook and when she'd answered it, Cassie Donovan's rich and mellow voice had commanded her full attention. Cassie had decided Hallie had been absent from her life long enough and that it was time for them to make peace. There'd been tears and name calling, but by the end of the lengthy phone conversation, they'd forgiven each other for the hurtful things they'd both said and done. Hallie had even swallowed her pride and spoken to Cassie's husband Nick, who'd started the unfounded rumors about his sleeping with Hallie in the first place. Though Hallie had to admit that she would have done far worse to anyone who'd come between herself and the man she loved, it still hadn't been easy to forgive Nick. His lies had cost her the last remnants of her father's affection and most of her surrogate family. Hallie knew he'd suffered for his actions as well. He'd almost missed the birth of his twins and lost Cassie permanently.

Hallie took a deep breath and opened the door. Ryker

pushed past her, slamming it shut behind him. "Who the hell have you been on the phone with? I heard you come in over an hour ago, and the line's been busy since then." Hallie took a look at his face and shrank back. Ryker followed until he towered over her. "Who were you talking to, Hal?" he repeated silkily, reaching out to play with a tendril of her hair. "You didn't forget what I told you about asking questions on your own, did you?" His eyes traveled the length of her. "I would hate to have to remind you of your vulnerability." He said the last word with a caressing quality and Hallie thought fleetingly that she just might want to feel a little vulnerable. The notion seemed a strange one to her, considering this was Ryker and remembering their history.

Hallie, mesmerized, let him play with the curl at his leisure. "I was talking to Cassie, actually," she answered hoarsely. "We've patched things up."

His pale eyes ground into hers. "You've never been very good at lying, Bishop, so I'll give you the benefit of the doubt—this time." His sensual mouth curved into a half smile, and Hallie found her gaze unwillingly drawn to his lips. He tugged at the strand of hair he held between his fingers to guide her closer. His eyes roamed over her, taking in the curves of her body that were seductively outlined by her satin robe. "Too bad," he whispered, his eyes coming alive with desire. "Right now the idea of disciplining you has a lot of appeal."

She tried to tear her eyes away from his mouth, and realized with mounting horror that she was wondering what it would be like to have that mouth claim hers. What would it be like to be crushed in a hard embrace and have those lips move slowly and sensually across hers. To feel his hands... She jumped back from him, and Ryker quickly dropped the lock of hair to avoid pulling it. He stepped back himself, and Hallie could have sworn she heard him mutter, "Damn you, Raveneau."

Louder, he said, "So how is the beautiful Mrs. Montoya?"

She cleared her throat, trying to recover. "Fine. The happily married mother of twins—no thanks to you or me." Ryker grunted, but offered no other comment regarding Hallie's reference to his part in Cassie and Nick's problems. In a moment of anger, Ryker had taunted Nick with the knowledge that he himself had spent a lusty night in bed with Cassie—albeit long before Nick reappeared in her life. Cassie had been humiliated and despite the rift in their friendship, Hallie had been furious. She'd slapped Ryker across the face as hard as she could. Ryker had slapped Hallie back just as hard.

"I wanted you to know that everything has been finalized," Ryker said suddenly. "My people are in place and the equipment is ready to go. I've planned for every alternative."

Hallie eyed him suspiciously. "What's going on, Ryker? Your people, the equipment? Are you going to help me, or invade a third world nation?"

"A little of both, and don't ask questions you don't want or shouldn't have the answers to. Some of those men I talked to today wouldn't sleep too well just knowing you'd heard their names." He continued with quiet, deadly intent. "I mean it, Hal: For your own sake, forget everything you heard. Those guys don't play as nice as I do." She nodded her understanding. Ryker took a folded piece of paper from his shirt pocket. "Here's the name, address and account number for a bank back east. First thing Wednesday morning, I want you to wire an additional thirty thousand dollars. If it's not there by Thursday afternoon, I'll take it out on your hide."

"I told you," Hallie said between clenched teeth, "money isn't an object."

"Fine," he said curtly, surprising Hallie by not throwing a sexual innuendo at her. "I'll see you in the morning then." As quickly as he had descended, he was gone. Hallie shook her head in bewilderment, then headed for bed.

In the hall, Jake Ryker cussed himself out roundly. He'd seen the growing awareness in her eyes as he stood there playing with her hair. It had shocked her to see him for the first time not as an arch-villain, but as simply a man who found her desirable, and one for whom she felt the distinct spark of attraction as well. For one hell of a smart woman, sometimes Bishop wasn't overly bright. He took the elevator to the floor below and strolled casually down the hallway checking the room numbers until he found the one he wanted. He rapped sharply on the door. Everything was in place. The only thing he needed to concern himself with, was controlling the wild card of the situation by putting it securely in his pocket.

"What the hell do you want?" Kelsey Hogan snarled angrily at the tall, dark-haired man in the hall. She kept her door partially closed both from habit and to insure this particular man's exclusion from her room. It didn't work.

"In," Ryker said, in a steely voice and with an indicative nod of his head. He pushed the door slowly and steadily with the tips of his fingers so that she was obliged to move or fall flat on her rear. Either one would have been fine with Ryker. Kelsey chose the former. Once she was out of the way, he crossed the threshold and closed the door with an air of finality.

Hallie sat in the cab sandwiched between Kelsey and

Ryker. No-man's-land, she thought glumly. She turned her head to glare up at Ryker as he shifted his arm to rest it across the back of the seat, then slightly angled his body. He'd contrived to form a niche that she found herself resting in uneasily while his fingers stroked the nape of her neck. That creep and his games. He'd seemed almost jovial when they'd all met this morning. At first he'd concentrated solely on trying to nonplus Kelsey, but at the attorney's staunch refusal to rise to the bait, he'd turned to Hallie. She stiffened and tried to pull away from the not altogether unpleasant sensations his light touch evoked. His fingers tightened ever so slightly on her neck and let her know she was required to stay put. As she relaxed, so did his grip.

"Comfortable?" he asked, as his eyes, full of mockery, stared down into hers.

"No," she hissed.

"Too bad," he replied. "I am."

Hallie's gaze came to rest on his jaw, and she wondered again about the scratches on it. She looked over at Kelsey, who was unusually silent this morning and angrily tapping her foot against the back of the cab's front seat. Hallie looked once more at Ryker. "What did you do to your face?" she asked.

"None of your business, Bishop," he said. Ryker gave Kelsey an insolent stare. Hallie noticed her attorney was returning it look for look.

"Never mind," Hallie murmured, "I'm sure I don't want to hear about it." The rest of the trip passed in silence.

Once at the departure gate, Kelsey was all brisk efficiency. She bid Hallie farewell, hugged her quickly and told her not to worry. She boarded the plane without so much as a backward glance at her client or the man still at her side.

Hallie turned to Ryker. This was it. He would get the job done, collect his money and vanish into whatever reality he normally inhabited. She'd probably never see him again and conflicting feelings of relief and regret coursed through her. He'd been her enemy, often her worst nightmare, sometimes her only source of security, and never really her friend. He was kind of like an ingrown toenail. It annoyed you and hurt like hell while it was there, but you became so used to it, that you kind of missed all the fuss when it was gone.

"Call me tonight, okay?" she said, looking down at the carpeting.

"I'll call you when I have something to say, not before," he replied sharply, and gave her an odd look. Of all the things he'd expected, the sad look in Bishop's eyes hadn't been a possibility he'd even considered. It didn't sit well with him. She was intending to say a permanent farewell to him. And even as thorough a bastard as he'd been to her through the years, she was going to miss him in her own way. He'd just have to see how much, he thought as he happened to glance down the concourse and an idea formed in his mind.

"Look, Ryker," Hallie began, "We've never been close or anything, I know, but—"

Ryker snorted.

"Well," she continued, as she studied the carpet, "don't...you know...take any unnecessary risks, okay?"

"Well, what's all this?" Ryker drawled infuriatingly. "True concern from Gal Hal Bishop herself? Don't worry, Angel, I never take unnecessary risks."

Hallie sighed and shook her head. What was the point in trying to be nice. Ryker didn't want nice, he'd probably rather have had her spit in his face. She turned to go, only to have his hand catch her arm. He set down his carry-on bag, and turned her slowly back toward him.

"There's just a couple of more things before I go, Bishop," he said. Before she had time to protest, he swept her into his arms and bent her backwards in a firm embrace. His mouth covered hers hungrily, his lips moving over hers, devouring their sweetness, and demanding a response. She was scarcely aware of her hands coming up to knead his massive shoulders, unsure if her intent was to push him away or pull him closer. His kiss became punishing as his mouth ground against hers and she felt breathless and weak as a warm, tingling sensation wound its way down her body. Ryker lifted his mouth from hers and searched her face with his molten eyes. His breathing was as rapid as hers and he looked as far from unfeeling and detached as a man can get. Suddenly, though, a devilish glint came into his eyes, and he gave her a slow sexual smile. "That one was for me, darlin'," he said in a husky whisper, "but this one is just for you."

His lips descended again, but this time they were tender and persuasive as they moved across hers. His tongue traced her lips and she automatically opened her mouth to offer him the entrance he sought. A little noise escaped from her throat and he drew her tighter against the hard, muscled length of him. Her body had a will all its own and she felt desire course through her as his tongue played with and stroked hers. Her brain screamed at her to remember this was Ryker she was kissing with such abandon—Ryker, for God's sake! Her body told her brain to shut the hell up and continued to press itself closer all of its own accord. Thank heaven it was still early and there was hardly any foot traffic on the concourse. Thank heaven he was leaving and he hadn't kissed her like this in her hotel suite. His lips left hers to nibble her earlobe, and she felt herself go weak in the knees.

Ryker whispered softly into her ear. "Now you don't have to wonder, Bishop. Now you'll know what it's like." He looked deeply into the warm, whiskey-colored eyes of the woman he held and saw the passion he'd placed in them slowly evaporate and fury take its place. He straightened himself upright and released her.

Hallie was a little unsteady on her feet. "You lowdown, dirty son-of-a-bitch! How dare you!" she fumed. "You are a first class prick, you know that!" Her voice got louder as rage destroyed every other shred of emotion he'd inspired in her.

"That's right, Angel Face, I sure am. And if I had some extra time, I'd prove it too. Damn, you sure can kiss, Bishop." He touched the tip of her nose with his finger and winked at her. "I'll be seeing you, Hal. You can bet on it." He turned and walked through the gate, leaving Hallie to scream her fury at his back. Just like old times.

"Ryker! You bastard!" Hallie kicked her flight bag, then snatched it up in frustration. She whirled to head for Horizon Air's gate and ran smack-dab into Tyler, literally. His eyes narrowed dangerously, and he caught her roughly by the shoulders.

"I can see why you didn't return my call yesterday, Hal," he sneered. "I guess you were too tired for a threesome."

"Get the hell out of my way, Nighthawk," she snarled. "I've been used and abused enough for one day, and in my present mood, I don't play well with others!" She shrugged off his hands and stalked away from him. "Men!" she threw at him over her shoulder. "You all make me sick! Somebody should find a pesticide and eliminate you from this planet! Don't talk to me—no—on second thought, stay the hell away from me altogether! Ride on the wing!" She was still yelling at him as she disappeared down the corridor. Tyler gaped after her, wondering why he felt in the wrong when it was she he'd seen in another man's arms.

❦ ❦

Ryker placed his bag in the overhead compartment and sat down by the slim, well-proportioned attorney. She had great legs, he thought to himself as he made a big production of settling himself in. He pawed through the magazine rack in front of him and accidentally brushed her legs several times.

"Try to touch me again, Ryker, and you'll get more than a couple of scratches this time," Kelsey Hogan ground out through clenched teeth.

"Oh really," he drawled, and raked his gaze over her. He smiled and withdrew his sunglasses from his shirt pocket and placed them on his face. "Next time you decide to use those claws of yours, counselor, I'm going to have you on your back with your legs spread so fast, you won't know what hit you." He leaned back in his seat and crossed his arms as if preparing to take a nap. "Bet you can really wrap yourself around a man with those long stems of yours, too."

Kelsey rolled her eyes heavenward. "Hal, you owe me big time for this one," she muttered.

Ryker chuckled.

"Really big time!"

Chapter 14

Hallie flopped sideways into the easy chair in her house and threw her legs over the arm. Shortly, she was joined by HB, who meowed steadily, chastising her for deserting him. True to her word, Mrs. H had taken wonderful care of him, and the last effects of his traumatic journey to Oregon had disappeared. Hallie stroked his ginger fur and listened contentedly as the mews of resentment changed to a loud, rumbling purr.

She promised herself to get to work in an hour or so, but right now, there was no place she'd rather be, or anything else she'd rather do than snuggle with her cat. The stress of the last few days had taken more of a toll on her than she cared to admit. Thankfully, she'd slept well last night—so well in fact, that she'd overslept this morning and had to scurry around packing her bag at the last minute. In her haste, she'd managed to lose the hair comb that she'd worn yesterday. A minor thing, but irritating nonetheless.

Much as it disturbed her to admit it, the reason she'd been able to sleep so well was knowing that Ryker was on patrol. She groaned out loud as she thought of those kisses this morning. He'd set her up royally. She knew she should have been suspicious from the beginning, but she'd been far too shocked at his actions, as well as at her own responses to them. Even now she blushed thinking about what could have happened in her hotel room. He must have seen Tyler walking down the corridor toward them. What better form of payback than to kill two birds with one stone by making her realize he could have taken her if he'd thought she was worth the effort, and throwing a monkey wrench in the relationship Ryker thought she was having with Tyler.

Revenge, tidy and cold, Ryker's favorite type. Still, she wasn't sure where Cass had gotten the notion he was cold and withdrawn making love. Those kisses had to be some indication, and there was no lack of feeling in them. Oh well, in a way he'd done her a favor. Now Tyler believed there was something between them, and that would probably end the lusty inclinations he'd been bombarding her with.

Tyler arrived back at the ranch about an hour after her. She'd locked the deadbolt and gone to unpack her suitcase, keeping an ear out for the sound of pounding at the door. None came, to her mixed feelings of relief and disappointment. Hallie shook her head, wondering why she'd let herself get so accustomed to Tyler's presence in her life. She gently moved HB and roused herself to go start a pot of coffee and begin to work.

Moments later, there was a gentle knock at the door, and Hallie observed the top of a blonde head through its high window. She opened it and gave Marlene a warm and generous smile as she shyly crossed the threshold.

"I saw you were back and I wanted to see how you were doing. I hope I'm not disturbing you." Marlene sounded a little nervous, as if she expected to have her head separated from her shoulders for arriving unannounced and uninvited. Hallie felt a twinge of guilt. In the past she'd done little to give this woman the impression there was anything between them but jealousy and animosity, yet in the short time she'd been home, Marlene had repeatedly shown herself to be a gracious and caring woman.

Hallie impulsively touched her arm in welcome. "Frankly, I'm glad for the company," she said, "I'm supposed to be working, but I think I'm going to play hooky for another day. I thought I might go riding later, when

Gen gets home. Would you be interested in coming too?"

Marlene looked pleased at the spontaneous invitation. "Yes, very much. I could use the exercise. There's nothing like a brisk gallop over the hills to blow away the cobwebs," she added with an impish grin that belied her forty years.

Marlene had never looked her age, and Hallie's father had often referred to her as his 'golden girl,' a term that had hurt and angered the lonely, neglected child Hallie'd been. Now, she thought firmly, it was time to stop all the childish resentments and establish some type of relationship with her stepmother. "Go on into the living room and sit down, Marlene," Hallie suggested. "I just made a pot of coffee. I'll get us some."

"Sounds good to me," the older woman replied. "I'll just get reacquainted with HB here. He looks much better these days."

"Yeah," Hallie called from the kitchen, "as long as I can keep Nighthawk from murdering him, he'll continue to improve." She heard Marlene giggle.

"He's home too, you know," Marlene began, when Hallie returned to the living room. She surveyed her stepdaughter with one raised eyebrow as she accepted a mug of coffee. "Ty isn't in one of his most charming moods. He can be gruff on occasion, but today he's downright surly." She tilted her head slightly to one side, inviting a response from Hallie. When none was forthcoming, she continued: "There're only a few things that can put a man in a snit like that, and they all involve a woman."

Hallie stayed absolutely still. The last thing she'd anticipated was a confrontation with Marlene, genteel or otherwise. The other woman didn't appear angry or indignant, merely inquisitive, yet Hallie wasn't sure Marlene would like the answers she received.

"Hallie," Marlene began softly, as if reading her thoughts, "I'm not here to expect, demand, or insist on anything." She leaned forward on the couch and looked down, as if studying her feet intently. She was weighing her words with careful deliberation. "I don't have the right to do that," she said finally. "None of us do. I just want you to know how much I regret not being there for you as a child." Marlene raised her large blue eyes to Hallie's face, as tears threatened to spill down her cheeks. Hallie knew that if Marlene cried, she'd be a goner herself. "I was so young when I married your father, Hallie. That's the only excuse I can offer. I was so terribly in love with him too. I couldn't believe that of all the women in the world, Tom Bishop would have chosen me. If I'd been more confident, perhaps I could have stood up to him when I should have—especially where you were concerned." A couple of tears rolled down the sides of her cheeks, and Hallie felt a painful lump lodge itself in her throat.

She lifted her hand towards Marlene in a gesture of understanding. She didn't trust her voice. Hallie'd dreamed of this moment all her adult life, and the only thing different now was the absence of her father. There was one thing more than anything she longed to hear, but the woman in front of her would be the last person in the world to say it.

"Cowardice is a pretty lousy excuse for emotionally abandoning you the way I did," Marlene rasped through the tears that were now streaming in earnest. "I stood back and allowed him to deny you your real mother—your heritage. When I questioned your father's decisions, he'd tell me not to trouble myself about you, that I was too kind-hearted, too inexperienced. What I was," she said, her voice quivering with emotion, "was too damn gutless."

"Please, Marlene," Hallie croaked, "it's all over. I don't

think dredging up the past..." Her own eyes were swim-
ming, and she had to cease any further attempt to halt
Marlene's confession. To her dismay, Marlene chose that
particular moment to move and kneel by the chair Hallie
was sitting in. Marlene looked up at her intently with her
wide, cornflower eyes.

"I know this is painful for you," she laid her hand on
Hallie's arm in a comforting gesture, "but if there's anyway
on earth we're ever going to be a family, there are issues
we have to resolve." Marlene reached up and gently
stroked Hallie's hair. "You understand that, don't you,
honey?" she said softly. That one touch, those few tenderly spoken words, unlocked the flood gates—and her heart.
Regardless of someone else being in the room, after years
of carefully schooling herself to always stay under control,
Bad Gal Hal Bishop lowered her face to her hands and
sobbed like a baby.

What was wrong with her? she wondered. She'd cried
more in the last two months than in the last ten years. Now
this soft, sweet woman, to whom she'd been an absolute
little monster, was kneeling at her side and apologizing—
apologizing to her.

Hallie felt Marlene's arm come around her and gather
her close, as if she was still the lonely, angry little girl she'd
been so many years ago. In truth, she was. Pains like those
didn't go away with maturation. They merely buried themselves deeper, nurturing old grievances close to a guarded
heart. Here was the threshold she'd been looking for since
childhood. She hoped she had the courage to step across
it.

"M...Marlene, don't...take all this on yourself," she
sobbed. "I was such a miserable little creep to you! I did
my best to make your life here a hell on earth. Oh God!
You don't know how sorry I am! I was such a little beast!"

She buried her head in her arms once more.

"Shhh, honey, it's all right," Marlene murmured. "You were a little girl. You'd lost your own mother in a horrible, tragic way. We should have handled things so differently. Back then there wasn't the information that there is today. Your father was a proud, stubborn man, and even though he had the money and influence to get us all the help we needed, his damned pride refused to allow it." Now she spoke with anger. Hallie could scarcely believe it. In all the years she'd seen man and wife together, Tom Bishop's word had been the absolute gospel law.

They rocked back and forth in each other's arms for some moments before Hallie gently separated herself and went to retrieve a box of tissues from her bedside table. They wiped their eyes, blew their noses, and sniffed loudly, without embarrassment. They relaxed in Hallie's living room and began, for the first time, to really talk. They talked about Loreli, her father, the company, and she even found herself trying to explain, without getting too deeply into particulars, her strange relationship with Jake Ryker and her disappearance with him after the meeting. A sudden knock at the door stopped them abruptly. Both women exchanged a knowing glance.

Marlene went to answer the door, understanding completely Hallie's reluctance to see Tyler. When she opened the door and he took one look at her red eyes, Ty Nighthawk lost all the hard-gained ground he'd made with his temper over the last several hours.

"What the hell is going on here?" he boomed, as he tried to step around Marlene and enter the house. The small woman effectively moved to block him. "If Hallie is working you over, Marlene," he snarled, still trying to side step her, "she's going to regret it." Marlene was still not having any of his interference and blocked him once more.

"Tyler," she said briskly, "I don't care for your attitude at all, especially when you're referring to my stepdaughter. Kindly take your disagreeable mood elsewhere. Hallie and I want to spend some time together."

Ty began to speak but found himself quickly silenced by the diminutive blonde in front of him. "We are in the middle of something, Ty," she said, softening her tone a little. "Hallie doesn't want to talk to you right now. Maybe later this afternoon, but not right now." Marlene lowered her voice for his ears alone. "We're planning on riding when Genna gets home. Why don't you meet us at the stable around four? We'll all go together. I think you two could use a cooling off period," she added pointedly. "We'll see you later." With that, she quietly and firmly closed the door, leaving him in shocked disbelief.

Ty stormed back toward the house. He wasn't completely sure what was going on at Hallie's, but he understood well enough that he'd been excluded in no uncertain terms. Part of him was glad to have Marlene and Hallie getting along well. It would make things easier in the long run for Gen and himself. He had limited success, however, in convincing himself that he was operating solely from his desire to keep close tabs on Hallie's actions.

The way she'd kissed that guy Ryker in the airport bothered him a lot. He'd been suspicious about the two of them since her adamant refusal of his company in Portland, and when he'd seen her in that son-of-a-bitch's arms this morning, he'd been ready to kill. Ty thought about the kiss he'd seen, the way Hallie'd been held tightly against this guy she professed to both fear and despise. Anyone would have been hard pressed to see daylight between them as the man held her reclined in his arms. Ryker had ended the embrace and was in the process of telling her he'd be back by the time Ty'd gotten close enough to do anything

about it. He would have done something about it too, and
to hell with all this garbage about how mad and bad the
guy was supposed to be. Hallie was his, damn it, and no
weekend warrior was about to take her away from him. He
was keeping her until he decided otherwise, and it was
time to establish that once and for all.

Obviously, Hallie's natural bed-hopping tendencies
were kicking in. According to rumor, she'd needed a
revolving door on her bedroom. It was time to put a stop
to that as well. Maybe Ryker didn't mind her extra-curric-
ular activities, but they were something Ty would never
tolerate. Once more, he thanked his lucky stars he didn't
love Hallie Leigh Bishop and never would. Women like
her made fools of men. It was one of their specialties. He
slammed into the house and stomped down the hall to the
library and his laptop.

Hallie spent one of the most pleasant afternoons she
could remember with Marlene as they continued to talk
and get to know each other. Marlene shyly asked questions about the upside of life as a celebrity and Hallie asked
tentative questions about her father. She hungered to
know if he regretted cutting her off as much as Marlene evidently did. What had he said to people at the ranch when
the teenagers died in Hamburg as the audience rioted and
rushed the stage? Was he ever proud of her musical triumphs? The questions hung on her lips, but she knew better than to ask them if she didn't want a straight answer.
She did, but she wasn't ready for the possible answers yet.
Eventually, as she knew it would, the subject turned to
Tyler Nighthawk and the reason for his foul mood today.

"Guilty," Hallie raised her hand impishly, giving her
stepmother a wink. "Nighthawk saw something he should-
n't have. More correctly, something that should never
have happened. I got set up by Ryker." She related what

had happened at the airport, drawing raised eyebrows from Marlene.

"I take it Tyler was less than—pleased?"

"I think the term would be more like 'red-faced-with-anger-and-disgust'. Then he starts acting all self-righteous on me, like since day one here he hasn't tried putting the moves on—" She stopped herself as she realized what she'd just blurted out in her anger at him.

"Hallie," Marlene said quietly, "has Tyler been acting in an inappropriate manner towards you?"

Hallie ran her fingers through her tawny hair, settling on one lock to twist nervously. "Um, well I guess," she said hastily, "it would sort of depend on the people and the circumstances to define what would be truly inappropriate, don't you think?"

"That inappropriate, huh?" Marlene asked dryly, arching an eyebrow . "Well, well. You'd have to be blind not to have noticed his interest in you. I just didn't think he'd decided to pounce yet."

Hallie gave the older woman a startled look. Marlene's last comment was something she'd have expected from herself or Cassie, or any number of people for that matter, but not her prim and proper stepmother. Her face relaxed into an open grin. Yes indeed, she liked this woman. "Marlene," Hallie said, rolling her eyes roguishly, "he's pounced, yanked, grabbed, and suggested things that would stampede the cattle."

The blonde woman on the couch threw back her head and laughed. "Lord, it's nice not to have to watch my words with an impressionable fifteen-year-old. So, are you going to take pity on the man? If there ever was a case of raging testosterone, it's Tyler."

"No way. I'm not about to take him up on his offers, not that they aren't as intriguing as hell, mind you, but, there's just too much antagonism and dislike." She shook her head and shrugged. "I'd never be sure what his real motivation was. He's still burned at me for ruining marital bliss with 'sweet, sweet Monica'."

"Seeing that you brought up that conniving little witch's name, I'd like to ask you myself why you did it," Marlene said, a thoughtful expression on her face. "For years I subscribed to popular theory—that you did it for revenge when your father refused to hold a *Quince Ñera* ball for you that summer. Since you've been home, I've developed my own theories about your reasons. I've decided they were much more altruistic than a simple chance to pay Tom back for denying you your debut. You had every right to be angry with him," Marlene said. She studied her hands in embarrassment for having failed Hallie in yet another instance. The younger woman assured Marlene it was all water under the bridge at this point. Marlene contemplated Hallie for a moment, then stated, "You caught her at something, didn't you?"

Hallie threw her legs over the arm of the chair once more and received a meow in mild rebuke for disturbing HB who'd recently returned to her lap. Marlene continued to surprise her. Hallie'd never heard her say a word against Monica before, but then she hadn't been overly devastated that the little slut had removed herself from Tyler's life either. "Truth is, I was ready to hate her the minute she set her size five, Italian leather pumps on this ranch," Hallie said, giving Marlene a sheepish grin. "As you recall, I was pretty good at hating anyone connected to this ranch at the time. Except for the hands, that is."

"So it was that bad of a crush, was it?"

"Sort of," Hallie answered evasively. "Thing is, I promised myself never to tell anyone else why I wrecked the engagement until the day I tell Tyler. Whether he'll believe me or not is another matter. Unfortunately, every time I start to, one or the other of us loses our tempers."

"I think it's time you have that discussion, Hallie, and I mean at the first available opportunity. If it doesn't present itself, then force it," Marlene said firmly. "He's always beat himself up for his beginnings, though your father and I went out of our way to try to assure him that he could make anything out of himself that he wanted. I know it's been important to Tyler from the first to fit in and not feel like a charity case." She looked sadly at Hallie and continued, "I wish now we'd shown you as much understanding as we showed him. I look back on it now and I see there was no earthly reason for Tom to deny you the same traditions as any other Latino girl, except he still..." An undeniable look of pain flared briefly in the older woman's eyes and Hallie, unsure of its real source, hurried into speech.

"No sweat, Marlene," she said, with a little more worldliness than she felt. "I got over it a long time ago. In the immortal words of Ryker, 'Bishop always lands on her feet.'"

"Really?" the woman curled up on the couch said, searching Hallie's face. "You know, he must be a very intriguing man in his own way. Has he always had feelings for you?"

It was Hallie's turn to burst out laughing. "Ryker?" she asked incredulously. "The only feelings that man has ever had where I'm concerned focus on death and dismemberment. That's why you could have knocked me over with a feather this morning when he kissed the hell out of me." She snorted in derision, "Of course it made all the sense in the world once I saw Tyler heading up the concourse. He thinks Tyler and I are lovers. It's just the sort of casual mayhem Ryker would enjoy causing before he left town."

Marlene's expression suggested that she found this to be a little too simplistic an explanation. She'd watched this Ryker in operation in the basement of Bishop Towers. The good thing about being perceived as an attractive yet somewhat dim-witted blonde, was that people frequently discounted her intelligence, leaving her free to observe humanity unimpaired. Her stepdaughter was obviously not ready to hear about the subtle tautness that had come over Ryker's face when he'd observed Hallie gazing warmly into Tyler's eyes. Perhaps those observations were best left for another time, or maybe best not disclosed at all.

Marlene cleared her throat. "In any event, Hallie, you've got to clear the air with Tyler. He's always harbored resentments toward you, and I think there was a lot your father could have done to prevent them. Tyler always regarded you as the princess of the castle, the one who turned and bit the hand of her father, the king, at every available opportunity. Now I'm not saying he was wholly incorrect, but he did idolize Tom, and Tom's beliefs and opinions became Tyler's. I think you could go a long way in helping him listen to his own voices by showing him that St. Monica had feet of clay."

Hallie was quiet for sometime; then she turned a bittersweet smile on Marlene. "You know," she began, "there's something I've been meaning to say to you for a while now. You made it clear to me today you think you let me down one hundred percent of the time when I was a kid. I want you to know that's not true." She stopped for a moment as the emotion she felt shook her voice. "At probably the biggest turning point of my life, you stood up and prevented something that would have caused the death of my soul. Remember the time when I was twelve, that day on Dad's birthday?" It was a token question. Everyone on the ranch who'd been present that day would never forget one of the few times Tom Bishop had vented his fury at his daughter in public. Marlene sighed and nodded at Hallie. "Marlene, he would have crushed my hands under the weight of the piano's key cover, all because I played like 'her,' my mother. I never thanked you for taking him on when it happened, or for refusing to allow him to take my music away. I know you were the one who encouraged him to buy me another instrument—my first guitar. 'Thank you' seems so little to say, but, thank you." Her eyes dropped to the floor as she heard the other woman's tear-filled voice respond.

"Think nothing of it, Hallie," she whispered.

Genna arrived straight from school without going to the house first. She was very surprised to find her mother lounging in her sister's home. Hallie picked up from her tone that she was a little miffed at finding what she considered to be her sanctuary invaded by her mother. She agreed to accompany Marlene and Hallie on their ride, though, and then danced off to change. Marlene excused herself shortly afterward, but not before extracting a promise from Hallie to join the family for dinner that evening. Once she'd left, Hallie got changed herself and headed to the stable.

She noticed a familiar figure casually resting his arms on the top railing of the corral. One foot was supported on the lowest plank, giving Hallie the chance to cast an appreciative glance at one of the nicest male backsides she was ever likely to see. His well-muscled thighs were nothing to sneeze at either. Her mouth turned a little dry and her cheeks flushed as she watched him, imagining caressing and gripping him as he plunged into her. She pursed her lips and exhaled. Damn, she'd always been a sucker for a pair of well-filled jeans. She debated turning around again

and locking herself in the bunkhouse until her own hormones got under control. Just then, as if he could feel her
eyes on him, Tyler Nighthawk turned around.

He watched her approach the corral with that lazy little
swaying walk of hers. Damn, he wished he'd been standing behind her so he could have enjoyed the back view.
The front view was hardly a disappointment, though. He
poked the brim of his battered cowboy hat back from his
eyes with his index finger and encouraged his mind to contemplate the treasures hidden underneath her clothes.

He was still angry with her, but once he'd cooled down
enough to think things through this afternoon, he'd decided she hadn't slept with Ryker after all. She'd told him herself she didn't sleep with men that didn't like or respect
her. Her anxiety and fear in the guy's presence had been
all too real. No, they definitely weren't on friendly terms.
The more thought he'd given it, the more the whole thing
smelled like a set up, with Hallie and himself as the vic-
tims. Still, he wanted to hear it from Hallie.

"Fancy meeting you here, cowboy," she drawled in her
bedroom voice. "Is holding up the fence part of your job
description these days?"

"Thought you knew I was invited along on the ride."
His eyes raked over her in fiery challenge. "If you have a
problem with that, maybe we should go somewhere private and work it out."

"Yeah, right," Hallie said sarcastically, as she joined
him at the railing. "Last one into the hay loft is a rotten
egg."

Tyler chuckled as he watched the horses in the corral.
He couldn't resist the urge to tweak her nose out of joint.
"I'm game if you are, Duchess. Are you missing your boy-
toy already?"

Hallie glared at him in fury. "Look, you stupid jerk, I

can't do a whole hell of a lot about you riding with us except to stay behind. I will not tolerate that smug, hypocritical attitude of yours a second longer, though. If you can't behave with the barest minimum of civility, go take a hike—preferably in front of a runaway bronc." She started to stalk off toward the stable, only to have Ty step in front of her. She was barely able to stop herself from really giving the ranch hands something to talk about. "You know, I've had about all I can stand of the opposite sex in general, and you in particular!" She punctuated it by jabbing her finger in his chest.

Ty's green eyes turned to darts as he glared down at her. He'd pushed her too far and if he didn't act quickly, she'd refuse to go riding, period; and manage to successfully avoid his company again. He was getting damned sick and tired of her calling all the shots. He took his hand and firmly covered the offending finger. He stepped closer until they were literally toe to toe, then he leaned down into her face. "Without a doubt, woman, you are the most aggravating, self-absorbed, spoiled brat I've ever seen," he ground out through clenched teeth.

"You bet your ass," Hallie snarled up at him. "So what's your point, Nighthawk?"

"My point is that for five cents I'd turn you over my knee right here and spank the living daylights out of you."

"Oh yeah?"

"Yeah."

"Well, let me tell you, buster," Hallie said, shoving her hands in the pockets of her jeans and thrusting out her chin, "I'd pay you a quarter just to see you try." Ty looked as if he was about to do that very thing when Luther stepped out of the barn and waved to her.

"Miss Hallie," hollered the grizzled old-timer, "that was Mrs. Bishop. She said her and Miss Genna are gonna be late so you and Mr. Tyler should head out toward Moon Mountain now, and they'll catch up with you in a bit."

"Never mind, Luther," Ty answered for her, "Miss Hallie won't be going riding with me." Then he added in a snide voice as he looked her up and down, "She doesn't have the guts."

"Luther," she immediately yelled, "let's get those horses ready!"

Ty watched her stomp to the horse barn, letting her get a little ahead of him before he smiled and said softly for his ears alone, "Works every time." He made sure he stayed behind her all the way to the barn so he could admire the view.

They rode silently, side by side, for quite some time. Hallie's nerves were stretched as tight as guitar strings and she refused to look over at Ty, even though she could feel his insolent eyes on her, demanding attention. He started to whistle low and slow. It was a tune Hallie recognized immediately as one of Loreli's big hits, "Never Tell A Lover." After all, she'd written it. It was the final straw, and she urged her horse into a gallop, leaving the source of her irritation in the dust. Soon she caught a side glance of Ty moving up on her left. She urged her mare faster and heard Ty angrily call out for her to slow down. When she didn't, he also increased his speed and moved his stallion closer until he could reach the bridle. He gradually slowed his mount, forcing hers to follow his horse's lead. He then turned both animals toward a copse of trees, ignoring Hallie's scathing words. When they finally stopped, he jerked the reins from her hands.

"Get down, now!" He barked the words at her. She sat where she was, defiantly. "Move it, Hallie. I mean business." When she still didn't move, he dismounted quickly, holding her reins, then yanked her from the saddle into his arms. She struggled and he tightened his arms around her. "Calm down, you little wildcat! I'm not going to hurt you. I just want to talk."

"Oh sure," Hallie sputtered, as she continued her futile efforts. "I suppose there's a hawk's nest at the top of that tree too. I walk over there and you take off with the horses."

"What the hell makes you think I'd do something like that?" he asked, his tone incredulous at her accusation.

"That's exactly what you did last time we stopped here on a ride," she responded hotly.

He looked confused for a moment, and then the light started to dawn. Of course, he thought: one of the first dirty tricks he'd played on her. How could he have forgotten? She'd pestered him for a week non-stop to go riding with her. The last thing a teenage boy wanted to do was play nursemaid to a scrawny, homely little eight-year-old brat. He remembered now, all right. He'd told her to go to the foot of the tree and be very quiet so as not to disturb the bird, and he'd stay with the horses. As soon as she was far enough away, he'd remounted and taken the horses back to the ranch. Hallie'd returned much later, limping badly from blisters caused by the new boots she'd worn for the occasion. He'd felt lower than a snake and immediately scooped her up and carried her to the house. She'd punched him in the mouth with her fist and used a string of four letter words no eight-year-old should even know. He recalled, also, that she was grounded for a week for hitting him and for the bad language, while he got off with a stern lecture from Tom about responsibility. In hindsight, he knew no matter how badly Tom's lecture had made him feel, he'd deserved far worse. Hallie, on the other hand, had been unfairly punished for her comparatively mild transgressions. Suddenly he felt guilty all over again.

"I'm sorry, Hallie," he said softly, as his hands began a slow massaging motion on her back. "I'd forgotten ditching you here. I was a pretty nasty shit myself back then."

"You sure as hell were," she said, somewhat mollified.

"Let me assure you, honey," he murmured, "the last thing on my mind right now is ditching you." He leaned down and gently covered her mouth with his. Hallie responded instantly, and her arms encircled his waist. It was a gentle kiss, asking for forgiveness and receiving it. He felt a surge of triumph as he deepened the pressure of his lips and felt her heartbeat quicken against his chest in response. He nuzzled her neck below the earlobe, then returned once more to drink passion from her mouth. She parted her lips and tantalized him with her tongue until he followed suit. Hallie stroked the inside of his mouth, slowly at first, and then with a sense of increasing urgency. Ty's own tongue responded feverishly, then took over the lead. Her hand slid into his hair, and she arched against him, almost past rational thought. Ty abruptly broke off the kiss and set her away from him.

"Oh lady," he whispered huskily, "what you do to me. We'd better stop this right now. We're expecting company at any time, and if I don't get a chance to cool down, we're going to shock the hell out of Gen and Marlene."

Hallie grinned up at him. "I think you might be a little surprised on that score. I know I was."

"What do you mean?" he queried.

Hallie relayed Marlene's questions and her amazing observations. She watched with amusement as Ty's face took on the same look of disbelief as hers had done earlier that day. "The woman is a constant source of amazement to me," she said. "I really enjoyed today. It's the first time I've ever sat down and really talked with Marlene. It meant a lot to me," she added shyly. A hint of wistfulness appeared in her eyes. "I think we might even end up pretty good friends."

Ty returned a warm smile. He didn't want to break the mood, but these few moments might be all the privacy they would get until much later. He had to know something for sure. "Hallie, I need to talk to you about this morning." His voice was inflexible, his gaze steady, demanding the truth whether he liked what he heard or not. "What exactly is this Ryker fellow to you?"

He saw her smile vanish and the warmth leave her eyes. "What you really want to know," she said bitterly, "is whether I'm sleeping with Jake Ryker or not. Right?"

His eyes narrowed at her bluntness and Hallie glared at him, saying. "Get over it, warden. It's what you want to know, right? I'm not one to mince words and you know it. There's no love lost between Ryker and me, so somehow the phrase 'making love' just doesn't spring to mind. I'm not a hypocrite." She turned and walked farther toward the trees and brush before facing him again. His expression was closed and guarded, yet she could see from the way his lips had thinned and his brows had furrowed ever so slightly that he was barely able to restrain himself from a harsh reaction. Hallie knew she should tell him 'no way' straight out, but she was still smarting from the sting of having him believe she'd casually hop into bed with any available guy, especially when he knew from personal experience that wasn't the case. His constant suspicions about her morals were aggravating enough, but the thing that angered her most was his point-blank refusal to see that if she was going to bed down with anyone, it would be him. Damn it. Lately her tongue had spent nearly as much time in his mouth as her own.

She said insolently, "What's the matter, can't believe Hallie-the-Turbo-Tramp would ever pass up a chance for a roll in the sheets?"

"Don't play with me, Hallie. Answer me." He spoke with a deceptive calm that belied his growing anger. If she kept playing this stupid game of hers, he would break his resolve not to shake the truth out of her.

She stomped back toward him. "No!" she yelled. "Is that direct enough for you?" Her face was red with fury and her chest heaving. Ty immediately went to her and tried to put his hands on her shoulders as Hallie continued to holler at him. She knocked his arms away from her and gestured to the world at large. "Attention, attention! To whom it may concern, I am not sleeping with that warthog from hell, Ryker! If I was going to sleep with someone, it would be this cretin here," she said, jabbing her thumb at Ty, "but I'm not going to sleep with anyone, and that's his hard luck!"

Ty found himself grinning broadly at her, but Hallie wasn't having any. She said, in a voice heavy with sarcasm, "Tell me, Tyler, how many men do you figure I've slept with over the years? Ten? Twenty? How about thirty, or do you figure I can't even remember the number?"

His grin faded, and he looked at her, eyes smoldering with some unnamable emotion. "It's in the past. I don't want to talk about it," he snapped out.

"Too bad, honey, because I do," she fired back. "In the grand total of twenty-six years of age, let me see now, exactly," she paused a moment for effect, before saying, "two." She placed her hands belligerently on her hips, and stood toe-to-toe with him. "Of course," she said slowly, wondering what reaction her next words would have on him, "I don't count my first time really, seeing as it hurt like hell, him being a sadistic pig and all. I ended up in the emergency room afterwards." Triumph ran through her as she saw him wince at her words.

"There weren't any affairs with the Stanton brothers, Pepe Ramirez or Nick Montoya, no liaison with either Randy Raveneau or Cassie Donovan, no endless orgies, not even a steady stream of one night stands." She meant to shut him up on the subject of her so-called promiscuity once and for all. "*Chico*, I happen to know for a fact, though, that your bed posts were so full of notches, you had to replace them by the time you left for college!" She was getting what she wanted. He looked positively dumbstruck.

"You see, I couldn't stand the idea of another man ever touching me after the first time, and it stayed that way until I was twenty-four. All the rumors were just that—rumors." She looked up into his emerald eyes, smoky with turbulence. "That's it, in a nut shell. No Ryker, nobody else. You can believe it or not, it's your choice." She turned away from him and folded her arms around her midsection. "God! I can't believe I just blurted all that out to you. The only people who know about the ER are Randy and Cassie. I never even told Sye or Toddy." She shrugged her shoulders as if to diminish the effect her admissions had on her, but kept her back to him. "Look, just don't treat me like some kind of nymphomaniac because I'm not. And don't waste your time on apologies or thinking I'm some kind of tragic little victim either, okay? Because I really couldn't hack that. Pride has gotten me through a hell of a lot in my life."

He realized that her last statement was probably the most insightful she'd ever given him. Gal Hal Bishop was hard boiled—one tough little cookie, but he wondered, after the lights dimmed and the crowd went home, how many nights had she spent alone, whistling in the dark, waiting for morning. What could he say? What was there to say?

From almost the day she'd turned fifteen, he'd accused her of, if not actually sleeping with a string of high school boys, everything short of it. Her own father had accused her as well. He was sure, himself, when he saw her at the Chicago concert hall that she was sleeping with the promoter. My God, she was still a virgin then, he realized. What would have happened if he'd followed his instincts at the time and kissed her as he'd pressed her against the wall. What if he'd taken her back to his motel room that night as he'd wanted to. What if he'd been her first lover instead of some monstrous brute. She would have had nothing to fear. He would have been kind and gentle, making sure he made it good for her too. He felt a swell of emotion in his chest. She'd told him. She'd opened up to him. He wouldn't do anything to make her close the gates of her fortress now. He'd walk on eggshells to keep the drawbridge open. He overcame his need to sweep her into a comforting embrace. In the end he said softly, "The one thing you're not is tragic, Hallie. You've got more grit and determination than ten people. You didn't owe me any kind of explanation, but thank you."

"Tyler," she said, turning back to face him, "Ryker was trying to get to me through you today. We've had a running war since the day we met, and he just wanted to make sure he got the parting shot." Her eyes had a burning, far-off look in them, as though she was still trying to figure it out herself. "I may have been frightened of him, but truthfully when we were heading through all the lights and cameras, I knew I was safe. You see, I've had a little trouble dealing with large crowds ever since the riot in Hamburg. I knew he wouldn't let anything happen to me, at least not from somebody else. After he was done snarling and intimidating me, he sent me to bed and sat guard duty so I felt secure enough to sleep. He's like that. But just when you think he's human after all, though, he does something horrendous." She gave Tyler a bittersweet smile. "Actually, what he pulled was quite mild for him. Before this morning, he's never so much as given me a peck on the cheek. A slap, yes—a peck, no."

Tyler's eyes blazed with sudden fury. "He's hit you? Damn it, Hallie, you should have told me! There's no way I'd have let you be alone last night!" He searched her face.

Hallie shook her head and examined the toes of her boots. "It was a fair fight, Tyler. I hit him first. I knew what he'd do, and he knew I knew. I was just too damn mad to care. Randy and Sye would have taken a shot or two at Ryker if they'd known. Anyway, Ryker just drew the line at letting me hit him a second time and I stepped over it, that's all." She quirked her lips in a half smile and added, "Now, if you don't mind, I think we've given Mr. Jake Ryker much more time and energy than he deserves. Besides, I have something I've been wanting to tell you for a long time."

Tyler arched an eyebrow and rewarded her with a larger smile of his own. "Dare I hope it's what I think?"

"What's that?" Hallie asked, eyeing him suspiciously.

Ty gave her his best bad-boy leer and answered suggestively, "That tonight's the night."

"I don't think so. It'll be amazing if you're still speaking to me at dinner tonight. I've been invited by the way. No," she began again, "what we need to talk about now is something I should have cleared up with you long ago— eleven years ago, to be exact. Monica."

Suddenly, Ty's face became grim. His voice hardened with bitterness as he said, "We have nothing to discuss in that arena, Hallie. You were young and I'm willing to try to make some kind of allowance for that, but I won't stand here and rehash it all."

"Tyler, I told you some pretty intimate stuff a few moments ago. This thing about your engagement is still between us, just like my alleged whoring. It would mean a great deal to me if you'd hear me out."

Tyler rubbed his hand over his eyes and said wearily, "You're not going to stop until you've destroyed every bit of ground we've gained in the past few weeks, are you? Okay, Hallie, have it your way. You always do."

"First, I'm very, very sorry, Tyler." He snorted and rolled his eyes. "Last time I tried to talk to you about it, I didn't explain myself well enough, and I gave you the wrong impression. I wasn't trying to hurt you back then."

"God help me if you ever really try," he muttered and walked away to put more distance between them. "Don't tell me. You humiliated me and the woman I loved in front of some of the most powerful and influential people on the west coast for the good of my soul. Right?" He laughed shortly and without amusement. "Well, we all know differently, don't we, Hallie. You were furious when your father refused to allow you a *Quince Ñera* celebration, so you took it out on me."

"Lord, give me patience," Hallie muttered to herself. "I'll admit I was furious with him, Ty. But who wouldn't be? His excuse was that his and Marlene's schedules were too busy. Ha! Less than a week later you announced your engagement and amazingly enough, their schedules cleared. How would you have felt when your own father..." Hallie stopped speaking and struggled to check her emotions. Ty was forced to admit that part of him did understand how she must have felt. Always the outsider, while he had been accepted and encouraged from the night he'd come to the ranch. If he hadn't been so hungry for the respect and stability Tom had offered him, perhaps he would have seen Hallie's plight a little differently. "It had nothing to do with Dad giving you and Monica an engagement party," she continued. "My method sucked, Tyler—I'm not denying that. But I did it because Monica didn't love you."

He glared at her in absolute fury. "Not after what you did, how could she? God, you must really have hated me to go to all the trouble of pouring my mother into a cab just to humiliate me."

She took a deep breath. Here it was, the moment of truth. "No, Tyler," she said softly, taking a tentative step toward him. "I thought I was in love with you."

"You thought what?" His tone of voice reflected the disbelief and shock in his face. He took a step toward her himself and his expression darkened. Hallie wanted to back away from him. Far away. Somewhere like New Jersey. Tyler sounded even more menacing when he said, "You're trying to tell me that you shot the hell out of Monica's and my life because you were jealous?" He didn't wait for an answer, but advanced farther on her. "My God, my life was turned inside out because of some stupid adolescent crush? What about the hell you put Monica through with your damned selfishness? Does anyone or anything ever matter to you except you?"

She winced at the hard unforgiving edge in his voice. Damn it, this time she would finish, she would make him listen. "Yes, Tyler, someone did. You, you big jerk! I was so full of angst and pathos, I was more than happy to sacrifice myself on the altar of unrequited love. I probably even had my funeral planned with you throwing yourself on my coffin in grief. What the hell did you expect? I was fifteen years old, for crying out loud!" Her face was as angry and red as his. "Then you know what happened, I caught pure, sweet, saintly Monica with her pants down, literally. In the hayloft with one of the hands. Roy, I think his name was." She thrust her hands in the back pocket of her jeans and glared at him mutinously.

Tyler had never wanted to hit her so badly in his life as he did right now. Monica was a virgin when they'd started dating. It had taken several months to get her to allow him to put his hands inside her panties, let alone sleep with him. She was shy, nervous and had only given in to his pleadings for sex when he'd told her how much he loved her and intended to marry her. Monica was the purest, deepest love he'd ever had in his life. She'd trusted and believed in him until she'd seen firsthand what kind of trash he'd sprung from. Her family had welcomed him with open arms, and the Bishops had welcomed her with theirs. Everyone except Hallie, that is. She'd been her usual spiteful, hellfire little self. Now he knew why. Everything had been blown apart, and not because of her hatred, but because Hallie Leigh Bishop had fancied herself in love with him. She'd probably invented that ludicrous story about Monica to justify her own actions, and told it over and over again until she'd begun to believe it herself. Sometimes it was sure harder than hell not to hate Hallie.

"I don't believe a word you've said," he growled. "Not about Monica anyway, and I'm not sure how much of the rest I'm willing to buy at this point either." He swept his eyes over her in mockery. "I can't help but wonder how much of that touching confession was to clean a little of the tarnish off yourself so it would be easier for me to swallow that horseshit about Monica. Nice try, sweetheart, but it doesn't wash."

"I didn't expect you to believe me, Tyler," Hallie replied through gritted teeth. "I think you'd better ask Marlene what she knows, because she's not any bigger fan of Saint-Monica-the-Chaste than I am." She started to walk toward her horse and turned back with an afterthought. "Oh, and about the rest of my confession? Screw you."

"I already told you, honey," he said in a falsely seductive tone, "I'm ready, willing and able. Just say the word and I'll make your girlhood fantasies come true." He focused on her breasts with a hot, insulting gaze. She mounted her horse without another word and rode off at a gallop back toward the ranch. He let her go.

Dinner that evening was strained, to say the least. Everyone with the exception of Tyler was polite, but his sullenness and his refusal to barely acknowledge Hallie's presence cast a pall over the entire event. Marlene and Genna tried to keep the conversation lively, but Hallie was withdrawn herself and only half-heartedly responded to their efforts. She stayed just long enough after dinner to be polite and promise to help Genna with dance steps and wardrobe selection for the upcoming dance this Saturday. Marlene was obviously disappointed at her stepdaughter's early departure and tried to induce her to stay with the promise of 's'mores later in front of a video tape. Hallie demurred, but before she left, she impulsively hugged Marlene and told her to come have coffee with her in the morning. Her stepmother smiled warmly, promising to be down early with some fresh baked goodies. Then quietly, Hallie slipped out into the night, leaving Tyler glaring at the spot where she'd stood.

Ty slammed the library door behind him and threw himself into his favorite chair. All evening he'd relived the horror of his engagement party, mentally flashing from scene to scene. He couldn't block it out—his mother arriving at the hotel ballroom slobbering, falling-down drunk, Monica's horror-stricken face, the startled gasps and whispers from the guests, Hallie's look of triumph directed at

Monica. And of course, the final obscenity of Lena Nighthawk vomiting on the maitre d' and himself as they tried to get the belligerent woman to leave. He'd refused to speak to his mother for the next two years, though he'd continued to support her until her death.

An hour later, Marlene knocked warily on the library door. The room had always been Tom's sanctuary, often shared with Tyler in earlier years, and sometimes enjoyed in solitude. It was meant to be a man's domain, with its leather furniture, dark woodwork, and heavy drapes. Generations of Bishop men had walled themselves off from the outside world and their womenfolk, Tom included. She hoped the next generation of wives and mothers wouldn't be nearly as compliant as she and her predecessors.

She opened the door to find Tyler sitting pensively in one of the wingback chairs. A gentle smile played at the corners of her mouth as she softly entered the room and took the seat opposite him. "Tyler," she began gingerly, "would you mind if I joined you for a while?"

He looked at her, but most of his attention still seemed fixed on some far-off point. Finally he said, "It appears you already have, Marlene. I think it's only fair to warn you, though, I'm not the best company tonight." He gave her a melancholy smile and added, "In case you haven't noticed."

"Yes, I noticed. I think everyone noticed, Ty. That's what I need to talk to you about." She sat back in the chair, apparently waiting for permission to continue. Ty indicated with a motion of his head that he was willing to listen to what she had to say. "I understand Hallie talked to you about Monica this afternoon." At the flash of anger in his face, she hastily added, "I ran into her coming back from her ride. That's why we didn't join you. She thought you might need some time to collect yourself. She didn't say what she told you, understand, but she said you'd probably need to talk this evening."

Briefly and harshly, he filled Marlene in on what Hallie told him earlier, punctuating her accusations about Monica with a disgusted snort. He waited for a similar reaction from the woman across from him. Minutes later he was still waiting.

At last Marlene said, as if putting kid gloves on each word, "I'm not sure how you're going to take this Ty, but I think it's true. I never saw anything as blatant as Hallie, but I saw enough to make me extremely suspicious, and with more than one man." His eyes burned intently as he scrutinized her. "Roy Dantine," Marlene said quietly, "was let go about a week or so after the party. You were still at the cabin at the time and very upset when you got back, so it's understandable that you didn't notice. Officially the reasons were poor work and lack of responsibility." She laughed shortly. "Well, it appears now he was responsible for something all right." She continued to speak as if to herself. "I never did like the way he looked at me, or Hallie for that matter. He used to make me feel like I was half-dressed. I was very glad when he was gone. I recall asking Tom exactly what led up to his being fired, but he got very abrupt and said it was business and not my concern." She sighed deeply, thinking about her husband's clearly defined place for her in his world and the humiliation she felt at his hands when she dared to step over his boundaries.

"When I told him how uncomfortable Dantine made me, he said the man was gone now and not to bring him up again, period. Hallie must have said something to her father in her own defense," she mused. "I always wondered why he let her off so lightly. She spent the rest of the summer at her Tia Augusta's. It was the only time Tom ever let her visit her mother's family. And even then he did it more for your sake than hers." She looked back at him suddenly. "All these years he must have known, Ty, but he chose to let you go on hating Hallie rather than hurt you with the truth."

"He begged me to forgive her," Ty said hoarsely. "He begged me over and over, Marlene." He shook his head in disbelief. "It was the one thing he asked of me that I couldn't do. It was the one request I refused."

"No, Tyler, stop it right now." Marlene said sharply. "He owed you the truth. He owed Hallie the truth also. He sacrificed her to protect your feelings. That was terribly wrong, Tyler. It was unfair to both of you. You were a grown man. The truth would have hurt bitterly, but not nearly as bitterly as spending all these years thinking it was because you weren't good enough." She shook her head in confusion. "I don't understand Tom's thinking about this."

"It doesn't really matter though, does it, Marlene?" he asked rhetorically. "The fact remains that no matter what Monica did, she still felt tainted by me, by my real family. I'm not a Bishop, never was. I'm the son of a drunken, woman-beating killer and the town whore. Once she knew that, what choice did she have? What choice would her family and friends give her?"

Marlene spoke with infinite patience, even though she was far from feeling it. "She had the same choices that any woman who truly loves her man has. She chose to break and run. Do you think those were the actions of someone who really loved you, Tyler?" Her speech became more impassioned. "For heaven's sake! Even at fifteen, Hallie had the strength of resolve to stand beside the man she thought she loved. She was willing to tolerate his hatred forever, rather than let him settle for a woman unworthy of him. That's the sort of woman a man needs beside him, one who knows how to love and trust deeply; one who won't turn tail and run under the first round of gunfire. She rose from her chair and gave him an appraising look. "I don't know about you, Tyler, but I think eleven years of mourning and self pity is way too much."

Ty watched her go, a glint of wonder in his eyes. That's the sort of woman a man needs—eleven years of self-pity, she'd said. Marlene was right, Hallie was right when she'd been yelling at him that night in her Jeep. All at once, the import of her words took on a totally different meaning. She'd been mocking him about himself with decent women, ridiculing his hyper-sensitivity so long after Monica, not his deservability.

With everything Hallie'd been through in the past couple of months, she was still taking it on the chin, asking for no special favors. He felt a brief wave of shame wash over him. It had been so much easier to loathe himself, his parents, and Hallie than to face the truth. Monica had never really loved him. Marlene and Hallie were right—his origins wouldn't have mattered a bit if she had. God, how he'd loved her, though. She was so small and delicate. Everything about her, manners, clothes, her very gestures and movements, proclaimed her a lady. She'd become the object of all his desires. When he'd pursued her relentlessly and won her, his heart had soared, feeling there was nothing he couldn't do or have if he only tried.

For years he'd limited himself to casual affairs and refused to allow his heart to completely engage for fear of hurting or being hurt. He'd blamed a fifteen-year-old girl for it all, when in truth the fault had been his own. He needed to think, to sort his feelings out. He needed to see Hallie. God! She'd shared a deep and personal part of her-

self with him, and he'd flung it back in her face as if it were
of no value. He'd be lucky if she ever spoke to him again.
A walk was what he needed. A walk in the cool darkness
would surely restore some much needed order to the chaos
in his head. Ty headed for the door.

❧ ☙

Hallie struggled with lyrics that refused to come together.
In the last hour, she'd lost track of the number of times
she'd bounced back and forth between piano, acoustic guitar, and notepad. Her mind and heart were in too much
turmoil for song writing, or at least this type of song writing, she amended mentally. She had lots to say for something that required bluesy lyrics.

Hallie glanced over at the three boxes carefully stacked
in the corner. One of the hands had brought them down
from the attic for her last week. They contained the sum
total of her mother's life and were all Hallie had left of the
woman whose warm light had all too briefly illuminated
her early childhood. Her mother—laughter, a whisper of
brightly colored silk, the scent of Givenchy perfume and
lullabies crooned softly in Spanish. Thankfully, her father
hadn't destroyed the boxes, but had instead relegated them
to one of the most remote corners of the main attic. She
still hadn't been able to bring herself to go through them.
Her emotions concerning Elena Bishop were always con-
flicted. She felt torn between the need for closeness to her
mother and anger that in the end, Hallie had been relegated to last place in the order of importance in her mother's
life. She tossed her head, unwilling to further contemplate
circumstances that could never be altered. Self-pity wasn't
her thing and she had more important matters to concern
herself with.

Kelsey had checked in about an hour ago. She hadn't
had much to report so far, other than the expected grum-

bling about Ryker. Evidently, he'd deserted her shortly after their arrival at the hotel. First though, she informed Hallie, she'd had the dubious pleasure of meeting Ryker's team, referring to them as a plethora of scumbags. Though Kelsey wasn't able to give her any concrete answers about anything yet, she admonished her client to hang tough and they'd contact her as soon as things started happening.

Hallie poured herself some juice and for the hundredth time since dinner, tried to stop the image of Tyler's face this afternoon from intruding on her thoughts. He'd been furious with her. Hallie's insistence on talking about Monica had felt like yet another betrayal to him and he'd responded by verbally striking back at her. It hurt, but she knew it was for the best. They had no future together other than heartache.

On impluse, she went back to her composition, reworking the tempo of the music and redoing her lyrics with much more success now. In no time at all she was playing her Martin and singing the finished piece. It was a little sad and poignant, and she sang with all the power and emotion she felt. Hallie was so far into the music she failed to notice Ty standing outside her door listening. As she finished the song, he turned quietly and walked away.

Chapter 15

Hallie threw herself into the flurry of activity surrounding Genna's first date. Outfits were selected and subsequently rejected at breakneck speed. Genna wanted nothing left to chance. It was a bittersweet time for Hallie. She was thrilled to be so involved, but nonetheless she envied her younger sister for the familial support the girl took for granted and for her mother who would never desert Genna in favor of a lover.

Hallie coached her sister on dance steps, cautioning her that most of the ones she'd used herself on stage were off limits to Genna's inquiring mind. Soon, the sound of laughter and music filled the house, managing to finally draw Tyler from his cave in the library. He watched the proceedings with amusement, and even volunteered his services as a partner. Hallie kept her manner toward him polite, yet decidedly cool. Evidently, her attitude only served to intrigue him further. He went out of his way to draw her into a conversation and even manipulated her into partnering him purely, he insisted, for Genna's instruction on basic dance steps. He worked diligently to draw her out, and Hallie found herself responding to his teasing smiles and remarks in spite of herself.

On Saturday night Hallie arrived shortly after dinner to give what help she could. Ty stood near the fireplace, his green eyes bright with desire as he regarded Hallie silently. She was wearing faded jeans that rode low on the hip and a short knit top that afforded him an unfettered view of her slender midriff and navel—and a navel ring. Attached to it was a small silver pendent with a glittering blue gemstone. It was a complete turn-on, and Ty practically drove himself crazy thinking of flicking it with his tongue and tugging it gently with his lips.

Hallie casually dropped her denim jacket on the back of a chair, smiled, and murmured greetings to him and Marlene. Mrs. H. appeared in the doorway looking totally exasperated. Genna was practically in tears and pleading for her big sister's help. Hallie sighed and excused herself, but Ty noticed she seemed pleased at the prospect of being needed. She left with Marlene in tow. He watched her head for the staircase, struck once again by the unconscious sensuality in her. The woman played with the sexual thermostat in a room by merely entering or exiting it. He wanted her, and he was damned tired of waiting.

He'd spent the better part of this week putting Monica's bones to rest, so to speak, and giving Hallie time to mend her wounded feelings. She was still being a little standoffish, but he was determined to be patient and bring her back around in a day or two.

He thought again of the song she'd played the night he'd stood listening on her porch. The words had spoken of lost dreams and the temptation to settle for second best. Through the lyrics he'd come to understand Hallie's need to follow her dreams to the end. Anything less would be a betrayal of her own spirit. Hearing the words and haunting melody had conjured images of yearning and sacrifice. That night he'd realized for the first time what a truly complicated person Hallie Leigh Bishop was.

He turned at the sound of laughter coming from the front hall. Genna pirouetted gracefully before the three admiring woman. He joined them, whistling softly. "Ah honey, you're a sight to behold," he said, drawing a shy grin from the teen. "I kind of feel sorry for this guy tonight, though, because he's going to end up having to let you dance with every boy in the place." Genna ran to him and hugged him tight.

"Thanks, Ty, thanks for the trip to Eugene, and for driving tonight," she said softly, and reached up to press a kiss on his cheek.

His heart swelled with emotion. "It's okay, honey, just seeing your face lit up like that is thanks enough." He hugged her again, and his eyes met Hallie's over the top of her head. Hallie's expression was unreadable. Her eyes were suspiciously bright, as if from unshed tears. She quietly went to the living room and retrieved her jacket. Damn, he thought, she was happy for Genna but sad for herself. There'd been no big family event preceding her dates; hell, as far as he knew there hadn't been a real date for her. Sneaking off to play at the roadhouse or hanging out with Deke Stanton and Pepe didn't qualify. If he didn't do something quickly, she would leave and wall herself up in the bunkhouse. For her own good and his, he wasn't about to let that happen. When she returned to the hallway with her jacket already on, he seized the opportunity.

"Great, I'm ready whenever you and Hallie are." At Genna's and Hallie's puzzled expressions, he said, "Of course you wanted her to get a firsthand look at this guy, didn't you?" The pleased light in Genna's eyes told him he'd found just the right ally. Before she could say anything, though, Hallie spoke up, saying she had a lot of work to do. Ty cut in, disallowing her protest. "Come on, Hallie, what's one night? This means a lot to Genna here. You've put a lot of effort into this yourself. Just come along with me for the ride. I promise I won't start a fight." Hallie eyed him suspiciously and looked to be on the verge of flat-out refusal when help came from two unexpected sources.

"What a great idea!" Marlene said enthusiastically. "Hallie can give us a second opinion and keep you company for the evening in town."

"Well I..." Hallie began.

"It's about time you went out and had a little fun yourself, Miss Hallie," said Mrs. H. briskly. "It's about time Mr. Tyler here showed you around some too."

"Wonderful!" Marlene said gaily, " It's all settled then. Hurry up now. It's time to go."

Even Genna entered into the spirit of the thing, grabbing Hallie's arm and tugging her toward the door. "Come on, Hal, let's get in the car. I'm so glad you're coming," she said with a sprightly twinkle in her eye, "because I can't wait for you to meet him." The look on her face would have melted a heart of stone, and Hallie resigned herself as the last nail was driven into her coffin.

She put the brakes on sharply at the front door and turned narrowed eyes on all the people present, saying, "All right, I'll go. But I want you all to know I can smell a scam a mile away." Then she allowed Genna to whisk her out the door and into the night.

Ty stopped at the door himself and winked back at the two remaining woman. "Thanks, ladies. I do appreciate the help."

The gym at Bishops Bluff High School was ablaze with lights for the Saturday night dance. Genna and Cole waved a jaunty good-bye and headed up the walkway of the school. "He's a nice kid," Ty said, as he wheeled Marlene's Mercedes from the high school parking lot. "I think she chose well."

"Uh huh, she did. I wasn't real happy about him calling me ma'am though," Hallie replied, grimacing.

Ty laughed and reassured her. "Don't worry, Duchess, you're not ready for the old folks' home by a long shot. What would you like to do tonight?"

Hallie studied him thoughtfully for a moment. Was this a date? Frankly, she doubted it, but butterflies spun chaotically throughout her stomach and she had to stop looking at him in an effort to get them under control. Part of her wanted to squeal like a giddy teen and part wanted to run screaming for the hills. Casual, calm, unimpressed, that's what she needed to be. Don't let him think it's any big deal. She immediately took herself sharply to task. It wasn't a big deal. He had an evening in town to kill and he'd asked her to tag along, that's all. It wasn't a date, not really. Finally, she said, forcing disinterest into her tone, "Whatever you were planning is fine with me."

He frowned slightly. "I was thinking we could go catch a movie at the Royal or do a little dancing ourselves. How does that sound?"

Hallie shrugged. "Whatever, it doesn't much matter," she said, sounding faintly bored. Ty whipped the car quickly to the side of the road and slammed it into park.

He turned to face her angrily. "Listen, Miss Hot Shot Rock Star, when I take a lady out on a date, I don't necessarily expect to knock her off her feet in the first ten minutes, but I do expect her to be polite and at least feign some enthusiasm at my company." He gritted his teeth and gave her a stony, leveling look. "Now maybe your manners are a little out of practice, I don't know. I'll give you the benefit of the doubt this time, but I'd better see a marked improvement in your attitude in the next twenty seconds or we're going to spend the evening doing a lesson on dating deportment." She stared wordlessly at him, but surprise registered on her face. "Well?" he queried softly.

She felt a new and unexpected warmth flow through her. "This is like a real date?" she asked a little nervously. She'd done it again, she thought. Rather than risk her feelings, she'd chosen the least threatening path and rebuffed him before he could rebuff her. He was right, she'd been terribly rude.

Ty smiled gently. "What the hell did you think it was, Hallie? It's not like a date, it is a date. Come here." He crooked his finger at her and she found herself unbuckling her seat belt and leaning across to him, more than eager for the taste and feel of his lips on hers. It was a sweet, gentle kiss, yet completely satisfying. Hallie found her breath quickening as a delicate tingle worked itself through her body. Ty set her away from him, but stroked her cheek with his hand to let her know he wasn't rejecting her. "I think that's enough kissing, at least for right now. If we don't stop, I'm going to make a detour out to the lake, and I promised myself I'd be a gentleman for at least two more hours."

Hallie shook her head laughingly and said, "You don't give up, do you, Nighthawk? I meant what I said the other day about not sleeping with you." More seriously, she said, "It would be a huge mistake for both of us. You know it would. Yeah, I'm tempted, but I'm not going to do any-thing about it. End of story."

Her words didn't seem to have much impact on Ty, and his face broke into that lazy, sexy boyish grin that did such marvelous things to her insides. "Whatever you say, Duchess. Far be it for me to destroy your illusions. Just remember, no matter how determined you are to resist temptation, I'm even more determined to create it." He tugged at a strand of hair playfully. "How about a little dirty dancing and beer?" Hallie nodded, but in the next instant Ty swore and slammed the steering wheel with his hand. He still had Paul Hanson's computer software in the trunk. Damn! He'd promised to drop it off this evening. He looked regretfully at Hallie's questioning expression.

"I'm sorry, I just remembered an errand I have to take care of. Some friends of mine asked me to pick up some software in Portland. I put off dropping it by all week, and

I promised it for sure tonight." He looked at her with a plea for understanding. "I hope you don't mind. We won't stay long, I promise."

"No problem, I don't mind in the least." She smiled genuinely and felt both disappointed and a little relieved at the same time. Dancing close to Ty was a divine madness. She probably would have ended up screwing his brains out in the back of Marlene's car. She felt a throb between her legs at the thought.

"Thanks," he was saying, startling Hallie until she realized he was thanking her for her patience, not the mental images that had been wreaking havoc with her body. "You remember Dottie Lang? I used to date her in high school."

"Oh yes, one of the multitudes. You guys were pretty tight as I recall."

"Yup, one of the few I remained friends with. Luckily, she married a fellow from back east who didn't have the good sense to resent my former relationship with her."

"She hates my guts," Hallie said matter-of-factly.

"No, she doesn't," Ty countered, coming swiftly to Dottie's defense. "Granted, she's never been any too fond of you, and I'm sure she's heard a lot of the gossip over the years, but she's a fair-minded person, and once she understands about why you broke up the engagement—"

Hallie interrupted him. "Understands? Do you believe me now?"

He nodded shortly. "I did what you suggested and talked to Marlene." He grinned ruefully. "It wasn't a very pleasant exchange for me. She slapped me around pretty good. I don't think much of your methods still, but," he paused before saying evenly, "I guess you were right about her."

Hallie quirked her mouth slightly and said in a voice filled with self-derision, "Tyler, unfortunately I have this stupid, God-given belief that no matter what, I know best and I'm always right. It even cost me my best friend, remember? 'I'm sorry' just isn't enough to say and likewise for 'I meant well.'" She sighed heavily.

Tyler's eyes burned into her profile, and she turned to meet his gaze, wondering what she might see there. His eyes were hot and glinting with pure carnal lust. "You know," he whispered, "I want to kiss you so badly right now, I ache. I don't dare, because if I do, I'm going to pull you into the back seat of this car right here and now."

I'd go in a heartbeat, Hallie thought to herself as he started the car and pulled away from the curb. The conversation was a little strained at first, but Hallie prattled on all the way to the Hansons' house, telling him everything she could think of to fill the air with anything but sexually tense silence. She gave him Kelsey's regards and the news of a reconciliation between herself and Cassie. He seemed genuinely pleased for her, and before she knew it, they were pulling up to the curb in front of the Hansons' handsome craftsman bungalow.

Hallie was nervous as Ty opened her door and offered her his hand. He smiled and brushed a kiss across her cheek. "Relax, Duchess, she won't bite. I promise, we'll be in and out of there in ten or fifteen minutes."

"Are they having a party or something?" Hallie asked, as the sounds of live music drifted from the basement of the house toward them. Tyler listened, then looked around at the cars parked nearby. He knew the answer.

"Shit!" he hissed. He turned to Hallie and slid an arm around her waist. "I'm sorry, Hallie, I forgot about Paul's band. I swear, I didn't even think about it."

"What band?"

"They play at the Moose and VFW dances, that sort of thing. What you call a garage band I guess." He ran a hand through his hair. He was afraid she'd think he set her up, that he'd talked her into coming tonight just so he could give his friends a thrill. Damn! Everything had been going so well too. "Look, do you want to wait in the car?"

"No, don't be silly. Let go see what's shaking." She grinned up at him, her nervousness a thing of the past. He was astonished—no temper, no tantrum, just 'okay let's go.' Then he realized something that gave him a deep rush of pleasure. She hadn't been worried because Dottie did-n't like her. She was used to people not liking her; hell, more than half the parents in America didn't like her. What was bothering her was that these people were friends of his and their opinion of her would obviously matter to him. His opinion of her mattered, and that meant he mat-tered. He didn't feel triumphant or victorious, he just felt unreasonably happy that he meant something to her. He kept his arm around her waist as he steered her to the trunk to retrieve the software he'd stored there earlier today.

❧ ❧

Ty was grinning like a kid who'd just won the whole bag of marbles. In essence, he had. Hallie had met two of his closest friends this evening and won them over. And Dottie, God bless her, had been one hard sell. Though Dottie was coolly polite to her, there'd been little welcome in her demeanor and Ty, feeling very protective of Hallie, had kept his arm around her through the initial part of the evening. Paul had been a different matter, however. A Loreli fan for years, Paul Hanson couldn't get over his luck at meeting their lead guitarist—in his own home no less. When Hallie had asked to meet his band, he'd looked like a kid at Christmas, practically tugging Hallie off her feet in his enthusiasm to introduce her. And Hallie? Hallie had been wonderful. She hadn't minded the impromptu jam session that followed. In fact, she'd seemed to enjoy it as much as the band had, even taking time to give Paul and Mark some quick pointers.

Ty'd taken advantage of Hallie's preoccupation with the band to talk with Dottie. His intent had been merely to explain why Hallie had gone to such lengths to destroy his engagement, but he found himself telling Dottie other things as well. About Hallie's kindness to her sister, her humor, her quick temper, her sensitivity—and of all things, her cat. Dottie had given him the same mysterious little smile he'd been receiving from Marlene lately whenever Hallie was discussed. He wasn't sure what to make of those smiles, but he felt much better ignoring them.

Hallie leaned back in the car seat, hardly able to keep the excitement from bubbling out of her. Paul's band had definitely lived up to her expectations. And Paul Hanson was a terrific bass player. If her plans to build a small recording studio in Bishops Bluff came to fruition, she'd be able to keep the band busy with all the work they could handle. She wasn't sure how Dottie would feel about that. Paul's wife had made it clear to all concerned that music was Paul's hobby and the print shop he managed for her father was his career. After all, as she'd pointed out, they had a small child to support and her salary as a substitute teacher would hardly provide enough for them to live on if Paul pursued his dream of music. Hallie couldn't resent Dottie's point of view. Bishops Bluff and the surrounding area would hardly provide enough opportunities for a local band, and Hallie seriously doubted Paul had the drive or the burning ambition necessary to make it to the top. If things went well, though, she'd be able to supplement his income nicely enough so Dottie would have nothing to be concerned about.

She planned on calling Paul tomorrow to see if she could arrange for them to help her out next Tuesday. Most of her new music was at a stage where she needed amplification and back-up. As much as she loved the roadhouse band, they were best after a few beers and with nothing very complicated.

She thought about the pretty blonde woman who'd married Paul. Dottie Lang had been Ty's girlfriend during his junior year and had remained a staunch and true friend through the years. She'd almost hauled off and slugged Hallie at the now infamous engagement party. She'd never said a pleasant word to her since, until tonight. Whatever Ty'd said to Dottie while Hallie was downstairs with the band had significantly changed her attitude toward the younger woman. Dottie still wasn't gushing with friendship, but the open hostility was no longer there. As it turned out, Hallie had gained more ground over the course of the evening.

Paul and Dottie's fifteen-month-old girl was teething and woke up around ten o'clock as the band members were leaving. Little Alison was very cranky and not willing to put up with the ministrations of either parent. Hallie's heart immediately went out to the tear-streaked, exhausted little face that lay underneath a riot of damp blonde curls just like her mother's. Without giving it a thought, she lifted the little girl from Paul's arms to her own and danced her slowly across the living room, crooning slowed-down versions of rock songs. The little girl was mesmerized by the lovely woman with the golden eyes. Soon her little head dropped to Hallie's shoulder, and she drifted off to sleep.

Dottie gave her a warm smile and thanked her as she took the sleeping child from her arms. Hallie glanced over at Ty and found him watching her with an intense expression on his face. It was neither a smile nor frown, but deep and thoughtful. She looked away uncomfortably. They left moments later, and Hallie said goodnight to the Hansons with Ty's arm securely wrapped around her waist.

"Hallie," Ty said, startling her from her musings, "I wanted to thank you for being so nice to Paul tonight. I know how much it meant to him, and I really appreciated it too." He paused and she knew something was bothering him. "I wanted you to know that I didn't set you up tonight. As odd as it sounds, I didn't think about the possibility of Paul's band being there. I wasn't trying to impress my friends at your expense. I wouldn't do that."

Hallie was frowning at him. "Of course you wouldn't, Tyler. I know that. No sweat. I enjoyed it. Anyway, you've never been particularly impressed with my music. Other than "Stumptown," I doubt you'd recognize much of my stuff."

"That's not true," Tyler countered, sounding defensive. "I've been plenty impressed with your music. I know when you were a kid I used to razz the hell out of you about it, but even I know how good," he grinned at her, "excuse me—great you are. I don't mention it because, one, you don't need me to tell you, and, two, I'm usually too mad at you to care how damn great you are." She laughed and reached over to give him a playful nudge on the leg. "Also Miss Gal Hal, though I never thought I'd admit this to anyone, much less you, I'm pretty familiar with Loreli's music. As a matter of fact, Paul and Dottie gave me a copy of the jazz CD you did with Eddie Melick and Cassie Donovan. His last before he—" He stopped himself. Shit, he'd just gone and reminded her of yet another loss in her life.

"Died," she finished for him softly. "It's okay, Tyler. It was a long time ago. He was a very talented man—a true genius. He was also a dear friend. I think of him a lot and I always smile."

"It's a beautiful piece of work, Hallie," he said simply.

"Thank you. Hey, if you're a big Melick fan, I've got some reel-to-reel basement tapes we did up at Cassie's apple farm in Washington. You should come over and listen to them. Other than the inner circle, you'd be the only one to ever hear them."

"The inner circle?" he asked.

"Yeah: me, Clance, Sye, Toddy, Cassie, Eddie, Randman, oh and let's not forget Ryker," she answered mischievously. "We always called ourselves the inner circle, meaning we all knew most, if not all, about the other members. Kind of our own extended family. It helped us out a lot when the press came gunning for us. "

Ty listened silently, slowly digesting the insights she'd given him. Tonight he'd been completely amazed at how little Alison had gone to her so easily and trustingly and then fallen asleep in her arms. God, but he'd envied that little girl. The last thing he'd ever imagined was Hallie Bishop being good with children. Since he'd seen her dancing and crooning to the toddler in her arms, he'd been driven crazy with images of her holding her own baby like that—his baby. Damn, he wanted to pull this car into a field, an alley, anywhere so long as it was private. "I didn't know you liked kids so much," he said a little hoarsely.

"Hardly goes with the image does it?" she said, turning a little sideways in the seat. "I love them. I want my own so bad I can taste it." She stopped talking suddenly and looked out the window in embarrassment. Would she never learn to keep her mouth shut around this man. "Anyway," she said after a moment, "I like kids."

Ty shifted gears in the conversation. "Is the offer still open to listen to the basement tapes you have?"

"You bet, anytime."

"Tonight, after we pick up Genna?" he pressed.

"Well, she's going to want to talk most likely," Hallie countered, sounding a little nervous. "That's what big sisters are for, you know."

He moved to block. "I don't care. I'll wait up and walk you back to your place. It's a date."

"Nothing is going to happen, Nighthawk. I already told you how I feel."

He smiled in the darkness of the car. Sure, he thought to himself: Her voice said 'no' in plain English but her body said something entirely different in a language all its own. "No problem," he assured her.

They reached the ranch shortly before midnight. Hallie'd talked Ty into stopping for a burger at the diner on the highway before dropping Genna's date off at his house. She'd threatened him with dire consequences when he attempted to get out of the car to watch Genna say goodnight to the boy. They dropped Hallie off at her bunkhouse and she promised to be up in just a minute to say goodnight to Genna. Ty winked at her and she blushed. Giving him a slight smile, she quickly darted into her house.

Ty dropped by his room to check the messages on the answering machine that was hooked up to his private line. There was only one, but he thought he'd listen now while he waited for Hallie. He smiled as he thought about the evening he'd spent with her. She'd liked Dottie and Paul, and with only minor reservations on Dottie's part, they liked her too. It pleased him, and there was little point in denying how he felt. He found himself becoming more fond of Hallie with each passing day. He shook his head ruefully as he rewound the tape.

The message was from Steve Shaunessy with Rose City Investigations. He had his answer, and as Ty listened to it, he felt the bottom drop out of his world.

"Ty, old buddy," Shaunessy said, "hang on to your hat. You were right about this all along. Deposits totaling over two and a half million have been appearing in Hal Bishop's accounts in LA. Looks like her people are scrambling to cover their asses too. The deposits appear to be dividends from investments in the Caymans. All routed to Persistence of Vision Corp., and guess who's named as principal owner and chairperson. One Hallie Leigh Bishop. Three guesses what the source money is for those investments, Ty—the missing funds from The Bishop Company."

Tyler Nighthawk didn't hear the rest of the message. His mind reeled and his gut burned. His hands curled into fists as he closed his eyes and leaned forward on the desk. She'd done it to him again. This time, though, she'd lured him with her body, her smiles, her sad eyes and her tender words. The whole time she'd been out to destroy him, destroy them all and everything her father had worked so hard to build. He muttered a curse, hating himself for his stupidity almost as much as he hated her for betraying him. All that had passed between them had meant nothing. Nothing! He walked downstairs calmly and stopped by the den to tell Marlene and Genna he'd just spoken to Hallie on the phone, and she'd had to cancel with Genna tonight because something had come up. It was a poor lie at best, but his stony face and distant manner kept both of them from asking questions. He excused himself, saying he needed some air before bed.

He was headed toward the bunkhouse, toward a final confrontation with Hallie. She'd never toy with their lives again. She wouldn't emerge unscathed this time because this time she had nowhere left to run.

Chapter 16

Hallie had barely touched one foot to the bottom step of the verandah when Ty appeared out of the shadows. As the light from the yard caught him more fully, she could see his handsome face contorted with fury.

"Oh no, you don't!" he snarled, moving with lightning speed down the steps. "Get the hell away from this house!" Ty swiftly wrapped his arm around her waist to half carry her back from the porch. "You thought you were real clever didn't you, Hallie?"

She stumbled as he let go. "What the hell? Have you gone crazy?" she yelled.

"Save it!" he thundered. "You were a conniving little brat when you were a kid, and the only thing that's changed is that now you're a whole lot more dangerous! I never thought I'd say I was glad Tom was dead, but seeing how low you'd stoop to hurt all of us would have destroyed him. You've tried your best to destroy us, and I'll be damned if I'll let you finish the job!" Ty shoved her in the direction of the bunkhouse.

Hallie whirled on him, eyes blazing. "Listen, Sybil, I don't know which one of your demented personalities this is, but you've got about thirty seconds to get a grip here and explain what the hell is wrong with you!"

Ty shoved her shoulder. "Move," he snapped, his tone dangerously quiet, "or I swear I'll hurt you. I owe your father, but I swear..."

Hallie shivered from the naked menace in his voice. He was clearly furious with her, yet refused to explain why. What could possibly have happened in the last ten minutes to account for this? She'd expected to have to defend her virtue from him tonight—but not her life. The

anger and frustration of years of false accusations and con-
demnation welled up inside her. No more, she vowed.
She'd had enough of this bullshit, and no matter if he
choked the life out of her, right here and now, he wasn't
going to get away with it!

"Owe my dad? Oh you bet you owe my dad. Big time,
right? After all, he picked you up out of the garbage and
gave you everything you have." Her voice got louder and
was edged with hysteria. "You came from nothing, would
have stayed nothing if it hadn't been for good ol' Dad!"

"Shut up, Hallie," he hissed, taking a step toward her.
"Shut up or so help me God—"

"'Shut up, Hallie,'" she mimicked, backing away
nonetheless. "Is that all you ever say? After eighteen years,
can't you come up with something new? But hey, with
your background that's probably real witty dialogue, isn't
it?" His eyes seemed to fasten on her throat as he took
another step toward her. She rushed on recklessly. "We
were talking about your gratitude to my father, though,
weren't we? All the things you owe him, right? Like
schooling." She saw the tendons in his neck tighten in an
effort to control himself. "Like job security, like your
stinkin' thirty-three percent!" Hallie was shouting now.
"Hey, maybe you should even thank him for the opportunity he gave you to try to screw one of his daughters, you
bastard!"

"That's it!" Ty bellowed.

Before his roar trailed off, Hallie had turned to sprint for
the relative safety of her locked door. She heard him close
behind her, even imagined she could feel his hot breath on
her neck. If he caught her now, he surely would kill her!
Like some mad thing, she'd gone into the bullring, waving
a red flag without a care as to what the bull was truly capable of doing to her. The bunkhouse porch appeared in

front of her. If she could just put a little more distance between them, she'd be able to slam the door and latch it. Hopefully Ty would vent the worst of his spleen on trying to break through. Hallie cursed herself for working him into such a blind rage. She jumped the steps two at a time, heading for the door. She yanked it open and pivoted to triumphantly slam it shut. Unfortunately, Ty's arm got there first. She threw all her weight against the wood, causing a string of curses from the enraged man outside. Suddenly, she felt herself flying through the air, coming to land in front of the piano. She scrambled to her feet as the door banged shut, closing her in with Ty—a man ready to tear her head off. She heard the deadbolt slide into place. Hallie scurried to put the piano between them. "Get out of here!" she hissed, picking up the thunder egg from the top of the instrument. "This is my home, and you can just get the hell out!"

"No way. Not this time." His green eyes trapped her with their cold fury, making her feel like a snared rabbit. "We're going to settle this once and for all." He stalked her with the slow, methodical progression of a natural predator, waiting for her to make one false step before he moved in for the kill. "You thought you could just waltz back here and toy with the lives of everyone, didn't you?" He stopped at the piano, never taking his eyes from her. "Well, you made a crucial mistake this time, lady. You picked on me. I'm sick and tired of your lies. How the hell someone like Tom could have sired a cold, heartless little bitch like you is beyond me. Of course," he paused, trailing his contemptuous gaze over her, "maybe you take after your dear *mamacita* in more than just looks. She could rip someone's heart out and hand it to 'em while it was still beating."

"You don't know what the hell you're talking about!"

Hallie spat at him. Her eyes now every bit as murderous as his. "She was a warm, loving person!"

"Right," Ty snorted. "I understand that was part of the problem. She was loving to just about any man she met. The fruit didn't fall far from the tree. You go plenty wild in my arms. Must be all that hot Latin blood." Wham! The thunder egg sailed through the air, just missing the side of Tyler's head, as it struck the wall behind him. "Your aim's off, Duchess." He smiled slowly and unpleasantly as he moved to the side of the piano.

Hallie instantly regretted throwing her only weapon. "Arrogant bastard! God, how I hate you!" She glanced around quickly for another missile, realizing her mistake too late. In that split second of wavering concentration, Ty was on her, effectively trapping her between the wall and himself. He placed his hands against the wall on either side of her shoulders.

"Now what are you going to do? You got nowhere to run, Duchess." He leaned over her, dark and ominous. She felt his hot breath against her cheek as he spoke low and close to her ear. "You should have kept your rock."

Hallie felt her throat go dry, not from fear, as she'd expected, but from the stirring deep within her. Damn it, every time he got near her like this she was gone, just like backstage in Chicago or that night by the Jeep. These feelings were something she'd fought almost as long as she'd known him. He smelled of soap and leather, and his face showed the dark stubble of a five o'clock shadow. His green eyes narrowed as they roamed over her. He was all man—sinew, muscle and arrogance. A war between panic and hunger raged within her. She answered the only way she could.

"God damn you to hell, Nighthawk," she hissed. Lifting her foot, she raked it down his shin and stamped painfully on his instep. Then with both hands shoved him backwards with all her strength. Hallie bolted for the door with the devil himself hot on her heels. Just short of her goal, two bands of steel wrapped around her arms. Ty spun her quickly to face him.

"You'll pay for that, Hallie!" he growled, as she struggled frantically in his arms. He tightened his hold on her, smashing her to his chest. Hallie continued to fight for freedom, but it was no use and she writhed against him in impotent fury. She felt his muscles hard against every inch of her body—her sensitive and vibrantly aware body. Her pulse quickened, and white heat began to spread from the pit of her stomach to her pelvis. As she twisted against him, she felt his erection pressing between her thighs. Hallie gasped and instinctively looked down.

Ty moved a hand to her hair compelling her head back in a none-too-gentle way. His glittering eyes captured hers. The very air was electric. Lord help me, she thought, he's going to kiss me.

As if she'd spoken out loud, Ty answered, "That's right. Damned if I know why, but I'm going to." Then he lowered his mouth onto hers.

His kiss seared into her, searching, demanding, forcing a moan from her as she opened her mouth to him. Ty shifted his grip, moving it from her hair to her rib cage, then began a light, stroking dance toward her breasts. Slowly, lingeringly, his hand closed over one tantalizing mound and his fingers began a well remembered sensual massage that left her trying to catch her breath once again.

He traced his thumb over the knitted fabric of her crop top to find her hardened nipple, alert and eager for his attention. Ty felt a corresponding tightening between his legs. He groaned against her lips, then moved his other hand down over her bottom as Hallie's arms came up around his neck. "This is totally stupid," he muttered against her mouth. "I know better than to have a damn thing to do with you now." The feel of her, and that damned fresh apple scent she had, were likely to drive him insane with need. He felt her stiffen at his words. God what an actress. She could pretend all the outrage and indignation in the world, but it wouldn't change the fact that she was and always would be a lying bitch. It also wouldn't change the fact that he still wanted her, and, by God, tonight he was going to have her. What lay between them was volatile and predestined. They both knew it. In spite of the reactions he felt coming from her body, though, she started to pull away. He encircled her waist, holding her firmly in place and preventing her retreat. The light glinted off the gemstone at her navel. He drew in a sharp breath.

"Ty...please don't do this," she pushed on his chest.

"Not now, Hallie," he rasped, straining for control. "For God's sake, not now!" His mouth claimed hers again, silencing her protest. His hands returned to move over her breasts, teasing the nipples as his kiss traced a molten path down her neck to her throat. Hallie gripped his shoulders, tilting her head back to offer more of the silken expanse of skin to his lips. His eyes, burning with passion, gazed at her breasts, wanting to see them and taste them. With a swift move, he roughly pushed her shirt and sports bra up and out of his way, allowing her bounty to spill free. She was exposed full and aching to his view. She whimpered deep in her throat—wanting his touch—needing it. As his mouth closed over one ruby tip, she dug her fingers deeply into his shoulders and arched sharply against him. Suddenly Ty broke from her and scooped her up into his arms. "Crazy or not, this time I'm finishing what I started," he said thickly. "You want it here, or in bed?"

"We can't do this. It's crazy. It's wrong. We can't..." Hallie protested as Ty walked back toward the bedroom.

"Too bad, Duchess. I get to choose the location by default, and I like my comfort. I'm taking you to bed tonight. Admit it. Be honest for once in your life," he said, his voice filled with scorn. "You don't want to stop any more than I do." He paused long enough to kiss her hotly before entering the bedroom. "Right now we have way too many clothes on." He kicked the bedroom door shut and stopped beside the bed. "Well?"

Her smart mouth was utterly failing her now. All she could manage was an uncharacteristic weak nod. If he changed his mind, if he didn't touch her again soon, she'd scream. He carefully placed her on the edge of the bed.

"You bolt for that door again, lady, and I won't be responsible," he murmured. He reached down taking her mouth gently with his, belying his harsh words. He softly bit her lower lip in a teasing, sensual way that made her breath catch in her throat. He kneeled down, slowly removing her boots, his eyes watching her face closely, as if looking for the slightest change of expression that might mean a change of heart.

She gazed at him warily. He was still so angry with her, and she didn't know why. This wasn't the man she'd spent the evening with, the one who'd been so full of concern when they were in Portland. She couldn't move her eyes from his. She was lost in deep forest pools that reached out and pulled her into their inviting depths. She might be drowning, but it didn't matter. All that mattered was that soon he would join her on the bed as naked and as hungry as herself. He unbuttoned his shirt, baring his well muscled chest and arms. Hallie sucked in her breath at the sheer beauty of him. He was tanned and firm. He was blood, muscle and raw animal instinct—and right now his animal instinct wanted her. She trembled with desire and apprehension.

Ty pulled off her top and bra, tossing them both to the floor with his shirt, then reached to unfasten her jeans. Easing her back to lie across the bed, he drew the pants slowly down her legs and let them join the shirts. Heaven help him, there was that infernal navel ring. A primal throb pulsed steadily between his legs. He quickly removed the rest of his clothing and stretched out beside her on the bed.

Ty looked at the woman lying next to him. God she was beautiful! She was still wearing a pair of dark blue lace panties. He wasn't sure what you called the style, but they were sexy as hell, and his hand came up to stop her as she started to remove them. He'd save that job for himself—later. This was the last thing he'd intended when he stormed through the door tonight. Liar, he told himself. He'd wanted this for years and he knew it. It didn't matter what he told himself his intention was, all thoughts of revenge had left his mind long ago, the first instant he'd touched her. He'd wanted her from the time she was eighteen, maybe before. He promised himself to stop at the first protest from Hallie, but he wasn't sure he could control the beast rising inside himself. His gaze took in her full ripe breasts and rounded hips. He brushed his hand lightly over her small waist and taut belly, and was rewarded with an immediate quiver. She was so responsive, he thought. He'd known it would be like this. Ty imagined what it would be like to be buried deeply inside her and drew a ragged breath. Soon it wouldn't be imagination.

He had to stay in control—he wanted it good for both of them. He was close to bursting, and he had to take her soon, or explode all over her quilt like some horny high school pup. Silently he reached for his wallet and the small square plastic packet kept there for just such occasions. His hands were shaking by the time he had it.

"Here," said the husky voice beside him, "I'll do that. Hallie opened the condom packet and gently holding his heavy erection in one hand, placed the rolled coin of latex at its head. Ty gasped as her fingers caressed him, slowly and sensuously unrolling the rubber upward.

"God, Hallie!" he groaned and pinned her arms to the bed. He bent his head to her breasts and captured a hard ripe nipple between his lips. She moaned low in her throat and rubbed her thighs together urgently. Steadily he continued his ministrations, first to one rich fruit, then the other. She twisted her hands in the quilt. Freeing her arms, Ty slid a hand beneath the edge of her panties to the silken thatch between her legs. Hallie arched wildly against his probing fingers. "Easy, baby," he whispered gently as he trailed kisses across her navel, "we're just getting started." His lips closed on her navel ring, giving it a gentle tug with his mouth. She sighed at the delicious sensation as his tongue slowly played with the silver loop and pendant.

Hallie was glad he couldn't see the naked need in her face. He had complete control of her, and he could do whatever he wanted and she would let him. She had to— such was her hunger for him. He brought her close to the edge of control and kept her there. She'd known passion with only one man before. He'd made her forget the agony of her first sexual experience and had taught her the meaning of desire. But this joining with Tyler was so much more intense. She'd expected lust, grinding animal passion, but not this tender, sensual assault that made her whimper and writhe. His mouth and hands were everywhere, coaxing and teasing. She felt his hands tangle in the lace of her panties as he slowly and seductively removed them. His fingers traced the entrance to her private citadel. Hallie felt the universe begin to tilt, and knew that no matter how hard she tried to balance the axis, it would continue to rapidly spin beyond her grasp. Suddenly his fingers were replaced by his moist, hot mouth. She cried out and clutched the quilt harder than ever. His tongue found the responsive bud in her center and began to tease it with a gentle, yet insistent flicking motion. For Hallie the stars exploded and the polar caps shifted, as wave after wave of orgasmic sensation washed over her. It stretched into eternity and out the other side, leaving her shaken and panting in its wake.

Seeing her face in the aftermath of climax proved to be Ty's undoing. He had to take her now. With a growl deep in his throat, he poised himself at her entrance and thrust deeply, filling her, stretching her to accommodated his size. Hallie tightened automatically and lifted her hips to meet him. She was warm and tight, more woman than he could ever remember having. She met him eagerly, thrust for thrust. Together they created an island of passion where anger and hatred couldn't reach them. He felt himself heading over the edge of time and space, and he began to thrust deeper and harder. She was coming with him; this incredible brat-child, woman. There was only sensation and raw need now. He rasped graphic and erotic words as he pounded harder and harder into her.

She was completely filled with him and still couldn't seem to get enough. The crest of the wave was in sight, and their bodies glistened from the heat of their union. Hallie's nails blindly raked Ty's back, but he took no notice. This was what she'd struggled so long to deny herself, yet she glorified in her defeat. When their mutual release came, it carried them both to the vanishing point between heaven and earth.

Ty collapsed on Hallie, trying to catch his breath. Slowly, he became aware of her fingernails still gouging his back. He swore softly. Realization dawned on her, and she released her death grip on him, wishing the bed would open up and swallow her. Hallie turned her head away. What gave this man, of all the men in the world, the ability to turn her into a mindless bitch in heat? Maybe, she thought, if I just lie still long enough, he'll get up and leave. Who was she kidding? This was too perfect an opportunity for whatever revenge he'd had in mind when he came roaring through her door. Her stomach felt queasy and she mentally winced at the scornful, crushing words that were bound to come. Ty rolled onto his back beside her. She felt a pang of sadness at his withdrawal from her body. Neither of them said anything for quite some time, both of them lost in private thoughts. When the silence became too much for Hallie to stand a second longer, she sat up and reached for her shirt. Ty's hand came up to stop her and she jumped off the bed as if someone had laid a snake on her arm. He raised himself up on his elbow to study her.

He was so smug, so damned pleased with himself, she fumed silently. He'd pulled her apart and put her back together forever changed, and he lay there unaffected, regarding her as though she were a curious species of animal he'd encountered. She'd made a complete fool of herself by giving him everything she had, everything she was. In the end all he'd done was screw.

Ty's eyes followed her movements greedily. Damn, he still wanted the little vixen. She was poison clean through, but that didn't stop the waves of desire already returning to his body. He quickly calculated his options. "Listen," he began, "I didn't want it to happen like this anymore than you did."

"Oh, shut up!" Hallie said morosely, snatching up her shirt.

"No. You and I both realize this deal doesn't change a thing. Are you listening?"

"No! And you're damned right, it doesn't change a thing! Here!" She threw his jeans and jockey shorts at his head. Infuriatingly, he caught them easily and set them aside with a chuckle. "You got what you've wanted since the day I moved back here, so get out, now!"

"Well, Duchess," he drawled, "you're right about that. I certainly did get what I wanted. I guess this settles the question once and for all if you like men. You're better in bed than I could have possibly hoped."

Hallie turned in a blind rage, ready to claw out his eyes and certain other areas of his anatomy. Suddenly he sat up and caught her by the wrist, pulling her down roughly on top of him. "Shut up and listen! Like I said, this doesn't change a thing." Was there a hint of something like disappointment in his eyes? He continued coldly, "Come sunup, we'll both hate each other's guts, business as usual. No quarter asked or given." His eyes glowed like a banked fire slowly returning to full blaze. "But the sun doesn't come up for hours yet." He rolled her underneath him, and said in a silky tone, "And I'm finding I'm still hungry, Duchess." He brought his mouth to hers.

After the kiss ended, Hallie met his gaze without embarrassment. "It's no damn good," she said softly.

"On the contrary, it's very damn good." His hand started to stroke her breast. "Outside of this room, this bed, we know what we think of each other. Make no mistake, sweetheart, you'll pay for this latest stunt of yours." His face hardened as he continued. "Of course, it's no big deal to you. You've spent your whole life trampling on everything your father built or loved—even yourself."

"What are you saying, Tyler? What the hell is this about?" Hallie began straining against his hold.

"Spare me the act. There's only one thing about you I'm interested in, and I just sampled it. If you could bring your-self to be honest for once, you'd say the same for me." He gave a snort of disgust. "I'm not expecting you to like me any more than I like you. It's not required."

"I'm surprised your nobility allows you to touch me," Hallie said resentfully, struggling to sit up.

"I didn't say I liked it this way." His eyes traveled over her, the self-disdain apparent on his face. "Like I said, I can't even pretend to know why, but I've got an itch to scratch where you're concerned, whatever the reason. Tomorrow we go to our corners and come out fighting. No one the wiser. But just for tonight we can enjoy our-selves—a lot." He rolled her nipple between his thumb and forefinger and proceeded to part her legs with his knee. "Jesus! If I don't get back inside you soon..." His voice trailed off as he bent his head to her breast.

"Just tonight, right?" she gasped.

His head came up and his eyes drilled into hers. "Tonight. No strings. No words. No regrets." His thumb traced a pattern over her nipple. "Just lots of good, hot and nasty sex." His lazy, mocking smile was back in place as he bent his head to take her nipple in his mouth once again.

This is crazy! Hallie thought to herself. What happened to the caring, compassionate man she'd spent the evening with, the one who cared what she thought of him, who cared what his friends thought of her. This man who suck-led at her breast, building her desire once more, didn't give a damn about her or what she thought and felt outside of this bed. She felt her groin tighten in response to the incredible talent of his mouth. She didn't know who this angry intense stranger was, but she seemed as powerless to resist him as the man she'd been with this evening.

She felt him hard and throbbing against her. He inserted three fingers into her, opening them wider and wider to deliciously stretch her passage. She gasped deeply for air. He began to move his fingers in and out of her steadily, going deeper with each return visit. He left her no time for rational thought, only burning pleasure building higher and higher. She moaned and clutched his shoulder. God he felt so good! He knew her body almost as well as she did.

"Well?" he said, leaning over her, grinning as her body began to quake beneath him. "Yes or no?"

"I've got condoms in the nightstand," Hallie gasped, pulling his mouth down to hers as her orgasm shook her.

The rest of the night passed in a haze of sensual pleasure. They explored each other's body—first one, then the other taking the initiative. Ty was an incredible lover: inventive, passionate, tender. Hallie reacted to him as she never had to another man, and instinctively she knew what he wanted, what would drive him wild, and when. The harmony and rhythm between them made it seem they'd been lovers forever. Hallie was experienced in many of the finer pleasures of the bedroom but still, she had an air of surprise in her own responses that made Ty realize she was more swept away than she'd ever been in her life. He felt a surge of triumph when she cried out his name and collapsed against him, weeping from the force of her pleasure. He cradled her gently to him and murmured tender words. Near dawn, Ty touched her once again, rousing her from half sleep. She murmured grumpily, "I'm exhausted. I won't be able walk as it is."

"Good," he whispered against her ear, "at least that'll keep you out of trouble." He began the happy task of arousing her one last time.

Later, as Hallie slept peacefully, Ty studied her, a thoughtful expression on his face. "Oh baby," he whispered softly in the darkness, "you've got trouble. I hate to tell you this, but one night with you just isn't going to be enough."

※ ※

Hallie stirred in the nest of tangled sheets on her bed. The clock on the nightstand showed eight-thirty in the morning. She moaned as she turned over, exhausted after last night's events. Tyler had left sometime shortly before dawn. Her skin burned red as she thought about the intimate acts they'd performed with each other. Thank God he'd left. She didn't think she could face him this morning. Facing him at all would be difficult enough.

She'd been so shocked the night before by his sudden change of attitude and by their explosive passions that she hadn't been able to think straight. Now, in the cold light of day, she would be able to make some sense of it all. Hallie sat up and winced from all her sore muscles and achy spots. Tyler's ardent sexual skills had left her well satiated, but somewhat tender in various areas. She moved gingerly from the bed to the bathroom, ran the bathtub and poured in her apple bath foam. A long, luxurious soak in the tub would be just what the doctor ordered. Maybe then she could figure out where the man from last evening and the board meeting in... That was it!

Now she understood. Somewhere, in between the time he'd dropped her off at her place, and then stood yelling in front of the house, he'd learned about the deposits and the money in the Caymans. Of course. She'd known it would happen sooner or later, but she'd hoped to be the one to tell him as she handed over all the evidence to him that was needed to convict the real criminal. On the surface, the information he'd received about her must have looked pretty damning. Being Tyler, and not trusting her much to begin with, he hadn't even considered questioning what he had learned. Hallie sank into the perfumed water, hoping it would soothe her aching muscles and troubled mind.

The arrogant jerk! He couldn't even give her the lousy benefit of the doubt. He couldn't even come to her and ask. As usual, she thought bitterly, he'd just assumed the worst. Now his accusations made sense. He thought she'd hated her father and the family so much that she'd destroy everything they all held dear. God, it hurt. How could he? She felt a sinking sensation deep inside as she realized that Marlene, Walt and the rest of the company would follow his lead. Oh God, Genna. She had to get hold of Kelsey right away.

❦ ❧

Ty set his mug of coffee on the desk in front of him. He leaned back in the chair and twirled around to look out the library window, staring up at the snowcapped peaks that rose majestically above the tree-covered foothills. The sky promised a beautiful, cloudless Oregon day. After a long, wet winter, days like these should be celebrated, he reflected.

She was probably still sleeping. He'd hardly allowed her a wink of sleep last night. He couldn't remember his hunger for a woman being so out of his control before. He hadn't meant to be that much of an animal, using her as long and hard as he'd done, but, except for the last time, he hadn't heard a murmur of protest. He shouldn't have insisted this morning, he thought, feeling a little guilty. She'd been eager enough, though, once she'd awakened. The whole night had been incredible, and damn it, he was still hungry for her. He exhaled sharply from between pursed lips. What the devil was he going to do?

He'd told himself at least a dozen times in the last couple of hours that what had happened last night was a one time thing. Even if he was insane enough to get any further involved with her, Hallie would never let him touch her again, at least not if she had a choice. Ty frowned. He planned to get all the details about her finances from Steve Shaunessy this morning. He wanted to know her strengths and weaknesses. He would contact the Bishop Company's legal team and have them take the steps necessary to prosecute Hallie and any of her cronies who had conspired with her. Kelsey Hogan's name immediately sprang to mind. His hand fiercely gripped the chair arm. He planned to talk to Marlene and Walt once he'd spoken to Steve. The sooner he did, the sooner they could go ahead with their original plans to get her the hell off the ranch and out of all their lives. Between himself and the company lawyers, they'd finish her off short and sweet.

Hallie gone. The bunkhouse dark. No more strains of music drifting through the evening air. Poor Genna. She'd never understand, never believe what Hallie'd tried to do to all of them. Genna would take anything Hallie said as gospel. He gritted his teeth, wishing Hallie's neck was within reach. One way or another, no matter what he did, Genna and Marlene were going to be hurt. Yet he couldn't just let Hallie get away with this. She had to pay for what she'd done. He narrowed his hardened green eyes.

Other images of Hallie sprang unbidden to his mind. She was holding and comforting a fussy child, helping Genna prepare for her date, patiently giving Paul and Mark guitar pointers. The most disturbing image was of her naked astride him, moving slowly and deliciously, taking them both to paradise. He shook his head to dislodge the unwanted image, but it was too late. He was already hard. He'd been right in the first place: One night in her bed just

wasn't going to be enough. Maybe it wouldn't have to be.
He picked up the phone and called Steve.

❧ ❧

Hallie poured herself a glass of wine, started a CD of clas-
sical music, and sank into her favorite easy chair. Within
moments, HB curled himself up in her lap. She'd never
been one for solitary afternoon drinking, but today she felt
entitled. Even after her soak in the tub, she was still slightly tender. She was also exhausted and frustrated. Her call
to Kelsey had been disappointing. She and Ryker still had-
n't turned up anything and there was no way Tyler would
believe her without hard evidence of her innocence. Even
now he was probably moving to have her arrested. Kelsey
had offered to return at once, but Hallie wouldn't hear of
it.   Her lawyer was safer out of the country, Hallie
informed her and believe it or not, safer with Ryker. Kelsey
sounded as though she seriously doubted Hallie's latter
comment, but agreed to stay put for the time being.

In hindsight, Hallie felt fortunate Ty hadn't killed her
last night. Luckily, he'd been more interested in keeping
her occupied in bed. Her cheeks turned pink again as she
thought about her uninhibited responses to him. She was-
n't a prude in bed by any stretch of the imagination, and
Remy had been an excellent lover, but last night had
shown her unknown heights of passion. Despite her tenderness, she was still aroused by the memories of her lovemaking with Tyler. Lovemaking? That was a joke! Maybe
on her part that's what they'd done, but for Tyler it was
only "good, hot and nasty sex." Never again would she
allow sex without some kind of emotional attachment, no
matter what. It hurt too much when the love was one-
sided.

All day she'd been hiding out in her house, waiting for
the other shoe to drop, waiting for Ty to swoop down and

pass sentence. Genna's visit to the bunkhouse this morning had felt like death by slow torture. Hallie'd been as nervous as a cat, waiting for something to happen. Luckily, Genna had been too preoccupied to notice. Nighthawk was probably leaving her hanging just to make her miserable.

Hallie hadn't been able to work, but she'd made some calls to set up arrangements for Tuesday. What chores she'd had around the bunkhouse involved cleaning up after last night. One of the hands would have to help her repair the plaster where the Thunder Egg hit the wall. Even changing the sheets had been difficult. The scent of their bodies had still clung to them, making the memories sharper and harder to hold at bay.

HB purred contentedly, and the music and wine began to tire her. She was brought instantly alert by a sharp knock at the front door. Without waiting for an invitation, someone opened the door and stepped inside. Hallie turned in her chair to see who it was, but she already had a pretty good idea. She glanced just in time to see Tyler Nighthawk close the door firmly and lock it. Hallie stayed put, furious at her own absentminded stupidity for having forgotten to bolt the door. "It's customary to wait until the door is answered before you enter," she said accusingly.

"If you're trying to discourage unwanted guests, you might try locking it next time," he replied coolly. He walked into the living room and regarded her with a level stare. "Are you all right?" he asked shortly.

"Of course, I'm all right. Why wouldn't I be? Are you?" she asked, rising to take HB from the room.

Ty's lips curved into a half smile. She was gutsy, he'd give her that. "You know what I mean. Did I hurt you last night?" He searched her face intently. She blushed and he fought the urge to laugh out loud. Hallie had the body of a goddess, and together they'd done the things of sexual fantasies the world over, yet she still blushed like a school girl at his question.   "Well?" he said, stepping closer to her. "Did I hurt you last night?"

"Of course not!" she snapped, and gave her cat a gentle scoot toward her bedroom.

"Look, if I was a little rough on you last night, I want to know. I'd never intentionally hurt you or any woman that way."

"I know that, Tyler," she said quietly. "It never crossed my mind that you would. I'm just a little tender from overindulging, that's all. Now could we please drop the subject?"

"I could take a look if you want." His eyes glinted with a mixture of mischief and desire.

"No!" she said sharply.   "You're demented, do you know that?" She walked past him and pointed at the couch as she sat back down in her chair. "Have a seat. Unless you've recently developed an unnatural interest in gynecology, I think you're here to talk about the account and the deposits. Right?" She shook her head. "I would have figured it out last night if I hadn't been so surprised by your sudden personality shift. I mean, really."

"Shut up and listen, Hallie. I don't have long because I have to catch a flight to Portland later tonight." His handsome face had become hard and unapproachable. He sat down on the couch across from her . "I have a little hands-on work to do with the auditing firm you hired. I hope, for your sake, they aren't up to anything shady."

"They have an international reputation, Tyler. You don't seriously believe they'd put it on the line for some half-baked company, do you?" she snorted contemptuously. "Bishop Company might not be anything to sneeze at by our standards, but these guys piss with the big boys. I had to call in a favor just to get the time of day from them."

"I bet you did," Ty responded, spitting out the last word. "They're in your back pocket, and that's exactly why I'm going to have people watchdogging them every step of the way." He glared at her angrily. "Do you have any remorse whatsoever for what you've done? Quiet!" he snapped when she would have answered the question. "You've made fools of all of us. You've tried to rob Genna of her birthright, and after spending all this time whining about how much you loved her. And the number you ran on Marlene is unbelievable. She thinks you're close to perfect. Then there's me!" He shook his head and laughed softly in self-deprecation. "To think I actually felt guilty that I'd misjudged you for so long! I bought every smile, every overture, every word—hook, line and sinker. You're real good, Hallie." His jungle eyes slid over her body, intimately caressing every curve. His voice became husky, and she knew he was remembering. "You're good at a lot of things."

Her throat was dry and she had to wet her lip before speaking. All Tyler's energy seemed to be focused on watching the tip of her tongue move across her lips. He quickly looked away, apparently disgusted at his response to her. "Kelsey will be able to clear all this up when she gets back, Tyler," she said hoarsely. "She's in the Caymans with Ryker trying to figure out who's framing me."

"Figure out who's framing you? Covering your tracks is more like it." His face filled with savagery. "Well, at least I know what Ryker was doing in Portland. No wonder he agreed to do your dirty work if you screwed him half as thoroughly as you did me." She blanched visibly. "Save your teary explanations, Hallie. The state pen is full of people who claim to have been framed. You'll just be one more." Her eyes widened and he saw real fear light her face. Good, he thought, steeling himself against any regret he felt for frightening her. Fear would make her more compliant when he dispensed his brand of justice.

"You don't have any idea what you're talking about, Nighthawk," she ground out, "but I'll save my breath because, as usual, you wouldn't know the truth if it came up and bit you in the ass. What did Marlene and Walt have to say about this new wealth of information?" He smiled at her question, and Hallie could tell she was going to hate what he said next.

"Why, Hallie, I haven't said a thing about it to either of them," he said in mock innocence. "I was a little preoccupied last night as you may recall." He was gratified to see her face flush. This was going to be sweet. "Probably a good thing too." In a voice that cracked like a whip, he added, "I warned you from the beginning that I'd do whatever it took to stop you. I meant what I said. I've thought about this all day." His hard eyes fixed on her soft golden ones. "They don't need to know at all, if you're smart. Are you going to be smart, Hallie?"

"What do you want, Nighthawk?" she asked softly.

He said just as softly, "A little penance for your sins, Hallie, that's all."

"Spill it," she snarled. "What do you want?"

"All right, here it is." He leaned back against the couch and stretched his arms across the top of it. "First, all the money you stole and all the interest will be put in Genna's name. Every penny. Then you'll arrange for your third of the profits and earning from the company to be added quarterly to Genna's funds. I can't strip you of your inheritance, but I can make damned sure you never get to use one red cent," he finished in a brutal tone.

"Already done," she stated flatly. "I had Dad's attorney named administrator. As for the earnings, that's fine. I don't need the money."

Ty glared at her. What was her game? He hadn't expected her to have already given the money to Genna. Was she securing the girl's future or merely creating a diversion from her real intent. "Second, you will sign an agreement that allows me to vote your interest in company matters—permanently." Hallie was on her feet in an instant, a vile name for him on her lips. He wasn't bothered by it in the least. "What a mouth you have, Duchess," he admonished smoothly. "Of course, I remember it from last night. Don't you think that particular name applies more to you than to me in this instance?" She tightened her fists and looked ready to swing at the next word from him. "You've already had your last warning, so don't even think about it," he said evenly. "Third, you'll stay here at the ranch, no high-tailing it off to California or anywhere else you might find allies."

"This is unbelievable! I was right, you are demented!" She walked toward the piano and turned, her hands clenching into fists that punctuated her frustration and disbelief. "What the hell made you think I'd agree to this?"

"Two things," he said simply, taking the gamble he thought might pay off. "Genna and a stretch in prison if you don't." His smile told her they both knew she had no choices except those he was willing to give her. "If you don't agree to those terms, I'll have you and your buddies arrested and prosecuted to the full extent of the law. Think about it, Hallie. Fifteen, maybe twenty years. You'll serve five to seven at least before you're eligible for parole. I'm afraid we'd all insist on it," he added easily.

The bastard was loving every second of this. She forced herself to try and block out his vengeful words, knowing that most of her agony came from having to face how much he loathed her. No matter what evidence was presented to clear her name, Tyler Nighthawk would never believe her—any more than her father would have.

Ty continued. "Seven years, Hallie. Your career will be gone, Kelsey's too. You'll be lucky to get a gig in a third-rate casino lounge in Reno. And then there's Genna. She'll know you stole from your own family. I imagine she can learn to hate you a lot in seven years. Almost as much as I do," he finished coldly. The look on her face told him she knew he was capable of doing everything he promised. "You've proven beyond a doubt how dangerous you are," he continued. "I won't stand idly by letting you ruin Genna's inheritance and probably her life. Rest assured, Hallie, I'll do it, and Marlene will listen to me, and her brother as well." He delivered another cold smile. "It doesn't have to come to this, though, if you're prepared to be reasonable."

"I'll think about it," she said, stalling for time. Ryker and Kelsey were no closer to answers than they'd been a week ago. My God, she thought, what would she do? She didn't stand a chance. Tyler was right; Marlene and Walt would never forgive what they thought to be her newest betrayal. She'd lose them all, just like she'd lost Tyler.

"You have until Tuesday afternoon. Three o'clock to be precise. You and I have an appointment. Wear something black and lacy." Her eyes widened as he meaning sunk in.

"I'm busy Tuesday. I have plans already."

"Cancel them."

"I can't."

"You can and you will," he said calmly, rising and moving to her side. "Don't even think about standing me up, either. This is a small town and if I have to track you down, I will. I don't think even you'd like the public embarrassment of being hauled out of somewhere over my shoulder."

"I won't allow you to do this to me," she responded hotly.

"That's your choice of course, but I think you'll come around," he said easily. He smiled without warmth, brushing a quick kiss across her cold cheek. Then he was gone.

Chapter 17

Ty wheeled the sedan into its customary parking space in front of the main house. It was a little before three o'clock, and he was relieved to see Hallie's vehicle parked beside her place. He smiled in satisfaction. He'd missed her. Last night had been pure hell as he'd tossed and turned in his bed. He'd kept remembering the feel of her silky skin against his, and the way she'd tossed her hair back out of her face as she'd ridden him. He'd lain there yearning to touch the fire of her soft, yielding core. Ty could have sworn the room smelled of apples. In feverish dreams, he had caressed her and loved her to the point of madness, only to awaken panting, with a painful erection and completely frustrated.

His Portland trip had proven more surprising than he ever anticipated. Ty had a frank, no-holds-barred discussion with the head of the independent auditing team, and was amazed to discover they'd received prior instructions to report all findings, good or bad, directly to himself or Hallie and absolutely no one else.

The meeting with Steve Shaunessy had been no less surprising. Ty knew Hallie to be a woman of contradictions, but it was almost as if he had been studying two diametrically opposed people. Her public persona had little in common with the astute business woman, the dedicated performer, or the driving force behind the many charitable works he learned of. Steve said she was worth a fortune. Ty had looked at the figures and given a low whistle. Financially, Hallie could have bought the town of Bishops Bluff with pocket change. He hadn't realized rock music was that lucrative.

Steve went on to explain most of Loreli's music had

been composed by Hallie herself or with Cassie Donovan, Randy Raveneau, and even Eddie Melick. Evidently, in the music business, being the songwriter made the difference between doing so-so or amassing incredible wealth. When Steve presented him with just the sample of her investment portfolio he'd been able to pilfer, Ty had been amazed. Astonishing as it seemed, Hallie had told him the truth. All missing funds and interest had been transferred to her sister's name.

The majority of the file contained matters of public record, some kind, many not so. Steve had labored to compile everything he could find about her and placed it against a time line of some of the Bishop Company's financial woes. Hallie's career had been going gangbusters and from the number of concerts, personal projects and recording sessions, it seemed unlikely she even had time to breathe, much less mastermind a plan for the downfall of the family business. The first round of thefts had appeared during a time when Hallie was engrossed in establishing her music publishing company. Some later thefts came close on the heels of Loreli's breakup, and anyone with half a brain knew she'd had her hands full there.

According to Steve, the alternative rock and grunge movements in the Pacific Northwest provided a bonanza for Vision Quest Music, Inc., Hallie's publishing company. Band agents and managers would approach Hallie with very select groups; she auditioned them, and if she felt they had a good shot with the right material and people behind them, she took them on. They recorded original music written and arranged by Hallie herself, and they were managed by Hallie's choice of people. She even involved herself by acting as mentor and image consultant, preparing a more polished product to attract the major recording labels. The success rate of her bands was very high, managing to cover her initial investments as well as supplying a tidy yield. Despite himself, Ty was more than a little impressed.

The biggest surprise of all came when Steve showed him the information on the various charitable organizations Hallie had helped to found and continued to help support. There were two youth shelters, one in Portland and one in Seattle, and an outreach program for former street gang members in LA that she'd co-founded with fellow band members Cassie Donovan, Randy Raveneau and Chuck E. Edwards. Steve told him it was anybody's guess how many kids they'd saved from God knows what and even sent through college, art and trade schools. Even with their personal and professional relationships strained or broken, as in the case of Cassie and Hallie, all of them kept up their commitments to these projects. Ty was having a hard time reconciling this Hallie with the Hallie who'd tried to destroy her father's company.

The back of the file included a variety of clippings of Gal Hal Bishop in various guises. Ty flipped through them, studying the kaleidoscope of events detailing the life of the enigmatic woman he knew simply as Hallie. There were photos taken at "American Music Awards" over the years, "The Grammy's" and even a couple of "Oscar" nights. In one of the more notorious photos, she was dancing on a tabletop with Cassie Donovan for a bunch of appreciative drunken men, including Randy Raveneau. Another article chronicled the food fight between a notorious bad boy of rock, Randy, Hallie, and a host of other famous musicians at an AIDS benefit dinner. Steve said what the article failed to mention was the healthy financial contributions all the people involved made to the cause, plus payment for damages. There'd been a glint of admiration in Steve's eyes. The picture that stole Ty's breath, though, was a picture of

Hallie in a black and white evening gown designed especially for her. She was the most gorgeous and elegant woman he'd ever laid eyes on. The event was a charity beaux arts ball for the San Francisco Opera. She looked more radiant and happy than he'd ever seen her before. He thought of how she'd looked the last time he'd seen her and his heart suddenly felt like lead.

As he was leaving, Steve stopped him at the door. "Ty, after going over the rest of this information, I have to confess to some serious doubts that she's your thief." He paused for a moment, then said sheepishly, "If I get out to the ranch, do you think you could give me an introduction? If I ordered the perfect woman out of a catalog, it would be Hal Bishop." Ty managed a tight smile, but only because he and Steve had been friends for so long.

"Sorry, Steve," Ty'd answered, "she's taken." There was no mistaking the look of disappointment on his friend's face.

Ty glanced down at the bunkhouse. The things he'd learned about Hallie didn't add up, and frankly, he couldn't be happier about it. He agreed with Steve: It was unlikly Hallie was their thief. He went to the passenger side of the car and took out the bouquet of flowers and bottle of wine he'd bought for her. He hoped a little bit of romance would help him regain some of the ground he'd lost with her. He felt a sharp prick to his conscience and wished he could rationalize it away. Granted, anyone would have believed her guilty after hearing even half of the evidence against her, but regardless, his attempt to blackmail her back into his bed was unforgiveable. He wouldn't blame her if she never wanted to set eyes on him again. He wouldn't blame her, but that didn't mean he intended to accept it.

His anticipation built with every step he took toward

the bunkhouse. He rapped smartly on the front door, imagining how he would gather her into his arms and kiss the hostility from her face. He hoped she liked the spring flowers instead of roses. She seemed more a spring flower type of woman than a two dozen long-stemmed sort. He rapped again. Still no answer. He wasn't that concerned. Her car was in the driveway and he'd expected some initial resistance getting in anyway. Ty reached out and tried the door. It was unlocked, so he let himself in and called for her. No answer. He checked all the rooms quickly and discovered that she wasn't home. Yesterday, he would have sworn his head off and vowed to wring her neck when he caught up with her. Today he simply chuckled because his little wildcat had called his bluff. Grinning, he headed for the kitchen, put the wine in the refrigerator and hunted through her cupboards until he located a vase for the flowers. So much for worrying about having broken her spirit, he mused, filling the vase with water and adding the blooms. In his mind's eye, he could imagine the flash of gold fire in her eyes and the unconscious sway of her hips as she'd stormed from her house in defiance. Ty felt his loins harden. What a woman. Humming, he left her place and strolled back to the main house to change into clothes more suitable for wrestling wildcats.

᪥ ᪥

The rivulets of sweat ran down Hallie's back as she ground her hips in time to the music. She'd been playing virtually non-stop since setup at about seven-thirty this morning. Her shoulders ached, two of her fingertips were cracked, and she hadn't eaten anything since noon the day before. She didn't notice any of it. The music was flowing, she was working, and that's all that counted. When they'd broken for lunch, she'd absently waved away the sandwich Pepe placed under her nose. While everyone else gobbled down their food, she'd run over some bars of music she still wasn't in love with. Gal Hal only knew one way to work: flat out, fast and hard driving.

Chuck E. Edwards sat at a table in the roadhouse watching Gal work with her new alternative rock band, Cheesey Weasels. The kids were good and they'd been taken under the wing of one of the best. The large burly man sipped quietly on his iced tea. They didn't come much better than Gal Hal. Chuck E. had been playing with her since the beginning of Loreli and, like every other male who came to know them, he loved Cassie Donovan and Hal Bishop completely. When his alcohol and drug problem had resulted in an overdose and near death, the first face he'd seen when he regained consciousness was Hal's, and she'd remained at his bedside until he was out of the woods. From there, she'd helped him choose a rehab center and gotten him signed up. He owed her his life—and for resurrecting his career once he was clean and sober. When she'd called him Sunday morning to drum for her and help whip her new protégées into shape, there'd been no question in his mind. He'd dropped everything and flown up last night. He'd stayed with her at the ranch and even gotten to meet her family.

Hal was in a good mood today. She'd only yelled four times, and no one was reduced to tears yet. She was getting tired though, he noted. She needed food and rest. The roadhouse had been rented till six, which meant they'd start the teardown a little after five. He glanced at the lead singer of the Weasles. Chuck E. didn't like the miserable little shit. He'd been a pain in the ass on the trip up here and had spent half an hour this morning whining about the motel Hal had footed the bill for. Luckily for him, she hadn't heard him. He'd seen this kind of macho, superstar wannabe shit before. Hal would cut him down to size in her own good time. He could hardly wait, because it was bound to be choice.

Dottie Hanson sat down across from him. He liked Paul Hanson. He really liked Paul's wife. Unfortunately, since he was playing with the guy and probably would continue to if Hal had her way (and she always did), the plump and pretty Miss Dottie was off limits. The door behind them opened and he noted Dottie's cheerful wave to the tall, dark-haired man who'd entered the bar. The man crossed over to them, looking surprised to see Paul and his wife. Paul, seated at a table near the stage, waved in salute.

"Hey there, Ty!" Dottie grinned up at him good-naturedly. She patted the chair next to her. "Have a seat. This is Chuck E. Edwards. He's a drummer." Chuck E. smiled at the woman. She hadn't recognized his name when they'd been introduced, so she saw no reason for it to mean anything to anyone else either.

Ty tipped his fingers to Paul, smiled warmly at Dottie and shook the beefy hand Chuck E. extended toward him. "It's a pleasure to meet you," he said. Personally, Ty thought the musician looked as though he'd be more at home in an outlaw biker gang than behind a set of drums, but he'd had the pleasure of hearing Chuck E's work and knew how tremendously talented he was. Before Ty had the chance sit down beside Dottie, he heard Hallie's voice.

She stood in front of the stage yelling directions at the oddest looking group of people Ty'd ever seen in his life. He assumed they were a band, though they looked more like sideshow freaks to him. There were three young males, or at least he thought that's what they were. But it was hard to tell with all the eye make-up and body jewel-ry. There were two females, one with a bootcamp haircut and the other with bright vermilion dreadlocks. They were dressed in items that would be better off in a rag barrel, in his opinion. The guy Hallie was yelling at looked like a poster child for world famine relief. He was tall and painfully thin, with dead-white skin and even whiter limp hair. His eyebrows and goatee were dark, like his eyes. He didn't look happy. As a matter of fact, he looked as if he could cheerfully strangle Hallie. It was a feeling Ty could empathize with. He'd felt that way many times himself. With a mischievious wink at Dottie and an easy grin to Chuck E., he sauntered off to make his presence known.

If the little dweeb opened his mouth once more other than to sing, Hal thought she would crawl down his throat and yank out his tonsils. She watched the milk-blonde lead singer pout to the bass player. His name was Seeto Benton and he had talent. Unfortunately, the little prick knew it, and he was determined to make all their lives hell. She'd let him have his head most of the day and shortly she'd take him out at the knees. Hal smiled with satisfaction at the prospect.

"Did you forget our date this afternoon, Duchess?" she heard a husky whisper behind her. Her breath quickened and her heartbeat jumped. She whirled around to see Nighthawk regarding her as intently as his raptor namesake. Damn. The last thing she needed right now was the distraction of those tight Levi's and his glittering green eyes. Part of her wanted to leap into his arms, demanding he take her home to bed, while the other part wanted to mount his head on a pike. Right now, it was a toss-up which part of her would win out. She struggled to remain calm.

"I told you I had plans today," she said evenly. "I'm busy right now. If you want to talk later, okay." Hallie turned back toward the stage.

"I want to do a lot more than just talk, Hallie," he murmured close to her ear.

She stiffened, but didn't turn around. "If you try making a scene, Nighthawk, I'll rip you eight ways to Sunday and if I can't, there are plenty of people here who can. Pepe and Deke for instance, and a couple of mean mother-bear roadies for others. Let's not forget Chuck E. either." She turned back to face him, her eyes snapping with hostility. "I'm not feeling an abundance of affection or patience for you right now, so I suggest you make a strategic retreat."

"I've never run from a fight in my life, Duchess, especially one that promised to be extremely—stimulating."

Hallie's face contorted in fury at the mockery in his eyes. "Take ten everyone! Now!" she shouted. "I'll be outside with Mr. Nighthawk here. No one, repeat no one, even think of disturbing us!" After saying that, she savagely kicked two chairs over and stomped to the door. The husky roadies standing by the bar stayed out of her way. Notorious Gal Hal was mad and they looked afraid. Deke Stanton exchanged a glance with Pepe and though neither one of them had any great love for Tyler Nighthawk, they both felt a little sorry for the guy. "Move it, Nighthawk!" Hal bellowed from the doorway.

Ty's mouth curved into a boyish grin as he observed the path of destruction Hallie had left in her wake. What a woman, he thought once more as he strolled after her.

No sooner had the door ominously banged shut behind them than Hallie launched her verbal assault.

"How dare you?" she yelled, pacing back and forth in front of him, too angry to stand still. "How dare you show up here with your threats and accusations! I won't have it! This is my world, damn it, and you don't have any right to be here." She trembled from rage as well as anguish. "I don't care what you believe I've done, you've got no right to interfere with the lives of those kids in there!"

"Wait a minute, Hallie," he began in a soothing tone.

She cut him off. "No, you wait a minute! There's no way I'll ever convince you that I never stole from my own father," she cried, the bitter desolation ringing in her voice. "I won't even try. What I refuse to allow, though, is for innocent bystanders to be hurt in your battle with me. Right now, nothing is as important to me as doing my job."

Ty heard the unspoken words at the end of her sentence, 'It's all I have.' He knew shame now, as he had never known it before.

"Do you have any idea how many people are depending on what gets done here today? No, you don't. You couldn't possibly." She gestured toward the door. "Those kids in there are just starting out, Tyler. It's a cold, nasty, bad-ass world out there. Talent is just a small part of what you need to survive in the music business." Her eyes took on an older, harder look. "You've got to have guts, determination, and an all-consuming drive, not to mention luck." She looked out to the mountains in the distance but her voice came from somewhere deep within herself. "Even then it's a crapshoot. Maybe one day you're in the right place at the right time, and you take your shot. Less than one percent of the shots you take will pay off, but it's your dream, your goal, and that moment of hope is worth all the nearly-made-its you get." She turned to study his face. "These kids took their shot, Tyler, and they ended up with me. I have a responsibility to them, my company and every person that works for me. Right now I think that's a hell of a lot more important than our personal war."

"I didn't come here to fight with you, Hallie," Ty said quietly.

"Like hell you didn't," she snarled.

"I came here to apologize," he stated in a clearer, firmer

voice. Hallie froze. "I was completely wrong about you," he continued. "If I had any doubts about your innocence before I returned from Portland, I don't now. You never would have hurt your family like that. You're not capable of it."

If he'd expected her to become dewey-eyed with grati- tude at his declaration, he was doomed to disappointment. Her chin and mouth quivered, betraying her pain. The shine in her eyes came from hard, brittle rage, yet the underlying emotion in her body language and expression was fear. Fear of believing him, fear of letting him come too close. She reminded him of a trapped animal wanting help, but ready to bite at any hand that came too near.

"Shut up," she whispered harshly, desperately.

"No," he replied with quiet insistence. "I'm sorry for the things I said to you, Hallie. And, though I don't regret what happened between us Saturday night, I am sorry I tried to blackmail you back into bed with me."

Hallie retreated a step. "I don't need this," she fumed. Grasping at straws, she tossed back, "I don't need you or my family."

"But we need you, Duchess," he whispered, adding silently, 'I need you.'

Ty stepped closer to her, causing her to retreat farther until the wall of the nightclub stood at her back.

"Don't," she pleaded, ducking her head against his invading presence.

"Don't what?" he asked. "Don't tell you that I'm sorry? Don't say that I missed you? Don't promise to do whatev- er it takes to make up for being such a complete bastard to you?" He sensed the fight draining out of her and leaned forward, brushing her cheek with his lips. "Don't tell you that you are, without a doubt, the most exciting, vibrantly alive woman I've ever known?" She made a slight whimpering noise in her throat as he pressed against her, tipping her chin up to bare her throat to his lips. He trailed lazy kisses down her cheek and along the column of her neck. Her breath came out in a gasp. "That's better," he murmured against her skin, taming the wildcat to his touch.

"You shouldn't get too close," she said, her voice husky, but steadier than before. "I'm all sweaty and I smell like a horse."

"I like you all sweaty." His voice teased her with its wicked intent.

"I'm tired and bitchy."

Smiling, Ty reached out and touched her cheek. "So what else is new?"

Hallie sighed and shook her head. "You're not going to go away, are you?"

"Nope, not without that fight you're so worried about." He stepped away from her. "I'll wait for you to finish working, Duchess, then we'll go—together."

"Okay," she said with a sigh of resignation, "but I'd better cover the ground rules."

"Ground rules?" Ty chuckled. "I thought I was the only one who liked ground rules."

The sparkle began to return to her eyes and she arched one eyebrow. "Uh,uh, Nighthawk. Welcome to Hallie World. I call the shots. You sit back with Dottie and Chuck E. Don't interfere, no matter what happens. I have my own management style and things might get a little hairy in a while." Ty nodded, more than happy to agree to her terms. "You're sure you believe me?" she suddenly asked, wary. "No doubts?"

"Not doubt one, Hallie," he replied firmly.

She smiled that liquid sunlight smile of hers that bathed the recipient in golden warmth. "Okay, then. Let's go." She headed back to the door then stopped with a sudden thought. "Oh, and play nice with Pepe and Deke. They might glare, but they mean well."

"What do I get if I do?" He felt heat and something else rising between his legs. God, she was hot when she was in control.

"How about if I just surprise you?" She winked, then stepped inside.

He took a seat at the table with Dottie and Chuck E. At a signal from Hallie, Pepe brought him a beer. He gave Ty a look that told him he was on probation as far as the taciturn club owner was concerned, and he'd better watch his step. Deke Stanton, who was standing at the bar in street clothes instead of his deputy uniform, gave him a similar warning look.

Chuck E. grinned amiably at Ty. "Nice to see you're still alive. Hal must really like you, 'cause it looks like you've still got your balls." Ty found himself laughing along with the man.

"Cut the hen session back there!" Hallie yelled from the stage area. "Okay, once more from the top. Seeto, don't try anymore of that damned improvisational shit this time! On the count of three. One, two—"

"Hold it a minute, Hal," Seeto said, holding up his hand. His fellow band members broke off the song's intro with a frustrated wail from the instruments. "I want to make some changes in this thing."

"I'm sorry, Seeto, what did you say? I didn't quite catch that." Hal said softly.

"Oh shit," Chuck E. rasped with apparent delight, "here we go!"

Ty shrugged an "I don't know" at Dottie, who then looked at the drummer inquisitively. He was too engrossed watching the drama on the stage to notice, however.

"I said that I'd like to make a few changes. I've given it a lot of thought and I've come up with a new arrangement that really burns." The singer was so caught up in his own brilliance that he failed to detect what was coming. The roadies lounging at the end of the bar closest to the stage abruptly left their beers and snuck to the opposite end, behind Ty and Dottie.

"Please, Seeto," Hal continued in the same soft voice from the floor below the stage, "enlighten us. We're all on pins and needles out here."

"Glad to, Hal." The egotistical little worm was warming to his subject and blatantly ignoring the cold fury building in her, Ty thought. He hadn't missed the roadies' strategic retreat or the fact that Paul and the other guys were looking at Chuck E. for guidance as they found themselves sitting in the middle of no-man's-land. Chuck E. crooked his finger and silently motioned them to move back as well. "You see, the thing is," Seeto continued, hardly able to wait for what he had to say next, "the way this is arranged just isn't us. It's not about who we are, Hal, and our music is who we are." He enthralled himself.

"I see." Hal turned toward the back of the bar. Her eyes sought out Chuck E. and she smiled at him. Actually, it was more like she bared her teeth.

"Paul," the drummer said carefully, "you might want to get your wife outta here. The rest of you, bend over and kiss your sorry butts good-bye, 'cause the Gal is gonna blow."

Then it happened. With apparent calm, Hal placed two hands on the top of the tall stool she'd been using, quietly picked it up and hurled it at the stage. She kicked over a table in her path, then slowly walked up the steps at the side of the stage. She seized the singer by his shirtfront. "Listen here, you sniveling little puke," she began, and the conversation went downhill from there.

Ten minutes into her tirade, three of the Cheesey Weasels were crying, the two girls and one of the guys. Seeto got paler than ever as he saw their big break going up in smoke. "So which is it?" Hal asked in conclusion. "I've still got things I want to do here today. I told you at the get go, my way or the highway. You guys choosing the highway?" The band members, Seeto included, fell all over themselves in a scramble to get back into her good graces.

She smiled, arching an eyebrow. She had him now. "Places everybody," she said, then turned to join the crowd at the back of the bar. She ignored everyone but Chuck E. as he regarded the stage. She leaned slightly toward him with a devilish grin, and asked, "Are there daggers pointed at my back?"

"Uh-uh, Gal—but I think you might have five people up there that need to change their underwear."

Hallie laughed, then abruptly spun herself to the stage shouting, "And, one, two, three, go!"

Ty watched Hallie, studying her intently as she quietly discussed the group's bass lines with Paul and Chuck E. He felt as if he could fly. This woman had just handed the kid on stage his head on a silver platter. She'd had a room full of men sprinting for cover and bending over backwards to do her bidding. She'd chewed him out, but in retrospect it was pretty tame stuff. This hellcat, this enticing temptress, was his. They'd made love, fierce and hot, and he'd brought her to tears with the depth of passion he'd aroused in her. She'd become soft and yielding and wonderfully sweet in his arms. Suddenly he was rock hard again. A woman like this made a man feel as if he could harness the stars. All he wanted was for this session to end so he could take her home to bed.

Chapter 18

They started the teardown promptly at five o'clock. Ty was amazed at how efficiently musicians and roadies worked together to get the job done. He was perplexed when he noticed that no one made a move to touch any of Hallie's guitars and equipment or help her in any way. She retrieved her own cases, unplugged the transmitters and the amps herself, and packed everything up. Ty, getting into the spirit of things, helped the roadies, along with Deke and Pepe, move amps and sound equipment out to the truck. When he saw Hallie working quickly by herself, his first impulse was to grab one of the other guys and give her a hand. Chuck E. saw his intention and quickly set him straight. No one touched Hal's instruments but her. On the road, she had her own roadie whom she actually let help her, but rarely anytime else. She was fanatical about it. He gave Ty a measuring look and went on to say that everyone walked on eggs around her while she was work-ing. Ty could barely contain his satisfied smile when he thought about the Hendrix Stratocaster of hers he'd held and how he'd lived to tell the tale.

He walked over to Hallie and casually asked her if she minded him giving her a hand with her equipment. She looked up at him startled, frowning slightly as she struggled with admitting him further into her world and relinquishing a substantial amount of control.

She remained silent for a time, the inner war clearly dis-played on her face. He turned to leave and she called his name. She looked a little unsure of herself for a woman who struck abject terror in the hearts of an entire industry. "Thanks," she said, pointing to a closed guitar case. "This is ready to go." Hallie watched him as nervously as a new mother leaving her baby with a sitter for the first time as he picked up the case and headed out to the truck with it. When she started to follow, he stopped and let her come up beside him. Hallie regarded him with caution, and uncertainty made her voice come out harsh. "Be careful. These are custom pieces, okay? They can't be replaced just anywhere." He set the case down with exaggerated care.

Stepping nearer to her, he bent his mouth close so no one else would hear what he said. "I promise to hold this rare and precious gem, carry it gently," he murmured, "and caress it tenderly through the whole night if you want." His eyes left little doubt as to what he was talking about. He caught her chin gently with his hand and tipped her face so he could slant a warm kiss across her mouth. He drew back and smiled as he saw the baffled look in her whiskey-colored eyes. He took charge with quiet confidence. "Why don't you go finish closing up the cases and take a break, honey. God knows you deserve it. We'll get them moved out safe and sound. Okay?" After a long pause, she nodded.

Paul, Chuck E. and the rest of the crew stopped dead in their tracks when they saw Ty emerge from the club carrying one of Gal Hal's guitars. He grinned broadly at their slackened jaws and asked one of the roadies where he should put it. After carefully placing the guitar where he was shown, he came back to join Paul and Chuck E. as they stood leaning against the side of the club wall.

"Ty, my man," the drummer said, heartily extending his arm, "I want to shake the hand that belongs to one of the biggest pair of balls I've ever met in my life." Ty shook his hand and laughed. "Not even that gutsy Donovan broad would've tried moving Hal's stuff on a bet." Chuck E. continued, "Guess that means you're part of the family now."

"Well, not exactly part of the family, more like a kissing

cousin," Ty answered lightly. The drummer chuckled as he headed back inside.

Paul's face broke into a leisurely grin. "Whatever it is, the arrangement agrees with you. I don't remember the last time I saw you look so darned pleased with yourself."

Ty nodded his agreement. Paul's voice dropped to a more serious note. "She has quite a reputation in this business, Ty, and not just for her temper or that tabloid crap either. She shoots square and she never sounds off on someone who is doing all they can. I was holding back this morning. I don't know, maybe I was too in awe to concentrate," he admitted sheepishly, "maybe I never really knew what I had in me. She sure knew though, and she wouldn't settle for less. Look, I guess what I'm trying to say is, don't believe all that junk you hear about her, okay? I know I sure don't."

Ty gave his friend a look of gratitude for his vote of confidence. "Thanks, Paul," he said simply. "Now, we'd better get this packed up before she's out of the shower. I don't want to be on the receiving end of a scene like the one with Seeto." The other man readily agreed, and within another twenty minutes they'd finished loading the truck.

When Ty came back inside after rechecking the tailgate lock, he found Hallie leaning back against the bar, deep in conversation with Seeto. Her mane of bronze-gold hair was loose, freshly washed and dried. She wore a form-fitting pair of jeans and some kind of white shirt under her navy blazer. She was a tempting morsel to any man, and he smiled at the images his thoughts evoked. Seeto was bending low to her ear, and Hallie laughed at whatever he'd said. Apparently, the guy didn't mind being treated like dirt, Ty thought irritably. The kid was totally captivated by her. Hallie knew it, damn it, and was flirting with

him. He strolled over to join them, jealousy burning a
hole clear through him.

"Hey Hal," Seeto said as Ty walked up to them, "I was
wondering if I could take you out to dinner when we go to
Seattle. It's my old stomping grounds, and I could show
you where the real Seattle Sound still plays, not this manufactured Nirvana-rip-off shit. What do you say?"

Hallie smiled at Ty and noticed his eyes had darkened.
It was a sure sign of his annoyance, though the rest of his
face remained impassive. Evidently, he'd heard Seeto's
invitation and, unlike herself, was hardly amused. She
turned back to Seeto and said lightly, "You keep your attitude like this and it's a date, okay?" She clasped him
warmly by the shoulder. "You did good today, kid—once
you got your head out of your ass, that is," she said with a
crooked grin. "You take care, and I'll be in touch."

Seeto bent quickly and kissed her full on the mouth.
He gave her a broad smile and winked before leaving.
"Why, that nervy little shit!" Hallie said indignantly, after
he'd left the building. "I was too easy on him!" Ty stood
glaring at her. She gave him a saucy wink and pulled him
with her toward the roadies and the drummer.

Her eyes took on a sad, wistful look as she said good-
bye to Chuck E. She launched herself into his arms, and
the gigantic man gave her a bear hug and a resounding
smack of a kiss before returning her to her feet. "As
always, Gal, it's been real. You tell your mom and sister
bye for me. And eat something, damn it!" he growled.

She waved away his concern. "I'm fine, I'll grab something at home."

He glared at Hallie. "How much sleep have you been
getting lately, Hal? I know for a fact you got squat last
night. I heard you up until at least two a.m. and you were
up and at it when I got up at six. You know you're gonna

start having them damn dreams again if you don't take care of yourself." He shook his head. "Never thought I'd say this but I miss the 'pit bull' right now. Ryker could at least make sure you ate and slept."

"She doesn't need the 'pit bull' anymore, because she's got 'the warden' now. Between me and Mrs. Hudson, she'll take care of herself," Ty said grimly, "or we'll have a major problem." Hallie gave both men a murderous look.

"Thanks,Ty, it would make me rest easier knowing someone was up here keeping an eye on her. She means a hell of a lot to me." He drew Hallie back into an embrace once more. "I'll see you this fall. You call me if you need anything, you hear me, Gal? Don't go giving Mr. Nighthawk here any trouble either." Hallie refrained from mentioning that she'd already done so in spades, and Tyler was one of the chief reasons she hadn't been eating or sleeping well. As annoyed as she was at the two of them tag-teaming her, she was secretly pleased that they liked each other so well. She whispered her thanks, kissed him on the cheek and left to talk to the others.

They said good-bye to Paul and Dottie at the door. Hallie told Paul she'd call him tomorrow and they would set a time to get together. Ty picked up her nylon workout bag and led her away as she was still talking, lining out items to discuss with his friend.

He noticed she looked a little pensive as he steered her toward his newly repainted Corvette. She'd never ridden in it before, even though she'd begged countless times as a kid. He hoped it would bring a little of the light back to her eyes. Initially, none of them at the ranch had cared what Hallie's move back to Oregon might cost her. She'd been an outsider since the first day she'd arrived at the bunkhouse. He felt a twinge of conscience again as he thought now about how terribly isolated she must feel at times. "You miss him already, don't you?" he said, wrapping an arm around her shoulders and giving her an affectionate squeeze. It felt so natural to walk with her like that, and he was happy when she automatically encircled his waist.

Hallie sighed deeply. "Yeah, I do. I miss him, and Randy, and Cass. I miss Mr. and Mrs. V, and my house, and believe it or not, LA. I guess I'm just lonely up here by myself. I don't think I realized how much until last night. I'm thinking strongly of going back to LA for good in the fall." If she thought he might breathe a sigh of relief or even offer to help her pack, she was mistaken. His response was short and to the point.

"No." His tone brooked absolutely no argument.

"Excuse me?" Hallie asked as she raised her eyebrow.

"I said no, Hallie. It's not a viable option." He felt her stiffen as if to brace herself for more of his threats. She was exhausted and the shadows under her eyes were more pronounced than ever. It gnawed at him that he was responsible for her lack of appetite and sleep. Very gently, he said, "You're obviously barely taking care of yourself as it is. I'm not going to let someone so important to me work herself into a sick bed when the solutions are so simple."

She was hardly able to concentrate on what he said after the words someone so important to me. Hallie couldn't remember the last time joy, so sharp and sweet, coursed through her. He'd made no threats, real or implied, declared no open warfare, nothing but five heart-warming words hung in the air about her. "What are your simple solutions, Tyler?" she asked, tilting her head upward, silently asking for a kiss. Ty smiled down at her and willingly complied.

"We'll discuss them over dinner. I'm taking you to get

the best and biggest hamburger and order of fries this side of the Mississippi. And you'll eat every bite," he said sternly.

Hallie's eyes lit up greedily. "Woolly Bill's sports bar?"

He smiled indulgently and kissed her again. "The same, Duchess. They even carry the latest micro-brews on tap. You game?"

"You bet! I'd bear your offspring for one of Woolly Bill's burgers. Last one to the cars is a rotten egg!" She laughed and took off toward his car. She stopped suddenly, stamped her feet in the dirt and thrust a fist triumphantly skyward. "Yes!" she shouted. "Finally, a ride in the Vette! This is gonna be so sweet!" She looked like a kid about to be given the keys to Disney World. "You got any Beach Boys in there?" she asked Ty when he caught up with her.

"What else?" He captured her waist and walked her the rest of the way to the vehicle.

❦ ❧

At the sports bar, they joined in warm, rich laughter—a sound that made the other patrons glance over in heartfelt appreciation. Lovers, they nodded sagely to themselves, and with smiles, turned back to their own conversations. Amid the clinking of glassware, the gurgle of the deep fryer, and the occasional boisterous shouts from the game, Hallie began to do something she'd considered impossible until now. She opened her heart to Ty.

They talked about her music, her life in LA, and her friends. Hallie was a good storyteller and more than once Ty had to wipe tears of laughter from his eyes. He felt envious of all those who knew her better than he did; all those who'd spent years basking in the light that surrounded her. Without considering the risks, he told her as much. Ty was gratified to see a soft, wondrous expression gradually steal across her face as she accepted his words, and he knew he'd made the right call.

Something unlocked in Hallie then, and she began to talk about less pleasant things, such as Melick's death so soon after he'd married Cassie, the band's breakup and the rumors surrounding her, Randy, Cassie, and Nick. There was an earnestness in her, a need to make him understand that compelled him to believe her without question. He'd known there'd been no scandalous liaisons between her, Randy and Cassie, but he was relieved to hear the truth about Montoya, even if it didn't cast Hallie in a very noble light.

Ty remembered Hallie telling him once that when she was guilty of something, she owned up to it. With Montoya what she'd been guilty of was trying to keep him and Cassie apart by any means possible, and when she'd succeeded, Montoya exacted his own brand of vengeance by setting up Hallie and making Cassie believe he was having an affair with her. Hallie not only lost her life's work, but her best friend as well. She didn't gloss over her part in her own downfall. She took it on the chin just as she always did, and in the end, Ty had more respect for her than ever before.

The drive to the ranch was accomplished in record time, and once they got there, it was all Ty could do not to throw her over his shoulder and kick the door down. He couldn't remember ever being this hot for a woman before in his life. Hallie giggled softly and raced up the steps with Ty literally hot on her heels. Once inside, she closed and locked the door after him.

He pulled her into his arms and kissed her roughly. "You little witch—*bruja*," he murmured as he trailed kisses down her throat. "What have you done to me?" He pulled her blazer from her shoulders and left it fall at their feet, and he started working on the buttons of her shirt. Ty walked backwards, letting his grasp on the fabric guide Hallie along with him. She gave a sudden cry and turned toward the cooking island in the kitchen. He shot her a curious look, then saw what had caught her attention. He let her go and she immediately raced to the vase of flowers he'd left there earlier in the day. The look on her face made his heart stop. Her lips curved into a breathtaking smile full of enchantment and wonder. Months later he would recognize this moment as the one where he'd lost his heart completely to Hallie Bishop. There was no struggle, no bloodshed. She simply reached in and seized his heart as if she had every right to it—and she did.

"Oh Tyler." His name was spoken as a caress. "You brought me flowers." The winsome quality in her voice made him wish he had a whole field of flowers to pull her down into and make love to her in again and again. She touched the bouquet with her cheek and nose, as if they were the rarest flowers in the world—more precious than diamonds. "I love it when someone gives me flowers," she said softly, her eyes shimmering with a golden glow.

"You know, Miss Bishop," he said, in a tender murmur, "you act like a woman who doesn't get flowers often. I bet your dressing rooms are loaded, and not with spring flowers either."

She inclined her head and laughed lightly. "Oh yes, orchids, roses, birds of paradise, even chrysanthemums arranged to look like a poodle, but they never mean much. These are from you," she stated quietly. "You've never given me flowers before," then amended, "unless you count the time you put the sprig of sticker bush in my bed."

She looked as if he'd given her the moon, and his heart swelled with an indescribable joy. He chuckled wickedly, "We'll count this as the first time, lady, because if I'm going

to stick you with anything in bed, it's going to be my..."
Hallie brought her finger up to his lips in a silencing
motion.

"I get your drift, Nighthawk," she said provocatively,
"and may I say it would be my pleasure."

"Oh yes, Duchess," Ty breathed out in response, "very
definitely your pleasure—and mine."

Hallie fought the blush that unexpectedly suffused her
face with a rosy glow. She reached out a hand to gently
touch the blooms in front of her. "I want you to know, Ty,
if I hadn't already arranged for Seeto and his fellow
Weasels to come up here, I most likely would have been
here today. Granted," she added ruefully, turning her face
to his, "I talked myself in and out of it several times."

"Hallie," he began earnestly. "I don't want just a few
quick thrills in the sack from you. I've had a taste of being
included in your world and I like the feeling." He reached
out his hand and carefully brushed her hair back from her
upturned face. "You know, I don't know where we're
going with this, but I think we should try walking the same
path for a while and see where it leads us."

Hallie cleared her throat in a effort to dislodge the
painful lump that had taken root there. Years dropped
away, and suddenly she felt like that fifteen-year-old girl
who'd waited in vain for her prince charming. But the
prince had chosen another from a neighboring kingdom.
Now, years later, he was holding out his hand again, to her
this time. All she had to do was have the courage to reach
out and take it. *Te amor,* her mind cried out to him, I love
you more than you could imagine. I always have, that's
why I waited for you. Hallie was more frightened than
she'd been in years. She'd admitted to herself that she
loved him, and that gave him the power to destroy her.
The only thing more frightening than this, however, was

the thought of refusing him here and now.

"You're saying the 'r' word, Ty. Are you sure that's what you want?" she asked, fighting to keep the anxiety out of her voice.

He smiled warmly. "I'm not sure what the word relationship implies about you and me. We've had a relationship of one sort or another for years, but yes, I'm sure I want to see what happens from here. How about you?"

She nodded, turning back to pick up the vase. "I know I like your company, and that I miss you like hell when you're away. Don't start checking out china patterns though, okay?" she added a little gruffly.

He laughed. "Deal. You either," he said, but couldn't quite get over the flash of disappointment he felt deep inside.

"No chance," she said, for once in her life lying smoothly. "I forgot to check my messages," she added quickly as she headed into the living room to place the flowers on the piano. Sure enough, the answering machine light was blinking, indicating three messages. She walked over and punched the play button, heedless of Ty's presence in the room. She had nothing to hide anyway. She was rewarded with an embrace from behind, and his lips nuzzling the back of her neck. "This will only take a minute," she said, moving her hips slowly to brush across the front of his jeans. Ty gave a sharp intake of breath, and pulled her hips firmly against him. She felt the firmness of his sex and sighed contentedly. Soon, she promised herself, very soon.

The tape finished rewinding and the first message started to play. Ty wasn't sure he could last much longer, and he hoped none of the people on the machine had been feeling particularly long-winded. The first message was from Clancy Redfern, saying she now had a list of tentative dates for the small Euro tour planned in the coming winter. He felt a sinking sensation at the prospect of her leaving him, even for a few weeks. Hallie's attention was snagged now, and she pulled slightly away from him as she reached for a notepad to take down the information. The second message was from no less than an icon of rock. When Ty heard the name and the cockney voice on the message, he did a double take and gave a low whistle. He knew Hallie hung out and worked with the major movers and shakers in rock music, but nothing brought the reality of it closer than hearing one of them on her answering machine, asking her if she would be interested in playing two or three numbers at his concert in Seattle next winter.

Hallie gave a pleased "very cool," and jotted down another note to herself to return his call in the morning. She looked up at Ty's astonished face and smiled. "He's just a man, Ty, albeit a very talented and gifted one, but just a man. He's also one heck of a nice guy. You'll like him." He was surprised and pleased at her automatic inclusion of him in her plans.

The last message on the tape brought both of them up short. Kelsey Hogan's voice asked Hallie to give her a call as soon as she got in, regardless of time.

"I've got to make this phone call. I hope you can understand," Hallie said hurriedly, already starting to dial.

"Of course," he answered, making no move to give her the privacy she might want. After all, he had a stake in anything Kelsey discovered concerning the missing funds.

Hallie beamed happily up at him, accepting his presence and perfectly content to lean back against him. She took his hand and gave it a tender squeeze. She'd kept the phone on the speaker, he noted, as if to assure him she had nothing to hide. The front desk of the hotel hurriedly complied with her request to be rung through to Kelsey's room.

Ty leaned his back against the desk, kissing the back of her neck lightly. The other end of the line was answered by a sleepy and decidedly grumpy man.

"Ryker, here," snarled the voice.

Ty and Hallie exchanged puzzled frowns, and Hallie quickly broke the silence. "Sorry, Ryker, it's Hal. The front desk must have rung the wrong room. I was returning Kelsey's call."

"No, they didn't," Ryker answered gruffly. "This is her room. As usual, Bishop, you've got impeccable timing. She's asleep now. If you'd called any earlier or any later, you would have gotten an earful."

"Oh God!" Hallie groaned in disgust and rolled her eyes at Tyler, who was busy trying to stifle a laugh. "Here we go again! I don't want to know, Ryker. I don't want to hear about it!" The man on the other end laughed unpleasantly. They heard a sleepy murmur from the woman beside him.

Hallie gave Tyler an appalled look. To Ryker, she said, "This is too weird, even for my life. I'll call back in the morning." Ty nodded his agreement. He had to admire Ryker's taste and his ability to talk any woman into bed with him though, especially one who disliked him as much as Kelsey Hogan obviously did.

"Just tell Kelse I'll talk to her tomorrow," Hallie said to the man on the phone, "unless you want to tell me in ten words or less what's going on."

"If it was up to me, I'd rather send you an explosive device in the mail," Ryker answered. When she made no response, he continued. "We found out what we needed to. Much good it does, though. The depositor of the other account is a Mr. Philip M. Phlam."

Hallie thought for a moment, then said "Phil M. Phlam—as in 'flim-flam'?"

"Give the the little girl a gold star, she can use her brain on occasion," Ryker jeered. Ty saw an angry flush darken Hallie's face. "Everywhere we turn we've got a new pun or anagram," Ryker continued. "At any rate, if you want to know more, you'll have to talk to Kelsey. You want to stay on the line? I was just about to wake her up when you called." He chuckled wickedly. "I'm afraid it's going to be a little while, though, before she can talk business."

"Urgh! I'm hanging up, Ryker. Trying to get decent answers out of you is impossible! Just tell Kelse I called, if you know what's good for you!" Hallie blasted at him.

"Bite me, Bishop."

"Yeah, like I'd want to catch whatever the hell you've got!" she snapped.

"Just one thing," he said blandly, ignoring her insult. "Keep your mouth shut—you hear? Trust no one. Especially pretty boy. Right now he's my favorite suspect for setting you up." His voice became sinister as he added, "I won't have you jeopardizing this investigation 'cause your hormones are in overdrive. You do that, Angel Face, and you and I will have a 'come to Jesus' meeting when I get stateside. Understand?"

She sensed rather than saw the furious expression on Ty's face. She didn't dare look at him. The verbal threats from Ryker were enough to deal with right now. "I understand, Ryker," she said and ended the call.

Hallie let out the breath she was still holding. Everything today had been like a dream and now the reality of their situation reared its ugly head once more. Hallie shuddered as she reset the answering machine, then turned off the speaker and ringer. She took in Ty's dark expression with trepidation. "It would seem you have suspicions of your own," he said with amazing calm.

"No," she responded forcefully, "Ryker does. You

never would have stolen from Dad."

"Well thank you for that much at least." He moved away from her and began to pace slowly around the living room. He ran his fingers through his hair and then paused to look at her. She'd expected him to be furious about Ryker's insinuations. He didn't look like an angry man, he looked like a tormented one. "Dear God!" he said finally. "I can't blame you. All the names I've called you—the threats I made. No wonder you think I'm capable of..." He couldn't finish—couldn't look at her.

"I told you 'no,' Tyler. I don't think that at all." There was such gentle earnestness in her voice that he brought his guilt-ridden eyes to hers. "Come sit with me. I have a lot to explain." She went to him and drew him to the sofa with her. Hallie told him everything—her father's phone calls, Clancy's discovery of the deposits, Randy's contacting Ryker and her subsequent hiring of him. Ty was stunned as much by her lack of resentment toward him as his own oblivion to the surveillance that had gone on right under his nose.

"Of course," Hallie was saying, "I had no idea myself that Ryker was at the cemetery that day until he told me. I wanted to kill him." She studied the hooded expression of the man seated beside her. "Try to understand. Randy was terribly worried about me." She laughed shortly and with limited humor. "He'd have to have been to call Ryker and get him involved. Randy knows I've never really gotten on well with you guys. Look, I don't blame you for thinking I stole the money—with all that evidence." She added in a somewhat defeated tone, "Dad would have believed it, too." He wanted to protest, but he knew she was right. She touched his arm gently, gazing up at him with her warm, whiskey eyes. "The only act of contrition I'm looking for from you, Tyler, is for you to hold me and make love to me. Not have sex—make love. Let's forget all this for tonight. We can deal with it in the morning. Right now," she murmured leaning toward him, "I just need you."

"Hallie," he whispered hoarsely as he pulled her into his arms to hold her close. He silently cursed himself for his own deceit. No, Hallie Leigh Bishop had never been the one with a hidden agenda. He had been, and God help him if she ever found out. "Are you sure this is what you want?" his guilt prompted him to ask. "I mean, if you wanted me out that door right now and out of your life, it would be no more than I deserve."

She arched one shapely eyebrow at him. "Are you offering to leave, Nighthawk?" Her eyes held an impish glint that refused to let him take himself too seriously.

"No," he stated flatly. "As a matter of fact, Duchess, I'd put up one hell of a fight."

"Good," she drawled in a husky whisper. "First one to the bed gets to be on top."

"Oh darlin', ladies first," he crooned in return.

Hallie raced off to the bedroom, and Ty heard the sound of the mattress bouncing as she threw herself on it. Suddenly, feeling as carefree and reckless as a teenager, he ran in after her and launched himself to land on top of her. They rolled on the bed laughing and tickling each other. Gradually, the tickling changed in intent and location. They worked on each other's buttons between kisses and husky murmurs, and soon they were naked on Hallie's bed. He enfolded her and trailed burning kisses from her mouth to her breasts, saying breathlessly, "I've been counting the seconds till I could do this." His eager mouth closed over the rosy tip of her right breast, "And this. *Quiero a hacer el amor contingo*," he whispered. Hallie quivered in delight at the thought of making love all night long.

Hallie tipped her head back, and arched her nipples against him. "I know! Oh lord, Tyler, I know. I've be dreaming of this since..."

"Sunday," he finished for her, and kissed his way to her other breast.

Much later, Hallie lay replete, covering Ty's powerful body with her own. He was wonderful, Hallie thought, wonderful in every way possible, and she was happier than she could remember being in a very long time. Three months ago she'd walked back into his life, demanding her due. Had anyone told her then she would end up sprawled on top of him after mind-blowing, body-searing sex, she would have laughed herself hoarse. But he felt so good, so right. She wanted this moment to last forever. She longed to look into his eyes and call him the words of her heart, *mi amor*. But it was too soon, too risky. Yes, he cared, he was enamored with her sexually, but he certainly didn't love her. She doubted he ever would. She sighed a little pensively, and Ty was on it in an instant.

"What's the matter, Duchess?" He began to massage her back in slow, sensual circles.

"Nothing, I was just thinking I want to stay like this forever, never move again." If he detected a false note in her voice, he said nothing.

"Mmmm," he murmured, as he planted lazy kisses on the top of her head. "Me either. It would present some logistics problems, however." His hands trailed over her skin in a southerly direction, coming to rest on the firm cheeks of her derriere. He began his massage again, stopping occasionally to cup and firmly squeeze her buttocks. He felt his shaft stir to life inside her. "Uh oh," he whispered, bringing his mouth to her ear, "see what you started?" His shaft throbbed again, a little more insistently this time, and he felt himself harden within her warm, supple body. He held her tightly as he rolled her underneath him. She encircled his neck with her arms and smiled up at him, her eyes shining with tenderness, and dare he hope, something stronger. Ty felt time stand still for him as he basked in the light radiating from her face. His heart swelled with exultation when he claimed her mouth as his territory. Yes, his, and God help any man or anything that tried to come between them.

Chapter 19

The sounds of bird song and the start of another workday on the ranch woke Ty later than usual. They'd both been completely and deliciously worn out after last night. He looked over at the woman who lay snuggled up tightly against him, sleeping on her side. He gently moved a long tendril of hair from her forehead so he could watch the morning dapple its light across her face. In truth, Hallie could use another hour of sleep. He'd tried to be as considerate as any normal, healthy man could be in bed with Hallie; however, they'd made love three times before he'd let her go to sleep. Somewhere after midnight, he'd woken to Hallie tossing and turning violently in bed beside him. He'd just decided to wait to see if she settled without him waking her, when she started moaning and swinging wildly with her arms in an effort to ward off phantom hands. He tried to shake her awake, but the nightmare was too reluctant to loosen its grip on her mind. Suddenly, she sat bolt upright and gave a blood-chilling scream of absolute terror. Ty'd felt panic and fear for her engulf him as well. It had been the very occurrence Chuck E. was afraid would happen due to her lack of sleep, grueling work, and poor nutrition. He hadn't been absolutely positive what the dreams were about, but as he'd watched her battle with the night demons in her head, he'd developed a pretty good idea: Hamburg and getting caught by the full fury of the mob on stage. The news accounts had dwelt mainly with the tragedy of the four teenage girls crushed to death in the onslaught. There was little or no sympathy in the press for the performers left to the mercy of the audience gone crazy.

He'd gripped her hard by the shoulders and shaken her

roughly. When the motion had failed to stir her from her night terror, he'd had to resort to slapping her sharply across the face. As he watched her now in the soft light of morning, he winced from the memory. After an endless, heart-wrenching moment, she'd become aware of her surroundings. With a broken cry, she had launched herself into his arms and clung tightly. Ty'd whispered gentle words, then he'd pulled her down to lie in his arms. After a while she'd calmed down enough for him to caress and kiss the rest of the isolation and fear from her. Even now in the warm morning light, he could still hear the need in her voice as she had pressed trembling kisses on his neck, pleading him to make love to her. And he had made tender and reverent love to her, taking his time to relax her completely before beginning the marvelous and delightful process of arousing her. Afterward, as they'd lain tightly in each others arms, she'd asked him to please stay the whole night so she didn't have to wake up alone. There had been no trace of the confident, dynamic woman he'd seen during the day. "Wild horses couldn't get me out of your bed, lady," he'd replied around the lump in his throat.

Hallie stirred sleepily beside him, and he watched with delight as the covers slipped from her shoulders when she rolled to her back. With a little encouragement on his part, they slipped further, offering him a full, tantalizing view of her creamy breasts. He couldn't see any good reason for resisting temptation, so he bent his lips to her nipple and began to suckle her gently. When she gave a soft murmur, he increased the pressure, then delicately drew his teeth over the strawberry tip. Hallie's eyes flew open and she gasped. "Good morning, Duchess," he said in a husky whisper.

An hour later, they rose and headed for the shower and another leisurely bout of lovemaking. Hallie dressed quickly afterward, then headed for the kitchen to put on the coffee. Suddenly feeling domestic, she frantically searched her cupboards for something edible to offer him for breakfast. She cringed, facing the deplorable condition of her larder. Chuck E. was right, she hadn't been taking care of herself. Her stomach rumbled in protest. She hoped he drank his coffee black, because even creamer wasn't an option. Ty came up behind her, hugging her at the waist as she set mugs on the counter.

"Hope you're not too hungry," she said with no small amount of embarrassment, "because Mother Hubbard never made it to the supermarket this week." At his stern look, she added, "I know, I know. You don't have to say it. If you hurry, I bet you can talk Mrs. H. into feeding you."

"Only if you come too," he responded in a no-nonsense voice.

"Can't." Hallie handed him a steaming mug of rich coffee, picked up hers, and headed for the telephone. "I've got calls to return, remember?" She pulled out the plain wooden chair at the desk and sat down.

"It's an hour and a half 'til lunch. I don't think I'll die of hunger by then, Hallie." Ty stood behind her and planted a kiss on the top of her head. "You're going to be taking your meals up at the house with the rest of us from now on anyway." She turned to look at him, a frown creasing her brow. "No arguments," he continued sternly. "I'm not having you forget nourishment for the sake of art and making yourself sick. Something tells me Marlene won't mind in the least, and Genna will be thrilled. As for me," he said, giving her an erotic look, "I'll enjoy flirting with you and making sexual innuendoes until you blush." He saw her turn a beguiling rosy shade immediately. Ty smiled. Who would have thought that Gal Hal Bishop would blush like a schoolgirl when confronted by a man's desire.

"Okay, okay!" Hallie turned back to the telephone in an effort to hide her reddened face from him, and picked up the hastily written notes from the previous evening. "Give me a few minutes to get business handled and we'll go up to the house. I know when I'm beaten."

"Glad to hear it."

The phone rang just as Hallie moved to pick it up and dial. She answered it, and Kelsey Hogan's voice came briskly over the line. "Hi, it's me. I heard you called last night." Obviously Kelsey thought the best way to keep Hallie's mouth shut was with curt efficiency. No such luck.

"Well, well. Sleeping Beauty finally awakens," Hallie chortled. "You must have been very tired." She turned to look at Ty over her shoulder and mouthed Kelsey's name at him. He gave her a crooked grin and mouthed "Be nice" in response. She stuck her tongue out at him and turned back to the desk. "So," Hallie chirped into the phone with false brightness, "tell me, how are things?" She could sense Kelsey's hostility through the tense seconds of silence.

"You know, Hal, it's moments like these that make me almost understand why Ryker hates your guts," her friend seethed.

"Yeah, well, he doesn't care much for the rest of me either." Abruptly, the insolent humor left Hallie's voice as she said, "I'm just concerned about you, Kelse, that's all."

"I'm a big girl, Hal, and the one thing I don't need from you right now is the position of Monday morning quarterback. Is that clear? I have no intention now, or at any time in the future, discussing anything of a personal nature with you." If Kelsey expected this terse oration to effectively silence Hal Bishop, she'd seriously underestimated the unmitigated gall of her famous client.

"Can I take that to mean you had a good time last night?"

"Hal! I'm warning you!"

"Oh all right, all right. I guess he must be a pretty lousy lay if you're this crabby the morning after. I could have told you so, would have too if I'd ever thought there was a snowball's chance in hell of you being tempted enough to find out. The selfish, sadistic type makes for a poor bedfellow—or so I've observed. What happened? Did you take your hormones with you and leave your brains in your other briefcase?" Hallie flashed Ty a devilish smile and wiggled her eyebrows suggestively at his frown.

"You're a menace," he whispered and rolled his eyes. "Hi Kelsey!" he yelled into the receiver. "If I were you, I'd ask Hallie what she was doing last night."

"Is that Tyler? Hal, you rotten little...I swear I'm going to kill you!"

Instead of Hallie being annoyed with either of them, she was laughing hard. "Okay, so I'm a hypocrite! What else is new?"

"Well now," Kelsey began calmly, but Hallie could tell she was anything but. Inside, Kelsey was fuming. "As a matter of fact, not all that much. Jake feels we've done all the checking we can here. The trail's leading back to the States. We're catching a flight out in a couple of hours, so as much as I'd love to stay and banter with you, we need to keep this brief. I want to run some names by you. See if they mean anything to you."

"Shoot."

"Don't tempt me, Hal," Kelsey replied dryly. "Okay, here goes. Lester Townsend?"

"Nope."

"How about George Kaplin?"

"Sounds familiar," Hallie replied as she jotted the names down on a note pad. "Of course it's a fairly nondescript name. Any others?"

"Just one, Roger Thornhill. Any bells?"

"Actually yes, I don't know why, though—nothing I can really put a finger on. Let me think about it for a day or two. What's Ryker's opinion?"

"That they're aliases. You're sure they're not investors, record executives—anything like that?"

"Damn it, Kelse, I meet so many people. For all I know one of them could be a stagehand who handed me a towel in Des Moines years ago. The names just sound familiar, that's all."

"Okay, well, get back to me as soon as you come up with anything," Hallie said. "Oh, and I wanted to let you know something else, too. I don't subscribe to Jake's particular theory regarding Tyler. I think you should tell him what Ryker and I are up to. He'd be a good man to have in our camp, Hal."

"Already done, Kelse," Hallie answered softly. "We've managed to work out some of the kinks between us lately." Ty grinned and leered at her from the sofa. "Just don't tell Ryker yet. He's threatened me with death and dismemberment if I tell Ty anything."

"My lips are sealed. But kindly return the favor. No more smart remarks about Jake and me, okay?"

"Done. Have a safe trip and thanks, Kelse. Thank Ryker too." Kelsey laughed, knowing as well as Hallie did what Ryker would say she could do with her thanks.

She sat at the desk after her lawyer had hung up, simply staring at the paper in her hand. After a while she joined Tyler on the sofa and handed the list of names to him. "These names mean anything to you? Businessmen maybe? Cronies of Dad?"

He frowned thoughtfully then handed her back the paper. "Sorry, honey, nothing."

His expression became hard and intractable. "Are these guys the ones behind Phil M. Phlam?"

"Maybe, but Ryker's pretty sure each one is an alias. Ty? Would you feel comfortable...I mean would you feel it was a conflict of interest to...help me out on this?" He noted a tightness around her mouth. She was afraid and she needed him, but like the Hallie Leigh Bishop he'd always known, she was reluctant to ask for help, as if it were a sign of weakness.

He stroked her cheek softly, yet the expression on his face was fierce. "Someone hates you an awful lot to do this to you, Hallie. They might even hate you enough to try to physically hurt you." She shivered. The same thought had crossed her mind more than once. "You're mine now, Hallie," he said in a voice edged like the fine sword. "I learned the hard way how to hold on to what's mine and keep it safe. Like I told you, I don't know where you and I are headed completely. I did realize something during your conversation with Kelsey." His eyes glinted into hers hotly. "Come hell or high water, we're going together. If you're not completely comfortable with that, tough."

Tyler Nighthawk was made of strong stuff. If he wasn't, she wouldn't love him so Godawful much. Suddenly the world opened up again with unexpected promise. He felt more for her than she ever dared hope. She didn't dare think in terms of love, but he was decidedly more than fond of her. In all honesty, she'd made her decision about him the night he'd kissed her against the Jeep. She was Tyler's, now and until he didn't want her around anymore. Probably longer. "Okay, cowboy," she said in a husky whisper, "enough with the sweet talk. Let's go get some-

thing to eat." They wrapped arms tightly around each
other and headed for the main house.

※※ ※※

The next few days passed in a glorious haze for Hallie. Ty
continued to oversee the workings of the Bishop Company
from the comfort of the ranch, spending his evenings and
nights with Hallie at the bunkhouse. She took her meals
with the family, and after the first day of evasions and stumbling over excuses, Ty made no secret of where and with
whom he was during the warm nights of early summer.
The guilt Hallie felt over everyone knowing she was sleeping with him was quickly put to rest by Marlene. She
assured her stepdaughter no matter how quiet and circum-
spect Ty was, they'd all guessed long ago how he felt about
her, even before Tyler himself knew. Marlene assured her
that while the arrangement was unconventional by Bishop
standards, her father would have definitely been pleased
by the affection between them. Hallie thought it was more
likely her father would have accused her of leading Ty
astray, but kept the observation to herself.

The evenings fell into a comfortable pattern, with Hallie
putting in two or three hours of work on her music, while
Ty worked on his laptop or quietly read. He listened while
she worked, occasionally complimenting the pieces he
liked, even criticizing the ones he didn't. Sometimes he
would request her to play jazz pieces on the piano. Often
they would knock around theories concerning the embezzlement from the company, but neither of them could
come up with any satisfactory culprits.

The nights were filled with passion as they continued to
learn each other's body and responses. Ty grew to know
the pleasure of holding a warm, loving woman as both of
them slept, and the aching joy of finding her still in his
arms at morning's first light.

Kelsey had informed her of all the goings on in the islands as soon as she was back in LA. Hallie was surprised to find her respect for Jake Ryker changed to full-blown admiration. She'd learned to her chagrin many times, never to let the man know she appreciated him on any level. It just made him mean. Instead, she told Kelsey to let the scumbag know she felt he'd completely bilked her out of thousands of dollars. She could hear Ryker laughing in the background as Kelsey repeated her comment to him. Evidently, their one night stand had blossomed into a full-blown love affair and Kelsey seemed to be in seventh heaven about it too. Hallie still worried about her friend, but wisely kept her comments to herself. Kelse had been right—it was absolutely none of her business.

As for Hallie's life, in spite of the shadow from the embezzlement scam, she was happier than she could have ever imagined. Who would have thought that the girlhood infatuation she'd held for Tyler Nighthawk would ever have bloomed to the deep, soul-stirring love she felt for him now. Certainly not she or Tyler. She had to fight the impulse to jump to her feet and run into his arms every time he walked into a room where they were alone. When he arrived at the bunkhouse, she fought to keep from leading him into the bedroom. More often than not, she failed in her attempts at self-restraint. And when she didn't, Tyler did.

Randy was due to arrive for a visit sometime on Saturday, so Hallie spent much of Friday restocking her kitchen with his favorite foods and cleaning. She wanted everything to go as smoothly as possible. Though it had never mattered before, it was now terribly important to her that Randy like Tyler and the rest of her family. She spent most of Saturday morning trying to placate Genna with limited success. Twelve days into summer vacation, her sister was positive that she was the most bored, unappreciated teenager in America. She was only moderately pacified with Hallie's assertions that she would get to meet Randy as soon as he arrived.

Mid-afternoon found her coming down the stairs from Genna's room to spot Tyler leaving the library. He saw her at the same time and joined her at the foot of the stairs. There was a careworn expression in his emerald eyes that made them look old and tired. Hallie felt a sharp stab of concern for the man she loved. This whole situation with the company money was eating him up. He was afraid for her, the future of the company, and wondering what direction the next assault would come from.

"Steve Shaunessy just called. He's finished checking out those three names for us. Nothing," he said tiredly, "not a single damned thing." His green eyes searched her face, as if to apologize for failing her.

"Randy and Cassie couldn't come up with anything either. Thanks for trying," she answered, and placed a reassuring hand on his arm. "Thank your buddy, the gumshoe, for me too next time you talk to him." Hallie furrowed her brow in mock anger. "By rights I should skin you alive for siccing a private detective on me."

"Hallie," Ty said, grinning unrepentantly, "I pulled Steve off any further digging as far as your private life is concerned long ago. Frankly, Duchess, your real life is pretty boring."

Hallie stuck out her tongue, then replied sweetly, "Told you so. You just wanted to believe my press."

"So when's Randy getting here?" A note of apprehension crept into his words. Hallie had spoken with her friend earlier in the week. Raveneau had been less than pleased, she'd informed Ty, that she'd formed any sort of alliance with him, much less a physical one. Ty wasn't sure if Randy would greet him as a potenial friend as Chuck E. had done, or punch his lights out, as he probably deserved. Whatever scenario unfolded, Ty was determined to win her friend over, and when the opportunity presented itself, Cassie Donovan as well.

"Relax, will you? I already told Randy 'no fights.'" She added with a devilish twinkle in her eye, "Did I happen to mention he's a black belt?" Ty groaned and she took pity on him. "Don't worry. I already told you he's going to love you once he gets to know you." She reached up and kissed him lightly on the cheek, then took his hand to pull him to the front door. "We've got to hurry. I want to make sure everything is all in place."

"Everything in place?" Ty laughed. "As far as I can tell, nothing in your place ever has a chance to get out of place, you clean freak!" All his teasing got him was a sharp jab in the ribs before she whirled out the door.

Chapter 20

Ty caught up to Hallie on the verandah, where she stood watching a red imported convertible honk wildly on its way up the drive to the main house. As it came to a stop behind Marlene's Mercedes, Hallie let out a war whoop and launched herself down the steps. Across the yard, a tall, lean man emerged from the driver's door to stretch and run his fingers through his shaggy blond hair. He spotted Hallie immediately and held his arms open to her as she raced across the ground to him. He caught her in mid-leap and twirled her around a few times before finally settling her at his waist. She instantly wrapped her legs around him, and he began to dance around the lawn with her. Genna, Marlene and Mrs. H. arrived on the scene, drawn by the honking and Hallie's wild shrieks.

Ty watched the horseplay in the front yard with a mixture of resentment and envy. He thought about all the opportunities he'd missed through the years when, perhaps, he could have been the one dancing with her across the grass. Life had taken them in such completely different directions. If he'd known her then as he knew her now, he'd have kissed her backstage in Chicago, taken her back to his motel room, then brought her home and married her and kept her safe forever.

The idea jolted him. Married to Hallie. He'd never thought in terms of having any sort of permanent relationship with her, or anyone else for that matter, since Monica. Not until he'd become so accustomed to his peaceful evenings with Hallie. Not until he'd begun to feel incomplete without her nearby. Not until he'd seen her folded up in the arms of another man. He felt threatened by the arrival of this friend, whose opinion she valued so much.

There was a tightness in his chest, and he didn't realize he'd been holding his breath until Mrs. Hudson nudged him, chuckling at their antics. Raveneau stopped at the bottom of the steps and put Hallie down. She was giggling like a schoolgirl, and it was all Ty could do not to reach out and shake the stuffing out of her. The two miscreants walked up the steps arm-in-arm to join the group.

"Everybody," she said, trying to catch her breath, "this is Randy. Randy, this is everybody, well almost. This is Mrs. Hudson, my stepmom Marlene, my sister Genna, and Tyler Nighthawk."

Ty heard the way her voice softened as she said his name and was instantly mollified. Randy hadn't missed the change in her tone either. He relaxed his watchful eyes and extended his hand to each of them in turn, thoroughly charming all the ladies with his easygoing manner and devastating smile. "Heard a lot about you, man," he said to Tyler with a twinkle in his eye. "That's funny, Hal, I don't see any horns or a tail." Hallie slugged him none too gently in the shoulder. Randy gave her a look of mock indignation. "Hey, I'm only repeating what you told me!" He turned back to Ty, "It's nice to meet you, really. I'm just razzing the kid, that's all. The redhead told me to scope you out and report in detail," he admitted amiably.

"The redhead?" Ty inquired with a slightly puzzled expression.

"Yeah, Donovan, who else? And let me tell you, man," Randy continued in a confiding tone, "you don't mess with the redhead."

Ty was amazed. In a couple of minutes, with no real conversation on his part, he'd been sized up, judged and accepted. He wondered why until he looked down into Hallie's face and saw the joy radiating from her eyes. Randy had seen it too and correctly assumed Ty was responsible for a good portion of it. He gazed at her, feeling a mixture of happiness and concern. How alone had she been in the midst of all her friends, he reflected, that one of them could instantly see she was happier than they'd ever seen her before? Hallie blushed softly. Her smile was almost shy as her eyes darted quickly between him and Randy. Ty stepped close to her and encircled her waist with his arm and dropped a light kiss on her temple. "Come on, honey," he said, "let's help Randy with his stuff." She nodded.

"Well, as I live and breathe," Randy said, a look of unabashed glee on his face, "Cass is never gonna believe this one. Gal Hal Bishop in love. Head over heels by the look of it too." He quickly moved aside as, predictably, his friend turned to slug him in the shoulder.

Later, as Ty stood quietly with Hallie on her porch and Randy settled into the spare room, he pursued the subject closest to his heart, her. He took an uneasy breath and said, "You know I'll do anything you want to make up for acting like such a complete ass to you, don't you?"

She was staring off into the distance at the mountains, looking thoroughly preoccupied, but there was no mistaking the mischief in her tone. "Anything, Tyler?"

"Yeah, anything," he answered, with a note of wariness creeping into his voice.

She fixed him with a hard stare. "Then get down on the floor and act like a duck."

He met the challenge in her eyes that told him clearly she didn't believe he had the gumption to play the fool for her. Then he bent his knees, squatted and started quacking. Hallie gaped at him. She'd never seriously considered he'd do it. She reached her hand down to draw him back up to her, eyes misty with emotion. He grinned at her and shook his head, perplexed by the tender affection he saw in her beautiful features. The strangest things touched this woman, and he silently vowed if he had to spend the next hundred years imitating barnyard animals, he would, as long as she kept looking at him just like that.

"I love you, Tyler Nighthawk," she said quietly, the evidence of her words clearly marked in her eyes.

He felt awed and humbled by what she'd just confessed. There was a boulder lodged in his throat, and he was afraid if he tried to speak, his voice might crack. So instead he grabbed her and hung on for all he was worth, and for the first time in his life, knew what it was like to be truly loved by a woman.

They were still standing like that when Randy came out. "Hey, Hal," he said seriously, "are you keeping ducks around here?" They both laughed.

༈

Hallie tidied the kitchen in the aftermath of two hungry men prowling for food while Ty and Randy sat hunched over Randy's laptop. Most of Hallie's larger and more complicated investments had been suggested by Randy. He had a knack for financial matters and was now showing Ty his latest stock acquisitions. Both men were babbling back and forth happily in some jargon Hallie had no hope of understanding. They looked up at the sound of her amused chuckle, and Hallie felt her heart turn over. The two most important men in her life were together in her home, enjoying each other's company, happier than pigs in mud. The bunkhouse finally felt like home.

Suddenly, the sound of spraying gravel brought her attention to the driveway out front. Walt had stopped his dark blue sedan on his way toward the main house and he seemed to be staring intently at the bunkhouse. Hallie had the eerie feeling that he could see her through the walls, watch her as she moved about the kitchen. The car moved on up the drive but Hallie could still feel his eyes on her. She shivered.

≈≋ ≋≈

Most of the family was gathered in the livingroom when Randy and Hallie arrived for dinner. Mrs. H, blushing like a girl, ushered them in. Randy was flirting outrageously with the older woman, but that was one of the things he did best. Hallie gave him a silent, murderous look meant to remind him he was supposed to be on his best behavior, and unlike Mrs. Verdoza, he didn't know Edna Hudson well enough to swat her one on the fanny. Ty grinned easily at them and came forward quickly to kiss Hallie's cheek and slide a possessive arm around her waist.

He caught the flash of cold eyes from across the room. Walt stood near the mantle with an expression of poorly concealed fury on his face. Walt had returned from Portland this afternoon, and he'd been in a piss poor mood all evening. He'd fought bitterly with Tyler regarding Hallie, insisting the family prosecute her. Walt threatened to call a meeting of the board and accuse Tyler of complicity. He'd gotten crude about the younger man's relationship with her and Ty had been close to exploding. Marlene had jumped between them and told her brother coldly that if he didn't believe Hallie was working in all their best interests, that was one thing, but she refused to allow him to say such disgusting things about her in her own home. If it didn't stop instantly, she'd expect him to leave. Walt was completely taken aback, and Ty had never been prouder of Marlene.

Walt raised his glass in a mocking salute and appeared to be on the point of saying something distasteful, when Ty asked Hallie and Randy what he could get them from the bar. He shot Walt a sharp, warning glare as he left Hallie's side to retrieve their requests. If Walt had had any intention of congratulating Ty on his conquest, the look of menace on the younger man's face served to dry up the words in his mouth. Ty wouldn't allow anyone or anything to distress Hallie or threaten their relationship. Not ever, not after she'd told him she loved him.

Hallie introduced Randy to Walt, then glanced around the room, noting Marlene was absent. "Where's Marlene," she asked, directing her question to no one in particular. Walt seized the opening with an almost malicious glee.

"I'm sure," he drawled in an acidic tone, "she's somewhere fortifying herself for the evening ahead." The cool look he gave Randy left no doubt as to what, or more correctly, whom, Walt felt they all needed fortifying against.

Hallie knew her friend well enough to be certain he wouldn't rise to the bait, but she was furious at Walt's blatant rudeness. She decided to temper her reaction for the family's sake. His actions lately left her completely puzzled and extremely irritated. He'd been treating her like a leper since her confession to Marlene about the deposits. She supposed she could understand his anger. Hadn't Ty been furious enough to think about doing her bodily harm? Walt was closer to open hostility with her than she could ever remember seeing him before. As he regarded her now, over the contents of his glass, she felt herself grow increasingly nervous and fought the impulse to glance down and make sure she still had her clothes on. Lately he'd been giving her these long, heavy-lidded looks that were beginning to make her skin crawl. His eyes spoke of a far deeper relationship, a relationship that had never existed between them. She watched with blatant relief as Ty crossed the room to hand Randy and her their drinks.

The dinner conversation was animated and amusing. Randy had been prepared to dislike Hal's family, and even do battle on her behalf if necessary. He glanced around the table, deeply searching the faces gathered there. Although Walt spent his time studying the liquor in his glass, the others watched Hal with obvious affection and respect. Randy put his doubts to rest. These people were willing to give Hal the chance her father had never given her during his life—the chance to be accepted for who and what she was and to be loved because of it, not in spite of it.

Hallie watched Randy turn the full force of his considerable charm on her sister and stepmother. The results were predictable. Genna gazed at him with absolute devotion, and Marlene alternated between blushes and a startling ability to flirt that Hallie hadn't known the woman possessed. Walt, on the other hand, tossed down more liquor than Hallie'd ever seen him do before, and she half-expected him to slosh when he walked away from the table. He was also getting more sullen and belligerent with each swallow. Randy kept the conversation light and flowing by regaling everyone with war stories from his long years with Hallie and the rest of the band. Everyone, with the exception of Walt, asked interested questions. He sat back looking bored and moody, finally leaving the table in a huff, to everyone's relief.

As the evening progressed, a lot of the gaps in Hallie's history were filled in by Randy. They were all shocked to learn that Hallie had met Sye Greenway while panhandling on a Chicago street with her guitar. She was broke, living on the streets, and hadn't eaten for days. It killed Ty to think of Hallie cold, hungry and alone. It was a miracle she hadn't just disappeared, been murdered, as had so many other young girls in similar situations. He and Marlene both drew sighs of relief when they learned Greenway and his life-partner Toddy Benedict had taken Hallie in that very day as a surrogate daughter. She'd lived with them for the next several months.

He went on to tell of the fiery meeting later that afternoon of him, Cassie, and Hallie. Considering the obvious closeness they'd all developed over the years, Ty was stunned to find out it had been mutual dislike and distrust at first sight. In fact, many weeks passed before the first bonds of friendship formed. Hallie and Randy alternated the narrative, laughing and joking about circumstances which, if presented in a less humorous way, would have drawn shudders and gasps from the audience. But their laughter was contagious, inviting everyone to join in.

After dinner Ty captured Hallie's hand and quickly raised her to her feet. He ignored her bewildered expression as he drew her with him from the room, leaving Marlene and Genna to entertain Randy. Ty slipped his arm around her shoulders and they crossed the yard toward the stables. She beamed happily at him and squeezed him gently at the waist. "I think dinner went surprisingly well," he began, "as soon as Walt left, that is."

"What the heck is the matter with that guy anyway?" Hallie asked. "I know he's furious about the missing funds, but lately he's either been looking at me like I don't have any clothes on, or I just slithered out from under a rock. I'm used to that from you, but Uncle Walt, for God's sake!"

Ty came to an abrupt halt and turned Hallie to him. "Has he tried anything with you, honey?" he said intently. "I swear if he so much as touches you..." There was a fierce light in his eyes that Hallie was very familiar with. Usually, it was directed at her not for her.

"Of course not. Why would he? I mean, so okay, he's not happy about our relationship, but face it, he's always been the kindest of everyone in the family. Even though I wasn't really his niece, he always treated me like I was."

"Hallie," Ty said gently, "I know for a fact that Walt

wasn't any happier about you coming home to live than I
was at the time." Even in the darkness he could sense her
discomfort and withdrawal from him at his words. He hurried on. "That's in the past, at least for me, sweetheart. I'm
very, very happy you came back into my life. I also know
for a fact that Walt hasn't thought of you as a niece in years,
if he ever really did." Ty frowned as he turned his last
thought over in his mind.

Hallie remained silent, remembering Walt's unnerving
embrace the night of her father's funeral and his offer to
come and sit with her at the hotel if she decided she needed him. Had he been being more than kind? Had he
hoped to get her alone somewhere in her pain and vulnerability and talk her into bed? And there were all those
unnerving looks lately too. After all was said and done, did
it come down to him desiring her and figuring she was an
easy lay? Hadn't Tyler? No, she reprimanded herself curtly, Ty was different now. He cared about her. He wanted
far more than a few quick romps in the sheets. His voice
broke in on her thoughts.

"I didn't bring you out here to discuss ancient history,
Hallie. I want you to be aware of Walt's interest, that's all.
And I want you to tell me if he ever steps over the line."
She nodded silently. "Good. Now, we have a lot more
important things to talk about," he murmured softly. "I've
been wanting to talk to you ever since your confession to
me this afternoon."

Hallie steeled herself against the gentle rebuff she
feared was coming. Something along the lines of, Gee,
honey, you know I never made you any promises. Or,
look, anyone can get a little carried away and say things
they don't mean in the heat of the moment. She'd promised herself that no matter what he said, she'd stand behind
her profession of love. But standing there waiting for the

ax to fall only made her want to escape.

"I didn't have a chance to respond properly when you told me you were in love with me," he stated in a gentle, quiet tone. Her heart skipped a hopeful beat. "I love you too, Hallie Leigh Bishop. Now and forever." He drew her into his arms and bent his mouth to claim hers in a deep, sensual kiss. He broke the contact and distanced her slightly from him. "Honey, I'm so sorry for all the cheap shots I've taken at you over the years. If I could go back in time, I'd have brought you back from Chicago that night. Back to me. I swear, if it takes forever, I'll make all those years up to you."

"Ty, hush," she whispered in a half-sob, throwing her arms around his neck. "It doesn't matter. We love each other. That's all that counts." She kissed his mouth, cheeks and throat in rapid succession. "Make love to me, *mi amor*. Make love to me now, please!" The urgency in her voice brought a moan from the man in her arms.

"Haybarn," he rasped. They were the only words he was capable of uttering as he grabbed Hallie's arm and pulled her along after him on his speed walk to the barn. She practically had to run to keep up. He stopped a little way from the barn, then quietly proceeded to open the side door, drawing her inside with him.

Within seconds he had her backed up against a rough wooden wall. Neither of them was in the mood for preliminaries. Hallie brought her silky leg up to his thigh and slowly rubbed it up and down the length of him. Ty's breath caught in his throat, and he mentally blessed Hallie's foresight in wearing a long skirt tonight. The satiny skin of her inner thigh seared his hip through his pants. He kissed her forcefully, pressing her even harder to the wall. He heard the small noise she made in her throat as he slid his hand under the gauzy material of her skirt to caress her mound. Her panties were already damp with need for him. He pushed the crotch of them aside and glided his fingers through her moist warm folds. He tested her readiness with his thumb and with an intense, possessive pleasure, heard her deep gasp.

Ty quickly undid the front of his pants and freed his hardened, pulsing shaft as rapidly as his trembling hand would permit. Neither of them made any attempt to remove a single article of clothing. There would be time for that a little later. Meanwhile, the hunger was too deep, too urgent to deny. He pressed the head of his engorged phallus around the crotch of her underwear, to her delicate grotto, gaining admittance with one deep thrust. Hallie moaned in pleasure as Ty cupped her bottom in his hands, while she brought up her other leg to encircle his waist. With two swift jerks he tore the lacy fabric of her underwear from her hips and discarded it in the hay behind him. Then he wrenched open her blouse and released her round, firm breasts from the confines of her bra. He seized first one nipple with his hot mouth, then the other, sucking strong and hard. Again and again he thrust into her, keeping her easily suspended between his arms and the support of the wall.

She wrapped her arms around his neck, powerless to do anything but receive him. And she did so willingly, over and over. *"Te amor, mi vida, mi cielo,"* Hallie cried out as she felt the tightening deep within her that signaled the approach of her fulfillment, Ty's breath came in ragged pants and he thrust harder and faster against her. Their cries, signaling mutual release, tore from their throats in one brief passion-filled song. Another hour would pass before the lovers could say their reluctant goodnights.

Chapter 21

Hallie sat on the floor of her living room, armed with a gigantic mug of black coffee, a yellow legal pad, an assortment of different colored pens and an impressive stack of cassette tapes. Clancy's latest shipment of young musical hopefuls had arrived a couple of days ago, but Hallie's mindset at the time hardly made her receptive to talent scouting.

Thankfully, by the time the tapes reached her, they'd already passed a two-level screening process. Of the twenty or so tapes she'd received, maybe one or two would contain that certain something she was looking for. Maybe none would. Randy strolled in from the kitchen and hunkered down beside her.

He took a sip of coffee from his own generous mug and inclined his head toward the stereo system in front of them. "Are we ready to go here?" he asked. Hallie nodded and pressed the play button. The first few tapes produced nothing unusual. The groups were talented, but there was nothing particularly unique in their sound, style, or approach. Hallie had a penchant for risk takers and a good ear for what would work. So far, all the groups were playing it very safe, cloning the styles of their favorite, most successful bands. Nothing was exciting her. As tape number seven started to play, Randy sighed, and she resigned herself to another dreary batch of polite notes saying thanks but no thanks. Tape number eight began and suddenly the two of them were sitting bolt upright. Hallie and Randy looked at each other, eyes widening, smiles growing. Here was what she'd been waiting and hoping for. They began talking excitedly, and Hallie grabbed the pad and pen to make hurried notations. On her signal, Randy rewound the tape, and she set to work analyzing the music. Her notes were color-coded as to instrument and particular bars of music played. She was still scribbling madly as Randy got up to answer the telephone.

She heard him greet Genna with enthusiasm and began to smile as she heard Randy's part of the conversation with her sister. "Yeah, babe, I understand. I'm sure it does sound like a totally bogus deal to you, but I've got to give your mom a big ten-four on this one. Hal would agree too. A NC-17 movie is not the best choice for your movie rental buck." He winked as Hallie began nodding rapidly at him. He chuckled at Genna's reaction to what he'd said. "Now come on, Gen, Hitchcock's films are classics. I love 'em. So does your sister. *The Birds* and *Rear Window*? Great! I'll tell you what, why don't we pop the old kernels and make a night of it?"

Hallie was so happy her family had warmed to Randy so quickly. Not only had she gained a sister since she'd come home, but Genna had gained another big brother. She remembered many an evening at her place or Randy's where the two of them had munched snacks contentedly while Randy had fantasized about Grace Kelly, Tippi Hedren—and who was the other cool blonde? She was in that one with Cary Grant—Eva Marie Saint. He'd played the ad guy who— She stopped cold, the color draining from her face. What was the name of that picture? Randy hung up the phone and his insistent voice called her back to the present.

"Hal? Are you okay?" She shook her head in vigorous denial. Randy got more concerned. She'd had a zoned-out look in eyes when he'd turned back to her. Her face was pale and she was deathly silent.

"Cary Grant, Eva Marie Saint. What's the picture?" she asked in a rush.

Randy thought for a moment and said, "*North By Northwest*—why?" But even as he asked, the light was beginning to dawn. "Holy shit!"

"I'm calling Ty!" Hallie dashed to the phone. There was no answer on Ty's private line and the main line to the house was busy. She suspected her sister to be the person ignoring the beep from Call Waiting. She swore and dug in the desk drawer for Ryker's number. He answered quickly, barking his name as usual into the receiver.

"Ryker, it's Hal. I know who Roger Thornhill is." She rushed on, giving him no time to respond. "He's Cary Grant."

There was silence on the line, then he asked with biting cold, "You're trying to tell me that Cary Grant is stealing your family's money from beyond the grave? You are a complete freak show, Bishop, you know that?" He swore. "I don't suppose Randy's there to tell me something that remotely makes sense?"

"Just shut up for a minute and listen to me. Roger Thornhill, Lester Townsend, and George Kaplan are all characters in Alfred Hitchcock's movie, *North By Northwest*. I should have figured it out sooner. I knew the names sounded familiar, but until Randy and Genna— that's my sister—started talking about Hitchcock's movies and I remembered Randy's thing about Grace Kelly and—"

"Jesus Christ, Bishop," he roared, "will you shut the hell up! Forget the extra details! I hate it when you do that shit!"

Hallie said nothing more until he'd calmed down. "Ryker, it's not as extraneous as it sounds, please," she said, hating to have to use the word in connection with him. "Roger Thornhill was Cary Grant's character. He was an ad man whose identity is mistaken for this guy George Kaplan." So far he wasn't shouting her down and Randy was giving her a thumbs up from the sidelines. "Soviet spies are after this guy, Kaplan."

"Who's Townsend?" he asked shortly.

"A United Nations representative whose identity is taken by James Mason's character—he's the master spy."

"So the whole movie is about mistaken identity," he said thoughtfully. It wasn't a question.

"Right, but the twist is that there is no George Kaplan. He's a red herring made up by the CIA to throw the Soviets. Far-fetched I know."

"Actually Bishop, it's one of the least far-fetched things you've ever told me. Believe me, I should know." She briefly contemplated the nature of his work. He was right; if anyone should know, it would be him. "That son-of-a-bitch," he continued softly. "He's playing games, laughing at us, twisting the knife with his puns and letting us know we're way off. What's the name of the movie again?"

"*North By Northwest*."

"Shit! The asshole's telling us we're looking in the wrong place. Good work, Hal," he said with grudging respect.

She took a deep breath and rolled her eyes at Randy, as if to say, well here goes. "Seeing as you're feeling a little more kindly toward me, I think I'd better give you some other news. I told Tyler Nighthawk about the investigation."

The explosion was large and immediate. "You dumb bitch. Some guy makes you come a few times and suddenly he's your fucking white knight. And they say only men think between their legs. He gives you a few good pokes in your—"

"Don't you dare, just shut your ugly mouth right there, Ryker!" she shouted. "You don't give a shit for my opinion, but obviously you do care about Kelsey's and Randy's.

Both of them agree with me. He's busted his ass for months trying to solve the thefts and if there's one person I know to a certainty is innocent, it's him."

He was surprisingly silent at first. He was only pausing for effect. "Well now, Hal," he began in a quiet, nasty tone, "let's think about this. Whoever is behind all this knows you pretty well or else why would they use the allusions to Hitchcock. They wanted you to figure it out. The person who would know that best would be Randy."

"What! That's crazy and you know it!"

"I do because I checked him out. He's clean."

"You're sick...you know he'd never do something like that!"

"Like I said, I do now. My point here, Angel Face, is this: Randy, for whatever dumb reason, loves you and I checked him out anyway. Now Nighthawk, well Nighthawk's never been real fond of you, has he? Especially after the night of his engagement party." Hallie gasped and Randy frowned at her stricken look. Ryker chuckled over the phone. "What does he want out of you? What are you worth to him, really? Control of the company? A little sweet revenge? Just a small brainteaser for you to work out next time you're in the sack with him. You just snuggle up with that thought." The line went dead.

༺ ༻

Hallie put the last of the rejected tapes back in the shipping box. The one tape she was excited about was carefully set aside with her sheets of notes. She'd contact Clancy first thing Monday to make sure contracts went out to the agent as soon as possible. She tried to remove Ryker's ugly comments and suspicions from her mind, but it was easier said than done. Randy managed to calm her fears somewhat by reminding her that Ryker's vicious words had been simply his way of punishing her for disobeying him. The urge to tell Tyler about the Hitchcock movie and Ryker's call, however, became too strong to ignore. More than anything, she needed Ty to kiss away her fears and insecurities and make her laugh at her own foolish imaginings.

Hallie headed toward the main house, walking a little more slowly as she approached the haybarn. She smiled softly at the memory of the unrestrained passion she'd shared with Tyler last night. The doubledoor of the barn was latched tight, but the small side door stood slightly ajar. Had they forgotten to close it all the way when they'd left? Perhaps Ty had returned to the scene, inexplicably drawn as she, herself was. Hallie quickly slipped inside. Her eyes adjusted slowly to the dim interior and a lazy half-smile played across her face as she saw the notorious bale of hay from last night.

"Looking for someone?" said a cold voice from behind her. She whirled around to find Walt glaring at her, disgust and contempt distorting his normally handsome face. "Will I do as a stand-in? Has sex in the hay barn become a new pastime around here or something?" The menace coming from him made her hastily retreat a step. "What's the matter, Hallie?" he asked in a disparaging tone, "You seemed more than willing to give Tyler what he wanted last night. It was quite inspiring really. Don't I deserve the same consideration? After all, I've wanted you more, waited for you longer than he did." His voice had picked up an ugly quality that made fear, sharp and bitter, rise in her throat. She'd heard that tone before from another man years earlier. Walt wasn't about to take no for an answer. Hallie tried to maneuver away from him, and at the same time not get trapped with her back to the wall. He continued to advance on her, apparently finding her efforts amusing. "You look just like her you know—your mother, that is—same hair and eyes, same face." He paused and smirked as he let his gaze wander over her in an insulting and demeaning fashion. "And apparently her same appetites."

"Leave my mother out of this, Walt," she hissed, "and get the hell out of my way. What gave you the right to spy on us anyway, you pervert? My relationship with Ty isn't any of your business."

He stopped his advance and gave full vent to his amusement. "But that's precisely what it is, Hallie Leigh—business." He gave her that condescending shake of his head he'd used on her countless times growing up. It had made her feel unimportant and not overly bright then—now it just made her furious. "Company business to be exact," Walt continued, oblivious to the warning flare of anger in Hallie's eyes. "Before you moved home, Tyler and I had many lengthy conversations on how to best ensure your 'compliance,' shall we say. He was sure if he got involved with you romantically, you'd fall right into line. Evidently, he was right."

Hallie's eyes drilled into his with golden fury. "You're lying. Tyler wouldn't use somebody like that. He wouldn't use me." Even as she said the words, she remembered Ryker's comments and felt an ugly doubt wrap itself around her heart once more. Ty's harsh statement returned to haunt her as well. *I'm not expecting you to like me anymore than I like you. It's not required.*

"Oh, I'm afraid that's just the sort of thing Tyler would do, Hallie Leigh," Walt said, his voice and manner becoming calmer and more persuasive by the second. "He hates you quite a lot, you know, for wrecking his future with Monica. He hardly ever went to see his mother before she died. Because of some whim, you took everything he ever cared about away from him that night. I'm afraid, my dear, he'd do a lot more than merely use your body if he got the chance." Her mind was reeling from the shock of Walt's words. Hadn't exacting revenge been exactly what she'd suspected Ty had been up to the whole time? "He'd lie, make promises—hell, he'd even tell you he loved you if he needed to." Walt's eyes took on the saddened, wise-old-man-look he habitually used to show his sympathy for her.

"And just what does he want out of me, Walt?" she snapped, wanting to claw his eyes out.

"Why, complete control of the Bishop Company. What else?" He began walking toward her again, the lust barely contained in his gleaming eyes. "Not like me, Hallie. I just want you."

She felt nausea coil throughout her stomach and fought to keep from retreating into the corner. "Walt," she began, with more calm than she felt, "I know you've always been fond of me. You've been nothing but kind to me over the years, but I've always thought of you along the lines of my uncle. You know that." She struggled in vain to keep the tremors out of her voice. "I'm sorry, Walt, but it's nothing like what I feel for Ty."

He snorted contemptuously. "Do you really expect me to take this little affair of yours with the half-breed serious-ly? You're a woman of strong passions, my love. You need a firm hand to govern them, guide them." He was close enough to reach out and touch her. Hallie was afraid if he did, she'd vomit. "With the proper influences, you could be every bit the woman your mother was." He stepped closer yet, and inclined his head to slant a kiss across her mouth. Hallie dropped back from him, her reac-tion short and sweet in the form of a right hook. Walt groaned from the impact and staggered back to regain his equilibrium.

"I told you, you son-of-a-bitch," Hallie snarled, "not to

bring my mother into this. Now you get the hell out of my way. And don't you ever dare touch me again."

Walt rubbed his injured jaw and regarded her malevolently. "That was a very big mistake, my dear. Very big. I'm afraid it's time to explain a few vital facts to you." He lunged at her and caught her upper arms in a vice-like grip. "You belong with me, Hallie. I'm the one who waited all these years for you to grow up. You were so desperate for love and approval, I could have taken you at seventeen if I'd wanted. I waited, though. I knew, sooner or later, we'd be together." His breath was coming in husky whispers. "All these years, I've dreamed of you coming home to me. I believed in you. I cared about you, Elena. He didn't."

"No, Walt," she said, not noticing his use of her mother's name. She tried to keep the pity out of her voice. "I've never thought of you in those terms. I never could. I appreciate all the care and support you've given me over the years, but..."

"You still don't understand, do you?" he said in a soft, yet chilling tone. He brought his mouth crashing down on hers. His kiss hurt and sickened her, and she prepared for the necessity of having to fight him tooth and nail. Walt was a good deal stronger than she, though, so she forced herself to remain calm and stop struggling. In order to escape him, she would have to choose her moment carefully. He took her sudden stillness for acquiescence and tried to open her lips with his tongue. Disgust roiled throughout her as she willed her lips apart and yielded to the frenzied jabs of his tongue. In an effort to make him drop his guard, she sighed softly. Walt responded immediately with a groan from low in his throat. "I knew you'd see reason," he whispered against her mouth thickly. "You want this just as much as I do."

"Yes, oh yes, please, Walt," she breathed back in fake

response. She brushed her knee on the outside of his thigh, triggering the actions she'd been waiting for. He eased the death grip on her arms. With one hand, he painfully squeezed her breast, as he used his other one to secure her to him by the waist. She held back a wince. "I can't wait much longer," she murmured. *Till I knock you on your ass.*

Walt chuckled smugly and said, "Soon, Hallie Leigh, very soon. But," he continued in a chilling whisper, " I think perhaps I might have to punish you a little for your stubbornness. Yes," he added almost to himself, "I think a little discipline is just what's needed here."

Hallie felt the hair rise up on the back of her neck and didn't waste another minute in seizing her opportunity. She brought her knee up fast and sharp into his groin. He went down. While he rolled on the floor of the barn in agony, Hallie raced to the door. She turned and regarded the man who still lay holding his crotch. Her face was full of loathing and disgust. She would shower and brush her teeth the second she got back to her place. "Listen, Uncle Walt. If you ever so much as think about touching me again, even to shake my hand, I'll cut off your balls and use them for castanets. Got it?" She didn't wait around for a response.

Ty was on his way to the bunkhouse when he saw Hallie running from the direction of the barn as if Satan himself was hot on her heels. He set out on a course to intercept her. "Hallie, wait!" he called. She stopped and he saw the fear, pain and anger in her face. *What in the hell was going on now?* "Hallie, what is it? What's got you so upset?" The abject misery in her face deepened at his questions. "Talk to me, sweetheart."

"Why did you tell me you were in love with me? You didn't have to, you know," she said stiffly. "I still would have signed over my vote. Hell, I'd do just about anything you asked. I love you, remember? Was I right in the beginning? Was it all just about getting even?" He could tell she had a lump in her throat, because he saw the difficulty she was having in swallowing.

"Walt's been talking to you," he stated, not needing an answer.

She gave a shrill laugh, "Oh yeah, he was talking to me, among other things. He told me all about your little plan to get me in bed. Guess it worked better than you figured." She shook her head and studied him with something akin to wonder in her expression. "So answer me, Ty. Why bother to tell me you love me when you already had everything you wanted?" Try as she might, she couldn't keep the pleading look out of her eyes.

He knew she was hurting, knew that somehow he had to reach her through her pain and get her to listen to him. "But I didn't have everything, Duchess," he said hoarsely. "I didn't have a damn thing because I didn't have you." The tears were pouring down her cheeks now. She made no move to staunch them. He couldn't remember ever seeing her cry like this and his heart ached to see it now. "You're everything to me, Hallie Leigh, everything." Cautiously, he moved closer. He couldn't afford to frighten her away at this point. If she ran from him now, she might never stop and he would lose her forever, as well as his soul. She stayed where she was, her shoulders heaving from her sobs. "I can't excuse how Walt and I planned to use you, Hallie. I think back on it and the thought sickens me. I sicken me. But please, sweetheart, please believe one thing. Believe I love you with all my heart." Hallie made a sound like a small, wounded animal. It broke his heart and he held out his arms to her. She ran into them.

Later, after carrying Hallie back to the bunkhouse and leaving her in Randy's care, Ty went to clean house. He caught sight of Walt leaving the barn and made a swift detour. The gingerly way the older man was walking reminded him of Hallie's comment. Ty knew what "among other things" meant. Relatively few things made a woman want to incapacitate a man the way Hallie evidently had incapacitated Walt, and that knowledge sent Ty into a fury. "Hi, Walt," he spit out with a plastic smile planted on his face. He was still smiling when his fist connected with Walt's jaw, and the other man was laid flat out in the dirt at his feet. Abruptly, the smile left Ty's face. He bent over and dragged Walt back up to his knees. "If you ever so much as look at Hallie the wrong way again, you'll get a damn sight worse. And," he said, punctuating the next promise by punching Walt in the eye and returning him to the dirt, " if you ever, ever touch her again, I'll kill you. Do you understand, Walt? I'll fucking kill you." Even in his dazed state, Walt recognized the cold, lethal certainty in Ty's face. He nodded weakly to the younger man, but when Ty's back was turned, his face took on a look of diabolical malevolence.

❧ ☙

Ty signaled the tall, blonde man who hurried into the library to join him at the desk. "Walt's left for his place in Portland. He won't be coming back for a long time, if ever," Ty said grimly. "How's Hallie doing?"

"Better than you might think. She's curled up with H.B., sipping tea and planning hideous vengeance on Ryker and Abrams."

Ty smiled softly, "That's my Duchess. Why Ryker, though?" he asked, aware of the edge that had come into his voice.

Randy related the story of this morning's telephone call,

the Hitchcock movie and the significance of the names. "Hal also told him that you knew everything now, and were helping out on the Portland end of the investigation." Ty grumbled an expletive and Randy nodded, confirming the other man's suspicions. "Yup, that's when it got ugly, Ty. Jake went for her jugular and made some very nasty inferences about you."

"And then Walt literally jumps her in the barn," Ty finished for him. "She got tag-teamed pretty good, didn't she? I'm sure you heard about what Walt told her." Randy's expression said it all. "Do you believe I set her up from the get go too?"

"Why don't you tell me your side of it and I'll judge for myself," the other man said evenly. Ty did just that, sparing nothing, from the night at Pepe's when he first realized he had to have Hallie, until today, when he'd defended her against Walt's advances. By the end of the conversation, he'd made a staunch ally. "The only thing I'm positive about in this whole deal," Randy said with an air of finality, "is that you're as crazy about Hal as she is about you. Anything I can do to help you, man, just ask."

"I'd be damned glad for your help, Randy." He permitted himself a weary smile. "Can I impose on you to stay another week or two here? Right now, the people I can trust are few and far between." Randy assured him it was no problem.

Now that the air had been cleared, Ty could redirect the conversation to the matters he needed Randy's assistance with. "Shall we get down to business now?" he began. "If we don't come up with some strategy today, everything Marlene, Genna and I have could be gone before we know it." He leaned forward to hand Randy several sheets of paper he'd recently printed out on the Desk Jet. "Ron Powell, the head of the auditing team, called me this afternoon. Someone's been wreaking some discreet havoc with the company's general ledger accounts. Ron says they might have missed it if whoever it is hadn't gotten a little careless last week." Randy accepted the sheets of paper and studied the highlighted dates and entries. "Once they saw the pattern," Ty continued, "it was simple to backtrack over the last two years. Our friend has been siphoning off corporate funds for some time now."

Randy flipped through the pages and gave a low whistle. "Any information on the disposition of the funds?" he asked.

Ty leaned back in his chair and exhaled a tense breath. "Yes and no. There's no connecting link to the numbered accounts yet, but it's got to be there somewhere. That's what I need you to help me with right now. I was going to have you act as go-between for Ryker and me, but I think under the circumstances, it's better if I settle things with him personally." Ty remained quiet for some time and Randy waited patiently. "I don't want Hallie involved in anything more, Randy," he said finally. "We all agree on one thing: Whoever's using her to cover their ass on the thefts has little love for her. This is bound to get dangerous. You know Hallie. She'll ride straight in with guns blazing, damn the consequences. The less she knows, the safer she'll be."

Randy nodded in agreement. He leaned toward the desk, resting his forearms on his knees. "She's not going to like being cut from the loop, I can tell you that. You know how she gets."

An involuntary image of Seeto Benton appeared in Ty's mind. Yes, he knew how she could be. "I'll handle Hallie," he replied, with far more confidence than he felt.

Chapter 22

The next few days were stormy at best. It took Hallie mere hours to determine that Ty and Randy had removed her from the "needs to know" list, permanently. As Randy had predicted, she wasn't happy about it either. She raged and threatened, but in the end only succeeded in alienating everyone at the ranch. Ty coldly refused to speak to her if she couldn't calm down and listen to reason. Randy ended up moving into a guest room in the main house and Marlene forbade her entrance to the house until she'd recovered her manners.

Ty and Randy camped in the library, toiling over reports with little success. When they emerged late one evening for a much needed break, things in the vicinity of the bunkhouse were considerably more quiet. Ty felt a stab of guilt. In his zeal to protect her, he hadn't stopped to consider how painful exclusion would be for her. Especially with the new and still fragile bonds she'd formed with her family and him. He wanted to kick himself for his own thoughtlessness.

When Hallie didn't answer her door, Ty let himself in. He found her in the living room, earphones firmly attached and papers strewn on the floor around her. God, how he'd missed her. Love coursed through him and he made the decision then and there to take steps to secure this woman to his side forever. Ty bent down and kissed the top of her head. Hallie jumped at the unexpected contact and spun around on the stool where she sat. Her face tensed as she saw him, but softened almost immediately by what she read in his face. She slipped the earphones from her head.

He drew her against him and pressed several gentle kisses on her upturned face. "I've missed you so much, sweetheart," he said tenderly. She returned his kiss warmly, making a soft, mewing sound of contentment. "Tell me, Hallie," he asked, scarcely managing to breathe, "do you want a summer or fall wedding?"

She stood up, watching him in absolutely silence. For one horrific moment Ty feared she would reject his proposal altogether. He knew it probably seemed spur-of-the-moment to her, but he loved her. He wanted a life with her, children—the whole nine yards. She closed her eyes and swayed against him. When she opened them, her answer was in their golden depths. "I'll have to get back to you on the date, Nighthawk," she whispered. "Gotta check with the bridesmaids, you know." She wrapped her arms around his neck and clung for dear life.

🖎 🖎

It was past ten the next morning before Ty woke up. The combined effects of little sleep over the last four days and a rewarding night in bed with Hallie had taken their toll on his energy. He'd slept the sleep of the dead, and now he sat up slowly, waiting for the grogginess to lift. Hallie'd long since risen, he noted with disappointment. In their short time together, he'd gotten used to the comfort of finding her warm, naked body curled against his. Waking her up was always a delight. The aroma of coffee brewing and breakfast cooking cleared his head completely and brought him out of bed like a shot. He was famished. He pulled on his pants, and headed toward the sounds of murmured conversation, and the soft, muted strumming of a guitar that came from the kitchen.

Hallie sat on a stool in the kitchen playing a song while Randy busied himself preparing what looked to be a four-star meal of bacon, eggs, cottage fries and English muffins. Three plates were set on the counter, along with an extra coffee mug. The scene had a warm, relaxed charm that made Ty wonder again about life in Hallie's house in LA. The stories both she and Randy had told of dinners, musical evenings and holidays had made him envious and hungry to experience such times with her himself.

She turned to smile brightly at him in welcome. "Morning, babe. I put towels and stuff in the bathroom for you." She winked. "Hope you won't mind a pink lady's razor."

"No problem," he answered. "First, I'd like to talk you out of a cup of that coffee, though. No, don't," he said when Hallie would have gotten up to get it for him. "You keep playing. It's sounds great." Randy greeted him with a wave of his spatula.

"You better be hungry, man, 'cause I made enough to feed an army, or a real hungry Hal." Randy grinned, then turned to the woman playing the guitar. "You got words for that yet?" She nodded almost shyly. "Well, what are you waiting for? Sing."

It was a love song with an easy beat and light, teasing lyrics. As she sang, her eyes flickered up to Ty every now and then as he stood sipping his coffee. Her face and voice spoke volumes about love, her love. Randy noted with satisfaction that Ty's green eyes responded in kind. He knew without a doubt that this song would be a hit. Of course, when Hal was inspired like this, how could it miss?

When she finished, Ty went to her and kissed her on the cheek, then held her chin in his hand as he feasted on the winsome beauty in her expression. "She's something else, isn't she, Randy?" he said as he gazed into Hallie's eyes. "I'm going to use that shower now, honey. Be sure he doesn't burn the breakfast. I'm starving." He kissed her lightly, then was gone.

Hallie gave her friend a self-satisfied smirk. Randy regarded her warily and her expression immediately became innocent. Too innocent. "By the way, Randy," she asked offhandedly, "is late summer or early fall better for you?"

Randy narrowed his eyes, unable to escape a feeling of being set up. "What's going on here, Gal?"

"I want you to give me away," she said, waiting for a reaction. All she got was a blank look. "To Tyler," she said. "At our wedding." For a moment she thought Randy was going to cry. He opened his mouth to speak and then shut it again. He turned back to the stove without a word and turned off breakfast. "Randy?" she inquired gently. "Are you okay? Aren't you going to say anything?" Before she could finish her sentence, he grabbed her like lightning and swung her around. The warrior yell he gave made Ty drop the soap.

❧ ❧

Marlene was as thrilled as Randy at the news. She slipped out to get Mrs. H, a tray of glasses, and a bottle of champagne. The elder woman came in wiping her eyes on the corner of her apron and offering warm congratulations. The ladies clustered around Hallie, chattering incessantly and making Ty wonder how she could make heads or tails of what they were saying. But when she caught his eye over Marlene's shoulder and delivered a sparkling smile, he knew she was in her element. As it turned out, all the ladies of the ranch decided to make an impromptu trip into town for the latest bridal magazines and catalogs. He knew that with one simple phone call Hallie could have a designer original gown flown in, but she would wear a flour sack as long as it meant she had her family's approval.

He motioned to Randy and they headed down the corridor to the library. Randy closed the door after them and moved to sit opposite Ty in one of the chairs by the fireplace. "I talked to Ryker earlier," Ty began without pre-

liminary conversation. "He got the information I faxed to
him. You were right. Once he'd verified it, he contacted
me."

Randy chuckled. "How did it go?"

"He let me know his opinion of me in no uncertain
terms, that's for sure," Ty answered with chagrin. "But
actually, once that was out of the way, he listened. I promised him complete access to company records and employ-
ment files, anything he needed to get the job done quickly. He was brisk and professional, even courteous to a
point."

"Not bad," Randy intoned as he tipped his head in Ty's
direction.

Ty focused his eyes sharply on the man across from
him. "The thing that made me the most curious was the
caveat he threw in at the end. He promised to make a special trip up here and personally take me apart if anything I
do puts "Bishop's ass in a sling" as he put it. Considering
there's no love lost between them, it's pretty amazing,
don't you think. "

"Not really," Randy murmured absently. "He's got
promises to keep, after all."

"What?"

Ty's question snapped him out of his reverie. "Oh,
nothing. Just thinking out loud." He automatically shuttered his face and continued. "I'm not surprised, really.
Ryker's invested a lot of time and effort in protecting Hal
over the years. He's being paid very well to get her out of
this. Hal's going to need smelling salts when she gets his
final bill," he concluded lightly.

Ty suspected there was more that Randy wasn't saying
but let the matter rest. "In any event, I'm glad he's on our
side. Even with the limited contact I've had with the man,
I can tell he's nobody you'd want to meet in a dark alley."

"A lighted one either," Randy added.

He shook his head. "You know, I look back on all the things I accused Hallie of, Randy, and I can't believe what a blind idiot I was. How could any of us have thought for a moment that she was capable of destroying her father's company."

Randy's normally friendly eyes hardened slightly and his words come out even and controlled. "I've tried to forget about it since I've been here, but to tell you the truth, it still makes me furious that you guys didn't believe in her to begin with.

Ty swore harshly in the next breath. "I guess I'm beginning to understand why she went to Mexico with you rather than come here for her father's funeral."

Randy frowned. "I don't know where you got the idea she was in Mexico the whole time, Ty, but she wasn't. She was in Boston sitting a death vigil over Sye Greenway—by herself. I didn't get there until the day he died. We stayed for the funeral, then went to Tia Augusta's so Hal could rest and we could patch up our friendship. She wasn't in any shape to be alone." At Ty's stunned expression he added, "Personally, I'm glad she didn't hear about her father until later. I hate to think what it would have done to her to try to make the decision about who to be with. As it is, the guilt is eating her up inside."

"I swear to you, Randy," Ty said earnestly. "I'll do whatever I can to help her. She's not going to be alone anymore."

Randy smiled in satisfaction. "I know. If I didn't think that you'd be there for her in the long haul, I'd have her bundled into the car, heading for LA."

✧ ✧

The ranch soon became a beehive of activity. Hallie called Cassie, who shrieked and squealed over the news of her friend's engagement. Bastian, Cassie and Nick's son from their first tempestuous marriage, demanded to speak with Auntie Hal and gave her a thorough interrogation about Ty. By the end of it, the boy sounded resigned, yet still a little petulant. Later, when Hallie asked Cassie to be her matron of honor, the other woman burst into tears.

Hallie favored the idea of an October wedding. Ty stated his preference to make it as soon as humanly possible, but there was so much to do, and she still had studio time scheduled for her new CD. She needed a miracle to accomplish everything that had to be done. Luckily for her, a miracle chose that moment to knock on her door. It was in the form of Marlene Bishop. Marlene, a veteran of innumerable committees, went straight to work. By the end of the first half hour, she'd helped Hallie make a schedule down to the minute of what was needed to pull off an October wedding. Marlene proved to be ruthlessly efficient when she was on a mission. The only thing left to do was call Clancy and work out some scheduling conflicts.

Clancy's reaction to the news came in the form of pure, unbridled joy. Hallie quickly introduced her to Marlene, informing her assistant that Marlene's word was law as far as she was concerned. If Clancy felt any surprise at her boss's unusual relinquishment of control, she kept it to herself and quickly set to work ironing out the rough spots in Hallie's very busy life. When Marlene referred to herself as mother of the bride, Hallie felt her eyes burn and her throat ache. It was more than she'd ever dreamed possible between them. She fervently wished her father were there to see this moment, as well as all the moments she'd come to cherish since her return home. She knew he would have been pleased to know she'd finally made peace with the family and planned to marry Ty.

Ty and Randy took advantage of the ladies' preoccupation with wedding matters to redouble their efforts to
unmask the real embezzler. All the females had made it
clear that, other than Ty's approval of the actual wedding
date, neither man's input was necessary or welcome. That
suited them just fine. They both had work to do. Ty
placed a call to Ron Powell and his own staff. Ron sounded more optimistic than he'd ever heard him before. He
told Ty all information on the illicit transactions as well as
pertinent employee files had been downloaded directly to
Jake Ryker as requested. Ryker had called Ron late last
night and asked some questions that, though they seemed
obscure at the time, paid off for the auditing team early this
morning. Two mysterious computer programs used to fil-
ter down and shift substantial amounts of company funds
between holdings had been located, thanks to Ryker's
scrutiny. The scales were finally tipping in their favor, and
for the first time Ty let himself share in the feelings of hope-
fulness. The long nightmare of suspicion and distrust was
almost over. The son-of-a-bitch responsible had failed, and
he'd be made to pay.

His conversation with his personal assistant didn't go
nearly as well. He heard that Walt had been on a rampage
for the last several days, and he was totally over the edge
at the moment. It seemed that the personnel files Ryker
had been chiefly interested in had belonged to board members and their staffs. Of those files, the ones of particular
interest to him were Ty's and Walt's and their respective
underlings. Walt had heard about it this morning. There
was no help for it. Ty would have to talk to him now. The
operator put him through to Walt's office. Once he'd identified himself, he didn't have long to wait for the explosion.

"What in God's name do you think you're doing,
Nighthawk? Who gave you the authority to hand over sen-

sitive information to some hired thug!" he roared.

"Calm down, Walt," Ty returned shortly. "Ryker comes highly recommended."

"Highly recommended for what and by whom?" the other man said contemptuously. "Did he audition in Hallie's bed like you did?"

"That's enough, Walt. We have some real leads, finally. Now you can go back to being part of the solution or you can become part of the problem," Ty said coldly. "The choice is yours."

Walt laughed unpleasantly. "She certainly must be phenomenal in bed, Tyler, because she's made sure you're only capable of thinking with certain relevant parts of your body. This fellow works for her, the auditing team works for her, she's the one who's been depositing the money. My God, man! Do you need a confession signed in blood?"

Ty gritted his teeth and continued to speak through sheer force of will. "I don't want you to say another thing against Hallie. Ever. I've asked her to be my wife and she's accepted. You will treat her with respect and you will stay away from her. Understand?"

"No!" Walt's disbelief came out in a choked rasp. "You can't marry Hallie Leigh. You don't love her." Walt's voice rose dramatically. "You've said yourself that she means nothing to you! You have no right to her!" The older man's forceful denials were incongruous coming from someone who still professed to believe her guilty of acts against her family and its company. Why should he care what Ty or Hallie felt for each other. No right to her? What the hell was all that about?

"Listen to me, Walt," Ty said sharply. "We're closing in on the culprits. Ryker is going to follow the money trail and have an answer for us in just a few days. In the meantime, I want you off the ranch for good. I'll have a couple of the hands pack up the rest of your things and have them sent to your place in Portland."

If Walt heard anything past Ty's announcement about marrying Hallie, he gave no indication. Instead, he whispered vehemently, "You won't ever marry her, you know. She doesn't really care about you. She couldn't possibly. You're not enough man for her. You haven't the slightest idea what she really wants—what she needs." Then he said absently, "No, you're not the one she wants. You never were."

Something in the other man's tone chilled Ty straight down to his soul. "Walt, stay the hell away from her. I'm warning you. You may be Marlene's brother and Genna's uncle, but if you ever show your face on this ranch again, I'll kick your teeth down your throat. And if I'm not here to do it, the ranch hands will be." He slammed down the receiver and met Randy's equally tense face. After brief conversation, Randy rigidly picked up the phone and dialed Ryker's number.

As it turned out, Ryker wasn't particularly bothered by the slurs and accusations Walt had thrown in Hallie's direction, deeming them par for the course where Bishop's concerned. What had brought swift reaction was Randy's recounting of Walt's attack in the barn and his eerie choice of words when he'd found out Hallie and Ty were engaged. Ty had cast an annoyed glare at Randy for deciding it was necessary to inform Ryker of either incident, but he was quickly appeased when Randy told him his own name had been removed from the suspects list and Walt's had been moved up several notches.

Ty found it hard to believe that the man Tom had relied on all these years, his own brother-in-law, could be capable of such vile actions. Why would he? Walt had been with Tom in one capacity or another since his graduation from college. Like himself, Walt owed much of his success to Tom. What if it had been Walt all this time? What if he'd been trying to take over the reins of the company systematically for years? How better to secure the transfer of power than to marry the boss's daughter. He mentally flinched. Scores of people were bound to say the same of him once his engagement to Hallie became common knowledge. They'd weather that storm together when the time came. In the meantime, he'd keep her safe from Walt, and when the culprit was found, whoever it was, he'd deal with him as necessary.

Chapter 23

"Okay, the way I see it, between you, Jon, Mark, Paul and Chuck E., I've got all the studio help I need to pull this thing together. But we have to put in some serious practice time and get the music up to tempo." Hallie was issuing her instructions for the day, holding court at the breakfast table. That's how Ty had come to think of it. For the past three days, Hallie had taken over all their lives. Ty couldn't help feeling he'd created a monster by encouraging her to pursue the recording studio idea. Randy laughed and assured him she was normally like this when she was working. The only person immune to her bossiness was Marlene. With all the wedding details, she was even worse than Hallie. Ty found himself longing for tomorrow morning when he would catch the flight to Portland. He planned to be gone until the end of the following week, depending on what developments Ryker had for them. Randy accused him of being the first rat off the ship. It was true. Unbeknownst to any of them, however, he'd arranged for help. With any luck, it should be arriving before lunch tomorrow.

"Damn it, Hal, you're doing it again," Randy was saying. "You just assume, because I agreed to help you with the songs, I'll go into the studio with you. Forget it. I've got my own life to live. In case you forgot, I've got a new book hitting the shelves. That means signings, talk shows, the whole bit. Hell, next thing you know, you'll try talking Cassie into coming back too!" Hallie just sat there giving him her cocky little half-smile. "Shit, Bishop! I should have known."

"Aw, come on, Rand-man," she said, winking at him. "This new work has Loreli stamped all over it and you know it. Consciously or subconsciously, half those songs I wrote were made for Cassie's voice with you and me in backup." She leaned forward to her friend, her eyes alite with a burning determination. "Is this how you really want to leave it, Randy?" she continued. "Is this how you want us all to be remembered—as a bunch of petty, egotistical jerks. I'm not saying we get back together for good 'cause it wouldn't last. We're all heading in different directions anyway. But this is our chance to end it right, to go out in style on our own terms." She spotted an answering gleam in Randy's eyes and pressed her advantage. "Don't try to tell me you wouldn't like a shot at rewriting that final concert." She had him.

"And I suppose you got Donovan to agree to this lunacy?" Randy demanded, a grudging note of interest in his voice.

"Not at first," Hallie admitted. "But when I put it to her like I'm putting it to you, well, what could she say?"

"Oh, I bet you put it to her, Hal. I swear, you've got the coldest brass balls in the business," her friend grumbled. "And just how is Nick going to react to all this? Or didn't either of you think about him."

For the first tim during the conversation, Hallie looked a little ill at ease. Ty joined Randy in giving her a hard and meaningful look. She gave them both tentative smiles. "Well, that was the one proviso I had to make for her. She insisted Nick and I get past our differences and become friends. Not try, mind you, but become real friends."

"Followed by which we'll see porcine aviation no doubt," Randy commented dryly. "That still doesn't tell me what Nick thinks of all this."

Hallie fiddled with her mug of coffee. "Actually, he agrees with me. Cass insisted we start working things out right away," she explained at Ty's raised eyebrow. He had-

n't known any of this was in the wind, and he wasn't sure
he liked the idea of her establishing any kind of relationship with Montoya. "Evidently, Cass hasn't been much
good in the studio herself lately. Randy, we all need positive closure on Loreli. All I'm doing is offering us the
chance." She waited for a moment, then asked, "Well?"

"I'm in," was all he said.

In short order, Hallie was back to barking out instructions and assigning tasks. She turned to point a finger at Ty
and was about to issue instructions to him when she got a
good look at the expression on his face. She was in imminent danger of getting the tip of her offending digit bitten
off. Hallie made a strategic retreat. She returned to the
bunkhouse to work with Randy for the rest of the day, causing both of them to miss dinner. A disgruntled Ty showed
up in the late evening to find Hallie and Randy playing a
new composition. Hallie frowned at him as he entered the
room. She and Randy had worked long and hard, but her
expression told him she wasn't ready to quit now. After
only one predatory glare from her intended, however, she
accepted the inevitable, albeit a little ungraciously. She
went to pack her overnight things and let the bedroom
door slam sharply behind her to punctuate her annoyance.

❧ ❧

Hallie woke shortly before sunrise to find Ty quietly packing his suitcase in preparation for the trip to Portland. She
stretched with feline grace and sat up to regard the man she
loved with an annoyed frown. "You weren't going to say
good-bye, were you?" she accused.

He turned and grinned in amusement at her. She
looked like a sleep-rumpled kitten, sitting up in bed with
the sheet drawn protectively across her breasts. He forced
himself to remember his flight time and turned his back
once more on the woman who could transform from kitten

into snarling lioness within a matter of moments. "I thought you could use the rest, Duchess. I was going to kiss you good-bye, though." He turned his head slightly, cocky smile in place. Hallie had turned a soft rosy shade. He couldn't help wondering if she were mentally counting all the love bites he'd left on her last night. He instantly regretted allowing his mind to move in that direction, as it led him to do some significant counting of his own. Damn. Maybe he should take a later flight.

"I'll miss you, too," she said. "But rest assured, I've got plenty of things to keep me busy. Now that the offer has been accepted on the property, I've got to get the permits handled and the recording equipment purchased. Not to mention trying to sweet-talk Dottie Hanson out of murdering me." At Ty's questioning look she explained, "You know how she feels about Paul chasing a phantom and leaving his family to starve. I've already guaranteed her he'll make more working for me than for her father, but she's still pretty lukewarm about the idea."

"She's just afraid the recording studio is a pipe dream that won't come true, hon. Try not to take it personally," Ty advised.

"I don't. I just need to convince her I take risks with my own career but not with investments and especially not with anyone else's future. If it didn't pencil out, I wouldn't even entertain the idea. As it is, I've had enough excitement in the project via industry gossip that I'm confident we'll make a go of it."

"So then you'll have your own label to record under, right?"

Hallie laughed shortly, "I suppose I could, for all the good it would do me." He was puzzled. After all, hadn't the Beatles done well with Apple? Wasn't creative control the brass ring all artists reached for? He voiced his ques-

tions. Hallie shook her head. "You've got to remember,
Ty, the key word in the term 'music business,' is 'business.'
Everything I told Seeto and Cheesey Weasels holds true for
me. I need the distribution and marketing power of a
major recording label just like they do." She gave a low
whistle, "Thanks for the compliment, but Lennon and
McCartney I'm not. I'll never have the success or clout
they had. What store, then or now, wouldn't want to carry
a Beatles album, regardless of the label name or distribution hassle. What we will be able to do, though, is plenty
of subcontract work for the major labels and a fair amount
of private studio work for artists from all music genres.
Like I said, I've already had plenty of inquiries. Actually,"
she said, giving him one of her most charming and dis-
arming smiles, "I could use some help in the business and
financial decisions if you're game."

Ty stopped his motions abruptly and turned to pin her
with a no-nonsense look. "No way, Duchess. I'll be more
than happy to listen to your music, encourage you when
you need it, sit with you at The Grammys and applaud like
crazy when your name is announced as winner. But other
than that, you're on your own." He went back to his packing, half-expecting an explosion. He had to establish their
independence from one another right away. Hallie was
too strong a personality for half measures. He closed his
suitcase, wondering what the conspicuous silence held for
him. He turned to find her doing a sexually charged stroll
toward him. Damn her, she was stark naked. A feather-
light hand stroked the top of his shoulder.

"Whatever you say, Tyler. That's just fine with me," she
drawled softly. He cursed and glanced desperately at the
bedside clock. Ten minutes. He could spare ten minutes.
She squealed as he roughly snatched her up and tumbled
with her onto the bed.

Twenty-five minutes later, Tyler Nighthawk was swearing a blue streak as he raced around the room frantically pulling on a suit. His other lay in a forlorn heap of hopeless wrinkles, where it had landed in his eagerness to be rid of it. Hallie was stretched naked across the bed on her stomach, with her feet crossed as she swung them casually up and down. Every so often, he directed a curse at her, but the only response he got was a saucy half-smile and a roll of her eyes. He finished dressing, kissed her forcefully, grabbed his cases and headed out the door. Hallie shook her head and reached for the phone. Within seconds, she'd been patched through to the one person who could help her out. "Deke? Hal here. Listen, I need a big favor fast. It's about Tyler." She chuckled afterwards as she replaced the receiver. She'd love to see the look on Ty's face and hear what he had to say when he saw the flashing lights in his rearview mirror.

Ty noticed the tense atmosphere in headquarters the moment he stepped off the elevator. He wasn't surprised. Between the auditing team and Ryker's less-than-discreet probing into various and sundry departments, everyone was bound to be on edge. Walt was conspicuously absent once again, and the nagging chill that had been plaguing Ty since his last conversation with the man turned into full-blown, icy fear. He tried Walt's home number, but all he got was an answering machine. Following a hunch, he headed briskly for Walt's office. The place looked like ground zero after the red button had been pushed. Files lay scattered, drawers pulled open with their contents dumped out in haste. Someone had been searching for something in one Godawful hurry. That, or they were removing evidence just as fast as they could. He hurried back to his office to page Ryker.

He felt surprisingly calm as he closed the door to his office. He'd strongly suspected that Walt was the perpetrator for the past several days. This just clinched it. The hardest part of the job was done anyway. The morning after Hallie's incident with Walt at the haybarn, Ty and Randy had had a very frank discussion with Marlene regarding her brother and his actions toward her stepdaughter. Marlene's first response had been denial. Who could blame her? After all, the man was her brother. The poor woman had been through so many shocks lately that, had there been any other course than to tell her, Ty would have gladly taken it. Shadows had come into her eyes that morning that still hadn't gone away. Right now, Ty had suspicions that would make her feel infinitely worse. Was Walt such a monster that he'd have thought nothing of killing Tom if the method and opportunity presented itself? Regardless of the man's terminal illness, his decline and subsequent death had come on very rapidly. Dear God, Ty thought, panic suddenly rising within him. Hallie. What would Walt do to Hallie if he got the chance. He paged Ryker and, luckily, his call was returned within a couple of minutes.

"Good timing, Nighthawk. I was just about to call you," Ryker began without preamble. "You can swear out a warrant today. And if I were you," he added darkly, "I wouldn't waste any time about it either."

"It's Walt," Ty stated flatly.

"Bright boy. I take it he caved in under the strain and tipped his hand?" Ty told him about the wreckage in the other man's office. Ryker grunted. "I'll get someone to check for plane reservations and exit visas. He's getting desperate and that makes him especially dangerous. It's personal with this guy. Where's Bishop and what does she know?"

"At the ranch and nothing as far as the company's concerned. She has her own suspicions regarding Walt though. As soon as the warrant is sworn out, I'm heading back there."

Ryker swore. "I'd say that's the first smart call you've made in this whole deal. I'm in Portland now, I've got a couple of errands to do, but I'll meet you at the ranch this afternoon."

"You're not needed," Ty snapped. "I can take care of Hallie just fine. I know she'd appreciate you keeping yourself scarce in her life from now on anyway."

Ryker chuckled. "Yeah, I'm sure she would. But not half as much as her husband-to-be would. Don't worry. You've got absolutely no competition, at least not from me. Personally, I wish you the best of luck. You're going to need it too, you poor, dumb bastard. You're in for one hell of a ride. I give your marriage a year—three years tops."

"I'm not interested in your pointless suppositions, Ryker. After I cut you a check for your work," Ty informed him coldly, "she's no longer any part of your life, and you're no longer any part of hers. Understand?"

"Better than you think, Nighthawk," came a soft, eerie reply. "Make sure you understand something, though. She gets hurt in any of this 'cause you're sitting around with your head up your ass, I'll make good on my threat. I'll tear you apart. The line went dead and Ty found himself sitting there with a death grip on the receiver, fervently wishing it was Jake Ryker's neck instead.

Chapter 24

The boxes lay open, their contents strewn haphazardly across the floor of the bunkhouse. Hallie examined each item with total concentration, her hands reverently stroking each object as she removed it from its box. It was like being with her mother again, her beautiful mother so long denied her. She set the photos and letters aside for later. Right now she wanted to see and hold all the trinkets and curios that she remembered from childhood. Objects that, by the grace of God and the foresight of her mother's Tia Augusta, had survived potential obliteration at the hands of Elena's enraged husband.

Hallie smiled wistfully through a fine mist of tears as she studied the figurine she held. It was one of those whimsical porcelain rabbits from England. Her mother had had many of them, and Hallie had loved to sit on her lap and listen with rapt attention to the stories Elena made up about them. They'd sat together for hours, whispering softly in Spanish. She set it down with loving care and gave a soft cry of delight as she touched a brightly colored piece of fringed material. Her mother's shawl. As she drew it from the box, she realized it had been used to protect an object carefully wrapped up inside. The snow globe, the magical Victorian snow globe. She could scarcely believe it. Hallie'd thought it long gone, lost forever, destroyed. The shimmering fabric fell away to reveal the figure of a prettily made woman from a bygone era, holding a flower basket in one hand and a sun hat in the other. The detail and craftsmanship were impeccable. The globe had been especially made for Hallie's great-grandmother on her mother's side, an anniversary present from her devoted husband. She carefully turned it over and wound the key on the bottom. As she righted the globe, the old-fashioned strains of "Fur Elise" drifted throughout the bunkhouse. The minute chips of pink and white represented a shower of apple blossoms from a spring breeze. She concentrated on the figure under glass with the same intensity she'd employed as a small child. So much so that she didn't hear Marlene's soft voice whisper her name. Marlene sat down on the floor beside her and gently asked Hallie to introduce her to her mother. Through Hallie's memories, the mysterious woman took on form and character. A portrait emerged of a fiery, passionate woman and a gentle, loving mother. Marlene listened quietly, slowly, at last able to make peace with the phantom who'd haunted her throughout her marriage.

They sat silently for a time, until Marlene stated matter-of-factly, "I hated her, you know." Hallie said nothing. Most people had reviled her mother, still did if given the opportunity. "I used to tell myself it was because she caused my husband so much pain, deserted her child to run off with her lover. I stopped lying to myself only a few years ago."

She reached out and took hold of Hallie's hand. Marlene's eyes filled with tears from the memories of the years she'd spent trying to gain her husband's love and respect by being the perfect wife. A live woman she could have fought and probably defeated. But how did one fight a ghost? She remembered a particularly ugly night between her and Tom. In tears of frustration at his icy remoteness, she'd asked him why he'd even married her. With his characteristic bluntness, he'd told her he'd married her to entertain his business associates, look good on his arm and give him another child. "You see, Hallie," Marlene continued, "he never stopped loving her, not for one minute." At Hallie's murmured protest, she held up her hand. "It's true," she assured the young woman. "He never forgave her for betraying him, or himself for letting her go that night, but he always loved her."

Hallie didn't need to ask for details to confirm the truth of what Marlene said. Her words spoke eloquently enough. Besides, the confirmation was all in the sorrowful depths of her stepmother's blue eyes. She leaned over to hug Marlene tightly. "I wish we'd known each other back then," she said, "because then we wouldn't have been so lonely." Marlene opened her mouth to form an apology for the past, but Hallie cut her off. "Let's just leave the past back there where it belongs and go on from here."

"I think that's going to be easier said than done for some time," the other woman said reluctantly. "Hallie, there was another reason I came down here this morning. Tyler called from Portland. He had some very disturbing news." At Hallie's concerned expression, she continued. "He would have told you, but I wanted to tell you myself." Marlene looked away. "It's probably my need to atone for what he's done to you—to all of us." If Hallie had been concerned before, she was now terrified by the expression on Marlene's face and the tone in her voice. What who had done? Not Ty, she was sure of that. He'd proven over and over that he'd lay down his life for any and all of them. "It was Walt," Marlene said in answer to Hallie's unasked question. "It was always Walt." Her voice sounded dull and numbed with pain. "He was the one trying to take the company apart. He wanted you to take the blame. For the love of God, I don't know why." She shook her head. "Tom gave him his first chance. Everything Walt has is because of Tom. He was his brother-in-law!"

"Maybe those were reasons enough," Hallie stated calmly. She wasn't all that surprised, really. She'd suspected him for some time now. But she knew what was

driving Marlene crazy. The same horrible thought haunted her. Had Walt killed her father? She studied Marlene
carefully. Her stepmother had received more than enough
information to torment her lately. She didn't need this.
"Should we tell Genna?" Hallie asked.

"She needs to know." Suddenly an anguished sob
forced its way from her. "Oh God! You're thinking the
same thing too, aren't you? Tom!" Marlene buried her
face in her hands, crying piteously. "Why, Hallie? His
own sister's husband? He couldn't be such a monster.
Tom might still be here if I..."

It was Hallie's turn to wrap comforting arms around
Marlene. "It's going to be okay, Marlene," she crooned.
"You're not responsible for anything he's done. You hear
me? We'll figure it all out together. Did Ty say if they've
sworn out a warrant yet?"

The other woman nodded affirmatively. "He said it'll
be done today. The DA is waiting to view all the evidence.
Some of it is coming from Mr. Ryker." Marlene went on to
explain the initial evidence the auditors had found, Ryker's
part and Ty's, and Randy's decision to keep Hallie out of
the investigation.

Hallie swore. "Sorry," she muttered at Marlene's
raised eyebrow due to her choice of expletive. "It's just
that I resent like hell their deciding to keep me in the dark."

"Hallie Leigh, the last thing anyone wanted was for you
to stage some sort of confrontation with a potentially dangerous person." Marlene sighed again. "After what he
tried to do to you in the barn, God knows what Walt would
have done if you'd accused him to his face." Hallie shivered at the truth in Marlene's words.

"Okay, okay. Point taken. So I won't get on their
backs." Marlene rose from the floor in a motion that made
Hallie envious. The woman was the definition of grace

under pressure. Although one would have to look closely
to see how much the events of the past few days had affected her, the evidence was there in the pinched look of her
face and the sadness in her eyes. Compassion stirred in
Hallie once more. All those years of strict tutelage under
her father had taught the woman the necessity of holding
in her feelings for the sake of appearances. "Everything is
going to be fine, Marlene. Honestly." Hallie forced confidence into her tone, "They'll find him. Did Ty alert the
ranch hands?"

"Yes, and the sheriff as well. Deke's on his way out as
soon as he finishes up with some project he's working on
for Tyler." Any further explanation was abruptly curtailed
by the sounds of squealing brakes and flying gravel. The
women exchanged curious looks and headed out front.

They arrived in time to see Deke Stanton open the passenger door and offer a hand to the petite, dark-haired
woman inside. Hallie recognized the mop of short curly
hair immediately. Clancy Redfern. She was laughing merrily at something Deke was saying to her when she caught
sight of Hallie. She waved and said, "Some friends you
got, Hal. Deputy Stanton here drives like a maniac. Half
the time I thought I was still in LA."

The deputy grinned broadly and reached to take the
suitcases from the backseat of the squad car. Hallie shook
her head in amazement. What in hell had made a dyed-in-
the-wool urbanite like Clance show up unannounced,
lock, stock and barrel, at her front door? "Remind me to
kick the crap out of that smooth-talking fiancé of yours
when I meet him, will you? He didn't say a thing about
having to live in the Goddamn middle of nowhere."

Hallie walked down the steps toward her friend,
employee, confidante and conscience. Her throat ached
and her eyes burned. Money and power couldn't buy this

kind of loyalty—not in a million years. She cleared her throat with effort and said gruffly, "It's about damn time you got here, Clance. What have you been doing anyway, except for sitting on your butt and collecting your paycheck, I mean?"

The other woman beamed happily at her and said with quiet intensity, "I missed you too."

Randy was as astonished as Hallie that Clancy had been persuaded to join the growing Loreli enclave in the Pacific Northwest—and just as delighted. She'd arrived at the ranch armed with her daytimer and her no-nonsense attitude. Marlene, Gen, Hallie and Randy all sat in the living room at the main house listening in absolute silence as Clancy took the floor. In short order, she'd brought them up to speed on what she'd been working on over the past several days. Chuck E. was now in residence at Cassie and Nick's house and the preliminary negotiations had already begun between all the agents and lawyers necessary to bring the former band back together for one final CD and concert tour. The record company was ecstatic, she told them, and had already made an optimistic announcement to the press. It never failed to amaze Hallie how fast the rumor mill worked. A lot of details would have to be worked out quickly for them to keep the studio booking Hal had in Seattle for the end of October. Kelsey's office almost had the contracts ready to go for the studio musicians Hallie wanted to hire and would be express mailing them up in a couple of days.

Hallie hadn't realized how much she'd needed Clance up here, making order of the chaos and establishing an efficient work pattern. Luckily, a certain green-eyed, high-handed man she knew had sized up the situation and had moved heaven and earth to provide her with what she needed. You had to love him.

Chapter 25

Ty paced frantically across the carpet of the district attorney's waiting area. He'd given his deposition, handed over the evidence faxed from Ryker, and now all he could do was wait. It was killing him. The wheels of justice ground on at a snail's pace and, as every second passed, Walt was slipping further from their grasp. At last, the office door opened and the DA motioned him inside.

For the next half hour, he answered question after question regarding the power struggle at the Bishop Company after Tom's death. The DA was a hard man to convince that Walt's actions were any more nefarious and the situation any more desperate than other white collar crimes. In his effort to give careful consideration to all the evidence, things came to a standstill. Ty finally had enough and used his cellular phone to call the federal boys in Washington, DC.

To his surprise, the mention of Jake Ryker's name alone shot him through the normal sea of red tape. In comparatively no time at all, a terse voice came on the other end of the line and informed him that a warrant would be issued by mid-afternoon. Simultaneously, the DA was summoned to an important phone call. He rejoined Ty a much more humble, cooperative man. It was all he could do not to flip off the DA as he left. The man was sputtering and back-pedaling as fast as he could to make amends. Ty left him still jabbering as he rushed out the door. He called his assistant and had her book the next available commuter flight south, which unfortunately was not until four. He didn't like it. So many things could change in the space of two and a half hours. Your own life and the life of someone who meant everything to you, for instance.

Hallie shoved the last box of personal items through her bedroom doorway. Already, Clancy was hanging up her clothing in the armoire as she grumbled good-naturedly about the hazards of wild animals, trees and fresh air. One of the hands would come by later to take the rest of Hallie's things to the main house. Marlene and Clancy had decided, in their mutually efficient way, to turn over residence of the bunkhouse to Clancy. Hallie's fax, computer and files were there—in total disaster, Clancy was quick to point out—making the appropriation the most sensible course. Hallie went into the spare bedroom to get her mother's letters and diary from where she'd tucked them. While she waited for the ranch hand to get there and Clance to finish unpacking, she decided to make a quick perusal of the items in her hand. She sat down on the narrow bed and began to thumb through the letters first.

Most were letters from Tia Augusta and a few friends. They talked of inconsequential things for the most part, but Hallie devoured each word as if they contained the cure to disease or the secret meaning of life. They were links to her mother, a woman she barely knew and certainly didn't understand. Occasionally one of her mother's friends would comment on some statement Elena had made regarding her unhappy marriage. There were also oblique references to him, the man her mother had been seeing at the time of her death. Evidently, her mother had described and discussed him without ever giving his real identity. Hallie swore under her breath. For some reason, it would have helped to know who her mother had left the house for that night. But there was no going back, she reminded herself. Her mother was gone. Her father too. The best she could hope for was to make peace with her memories and the shadows that haunted the back of her mind. Thank

God for Tyler. Even at her happiest times, she'd never felt completely free to give her love without reservation. She hadn't dared. It was different now. She was different. She picked up another letter, this one from a girlfriend, skimming it for more clues. A paragraph jumped out at her:

Elena, listen to me. Get away from this guy! He may be exciting but he's dangerous. You're right. There is something dark and wicked in a man who likes games like that. Sooner or later he's bound to lose control and hurt someone. Please don't let it be you. Think of your little girl. I know how much you love her. You've said time and again that she's the most important thing in your life.

Hallie's eyes stung. If she'd been the most important thing in her mother's life, why would she have left her that night? Why would she have run off with a man about whom she'd confided serious doubts to her friend? It didn't make sense. She set the letter aside and hastily picked up her mother's diary. Hopefully there was some clue inside. The entries in the last portion of the diary made more and more references to a man whom she referred to as her "dark knight." Whoever the guy was, he'd evidently impressed her mother. He'd demanded an end to her nocturnal explorations with other men and Elena had willingly agreed. As the entries progressed, even Hallie was shocked. It wasn't necessarily the nature of the sexual games they played that shocked her as much as the fact that it was her mother she was reading about. In the weeks before her death, her mother had become frightened of her "dark knight." His control over her was becoming stronger, as was the intensity in the games. When her mother had tried to end the affair, he'd become irate and threatened to go to her husband with photos and make sure Elena couldn't get custody of a fish, much less her daughter. Hallie shook her head in silent torment for her mother. She'd foolishly followed her passions and needs into a dangerous and humiliating situation. There was no doubt in Hallie's mind that her father would have cast her out from their lives when confronted with hard evidence of the type of debauchery her mother spoke of.

The following pages were filled with sorrow and remorse for all the things she'd done and the hideous mistakes she'd made. He was her punishment, she said, for her wicked indulgences. Finally, the man's demands had become more and more outrageous, and on more than one occasion, Elena had been left much the worse for wear. The last entry confirmed Hallie's mounting suspicions. Her mother hadn't left the ranch that night to run away with her "dark knight"; instead, she'd headed to Portland to do whatever it took to get the photos back from him. Then she planned to return to Bishops Bluff and, in her own words, spend the rest of her life trying to atone to her husband and daughter for all the terrible things she'd done. Her love for her daughter would give her the courage, she wrote, to do what must be done.

Hallie closed the book and set it in her lap. Her poor mother had never gotten a chance to make things up to her family. She'd died that night on the highway, the victim of a drunk driver. She'd died with the censure of an entire town and the disgust and hatred of her husband. Her poor beautiful and vain mother. For years, the little girl she'd sought to protect had paid the price for her mother's infidelities. She hated this unknown man. Her heart burned to discover his identity and even the score. But who was he? She believed from some of the remarks her mother made in her journal that he'd been well-aquainted with Hallie's father. She was mulling over all the implications and possibilities when she heard a muffled thud from the bedroom next to her.

"Clance?" she called as she headed toward the sound. "Don't tell me you're rearranging furniture already?" The chuckle died on her lips as she saw her friend lying unconscious on the floor. "Clance!" She rushed to her friend's side, then turned quickly at the sound of the bedroom door being quietly closed. Walt stood in front of it, a gun in one hand and a rag in the other. He was unkempt, his clothes wrinkled, his face unshaven. His eyes had a wild, unholy look about them. Before Hallie had a chance to scream for help, he was pointing the gun at Clancy's head as she lay helpless.

"I'll kill her. I swear I'll put a bullet through her head if you try to call for help." Hallie mechanically turned her head in the direction of the barn. "It wouldn't do you any good anyway. The erstwhile deputy has gone off somewhere. I've waited all day for my chance, you naughty little bitch," he said, shaking his gun at her in admonishment. "You were supposed to be alone. But I suppose it's just as well she was here. You won't give me nearly the trouble you might have otherwise." He gave her a menacing grin and swept her over with bright, feverish eyes. "I don't want to hurt you, Hallie. Not just yet anyway."

The words rushed at her, freezing her with dread. What had he said in the barn that day? Nausea roiled in her stomach. He'd said he would need to discipline her. Discipline—as much a woman as your mother was—I don't want to hurt you—yet. He'd called her Elena. "Dear God," she whispered in disbelief. "Dear God, it was you. You're her 'dark knight.'"

He smiled at her with genuine pleasure. "I knew you'd figure it out, my darling. I knew you've just been waiting for me. It's time to go now, *mi flor*. It's time to start our new life together." He was pointing the gun at Clancy once again, in warning. He crossed warily to Hallie and held up the rag to her nose. She coughed and gagged at the sickly-sweet smell and automatically turned away. "Ah, ah, ah, my darling," he said. "We don't want a bullet hole in our pretty little friend's head now, do we? Be a good girl and breathe deep." Hallie did as she was told, and in just a fraction of a second, the room began to spin and the world went black.

❦

In an artfully restored Tudor-style house, in one of the more prestigious neighborhoods of Portland, Ryker skillfully and patiently searched for the information he still needed. He kept his cell phone on, waiting for his quirky but highly accomplished computer hacker to call. Miri had never let him down before, and he knew she'd come through for him again. He just hoped it was soon enough. He'd given her a list of names he felt Abrams might use. The asshole liked to play games. Once Jake had figured that out, it had been a simple matter to spot the puns and anagrams that peppered the fake names he'd used for the transfers and acquisitions. Miri had a whole world of plane and ship reservations to check, but she'd get the job done.

What Ryker didn't understand was Hal's importance in this whole business. Abrams had attacked her in some barn and made it clear, in a creepy way, that he felt she belonged to him. Why? In all the years in LA, this man had never once come to see her. Yet he felt he had some warped, vested interest in her, some entitlement. His actions against her cried out hatred, not love. Unless Jake missed his guess, the bastard wouldn't leave without trying to see her again. Or if he did, he wouldn't stay gone long. The electronic buzz at his hip snapped him to attention.

"Ryker here."

"Hey, Jake!" said the cheerful young voice on the other end of the line. "Canada. He's planning on getting to

Canada somehow, probably by vehicle. And he has reservations for two. Destination: Argentina."

"Two, huh?" Jake replied, an ugly feeling settling into his gut. "What names?"

"Right again, Jake. Mr. and Mrs. George Kaplan."

"Shit! Thanks, Miri. I owe you one."

"No, you don't. I still owe you plenty. Call me when you're back in town."

"Right. Take care, sweet thing." He hung up and turned to the elegant blonde watching him with concern from the desk she'd chosen to search. For someone not used to operating on the wrong side of the law, she'd taken to it as if it were second nature. There was a hell of a lot to admire about Ms. Kelsey Hogan. She feared little and didn't mind getting her hands dirty for the right cause. "He's planning on taking someone with him," Jake told her. "Who, I can't say for sure."

"But we both have a pretty good idea who it might be, don't we," she said, her voice full of concern. Jake nodded. Kelsey slapped the fistful of papers she held sharply on the desk. "Why? Why go to all the trouble of setting her up and then run off with her? It just doesn't make sense."

Jake shrugged and turned back to the closet he was searching. "It makes sense if you plan on convincing the person you're framing that running away with you is the only hope they've got." He frowned. The ceiling of the closet was suspiciously lower than the ceiling of the room. He stood inside the closet, turned to face the room and ran his fingers over the area where the ceiling met the wall. Ah. Just as he thought, a soft spot in the surface. Jake pressed carefully. There was a slight clicking sound and half the ceiling dropped to reveal a compartment. "Jackpot," he whispered, and summoned Kelsey to take the items he handed out. Jake searched the compartment thoroughly, then closed it and joined her at the desk. Kelsey had opened the tin box without waiting for him. She was busy studying some photos when Jake returned to her side. She looked ill.

"It can't be," she whispered in disbelief. "Hal wouldn't—she'd never..." Jake took the stack of photos from her nerveless fingers.

"What the hell?" he asked, feeling speechless for one of the few times in his life. The pictures chronicled the bedroom adventures of Walt Abrams and a woman, who at first glance appeared to be Hal Bishop. Jake flipped through the stack, pausing at one of the less graphic ones. Something wasn't right. As Kelsey said, Hal would never pose for the mildest of these, let alone the ones that were downright degenerate. A startled gasp from the woman beside him brought him up short.

"Jake," Kelsey said, her face pale, "I think you better take a look at this."

He put out his hand to take a folded double picture frame from Kelsey's hand. "Jesus!" he exclaimed as he glanced quickly at both pictures. He knew the teen in the graduation photo immediately. Her pretty face showed excitement and the promise of the beauty she would one day be. The other photo showed the same face, years older, very beautiful indeed, but harsher and more jaded than the girl in the graduation photo would ever look. Next, Kelsey handed him a clipping of a society page from a 1971 newspaper. The photo identified Tom and Elena Bishop as well as Walt Abrams. His fingers hurriedly dialed Nighthawk's number.

Ty didn't think he'd ever seen an afternoon go so slowly. He still had an hour and a half before he needed to head for the airport, and he knew he'd be better off wait-

ing here in case something unexpected happened. He'd
talked to Deke about forty minutes ago. He'd assured him
everything was fine, and that Hallie was thoroughly occupied with Clancy's arrival. Deke warned him that because
Clancy was moving into the bunkhouse and apparently
didn't get along any better with the cat from hell than Ty
did, Hallie was taking him to the main house with her.
Ty'd winced at the memory of those ferocious claws and
thanked Deke for the warning as well as the police escort
he'd provided him with to catch the plane. He smiled to
himself as he thought about the pleasure of seeing Hallie
later. He would make sure they retired early tonight and
got up late tomorrow. The phone rang and before he could
form a greeting, a voice broke in urgently.

"Nighthawk, it's Hal." Ryker barked. Ty fought the
steely panic gripping his heart. "This whole deal is about
Hal. Abrams was having an affair with her mother. When
she died, he became fixated on the daughter."

"Christ!"

"It gets worse. He's planning on leaving the country
with her. Argentina. No extradition. There are a million
and one places he can hide her once he's got her there."

"He'll never make it that far," Ty seethed. "I'll kill him
first."

"Well, you've got to get to him first," Ryker said tersely. "He's going to be wherever Hal is. I'll have a chopper
on the roof in twenty minutes. Meet me up there. Don't
make me sorry I'm bringing you along, Nighthawk," he
said sharply. "Don't ask questions and when the time
comes, don't get in my way." Ty agreed, without argument. Anything to protect Hallie. "I'll call the ranch and
put them on alert."

"Wait a minute, Ryker," Ty said. "How much do you
know about Elena Bishop's death?"

"Just that she was killed by a drunk driver. Why?"

"The rumor at the time was that she was leaving to run away with her lover that night."

"Abrams."

"Yeah. This explains a lot of things that happened in Hallie's life. Listen, don't say anything to them at the ranch about Elena. Walt's sister Marlene is almost over the edge as it is. I'll meet you in twenty." Ryker agreed and abruptly hung up.

Ty called the ranch but only received a busy signal. He hung up the phone and even though he knew it was too soon to meet Ryker, he headed out of the office at a dead run, not even taking the time to check out or give last minute instructions to his staff. He paced the waiting area of the helipad like a man possessed as the minutes ticked by in agonizing slowness.

❧ ❧

The small truck lurched and bumped its way over the rocky access road, struggling to avoid the gullies and ridges that had formed through neglect and misuse. The man at the wheel hummed pleasantly to himself as he maneuvered the wheel in an effort to outwit the hummocks and hollows. Every once in a while, he risked a glance at the woman slumped against the door. His prize. His reward for years of patience. Things were back under control now. They were the way they were supposed to be. Hallie, that naughty little minx, had almost ruined everything by getting herself engaged to Tyler. He hadn't minded her enjoying herself with another man or two until he was ready for her. It couldn't be helped. She was like Elena—hungry for it. Now he was ready to claim her, and as he'd told her that day in the barn, she belonged to him. He licked his lips in anticipation. Tonight he would begin her instruction. She would have to pay for angering him as she'd done, of course, but once she knew how much pleasure he could give her, she'd be willing enough. His Elena always had been. She'd protested and pleaded in the beginning, but she'd enjoyed it, no matter what she'd said. So would her daughter. He permitted himself a chuckle. Yes, he'd been very clever. Few people remembered this old logging road. He'd planned for everything, had even carried her quite a distance to the waiting truck to avoid tire tracks. She might wake up before they reached their destination, but it wouldn't matter. He had securely bound her wrists and gagged her. Actually, he hoped she would awaken. He would enjoy watching her struggle and strain against the ropes. Yes, he would enjoy that very much.

He continued to hum, congratulating himself on his enterprise. He was so busy congratulating himself that he failed to notice the young rider watching him from the shelter of the trees, watching with growing alarm.

Chapter 26

Deke kicked the door to the main house open with a booted foot. It crashed back on its hinges, sending an alarming noise reverberating throughout the rooms. He carried the half-conscious woman into the living room, calling for anyone within earshot. His cries brought Randy, Marlene and Mrs. H. running.

"What the hell? What is..." Randy began.

"I found her on Hal's bedroom floor," Deke answered. "I'm calling for backup. That bastard's nabbed her."

Marlene moaned and Mrs. H put supporting arms around her. "What has he done?" Marlene choked. "Why, Walt? Why in God's name do you hate her so much?" She was sobbing into Mrs. Hudson's arms by then.

Randy bent over Clancy while Deke sprinted to his radio. "Clancy, can you tell us what happened?"

She tried to sit up, but Randy held her back gently. "I'm sorry, Randy. I didn't see what he looked like," she said, tears filling her eyes. "It all happened so quickly! It was a man. That's all I know. His arm came around me and he held this awful smelling cloth to my nose and mouth. I'm so sorry! I couldn't even help her." He squeezed her hand and turned away, trying to hide his distress.

"It's all right, Clance. We'll find her. We've got to." He didn't spare Marlene a glance as he rushed from the room to call Ty. He didn't dare. He knew his expression was savage, and if she met his eyes, she would see the hatred there and think some of it directed at her. No, it was better Mrs. H comfort her now.

Deke was already mobilizing the hands into search teams. Hallie had become very popular with the men. Once she'd gotten to know them a little, she'd taken time to ask about the people and events important in their lives. They were outraged that someone, especially one of their own, would come on Bishop land to harm her. Deke knew his biggest problem would be guaranteeing Abram's safety from them once Hallie was found.   Randy joined him shortly. Ty had disappeared from the office in a rush moments before, Randy told him, and no one was sure where he'd gone. He'd been scheduled to fly out, they said, but not until later in the day. Randy had had him paged at the airport but to no avail.

No one had seen anything and Deke, who'd been on duty, was beating himself up for letting Walt get to Hallie right under his nose. They sent groups of the men out on horseback to scout the outlying areas, but they were afraid he'd already removed her by car. As near as Clancy had been able to pinpoint it, Abrams had well over an hour, possibly two, on them. Soon, the rest of the police arrived and an officer was stationed in the main house, while Deke, Randy and the rest headed out.

Genna didn't notice the hubbub in the front yard. She was too frantic to get to her mother. She raced up the back steps and into the kitchen calling for someone—anyone.

The phone was ringing and in a half-sob Genna answered it. "Hello?" she said in a wobbly voice.

There was a brief pause before a man snarled at her. "Is this the Bishop ranch? Who the hell am I talking to?"

"It...It's Genna. Please, I need someone. I need help," she sobbed.

The voice softened slightly in response to the girl's ragged state. "You're the sister, right?" Genna murmured she was. "Okay honey, listen. This is Jake Ryker. I'm a friend. Tell me what's happened."

"I don't know really. It's my Uncle Walt. He's doing

something to Hallie. I saw him. He tied her up and she was knocked out or something."

The man on the other end swore. "Is Raveneau there?"

"I just came in. I don't know. Mom!" she cried as Marlene rounded the corner into the kitchen in answer to her cries. "Mom, quick! Uncle Walt's got Hallie tied up! What's going on?"

Ryker shouted at her to give the phone to her mother.

"Mr. Ryker! Thank God!" Marlene exclaimed as she took the phone. She quickly brought him up to speed. Ty hadn't checked in for his flight, she told him, and wasn't answering his cell phone. To her relief, Jake told her that even now he was preparing to land a chopper atop Bishop Towers to pick him up. He and Ty would be there as fast as possible. Genna pulled on her mother's arm.

"Mom, I saw him in some truck. I know where he is."

"Where?" Marlene demanded.

"On one of the old logging roads on the south side of Moon Mountain. I was riding in the hills. He didn't see me—I was in the trees."

"Did you hear that, Mr. Ryker? He could be heading for the family cabin on Moon Lake or planning on taking the forest service roads out of the area. The whole mountain range is honeycombed with them. I'll have the sheriff's office radio the patrols. Ty can direct you," Marlene said anxiously.

"Yeah. We'll fly straight there." The line went dead, and Marlene could only hope Ryker was as good as his word. She turned to her daughter and said softly, "Honey, come sit down in the living room with me. I've got to tell you something." She led the confused and fearful girl away.

Tyler Nighthawk watched the chopper's approach with

relief. Ryker was ten minutes early. Wherever he'd been, he must have broken speed records to get here this quickly, he thought. Obviously he was as concerned about Hallie's safety as Ty himself was. Walt was in hiding. And if Ryker was right, the thefts had all been about his obsession with Hallie.

Things were starting to make sense. First of all, there were the phone calls and the telegram Hallie said she never got at the time of her father's death. Walt had been in charge of them, and, at the time, no one had questioned whether or not he'd actually done as asked. It had been so much easier to blame Hallie for not caring. When Hallie arrived, she'd been shunned and neglected, making her the perfect victim for good ol' Uncle Walt's condolences. Walt had been the first to suggest that either he or Ty establish a romantic relationship with her, and doubly quick to point out that Ty would have little, if any, success in that area. He flashed quickly through all the years and every instance where Walt had defended Hallie—offered her comfort. Walt had been simply marking his territory. The chopper had barely touched down before Ty was running toward the passenger door. In record time he'd buckled himself in and signaled Ryker to take off. The other man watched him ominously, giving Ty a sinking sensation in the pit of his stomach. He put on the headset that Ryker indicated.

"We got trouble," Ryker said via his microphone.

It was stuffy and dark and she ached all over. Her head felt like two construction workers were using sledge hammers on it, and she was desperately fighting the need to vomit. Her mouth was sore and dry, and she suspected that at one point she must have been gagged. Hallie tried to sit up but her hands were bound tightly in front of her. Oh God!

Walt. She surveyed her surroundings in the dim light coming only from the cracks around the door. He'd put her
somewhere—a closet maybe. Hallie concentrated on the
pain in her wrists. The sadistic son-of-a-bitch had practically cut off the circulation. Panic surged through her at
the thought of possible nerve damage to her hands. She
breathed and choked it back. She had much more important things to worry about right now—like getting out of
this alive.

The doorknob turned and her prison was suddenly
flooded with harsh light. She squinted her eyes shut
against the glare and felt herself being roughly dragged to
a standing position. She stumbled forward into Walt's
arms. As her eyes adjusted, she took note of her surroundings. Though she hadn't been here for years, Hallie
knew immediately where she was: the cabin at Moon Lake.
She glared at her captor. He'd obviously made good use
of the time she was unconscious. His hair was wet from a
recent shower, his face freshly shaved and his clothes
clean. She smelled his familiar cologne and wondered
how she could ever have found the scent pleasant.

He pulled her toward the bedroom. Hallie was stunned
to find the heavy drapes closed against the afternoon sun
and the room bathed in candle light. A chill crept over her.
He'd gone to a lot of trouble. The bed was turned down
and an ice bucket complete with champagne stood on one
of the nightstands. It was as though she were looking at
some grotesque parody of a bridal suite. She knew what
role he expected her to play. On the foot of the bed lay a
filmy negligee in a soft green hue. Walt pushed her hard
against the doorjamb and held her wrists up over her head.
She turned her head away from him, only to have him grab
a fistful of hair and yank her head back around. He
laughed at her cry of pain, then kissed her. When he final-

ly released her mouth, he let go of her hair and roamed his free hand over her body, alternately stroking and pinching.

"That's right," he murmured in a husky voice. "You remember, don't you, Elena. You remember what it was like." He ran the tip of his tongue along the line of her jaw and Hallie fought the reflex to gag. "Oh my passionate goddess," he breathed as he nipped painfully at her earlobe. "It's been so very, very long."

"Walt," she said as carefully and calmly as if she were talking to a child, "I'm not Elena, I'm Hallie. Remember? Hallie, Elena's daughter."

He looked momentarily confused. "Hallie? Tom's miserable little brat? She's not important. Leave her with that prick who sired her," he said viciously. "We'd have been together long before now if you'd done what I told you." Without warning, he drew back his hand and slapped her hard across the face. Hallie felt the blood trickle from the corner of her mouth and the sting of hot tears in her eyes. Almost immediately he was back to stroking her cheek and whispering endearments. "I'm going to untie you, darling, but just for a while. See?" he said, pointing to the gown at the foot of the bed. "I kept it for you. Go put it on. Make yourself beautiful for me."

Okay, Hal, she said to herself. If you want to stand a chance of getting out of this, you have to play along. Stall for time—stall 'til Ty gets here. He would come. He had to. She smiled coyly at Walt. "How did you know that was just what I was thinking, my dark knight?" she purred. His eyes flared bright with desire, and he allowed her to lower her arms. He pulled out a pocketknife and quickly severed the chords binding her hands. Hallie gasped with pain as the blood started flowing again. Walt murmured with pleasure and nudged her further into the bedroom.

Helicopters always made you feel like you were flying face first, Ty observed. All the goddamn hills looked alike from up here, he thought. He felt disoriented. He knew these hills like the back of his hand, but he was unable to give them his full concentration. He was too frightened for Hallie, for what Walt might be doing to her right now. Suddenly, Mount Baldy rose underneath them and he pointed to the left, speaking tersely to Ryker over the head-phones.

"Head left and drop behind that ridge line. You can follow it all the way to the backdoor of the mountain. We'll still be a ways from the cabin, but if he's there, it's as close as we dare to come without spooking him. You'll have to come in easy, but there's a small clear cut where you can set her down."

"Listen, hot shot! I can land this thing under heavy fire on a dime and give you eight cents change. Don't tell me how to fucking fly!" Ryker snarled. For once, Ty didn't take offense. He knew Ryker was furious that they'd all gotten caught with their pants down, and though he'd probably die rather than admit it, he was concerned for Hallie's safety too. "That little bitch is nothing but trouble," Ryker ground out as if in response to Ty's thoughts. "Hope she's worth it to you."

Ty glared at him, but his voice sounded bleak as he said, "She's worth everything I have."

"Yeah?" Ryker asked mockingly. "Well, knowing Bishop she'll give you the opportunity to prove it too."

⚜ ⚜

Hallie faked a silky laugh over her shoulder as she ran her hands over the negligee.

"You see, darling," Walt was saying, sounding almost like a school boy trying desperately to please, "I still have it. Remember the last time you wore it? I even have your

favorite champagne. I wanted everything to be perfect."
She didn't like the feverish look coming back into his eyes,
and the last thing she wanted to do was go anywhere near
him, but she had little choice.

Hallie swayed her hips in invitation as she sauntered
toward him. Her hands still felt weak and she was still a
little woozy. She doubted her ability to fight him off successfully right now, as she had in the barn, or even outrun
him if she got the chance. She'd have to bide her time until
her strength returned and hope she could postpone Walt's
plans. She reached out and ran her hand over the top of
his shoulder and down his arm, capturing his hand. Hallie
brought it to her lips, resisting her natural impluse to bite it
to the bone. She kissed it leisurely, then gazed up at him
with what she hoped he took for longing in her eyes. "I'll
just be a moment, darling," she said in a seductive whisper.
"I want to freshen up for you. You know, like you said,
'make myself beautiful for you.' I'll take a shower and
change." She started to turn away, but in a flash Walt
reached out and grabbed her.

"You think you're so clever, don't you? You think I'll
believe your sweet words and your lovely face." He
laughed shortly. "The second I give you the opportunity,
you'll go hightailing it back to him, won't you?" Hallie
wasn't sure at this point if he was referring to Ty or her
father. Even in his confused mental state, though, it was
apparent he held some dim memory of how she'd tricked
him in the barn. "*Nunca te voy a dejar ir, mi flor, mi vida.*
Do you think I've waited all this time, planned everything
so carefully, to let you get away now?" he whispered softly. In the next moment his voice became hard and frantic.
"He won't come for you. And even if he did, he won't
want you after you've betrayed him with me. You won't
want him anymore either. He'll never satisfy you like I

can."

Hallie took the chance that he was still confusing her with her mother, hoping to draw him into a conversation and obtain the answers to her questions. "Tell me," she whispered. "Tell me about everything you planned." He looked at her skeptically, and she hurried on before he had too much time to ponder the import of her request. "Prove to me how much I mean to you."

Walt studied her for a moment, and Hallie was afraid he was about to refuse her request. But he bent his head and kissed her mouth. Hallie pretended an ardor she could never feel for this man and responded.

When Walt ended the kiss, he smiled down into her face and said, "All right darling, I'll tell you." He drew her to the bed and pulled her down to sit next to him, looking very pleased and proud of himself. "I've worked for this since the day they took you away from me," he said.

"Who is 'they,' Walt?" Hallie probed gently.

"Why, that bastard you married and his little brat, of course. It would have been so much simpler if you'd run away with me like you promised." His face shadowed and filled with dislike as he stared off into the distance. "But I didn't have enough money, and you wouldn't leave that kid of yours. I told you I'd take care of you. I was only twenty-four. I had my whole career ahead of me. We could have had other children if you'd wanted them."

"It was an accident. Dad...I mean Tom and Hallie weren't to blame," she said, hoping he didn't catch her slip-up.

"You wouldn't have been there that night," he muttered to himself, oblivious to Hallie's presence. "You wouldn't leave the brat—wanted to stop seeing me altogether." He suddenly turned and glared venomously at her. "It wasn't just an affair! We loved each other! We belonged together!"

Hallie shrank back, afraid for herself if he still thought she was Elena, but more afraid of what would happen if he realized she wasn't. "How did you make them pay, Walt?" she asked as she tried to defuse his rage by stroking his arm. It appeared to work for the time being. He gave her another one of those eerie, disconnected smiles and leaned over to place feather kisses up and down her neck. She forced herself to sit still and not make a sound, although she had never wanted to scream so badly in her whole life. He chuckled deeply against her throat.

"I made him start paying the day after the funeral. And you know how? I became his friend." He sat back from her and traced the faint line of blood at the corner of her mouth. "He was so distracted, so dependent. You see, even though he knew how many beds you'd been in and out of and no matter how much you sickened him, he still wanted you. And me, good friend that I was, I was right by his side to drop a little word here and there—enough to remind him what a whoring little bitch you'd become. I made hints about your brat too. I warned him that she was just like her mother. Nothing obvious, you understand. That was the trick, you see, to slyly imply, cite evidence, stand back and let him draw the conclusions, then say 'tsk, tsk' at the most significant times. It wasn't that hard, really. You know what a sanctimonious old goat he was. I began to take away the last thing of you he had. Hallie."

She was numb—horrified. He'd taken the most negative traits Tom Bishop possessed and exploited them. This man had sat like a spider, spinning his webs of intrigue, while he whispered his poison in her father's ear. Her breath felt ragged. Walt looked at her in surprise. "Really, darling, he had it coming. And as for little Hallie, well, I never liked the brat anyway." He paused as though mulling something over.

Oh God! Someone help me! She'd never be able to sit here calmly and listen to his filth. Hallie began to detach herself as she'd done countless times when cornered by an unrelenting press or an overwhelming situation. This time there was a difference though, she was tightly controlling how far she went. That little lost girl who'd been a pathetic victim of Walt's insidious evil was someone else right now—not her. She'd deal with the pain later. Right now she had to survive. She heard her distant voice ask, "And Marlene?"

Walt shrugged, "What he thought he wanted more than anything in the world was a pristine little virgin who wouldn't say boo to a goose. I served him one on a silver platter." He snickered. "Marlene had been harboring a secret tendre for him since she'd met him at the funeral. Be careful what you wish for because you might get it. The novelty wore off soon after the honeymoon. Virgin brides can be so...limiting." Walt drew in a shaky breath and reached over to cup her breast. "But that's one thing you never were, isn't it, Elena?" He unfastened the button in the V of her shirt.

"Hallie, what did you do to Hallie Leigh?" she asked quickly, in an effort to distract him from his amorous pursuit.

"Well," he sighed, straightening away from her, "Like I said, I simply reminded Tom how much she looked like you and played on his natural fears about her turning into a little whore. Once he truly believed she'd slept with the Ramirez boy and the Stanton brothers, she had no one to turn to. Not Tom, not Marlene, and certainly not Nighthawk. No one except me. She was so pathetic that I almost felt sorry for her." He was off searching the distant horizons in his fragmented mind once again. "After the debacle at the engagement party, everything was ridiculously simple. I didn't have to work at tearing father and daughter apart. Hallie did my work for me."

A painful knot formed at the base of Hallie's throat. There was truth in what Walt said. Whenever possible, Hallie had begun defying her father at every turn. She'd become an easy victim for Walt's machinations. She slowly and carefully rotated her hands, flexing them as surreptitiously as she could to gauge their strength. She was getting stronger, and the light-headed, nauseous feeling had all but gone. Her limbs felt steadier, and if she could just determine that the gun he'd used to threaten Clancy with was out of the equation, she could make her move. She was desperate to get away, but she didn't want to get herself killed in the process. Hallie realized that she might have to stall for quite a long time yet, and if she wasn't careful, one of two things would happen to her: She would be forced to submit to Walt's sexual demands or he would further lose his grip on reality and kill her. Neither alternative held much attraction. Walt became lost once more in his verbal musings.

"It was that night of Tyler's engagement party that I first realized that Hallie was you come back to me. I held her that night, you see, and I felt the promise in that young body. I wanted to take her a dozen times or more before she ran away, but I knew it would be better to wait until she knew she belonged to me. When Hallie started getting famous, I made sure Tom and Tyler saw every despicable article, heard every ugly rumor." He laughed loudly. "That was the best thing, watching Tom's puritanical soul in torment. It was even better than hurting his precious company. There he was, lying around at the end, just waiting to die, knowing he had no one to turn the company over to but Nighthawk, that half-breed bastard."

Hallie let the rage wash over her. She would put it to

work for her shortly, focusing its power on the object of her hatred. Right now, there was one more question to ask.

"What about Tom?" she asked softly. "Did you kill him in the end?"

He turned and smiled benevolently at her. "Yes. A slow acting poison to start his decline, then a simple overdose of his pain medication at the end. He was too weak to stop me." Walt's smile broadened. "You should have seen the confusion, the horror, the panic. It was quite rewarding, really. I even made sure the old bastard never even got to say goodbye to Hallie. I never called her or sent the telegrams. Of course," he said in an offhand manner, "I had to move up the timetable somewhat. He'd been calling her, urging her to come home and help him find out who was stealing his precious money. I couldn't have that, now could I. Her coming home and making up with him would have spoiled everything. I had to move faster than I'd intended, make the deposits and secure Hallie's guilt in the eyes of the world. Then she'd have to come to me for protection and bring you with her."

Hallie clasped her hands together as they lay in her lap. It was time. With every ounce of strength in her being she swung her locked hands, catching him on the side of the head. He went down across the bed, and Hallie raced out of the room heading for the front door. The murdering son-of-a-bitch had foreseen the possibility of escape, however, and installed a deadbolt at the top of the door, just out of her reach. With a frustrated cry, Hallie whirled to look for another avenue of escape. Walt was already staggering from the bedroom, a string of foul oaths coming from his mouth. Instead of charging her, he lurched toward the desk in the living room. Hallie's worst fear was realized. He was heading for the gun.

Ty didn't wait for Ryker to shut down the engines after landing. He ran as fast as possible, maintaining a low crouch until he cleared the deadly blades, his only thought to get to Hallie as fast as humanly possible. Seconds later, Ryker, now fully armed, was sprinting along with him. He prayed they got there in time.

❄ ❄

Walt pointed the gun at Hallie with deadly precision as he approached her. "All right, you little bitch!" he roared. "What have you done with her this time? You bring her back to me right now! Right now! You hear me? Give me back my Elena!" He was in a murderous rage. Hallie pressed her back to the wall and tried to slide herself farther away from him. He bellowed his frustration and rushed her. He caught her arm and swung her roughly to the middle of the room, then brought the back of his free hand across her face. She went down. He grabbed her hair and dragged her back to a kneeling position. Wham! He hit her again. He dragged her up again, and this time placed the barrel of the gun underneath her chin. "No more games, Hallie Leigh," he said with lethal force.

"You know what I want. Give me Elena." Her head swam from the pain of his blows, and her eye was swelling, obscuring her vision. She prayed for the strength to go through with what she must do in order to survive.

❄ ❄

The cabin was just ahead of them now. Everything seemed quiet and there was no sign of any vehicle. It didn't mean anything though, Ty reflected. A man clever enough to do the things Walt had done was surely clever enough to cover his tracks.

"Okay," Ryker snapped, "we stop here. I'll approach the cabin. You wait here for my signal." He handed Ty his handgun and swung his rifle from his shoulder, ready to go. "Just in case," he said tersely, and he was off, moving with the stealth of a panther among the trees. The seconds stretched out like hours. Finally, Ryker motioned Ty with a single short wave of his hand. Ty followed.

❦ ❦

He'd dragged her to her feet, keeping a painful grip on her arm to keep her from falling to the floor. "You've forgotten your lessons, darling," he said, his voice high- pitched and shrill. "You almost let them take you away from me again. It's time to remember what we shared together." He was propelling her toward the bedroom once again.

Everything in Hallie's being rebelled. To allow this man to profane everything she'd shared with Tyler, to once more be the victim of his foul plots and demented fantasies, was more than she could bare. Even though she wanted to survive for Ty, she'd rather die here and now than let this man claim any more of her. Time had run out for her and Walt would ultimately have what he wanted. She just couldn't bring herself to let him enjoy it. "Go ahead, *cabron*. You murdering, scum-sucking bastard," she said hoarsely, "but remember something. *Ella nunca te amor.* How could she love a weak, pathetic fool who had to resort to blackmail to keep her in his bed."

He recoiled from her as if she'd struck him. "You're lying," he whispered. Hallie shook her head slowly. "You're lying!" he said again, yelling this time. "Keep your filthy, lying little mouth shut!" He shoved her against the wall and closed his hand around her throat, squeezing harder and harder. She tried to push his hand away, but the combined effects of his powerful blows and her rapidly dwindling air supply made her arms feel like lead weights. There was a steady roar in her ears and her vision began to dim around the edges. She heard someone gasping, struggling to breathe, and was dimly aware it was she.

As she started to lose consciousness, she heard an indistinguishable noise coming from the front door. Hallie wished she could live to see what was happening, but just then the room went totally black.

As soon as they heard Walt yelling, Ty and Ryker sprang into action. "Cover me!" the mercenary shouted. Taking careful aim, he shot out the upper deadbolt at close range. Then he delivered a thunderous, well-placed kick, shattering the wooden door and gaining access to the cabin. Ryker entered first, his rifle ready. Ty waited, his body pressed against the outer wall and his handgun poised to be fired in the flash of an eye if necessary.

In a split second, Ryker located his quarry in the small front room. Hal was limp, secured to the wall by Abrams' strangling hand. Damn, he couldn't get a clear shot. "Let her go!" he shouted. He hoped to get him away from her long enough to take him out. He didn't see the gun until the man turned, and by then it was too late.

Ty heard Ryker groan as the slug hit him, and not waiting to see what happened next, he came around the corner in a crouch. He had the advantage of knowing the placement of the furniture in the room and used his knowledge to dive behind the end of the sofa. Walt fired, narrowly missing him. He heard a low moan from Hallie and relief overtook him. She was alive. "It's over, Walt! Put down the gun," he yelled.

Walt screamed hysterically, "I'll kill her, goddamn it! I swear. I'll put a bullet in her and then in me! I won't be separated from Elena again! You hear me, Tyler? I'll do it!"

Ty's heart stopped. Walt was completely over the edge now. Dear Lord, he thought Hallie was her mother! Any more pressure and Walt would surely snap and kill them both. He couldn't let that happen. He'd have to back off. He risked a quick glance over at Ryker. His rifle lay out of reach and, if he went for it, Walt would kill him. The man had taken a hit in the shoulder but was awake and alert. He shook his head vehemently at Ty. He knew what Ty was thinking and wanted to convey the message that as far gone as Walt was, he'd kill himself and Hallie regardless of Ty's decision. Grimly, Ty understood that they had nothing to lose. There was no time to waste. The deputies could be here any second, and that would be enough to make Walt carry out his terrible promise. Hoping he could give Ryker a chance to go for his rifle, Ty rolled from behind the edge of the couch and gave Walt a new target.

Hallie became dimly aware of what was happening, but she couldn't get her limbs to cooperate. The blackness slowly receded with Walt's grip gone, but she still wasn't in any real condition to help her rescuers. Terror ripped through her at Walt's threat, and she knew that no matter what Ty did, Walt would kill them all if he could. She wanted to cry out a warning as she saw Ty move into the open to draw Walt's line of fire but her throat was far too sore. As she saw Walt pivot and take aim at Ty, she used her last remaining strength to kick out at Walt's leg. The sound of Walt's gun firing was followed closely by a second shot. Hallie sobbed Ty's name, but a pathetic croak was all that came out. She heard the sound of something heavy falling, and Walt's lifeless body was suddenly beside her on the floor.

Ty stood up slowly, looking at the body of the man he'd known for years. If Hallie hadn't managed to kick him hard enough to make his shot go wild, Ty could very well have been the body on the floor. He rushed to her side and bent down to look into her battered face. He drew her up to stand beside him, slowly and carefully. With the utmost tenderness, he folded her into his arms and rocked her as though he couldn't bear the thought of ever letting her go again. "It's all over now, sweetheart. I'm here. You're safe." It was almost as though he were trying to convince himself, Hallie thought, and she weakly brought her hand up to stroke his cheek. "Dear God," he said, his voice breaking with emotion, "I thought I'd lost you back there, and I've never been so frightened in my life. I love you so much, Hallie." Ty kissed her softly on the cheek, mindful of the terrible bruises already forming. She winced anyway. "Oh Duchess, your poor face," he said with tender concern.

She looked up into his face with her lovely golden eyes full of courage and the determination to overcome her pain. "He killed Dad. Bragged about it." She hid her face in his shoulder. His arms tightened around her and he whispered words of comfort.

They turned at the sound of Ryker's frosty voice. "If you two lovebirds are ready, there's a man bleeding to death over here."

A moment later, the sounds of cars and choppers filled the air. Soon the place would be swarming with deputies and later, press and curiosity seekers. For now, the most important thing was to get help for Ryker and Hallie. Ty kissed her once more tenderly, then helped Ryker to his feet. With one arm supporting the wounded man and the other securely wrapped around his future, they headed out into the sunlight.

Epilogue

The concert had about fifteen minutes left to run, and with curtain calls, that would make it thirty, maybe forty minutes before Tyler Nighthawk could escort his wife backstage to the dressing room and their three-month-old daughter. Addie was probably waiting impatiently in the arms of Gramma Marlie for her mother to come and feed her. If Tyler had been impressed with Hallie dancing little Alison Hanson around the room all those months ago, he'd been speechless with wonder the first time he'd seen Hallie take their little baby to her breast. He smiled at the memory of a shy, timid Hallie telling him the big news—there was one thing the doctor had found different about her during his examination after her abduction. She was two months pregnant. Ty had been ecstatic.

He watched her out on the stage, ready for her solo. The critics said she'd surpassed "Stumptown Boogey" with this piece called "For Keeps." Cassie and Randy stood in the background taking a much needed break while Gal Hal swept the audience away. The latest and last Loreli CD was outselling anything they'd previously recorded, and everyone in the industry felt the band was sure to garner more than its share of awards at The Grammy's this year. The limited concert engagements had all been sold out, and three more dates had been added. At that point, Tyler and Nick had put their respective feet down. They wanted their wives home with them and their children. There had been more than a little tension between Hallie and Tyler during the ensuing battle, but he'd stuck to his guns, and she'd finally backed down. The making up, as usual, had been fantastic.

Cassie turned at that moment and waved to her husband Nick, who was standing beside Tyler. She gave Ty a cheery thumb's up and he responded in kind. He'd liked Cassie immediately, though for obvious reasons, it had taken him somewhat longer to make that determination about Nicholas Montoya. Five days after the ordeal at the lake, the Montoyas and their children, with Chuck E. in tow, had arrived bag and baggage at the ranch. Marlene and Hallie wouldn't hear of them staying anywhere else, and in short order, the third floor was opened up and whisked into shape. Cassie, who'd been unable to stay away from her best friend after this almost-fatal crisis, had taken one look at Hallie's bruises and burst into tears. Ty had thought wryly at that time that Tom would be spinning in his grave at the thought of his beloved home being overrun with rockers, but it was Hallie's home now. And quite frankly, the place had seen more life and happiness in the past year than he could ever remember seeing there before.

The hardest thing in the world Tyler had ever had to do was meet Marlene at the hospital that day and tell her he'd had to kill her brother. She'd gone into a state of depression for a period, but, thanks to Hallie's and Genna's love, she came out on the other side of it stronger than ever.

Genna hadn't been able to understand all the nuances of what had occurred; after all, she was only sixteen. In fact, Ty wasn't sure if any of them would ever fully understand the years of sorrow and misunderstanding brought about by one man's obsession. The past few months, however, had made Genna bloom. She was in the center of a constant social whirlwind at school. Her poise and self-confidence had grown by leaps and bounds as she stayed firmly cloaked in her family's love and support.

Hallie'd had her hands full between recovering, worrying about Marlene and her sister, and visiting Ryker in the hospital. Even Clancy and Ty together hadn't been able to slow her down. Ryker hadn't been happy in the least to see her and had punctuated his annoyance by throwing anything that wasn't nailed down. Only Kelsey's timely arrival had prevented him from doing serious damage to the hospital, himself or Hallie. True to his contrary nature though, Ryker had left a phone number for Hallie to use if she ever needed help. It had a Washington, DC, area code. Ty suspected that it was a direct line to Ryker's federal employers.

Much to Ryker's and Hallie's displeasure, however, their lives seemed destined to be continually linked. Ty frowned as he thought of the new uneasiness that had so recently sprung up between his wife and the cold, arrogant soldier of fortune. He assumed it was due to Ryker's continued involvement with Kelsey Hogan, but his wife was being particularly tight-lipped about it.

As far as Ty could tell, the only thing Ryker seemed to fully approve of was Addie. He'd even sent a present at her birth, little pink boxing gloves with a card signed "Uncle Jake." When he and Kelsey had shown up on tour to attend a particular concert, he'd spent a considerable time standing over Addie's bassinet, simply watching her with an inscrutable look on his face. Marlene liked to remind them that a high regard for children said more about a person's character than a rough exterior.

Randy was going forward now to join Hallie with his bass. Twenty minutes to go. Barbara Walters had even talked Hallie into an interview. The public, notoriously fickle with its opinions, took Hallie's sorrows and triumphs to heart. Her formerly tarnished image was now shiny bright, and she'd been named one of the most fascinating people of the year by a popular magazine. None of it seemed to impress her very much, though. As she put it, she knew who she was and where she was going, and that's all that mattered.

Cassie was undulating slowly toward the front of the stage to join her partners for the end of the song. Ty saw Chuck E. grin and glance at Nick. It was a well-known fact that Nick didn't like the provocative stage choreography the band used. Ty heard his friend growl and turned to give him a commiserating grimace. He felt the same way. Hallie and Cassie had toned things down in deference to their spouses, but both he and Nick knew it would make no difference if they were wearing baggy sacks and army boots—they'd still be the sirens luring men with their music. But that was okay, he thought, smiling to himself. Because both he and Nick knew it was the love of their husbands and children that would lure their wives home each night. It always did.

INDIGO: Sensuous Love Stories *Order Form*

Mail to:
Genesis Press, Inc.
315 3rd Avenue North
Columbus, MS 39701

Visit our website at

http://www.genesis-press.com

Name————————————————————

Address————————————————————

City/State/Zip————————————————————

1999 INDIGO TITLES

Qty	Title	Author	Price	Total
	Somebody's Someone	Sinclair LeBeau	$8.95	
	Interlude	Donna Hill	$8.95	
	The Price of Love	Beverly Clark	$8.95	
	Unconditional Love	Alicia Wiggins	$8.95	
	Mae's Promise	Melody Walcott	$8.95	
	Whispers in the Night	Dorothy Love	$8.95	
	No Regrets (paperback reprint)	Mildred Riley	$8.95	
	Kiss or Keep	D.Y. Phillips	$8.95	
	Naked Soul (paperback reprint)	Gwynne Forster	$8.95	
	Pride and Joi (paperback Reprint)	Gay G. Gunn	$8.95	
	A Love to Cherish (paperback reprint)	Beverly Clark	$8.95	
	Caught in a Trap	Andree Jackson	$8.95	
	Truly Inseparable (paperback reprint)	Wanda Thomas	$8.95	
	A Lighter Shade of Brown	Vicki Andrews	$8.95	
	Cajun Heat	Charlene Berry	$8.95	

**Use this order form
or call:**

1-888-INDIGO1

(1-888-463-4461)

TOTAL _____

Shipping & Handling _____

($3.00 first book $1.00 each additional book)

TOTAL Amount Enclosed _____

MS Residents add 7% sales tax